GIRL, INCORRUPTED

GIRL, INCORRUPTED

A LOVE-HORROR STORY

MEGAN BLEDSOE

Arched Brow Books
VANCOUVER

Content guidance is available at meganbledsoe.com/cw.

This is a work of fiction.
Names, characters, places, and incidents either are the product of the author's imagination or are used fictitiously. Any resemblance to actual persons, living or dead, events, or locales is entirely coincidental. Except for the postergeist.

GIRL, INCORRUPTED

Copyright © 2023 Megan Bledsoe

All rights reserved.
No part of this book may be reproduced or used in any manner whatsoever without written permission of the copyright owner except for use of quotations in an article or book review. For more information, address: megan@meganbledsoe.com.

Designed by Megan Bledsoe

Subtitle text image and vector artwork
by SuYuk, RATOCA, and gengdev
via canva.com

Bledsoe, Megan, 1980–
Girl, Incorrupted : a love-horror story / by Megan Bledsoe.
First Edition. | Vancouver : Arched Brow Books, 2023.
FICTION / Horror. FICTION / Fantasy / Dark Fantasy.
FICTION / Occult & Supernatural.
Library of Congress Control Number: 2023907292

Summary: While trying to become the kind of girl her boyfriend says he'd marry, college senior Daphne James entangles herself with the local vaudeville star, an incorrupt corpse who thinks that Daphne can help reanimate her body.

ISBN 979-8-218-18734-7 (hardcover)

First Edition: September 2023

For Mom,
without whom...
And for DAD:
I hope they get this on audio
where you are

When you aim beyond them,
how can you not deserve your desires?
—Daphne James

Love is something you do,
not something you take.
—Nechai Chaiprasit

GIRL, INCORRUPTED

CHAPTER 1

DAPHNE - 62 days left

I would have done anything for Andy. But the night I vandalized the starlet's poster, I began wondering how to make Andy do anything for me.

On Monday, January sixth, I spied him down in the Urban Plaza, by the fountain, his golden hair shining in the last of the sun. He looked funny. Something wrong with his peacoat. The navy-blue wool was bulging on one side, right around the...

Omigod.

He had it in his pocket.

I hurried down the redbrick steps, backpack bouncing against my tailbone, and zagged a path through the crowd, keeping out of Andy's sight.

Across the plaza, Andy kicked a fidgety toe against the fountain basin and stuffed his hands in his pockets—but his right hand wouldn't fit! His elbow bobbed as he wedged in his fingers, as if the item in his pocket took up so much space.

Too much space?

Nah, he probably had it in something protective.

I dodged a bicyclist and hid behind a band of fellow college students gleefully recounting their winter holidays. A MAX train wrapped in a map of Portland glided down the street, and Andy looked over his shoulder to watch it sail by, turning his back to me. *Perfect.* I darted up behind him, was just about to spook him when—

He spun around. "Boo!"

I screamed and whacked his shoulder, and he curled me into a hug. I loved this, the way he held me with both arms and pressed his lips to my crown. And I definitely felt something hiding in his coat.

And here I'd been worried he might not do it in time.

I vowed to just let it happen, to let it be all Andy so that I could be one hundred percent certain our future was true and not precariously based on him feeling pressured.

Andy squeezed me tighter, then let me go.

Behind him, a poster clung to the window wall of the rec center. Someone had managed to stick it to the second story. All I could make out was shades of white on a black background. Dress ruffles? Or maybe rose petals? Either way, those shades of white felt affirming.

Especially when Andy took my hand—my left hand.

He turned to face me, smiled down at me with those defined lips, those copper-colored eyes. I tried to smile back, but my lips were clamped between my teeth. I couldn't stop darting looks at his pocket, and I didn't trust myself to keep quiet.

Andy's smile faltered. He looked down and shifted his weight, probably thinking the red bricks were too damp to kneel.

So don't. Who cares? What mattered was he was doing it. Here. Now. And soon he'd reveal what was in his pocket.

I squeezed his hand to encourage him.

He said, "I gotta stop by career services before the party. Did you apologize to Hannah yet?"

I stood numb for a moment, aware of nothing but the four words he'd failed to say.

But then I heard rollicking laughter from a group of passersby.

Chortling from the fountain water.

Even the poster, whose top corner had peeled away from the glass, was now lolling in the wind, as if pointing at me with a taunting finger.

The party was in the Lloyd District. We took the MAX, and as I sat in my yellow train seat, I decided that Andy must've gotten overwhelmed by the plaza's growing crowd. Panicked a little, started rambling. Decided he could do it later, in private, after the party. So cute. So long as he did it soon. We had too few days left before graduation ripped us apart.

The train was full, and Andy ended up standing by the bike rack, one hand on the stability pole, the other pinching his bottom lip. Across from him, a girl in a pink hoodie flipped her dark hair and posed for him, but her growing pout said she wasn't getting his attention. I wasn't surprised. I never caught him ogling the girls who ogled him. Not that I blamed them for looking. Andy was tall, well groomed, and you could tell by the way he carried himself that when life got hard, he wouldn't crumble and make it harder.

The person next to me got up to exit the train. I waved at Andy and pointed at the empty seat. He'd stayed outside while I'd run into my on-campus apartment to ditch my backpack and swap my functional shoes for something cuter. I'd been worried that after flubbing today's practically perfect moment, Andy might have stashed the proof of his commitment in some hidey-hole, saved for some mythically perfect day. But when I'd returned, I'd found his pocket still full and him slumped on the low wall, staring at his hands.

He now slumped into the seat next to me, resuming the position.

"So," I said, perking up my tone. No one commits to someone else while they're both sulking out their respective windows. "First day of term, how was it?"

Andy seized my hand and rubbed my knuckles. I could almost see an apology in his eyes, the appreciation for the opportunity to just gloss over the almost-fight at the plaza. He clearly hadn't meant to start one, especially not over Hannah: New Year's Eve had been her fault—I'd told him as much (and, thankfully, that's all I'd said).

"Bryant put us in these project teams for marketing," he said. "I'm trapped in one all term. Our first meeting is Thursday."

"Teams are good." I squeezed his hand. "Teams lighten the load."

"Not when one member's a problem."

I nodded concession. "What about the others?"

His shoulders hunched and his neck rolled like his shirt collar was choking him. "We'll see."

I patted his knee. He might resist at first, but once Andy made something a part of his life, he saw it through with his best effort and an optimistic attitude. This made him not only my heart's choice, but the smartest choice I could ever make. If Andy proposed tonight, I knew that we would last and that we would be happy.

"It's only ten weeks," he said, bumping his knee against mine. "How about you? How was your seminar?"

Ugh.

"Good news is I now have Monday afternoons free." I pulled from my pocket the reason I'd been late meeting Andy: a quarter sheet of pink paper. The instructions for dropping a class.

"Sullivan cut you?" he said. "Why?"

I glanced at his pocket. In word, deed, and presentation, I'd been a perfect girlfriend for two years, but apparently not perfect enough. Something—maybe the thing with Hannah on New Year's—had Andy withholding what was in his pocket. I shifted in my plastic seat, wondering what I could say about getting cut that wouldn't further jeopardize how he saw me.

I'd gone to Sullivan's office hours to correct the drop slip, but she'd said the cuts were no mistake. The registrar had overbooked her seminar (a not-uncommon glitch that professors used to audition students and create the optimal class rather than settle for any and every nincompoop who signed up). Sullivan said that because her area of study was so new, she was relying on the seminar to triple-check that she wasn't overlooking any ideas that warranted exploration, and so she had to slash the roster to "facilitate discussion."

"Okay," I said, "but now it makes absolutely no sense why you'd cut me."

She'd handed out the drop slips after having us introduce ourselves: name, year, major, and why we were interested in the biology of paranormal phenomena. My classmates had said the topic was new or different or their life's obsession (wow). But I'd had Sullivan as a TA before, so I knew what kind of response she'd want to hear: "Hi! Daphne James. Senior. Biology." Not my first choice of major, but my scholarship was science-specific, and biology is better than chemistry (all those labs) and way better than physics (kill me now before the math does). "I'm interested in your class because I'm hoping we'll get into details about the whole mind-body connection thing."

Sullivan had leaned forward. "Like ringsels?" she asked. "Silver cords? Incorrupt corpses?"

Corpses? Gawd, I hope not. "For starters," I said, and I flashed a big smile.

I'd thought I'd been earning my A already.

"My introduction was the only one that prompted you to ask a follow-up question," I reminded her at her office. "Isn't that *discussion*?"

She scoffed. "Your introduction. Did you even hear anyone but yourself? I've been watching you in class for years now, and you're still too busy posturing to be...*engaged*."

"Excuse me?"

She leaned against the door frame, pleased with her pun. "I know you think of the science department as a dating pool, but *my* class isn't Husbands 101, and I'm not chancing my PhD on someone who's only here for her MRS."

I'd stared at her in stunned silence, wishing everyone could just want for others what others wanted for themselves.

Back on the MAX, I shook away the rest of the memory (it wasn't very Andy-worthy) and told Andy about why I'd been cut.

He said, "Sullivan thinks *you* don't try hard enough?"

I might have fudged the details. I wanted Andy proud to call me his girlfriend. Or fiancée.

He said, "You try harder than anyone I know."

"Meh," I said. "The class was bogus anyway." The Biology of Paranormal Phenomena. It was the *oxy* to Sullivan's *moron*. "This'll give me extra time for physics."

Andy nudged my shoulder. "And me."

I grinned and nudged him back. "And you."

Andy stretched out in his seat, finally abandoning his slumped posture. I closed my eyes, thankful that we'd been able to reconcile so quickly, then sighed and looked skyward—and on the train car's ceiling was a smaller copy of that strange and alluring poster.

The box lights running alongside it seemed to spotlight the woman in its image. A vaudeville star. She had long dark hair and wore a short white dress.

A wedding dress.

I thought I'd want a gown, something classic and sophisticated, but I loved the starlet's sexy pin-up style. I glanced at Andy, wondering if he might love it too. I imagined us standing before the officiant: me wearing the starlet's corset and her short, ruffled skirt; him lifting the veil of her tilted white hat; me looking over my bare shoulder and tossing her pink-and-mint-green bouquet.

Although, really, I'd exchange vows in a white plastic garbage sack so long as Andy—

The poster flickered, and I jumped, shrieking a little.

"You okay?" Andy asked.

I shook my head and laughed at myself. What I'd seen was just the headlights of a passing car glancing off the poster and brightening the dust in the air.

Had to have been.

But I buttoned my coat as if the winter wind were forcing its way through my skin. "Just chilly, I guess."

Andy pulled me close and rubbed love into my arms.

The MAX lurched onto the Steel Bridge, and a crayon rolled out from under our seats. Still rubbing my arms, Andy pointed at it. "Harry says hi."

I buried my head against Andy's shoulder, loving that he not only remembered my thing with Harry and crayons but was willing to play along with me.

When I was little, Harry had bought me crayons. Not to keep me out of the way or even for my birthday, but because I'd been drawing in the dirt, making mountains out of molehills and copying the neighbor's sunflowers, like in a documentary I'd watched with my mom on Van Gogh and Gauguin. He'd brought them home with the pizza. He drove a truck, short-distance hauls, and every night he'd come home with takeout from some new restaurant.

Until one night he didn't. I was seven. He and Mom weren't married, so everything went to his next of kin. Mom received their eviction notice the day she received Harry's ashes. She didn't fight it. Easier on the soul to just move on, she said. But I don't know. I thought she could've at least tried. Might've reduced my *childhood instability*, so called by my Psych 101 textbook. It predicted I would learn helplessness. I didn't. But I suppose I'd learned other things.

I picked up the crayon. It was brand-new and double-ended, which usually comes in red and blue or yellow and green. This one was pink and green. Same as the starlet's poster. I puzzled up at her, at the pink and mint-green details on the dress she wore, the dress I now wanted—then side-eyed the man I wanted.

"What?" he said.

I'd told myself to just let it happen, and that's still how I preferred it: all Andy, all us. But time felt like it was running out. I knew two other girls who'd already gotten engaged—the copycat effect was gaining momentum among Andy's friends but wasn't (yet) benefiting me—and I was having a harder and harder time with waiting patiently. And judging by the looks of Andy's pocket, he'd already made his decision. He was just delaying its announcement unnecessarily.

Anticipation. They say it's desire's best part. Not so. Satisfaction. Relief. That's the best part.

I reached across Andy's lap.

He lifted his arms, laughing. "What are you doing?"

I prodded his pocket. The contents felt dense, spongy beneath the wool. Not the customary box, then. A novelty box? Come to think of it, a novelty box sounded just like Andy.

"Oh yeah," he said, and he revealed his surprise.

He'd wrapped it in a napkin. Many. The last one grease-stained.

A muffin? It was a muffin, a blueberry muffin. Blueberry's my favorite, but still. It was a free-food-event muffin we could've shared at any time, so why was he—

Wait a minute.

I closed my eyes and savored the feeling, his cleverness, the trembling of my fingers. I rubbed my thumb across the muffin's bottom, searching for the puncture in its paper cup.

The cup felt smooth. But of course it would. Andy would've fixed the tear with a toothpick.

I flipped the muffin over. The paper was pink and still intact.

I tore the muffin in half, into chunks, into crumbles and confetti on the floor. There was nothing else in it. I gaped at Andy.

His face grew stoic, like he used to think he was just being a nice boyfriend getting his girlfriend a muffin but was now realizing that the way he'd handled its delivery had invited me to think it was something more.

"Patience," he said, renewing my expectations—but I couldn't discern his tone. Was he apologizing or admonishing? Or teasing?

"Patience?" I said, hoping he'd repeat himself and I'd get another chance.

He only nodded. But I thought I detected a smile behind his composed lips, his copper eyes. And his pocket, it still looked a little bulky.

"Tonight?" I asked.

He snorted and a smile broke through. Just teasing, then?

After the party. Andy would save us after the party. He would.

But what if he didn't?

I admit I knew Andy's inclinations (or disinclinations) toward matrimony, and I was pretty sure that he knew mine, though probably not to their full extent, since I did my best to hide that—but we'd never discussed getting married. Doing so offered no benefit. The gist of the conversation would go like this:

I want to get married.

I'd rather not.

So you want to break up?

Well, no...

And I didn't want to break up either. So here we were: each in denial (him unknowingly more than me) about our incompatible intentions; each hoping the other (me far more than him) would change their mind.

And I clung to every reason that let me believe that Andy was changing his mind.

Andy and I followed the too-sweet smell of frosted cupcakes down the hall to Hannah and Madison's apartment and found the door ajar. Andy pushed it open. "After you, my lady."

I usually played along—*why thank you, kind sir*—but New Year's Eve kept haunting me. I'd revealed too much that night. I'd let Andy see the raw and ugly me, the unworthy me. I needed to show him, fast, that that version of me had been a fluke; I was still the polished, carefree girl I tried so hard, for him, to be.

In the living room, Madison's boyfriend, Tyler, was tugging the couch away from the back wall. I shrugged off my coat, wondering what manner of horror he had planned for us tonight. My best guess was charades.

Reality would prove itself worse.

"You need any help?" I asked.

Andy winked at me—these were his friends more than mine—then took my coat and hung it with the others on a hook next to the door. Bonus, Tyler said no:

"But could you keep everyone else outta here?"

"Hey!" everyone called as we entered the kitchen. Most were hunkered around the tiny table, munching chips, but Madison stood at the tiny island, making drinks. I didn't see Hannah.

See, Andy, even Hannah knows New Year's was her fault.

I told Madison happy birthday and complimented her sweater. She offered to make me a daiquiri, except we were out of ice.

"Hannah went to get more."

"Oh, is that why she's gone?"

"Hm." Smiling tightly, Madison plucked a filbert from a bowl of holiday nuts and cracked it with a nutcracker. "I heard Andy's parents wouldn't let you stay for Christmas."

I hugged my elbows and shot a frown at Andy. "I got to stay." *Mostly.*

"That's not what I heard." *Crack.* "I heard you spent Christmas Eve schlepping back to Portland on a bus."

"*Psh.* No, I didn't."

I'd taken the train. Andy had driven me to the station after his mom decided she wanted Christmas Day with just family. I wasn't the only one asked to leave. Andy's younger sister's boyfriend had to leave too. But his older sister's *husband* got to stay.

"Poor thing," Madison said. "So *awful*. Was that your problem on New Year's? Why you rotted all over Hannah?"

We'd all gone out to the Roseway Manor and were exploring the grounds when Andy pulled me away from the group. He'd met us there, straight from a last-minute visit with his grandmother. His sisters had teased him all vacation about a McBride family ring. They'd told me not to get too excited because it was ugly, but I didn't care. I just didn't want to end up like my mom.

Andy had shown me the Roseway's herb garden and kissed me on the tiny bridge. We'd stopped to look at a giant tree. The whole time, he was aw-schucks-ing and swinging my hand...

But here came Hannah, even though she knew, even though I'd taken a chance and confided in her on the ride over. She came racing across the grass, interrupting our engagement to brag about her own. Andy congratulated her, because he's nice like that, and our moment was lost. I don't remember what I said to Hannah. It didn't really matter. What mattered was that I'd yelled. A lot. In a tone Andy had never heard me use before. Using words he'd never heard me say. What mattered was the way he had looked at me after.

I hugged my elbows, trying not to relive how he had reassessed me from beneath his New Year's hat, his smile slipping, his hands hiding in his coat, his body angling for the parking lot.

"Everything okay over here?" Andy squeezed my shoulder.

"I'm good," I said, but I choked on the words. I grabbed his glass and chugged.

"So, Mads," he said. "Tyler says you're thinking of studying abroad next term."

"Italy," Madison said. "Or maybe Portugal."

"Nice."

"What about Tyler?" I wiped the rum and Coke from my mouth and tried to match the upbeat tone Andy had so easily established. "Could you really go without seeing your boyfriend for three months?"

I wouldn't want to go without seeing Andy for three months. Three months has a way of stretching into the rest of your life.

Andy looked down at me quizzically, then, as if noticing I was looking back at him, gave me a sympathetic smile.

Madison shrugged. "It'll work out."

I stared at her, unable to fathom feeling that indifferent about Andy. "I'll be right back," I said.

I feigned a pee, but really, hiding out in the bathroom was better than hanging out in the kitchen, listening to people like Madison remind me that people like Hannah were getting engaged while I was not because—hey, nobody wanted to spend even Christmas with me. Why would they want to spend their whole life?

Then I heard Hannah come back with the ice, and everyone started praising that dust fleck of a diamond on her finger, and suddenly hiding out in the bathroom became way better than hanging out in the kitchen.

It was a lot to bear.

And I was missing out on Andy's laugh. I could hear a ghost of it through the walls. I loved how his wholehearted tenor could lighten my mood, no matter where my mood had started. All I wanted was to never have to rely on a memory of that mood-lifting laugh.

"Okay, I'm ready," Tyler hollered. "Come to the living room."

Voices and footsteps meandered down the hall, no big hurry, but then someone gasped, and up rose a chorus of *oh*s and *omigod*s. I left the bathroom and got to the living room just in time to see Tyler grab Madison's hand and pull her away from the group. She covered her mouth and looked back at us. The room's far end was cleared of furniture, and on the wall hung a floor-to-ceiling sign that read *I love you, Madison Green*. Still holding her hand, Tyler shushed us. And he lowered to one knee.

My ears burned.

Love was baiting me again.

There was lots of squeeing and excited hands. There was pushing and movement around me. There was talk of her ring and talk of her surprise—

There was threat of some talk of my own—

But there was Andy: "Daph?"

A warning numbed my body. *Don't repeat New Year's, Daphne.*

No, not in front of Andy. I mustn't embarrass Andy. But the urge... Envy blazed within me, begging for release. I exhaled slowly and stretched my fingers to keep them from clenching into fists.

There was a pop of champagne and the filling of cups. There were cheers and toasts for the couple. There was talk of dresses and talk of colors.

And there was Andy: "Congrats, you two."

He left me alone to go talk to our friends, so I backed even further away, into the couch, now placed alongside the TV, and sank into it deep, closing my eyes and trying to ignore all the happiness around me.

The only person I listened to was Andy: "Hate to leave, but I've got an early study group tomorrow....Nah, you did good, Tyler....Yeah, we'll see you later. Congrats, Mads."

Mads. She didn't even care if she left Tyler for three months. She didn't even care. She didn't—she didn't deserve this.

There was boisterous laughter and attentive sighs. There were suggestions and cautions for the honeymoon. There was talk of bridesmaids and talk of dates.

And there was Andy.

Keep it together.

He pulled me up from the couch and wrapped me in my peacoat. He was already wearing his.

"I got you, Daph."

Sure, now, but always?

"Did you know Tyler was gonna do that?" I asked.

We'd gotten off the MAX early and were walking the rest of the way home through the Park Blocks, a twelve-block greenway lined with century-old elm trees. The walk was Andy's idea. And that gave me hope.

Andy glanced at me—I was struggling to keep up with him in heels, and he slowed his pace to our normal, matching stride—but he didn't answer. I squeezed his hand to prompt him. He exhaled a thick white breath into the cold night air. "Nope."

"You say that like we might've stayed home if you had."

Andy's mouth twitched a quick smile that warmed my whole body. Twice now he'd seen my unworthiness, and at the party, he'd still chosen us, me. He'd lied to Tyler about his study group (it was

Thursday, not tomorrow). He'd put my need to leave on himself. To help me hide my ugly side.

I hugged his arm, squeezing my eyes shut and pressing my face to the wool of his sleeve. Mine. Andy was mine, and tonight he'd more or less claimed me as his. I wish I could have let this all be enough, but his encouragement only spurred my desire for more. And now was the perfect time. The park was magical at night, with the moonlight shining through the skeletal trees and the streetlights illuminating the mist at our feet. So romantic. I squeezed Andy's hand to let him know I was ready.

He kissed my knuckles—and kept walking.

"Andy?"

"Yeah."

"When do you see us—"

He stopped and took me by the arms, tried to look me in the eye, but I focused on his shoes, his ruddy-brown ECCOs, their laces a festering cream.

He said, "I need to focus on school right now. Okay?"

I closed my eyes and turned away from him.

"Daph?"

The night was colder, looking away, the air thicker. Hard to breathe. Andy stepped up behind me and wrapped me in his arms, kissed the top of my head and laid his cheek on my hair. I snorted. I loved it when he did that. And he knew it.

"We're good," he whispered. "Don't you think we're good?"

The best. That's why securing our future was so important.

"Come on." His tone was kind. When I didn't move, he toed my heel, and we took a step forward together. Then we took another. Two more steps and he let me walk on my own. Another block and he grabbed my hand. But then, out of the blue, he said the words that broke me.

"Now *there's* a girl I'd marry."

It started in my chest, this frozen feeling that wouldn't let me move: my inner shields were surfacing to protect me.

A static filled my ears. *Just don't listen, Daphne.*

A haze blocked my eyes. *Just don't look there, Daphne.*

They promised to make this easier on me—to slow the momentum, to minimize the pain—if I'd just relax and let Andy's comment pass.

But I couldn't.

A cloud fogged my brain. *Just don't ask him, Daphne.*

Hysteria shook my voice. "What did you just say?"

"Let's go. It's getting cold."

He tried to pull me with him, but I stumbled back, putting a sidewalk crack between us. *Breathe.* I couldn't breathe. My face was on fire.

He said, "I don't know why I said it. I was just kidding, lightening the mood."

A throbbing seized my heart. *Just believe him, Daphne.*

"Who?" I twirled, searching for her, but the fog was so thick, I couldn't see anyone, let alone someone Andy would marry. "Where is she?"

Andy pointed to the left. All I saw was fog. But the spot he pointed at—it was like moonrays were cutting through the trees just to highlight that spot. The fog glowed.

I stepped closer and tried to wave away the fog but only whacked my knuckles on a stone building. I rubbed my hand. The wall was covered with homemade ads for roommates and tutoring, all fringed with phone numbers.

"Where, Andy? I don't—"

But then I did. Nestled among the ads. That same black poster promoting the starlet in white.

My upper lip curled. "*Her?*"

She knelt at an angle, sitting on her heels with her back erect. Her corset pushed up vulgar cleavage and topped a barely-there skirt, the ruffles all white and shades of white. Her bouquet, which she pressed suggestively into her fishnet lap, matched the pink-and-mint-green streak in her tousled dark hair. She looked straight at us, chin down. Assertive. But I couldn't see her face. Her tilted white hat had a veil.

I read her caption with as much disdain as possible. "*The Pin-up Bride*? Seriously, Andy? You'd marry *her*?"

"I said I was kidding." He forced a laugh, but that just made it worse.

"Why her?"

He grabbed my hand, tried to pull me away from the competition, but I wouldn't budge.

"Well, what is it about her?"

"Come on. Let's get you home."

"The nasty hair?"

"Come on, Daph."

"The tramp outfit?"

"*Daph.*" He smacked the poster with the back of his fingers. "Like I could really marry Fausten Cotter."

My whole face dropped. "You know her *name*?"

His expression shifted from consoling to confused, and he stuttered nonsense, like he'd just realized his mistake. His nose kissed the paper as he scanned the poster's fine print, like he was looking for her name, like he wanted to prove to me, to himself, that he had never heard of this girl before tonight.

"Whatever." I rubbed my aching temples. "She can't be that great if she's hiding her face."

And that's when something crazy happened. So crazy, I wanted to blame it on alcohol-impaired vision, but I was sober, especially after a freezing walk home in heels.

The Pin-up Bride, the two-dimensional girl in the poster—she took on a third, hazy dimension and she leaned forward. Out of the poster.

She leaned toward Andy like a ghostly pop-up centerfold, and she lifted her veil.

I shrieked and ripped her from the wall, crumpled her poster tiny, and drop-kicked that wad of trash past the next streetlight, where it disappeared in the gutter. My shoe, trailing after it, skidded along the pavement.

Andy remained facing the wall, staring at where the Pin-up Bride's poster used to be and touching his cheek. He was so still, I wasn't sure he was breathing.

"Andy?"

He shook his head, and his hand dropped to his side, revealing a softly glowing kiss print. I blinked and it was gone. I told myself it was just glare—the kiss print, the postergeist—I told myself it was all just glare, just glare from the streetlight or maybe the moon.

I actually told myself it was nothing to worry about.

I hopped toward Andy. He looked at my bare foot, then jogged down the sidewalk and picked up my heel. When he returned with it, he stooped to one knee and held it out to me.

If only it were a ring...

"I didn't mean anything by it," he said, his lips quirking into a remorseful expression I never could resist.

I slipped the heel on, feeling nothing like Cinderella, then pulled him up to standing, kissed us all better, and aimed us home.

But our strides wouldn't match. Our hands refused to hold. I blamed the crumpled poster. If only it had fallen down the drain.

The wad was rustling and glowing in the gutter, but that wasn't what interested me about it, although maybe it should've been. And it wasn't that I felt guilty for littering either, although that's what I told Andy as I snatched the poster from the ground.

Obstacle or opportunity?

I stuffed it into my purse.

CHAPTER 2

DAPHNE - 61 days left

Andy fell asleep as soon as we got to my studio, but I couldn't stop thinking about her. I couldn't stop looking at Andy as I thought about her, as I worried about *him* dreaming about *her*. I tortured myself so much it felt like she was helping me do it, like she'd burrowed into my brain just to spawn fear about herself. All these thoughts about them, about *her*, they were a dreadful tune I wished I could stop humming—an earworm.

They would become my constant earworm.

I slid from the covers and padded across the carpet. Harry's crayon box sat on my desk. I'd worn out most of the original crayons long ago, but I enjoyed replacing them. I pulled the double-ended crayon from my purse and added it to the box.

Still in bed, Andy rubbed his face and flipped over. He sometimes reminded me of Harry. His lack of temper. His quiet way of knowing what people needed. Harry had always seemed hesitant, unsure about being a dad, but I'd trusted him, and he'd always come through for me. Maybe Andy shared that too.

I pulled the crumpled poster from my purse and smoothed it out on the desk. And there she was: the kind of girl Andy would marry. Even in minimal light, she had an eerie glow about her. Like the glow in a Thomas Kinkade painting. Only ominous.

The poster's bottom-right corner listed performance dates from two summers ago, all for a theater called the Orphic Starlight. The phone number for the box office had a 213 area code, wherever that was. I had no idea how her posters had made it onto Portland walls, but given that they were obsolete, she probably hadn't come with them. Good thing.

As for her real name, it might have been printed on the poster's bottom-left corner, which hadn't survived the tear-down, but I didn't think so. No, her real name had never been at hand. And yet Andy knew it, knew her. Enough to prefer her.

"Why?" I asked her image. "What's so special about you?"

I powered my laptop. Chimes rang from the speakers, and I fumbled for the mute button. Andy hugged his pillow to his ears but didn't wake.

After three and a half years of accumulating college crap, my trusty old computer had gotten slow. When the cursor finally stopped spinning, I opened the browser and whispered to myself as I typed. "*The Pin-up Bride.*"

The PuB had a website, but it was under construction. I had better luck with a fan site, though not much. The only picture was the same as the poster; the calendar showed no appearances in the last eighteen months; and the links to the PuB's videos were all broken. I searched YouTube directly and found some playlists, but most of her videos had been removed. The titles were still there, though, things like "Rising Starlet Spells Success" and "Overnight Success—Literally." The only watchable video was a thirty-second news spot. A KTLA talking head, on location at some high-end theater, rambled on about Fausten Cotter being that night's headliner.

"The newest sensation to hit the vaudeville revival circuit might have played a tavern last week, but her show's sold out for the next six weeks here at Los Angeles's Orphic Starlight."

California. Good. That was plenty far away.

Behind the reporter, Fausten Cotter rehearsed a dance. A slinky, sexy movement. She wore the same veiled hat as in the poster, but her outfit was family friendly, a '40s-style calf-length dress with strappy peep-toe heels. All white, of course. She kept her distance from the camera, but that didn't stop her from flirting with it. She was intriguing, this Fausten Cotter. I didn't like her.

But I kept reading. I searched for Fausten Cotter and found something encouraging, a forum called *Where in the World Is Fausten Cotter?* Apparently, after rising to fame overnight, she'd disappeared just as quickly. There was no official comment, but her fans insisted she was at an ashram. Her trolls said obviously rehab.

Either way. I sat back and tapped at my teeth. Andy's crush was probably off slacking in the hills, hiding her issues. Andy had little tolerance for issues.

And yet he'd said he'd marry a girl like her. Something about her impressed him enough to compensate for her faults.

Maybe it could compensate for mine.

My gaze strayed from my laptop screen to her poster. To her glow. To her bygone theater dates and her missing name. Even though a veil shrouded her face, it felt like she was laughing at me, at how I'd never extract her secret.

I pulled out my phone to dial my friend Brenda, but my dumbphone was out of minutes. Irritating, but Mom and I had had enough phones shut off or stolen when I was growing up that I still preferred prepaid.

Andy's smartphone lay on my desk. I woke the screen and slid my finger over the path of his pass code. The numbers used to match his dog's name, but now they matched mine.

Brenda sounded wide awake. "This is Daphne, isn't it?"

Brenda's reading light used to keep me up all night freshman year, but we otherwise understood each other. Quiet, private, selective about who and what we gave our energy. Andy was similar. I saw Brenda less since finding him. She only hung out when the group was big enough to include plenty of singles and conceal an early exit. (I wished I could too.) But the best thing about her was that we could go weeks without hearing from each other and then pick up right where we left off, no hard feelings.

I took my laptop into the hallway, sat on the floor, and closed the door most of the way. "Hey," I said. "You ever hear of the Pin-up Bride?"

"Fausten Cotter? Yeah, why?"

Just like that. *Yeah.* Like she was some big thing. *Yeah, I know her. Who doesn't?*

"What's the appeal?"

"I dunno. Beauty. Talent. Torment. Mystery. Puts on a good show. She's kind of the whole package, you know? Why?"

I didn't like that answer. I couldn't emulate any of those qualities, and anyway none of them gave me insight as to what about her appealed to Andy.

So how could I reframe the question to get an Andy-specific answer without revealing what he'd said about her? I'd rather confess to tearing down the PuB's poster to vanquish a ghost, like a superstitious twit. Or, worse, a hallucinator. Although, really, given Andy's betrayal, a shock-induced hallucination was still me taking it pretty well.

"Daph, I love you, but I'm *loving* my book. Why are you calling about Fausten Cotter?"

"Andy said he'd marry a girl like her."

"*Pfft.* I'm sure he was joking."

"So he said. But the thing about jokes is that they're funny because they're partly true."

"Relax. Andy loves you. He'll come around."

I wanted to believe that, but when—when would he come around? He'd come around no problem for Pin-up Girl here, but for me?

My voice shrank. "But what is it he likes about her?"

"Aww, Daph. I know your relationship doesn't look like you want it to, all official or whatever, but you've got what you want—what we all want. You're lucky, Daph. Trust me. You're lucky."

"But what is it? I tried to find her online, but all her videos have been pulled."

"Yeah, she refused my interview, too."

"What interview?"

"For my Channel 8 internship. She's doing a show at L'Aornum."

"Never heard of it." I typed a search.

Brenda said, "It's that building they're redoing on Park."

My hand stilled above the trackpad. California held her safely away, but if the Pin-up Bride was in town, if she was *just down the street...*

I opened the door and peeked at Andy. He was still asleep in my bed, so cute with his arm thrown over his head. Andy was perfect, but perfect is subjective, and in town or not, this girl was still famous—still busy, still troubled, still distant. Still beyond his potential.

Still...

Brenda yawned. "Can I go back to reading now?"

"One sec." It took some digging on L'Aornum's website, but I found her: Fausten Cotter, the Pin-up Bride. Her bio called her *Queen of the Vaudeville Revival,* but other than that it lacked personality. I hoped that was because she didn't have any.

But I'd know for certain soon enough.

"What are you doing Friday?" I asked.

"Probably nothing. Why?"

My earworm buzzed: I didn't want to compare myself to a standard I couldn't match, but if I was going to be the girl Andy *did* marry, I first had to become the kind of girl he *would* marry, and if there was something—anything—I could do to make Andy feel about me what he had said about *her*, I would do it. I just needed to know what that something-to-do was.

"Want to go see a show?"

CHAPTER 3

DAPHNE - 58 days left

On Friday night, a few hours after sunset, I headed to the Park Blocks to get tickets to see Andy's crush. I found myself in a throng of people, all of us beckoned to the same spot by the flashing globe-light trim of a new marquee jutting over the sidewalk. It read, L'ADORNUM THEATRE.

Beneath the swooping font, a black-and-white readerboard (missing some Os) read:

INAUGURAL EVENT, FRIDAY 8PM
LUCAL ACTS, W/HEADLINER
THE PIN-UP BRIDE
ALL DAY MAUNDAY – B&W FILMS
HELP WANTED

And beneath *that*, a line of people stood along the wall, four people abreast: retired folk in REI couture, hipsters in secondhandmade bohemia, men in suits and blazers, but mostly women in short skirts and halter tops, all fussing with dark wigs or veiled hats.

All wearing white with hints of pink and mint green.

I smoothed my plaid scarf and tried not to regret wearing the dark blue top that Andy liked. As part of my self-torture, I'd considered dying my hair black and swapping my dark jeans for white dresses, but Andy wasn't that superficial, and even if he were, he complimented me most when I was classic and sophisticated. Looking at the line, I told myself to be glad that I hadn't changed my appearance. Some of the girls had nailed the PuB outfit, but none of them had captured her appeal. Too bad, really. Copying her style would've been easy.

"There you are," Brenda said, grabbing my shoulder. "Do you have the tickets?"

I'd never seen Brenda in a dress, but she was wearing one now, pale pink with white peep-toe heels.

"Nice flowers," I said.

Brenda patted her short dark hair. "Do they look okay? It was the best I could do."

"Yeah. Can I have one?" Before she could say no, I plucked out a fake white daisy. Bonus! It came with a clip. I handed it to her. "PuB me."

Brenda pulled some long honeyed strands away from my temple, teased them a bit, and clipped in the flower.

"Good?" I asked.

"Yeah," she said with a miffed shake of her head.

I gave her a thankful hug and said, "You know you love me."

"Yeah. Do you have the tickets? 'Cause we should get in line. It's already curved around two corners."

"What?" The Cultural District saw crowds during festivals, but I'd never seen one for a solitary show.

I looked around and found the ticket booth behind me. A handwritten sign taped to the window read: *Will-Call Only — Show Sold Out.*

"Crap."

"You didn't get tickets?"

"I thought we could get them at the door, like we usually do."

"It's the Pin-up Bride."

I shrugged. "Never heard of her until a few days ago. Never heard of this theater either, and I walk by here every day."

Brenda sighed and looked around. "Then what do you wanna do tonight? Movie? Powell's?"

She looked so bummed standing there all dressed up, and I admit all the fanfare had me even more curious to see the show, to see what could inspire so many people to such commitment.

"Hold on," I said.

I approached the ticket booth. A lanky guy with full lips on an otherwise skeletal face topped with a gradient-blue fauxhawk—dark blue roots, light blue middle, fluffy platinum ends—generously gelled into a victory-roll ocean wave was counting the till.

"Show's sold out," he said without looking at me.

I pointed at the handwritten sign. "When do you release the leftover will-call?"

His bony fingers plucked the sign from the window, tore it in half, and taped one half back up: *Show Sold Out*.

"Okay, then, when's the next show?"

"Sorry. I think there's an amateur night next week."

"Still no tickets?" Brenda said when I returned.

I shook my head. If there were no more shows, then the PuB must be leaving town. She'd be out of my sight and hopefully out of Andy's mind.

But her absence would teach me nothing. I'd finally had an opportunity to make progress with Andy, and I'd squandered it. I felt sick.

"I have to see her," I said. "It's now or not at all. After tonight, she's leaving."

"She's not leaving," said an eavesdropper. She and her friend stood in line, each wearing a veiled white hat and a frilly white dress topped with a raincoat. "It's just that she's been away from the stage for over a year. They'll extend her appearances if she can still perform."

"Why wouldn't she be able to perform?"

They looked at me like I must've recently come out of a coma.

"She got hurt onstage," said the eavesdropper's friend. "Knocked herself out doing a trick."

"What kind of trick sets you out for a year?" I asked, and then, daring to hope: "Is she a gymnast?"

Andy got bored when I watched gymnastics. If she were a gymnast, I could chalk up his heartbreaking declaration as the joke he'd claimed it to be.

But their expressions said not even close and how bizarre that you're so clueless. "If tonight doesn't go well, she'll retire, is what I heard," said the friend. "Heard she might go to Stumptown State."

"Wait," I said. "Either way, she's staying?"

"Cool, right?"

Not even close. If the PuB was staying, if Fausten Cotter was reentering average society by way of my university—walking past Andy on campus, sitting behind him in econ, inviting him to tutor her at her place... My hands shook at my sides.

"Don't look at me," Brenda said to me. "You're the one who didn't get tickets."

"You need tickets?" The eavesdropper pointed behind me. "I think that guy has tickets."

He was standing by a light post in a green puffer jacket—and I was suddenly tugging his sleeve.

"Please tell me you have tickets."

"Two premium," he said, not bothering to pull out his earbuds. "They'll get you into the front two rows."

I'd be able to see her sweat.

"How much?" I asked.

"Hundred dollars. Each."

"That's double the price," said Brenda.

The scalper sneered. Behind us, the doors opened and the line began to move.

Brenda said, "I don't need to see the Pin-up Bride that bad."

But I did. Fausten Cotter was staying. I had to know what I'd be up against. I took a mental inventory of the money in my purse. It wasn't much. "I assume you're cash only?"

The scalper flashed me his phone and its attached card reader. "I can do credit."

Pfft. I didn't have much money in my debit account either. My scholarship people still hadn't disbursed my funds. I dug in my purse for my wallet. "I'll give you a hundred for two."

The scalper laughed.

"Come on," Brenda said. "Her boyfriend's got a crush on Fausten Cotter, and she's never seen her perform."

"I should charge you five hundred," he said. "Each."

I pointed at the line moving into the theater. Anyone interested in the show who might have been willing to pay extra was already shuffling toward the entrance with a ticket in hand. "Would you rather sell them for cost or take them home with you?"

The scalper scanned the sidewalk in both directions and the park across the street, but Brenda and I remained his only option. He glanced back at us with a resigned look on his face.

I grinned. *Who has the upper hand now?*

"Tell you what," he said. "I'll give you two tickets for one-fifty and a demonstration of your fandom."

I looked to Brenda for an explanation, but she, too, looked confused.

"My what?" I said.

"You've got the white flowers," he said. "You've got the crushing boyfriend. Now show me you've got the moves."

"The moves?" I said, but Brenda said, "Like her intro?"

The scalper shrugged. "Sure."

"Two for one hundred," Brenda said, "and I'll show you her moves."

The scalper pointed at me. "She shows me the moves."

"For one hundred," Brenda said.

"For one-twenty."

Brenda acquiesced with a sigh. She had to be kidding.

"I don't know the moves," I said.

"It's easy," she said. "We'll get everyone to do it."

Easy, huh? I liked that. I liked that the PuB's crushable moves were so easy anyone could do them. Then again, if her moves were so easy, then they, like her style, were not the secret of her appeal. That was still something else.

Brenda turned to the line shuffling along behind us. "Hey, ladies"—female heads turned—"how does the Pin-up Bride intro go?"

Their faces lit up. A few of them stepped away from the line and crouched to the ground. The rest clapped a rumbling drumroll as they continued toward the doors. On a cue I didn't catch, the crouched PuBlets twirled in a tight circle, slowly standing as they undulated their torsos and drew their hands—wrists circling—up the length of their bodies. The whole move, one I doubted I could do, took several seconds and finished with feet together, one knee popped, and arms raised in a high V.

"Shuhga," some of them said—her catchphrase, Brenda told me later, given to her by her fans. Too bad. If she'd come up with it herself I'd know for certain she was ridiculous.

"Andy wants a demented belly dancer?"

"It's just her intro," Brenda said. "Just do it."

Never mind, I thought, testing the words—I was tempted to just accept this stupid little dance as the proof I was hoping for, that Andy's statement really had been a meaningless joke, a joke based in irony rather than fact—but the words never left my tongue. I needed to see the girl do her whole stupid little show before I could dismiss her as a threat.

I scowled at the smirking scalper. As if it weren't enough that Andy would marry another girl but not me, I now had to make a fool of myself, for this guy, just so I could check her out. I squatted in my tight jeans and stood quickly—spinning once, nearly tripping in my boots—and raised my arms overhead. A clumsy hack job.

The scalper held a hand to his ear.

Kill me now. "Sugar."

The scalper laughed, barely a puff of chuckle, certainly not enough to make it worth the torture. I snatched my purse from Brenda and dug out my debit card. The scalper punched something into his phone and held it out to me.

"Sales tax?" I said. "Really?"

He shrugged.

"You do know we're in Oregon, right?"

He grinned.

"So much for eating this week." I slid my debit card through the chip reader and authorized this jackass to take one hundred and thirty-two dollars from my checking account. He pulled two tickets from an inside pocket. I plucked them from his fingers and gave him a finger of my own.

And then Brenda, normally more reserved, stuffed a wad of cash into my purse, snatched her ticket out of my hand, and galloped me to the back of the line, squeeing, "I can't wait!"

CHAPTER 4

DAPHNE

The line crept along but still moved too fast.

To distract myself from dreading the show I'd come to see, I asked Brenda about the guy she'd been dating.

"He said he'd call over break, but he never did."

"So call him."

She shrugged and ran her finger along the grout in the theater's stone wall.

I tried a new topic. "So what is a Pin-up Bride anyway?"

"It's just a reference to this one show she did. She's always got that '40s pin-up look, but for one night"—Brenda pointed up ahead, at a poster like the one I'd torn down with those old California dates—"her act included a ceremony."

"She's married?" *Ha! Take that, Andy.*

"I don't think so," Brenda said. "That was the night of her accident."

We reached the main doors, ten-foot slabs of dark wood carved with a swirled design like vapor, and weaved around an A-frame sign that warned us the show would use smoke effects and flashing lights. A man scanned our tickets and handed us pink programs as we stepped inside. The theater smelled of fresh peaches and hummed, not unlike my earworm, with chatter about Fausten Cotter.

Domed crystal-basket chandeliers, four big ones and a dozen

sconces, dimly lit the length of the brown-and-burgundy lobby. We passed vendors at tiny tables, selling T-shirts, white hats, strips of pink-and-mint-green clip-in hair. The lanky guy with blue ocean-wave hair saw me looking and handed me a vial of something clear and glittery.

"PBP," he said with a wink. "Pin-up Bride pheromones. Wear it and be lucky in love."

"Uh-huh." The PuB's secret couldn't be that crass, but we would see. I'd handed the vial right back, but just holding it had left my hand smelling like peaches.

We made it as far as the second dome light when traffic stalled. I strained to see over the crowd but could only glimpse the rise of a grand staircase at the end of the lobby and, at its foot, a warm glow of light.

"That must be the bar up there?"

"Bar's right here," Brenda said, patting a slab of shiny walnut to her right. "What you came to see is up there."

"She is?" I'd thought she'd be backstage. I elbowed my way to a better view, and the sight of her nearly choked me of air. "*That's* Fausten Cotter?"

"Well, yeah," Brenda said, squeezing in on my right.

"I thought she was supposed to be a pin-up bride," I said, "all short white dress and veiled face and stupid dance moves."

"That's just her most popular act."

Well, she wasn't doing that act now. In fact, she wasn't doing anything. She was just standing there—just standing—and still a terrible patter of inability-to-compete raged in my chest.

I'd seen living statues before, but not like this, not uplit in a way that created an ethereal glow, like a full-body halo. I didn't see a light source or any electrical wires, but however it worked, her brilliance seemed sourced from within. Fausten Cotter, twentysomething, was a goddess.

She was Venus, posed in a Botticelli clamshell. A pink pearl hid her feet and accentuated slender ankles, the backs of her calves, the bend of her left knee. A gauzy strip of translucent fabric—her only clothing—draped over her thighs as if it had slipped from her hips.

By now, I'd seen enough—my stomach had dropped out of my body, probably in an effort to join hers—but I gawked at each individual vertebra in her arched spine. It twisted as she looked back at us over her shoulder, her hands mussing her dark hair. A titillating pose more De Berardinis than de Milo.

She'd been painted. But not with that garish metallic grease I'd seen on street performers. This glistened like mineral oil on grade A marble worn smooth by millennia, all polished to a dewy glow.

At least I hoped it was just paint. There was no way her skin could be that luminous. I shifted my weight and scratched self-consciously, and all the while, she stood there, perfectly still. I couldn't see her breathe, and I never saw her blink. The only tell that she was real was her skin. Every time someone opened the front doors, they let in a rush of icy wind, and all the delicate hairs on her arm stood erect on the tips of chill bumps.

I wanted to warm them. I wanted to feel—to prove to myself that her perfect skin really was just makeup; that she really was just a girl, just like any other girl, just like me, even; that it really was doable for me to develop in myself whatever it was about her that had captivated everyone, that had captivated Andy.

But the velvet rope separating her from the spectators in the lobby only belabored what I instinctively knew: Fausten Cotter was distinct from us. Better. She had an advantage, a certain *je ne sais quoi* inherent to her, to only her, something I might never pinpoint, let alone emulate.

But I wanted to. I wanted to radiate. I wanted to mesmerize like Fausten Cotter.

"I warned you."

The voice cut my reverie like a scalpel scraping bone. It came from my left, from a slender person in a tomboy suit. Tall for a girl, just average for a guy, and with a shaved head, leaving just enough jet-black hair on top to sleek it to the side.

The person scrutinized Fausten Cotter's statue through blue-lensed glasses.

Something hit my foot. I looked down as it ricocheted toward Blue Glasses' heeled boot. An empty quarter-ounce vial. It looked to me like someone's used PBP souvenir. But Blue Glasses picked it up, chuckled a creepy chuckle (that made my skin crawl as if covered with flies), and asked Fausten Cotter if she was "still demanding more."

At least I thought that's what Blue Glasses said. I leaned closer and—*ewgh*—smelled something worse than rotten pork brined in lemony dumpster juices.

"I'm not here to help you," said Blue Glasses, still taunting the PuB in that creepy bone-saw voice, a voice that had me thinking of Blue Glasses as *the creepy fan*. "I'm not here to give you anything."

Poof! Fausten Cotter's clamshell emitted a mushroom cloud of fog. The crowd gasped. Most people clapped and retreated from the crowd-controlling smoke as it billowed around us.

But not the creepy fan.

"So *this* is what you've been working on all year." The creepy fan held out both palms and surveyed the scene through those blue-colored glasses, delighting in the smoke as if it were rain.

Or as if it were camouflage. The fog now concealed the remaining few of us from the rest of the lobby. The creepy fan looked around, saw me watching, and flashed me a smirk—then leaned over the velvet rope anyway and stretched out a hand. The creepy fan was reaching for the statue, was trying to touch—

Thwack! I smacked that violative arm.

"What are you doing?!" Brenda grabbed my sleeve and pulled me away from the creep, away from the fog, away from Fausten Cotter.

I looked back at her still mussing her hair in her clamshell. Only then did I actually see her face, really see *her*. She was gorgeous, of course; even with monochrome makeup she was gorgeous. But her hazel eyes had a look of longing that belied the pose. That endeared me to her. I wanted to save her from the creepy fan. I wanted to know her rather than resent her. I reached out to Fausten Cotter, and—I swear it—her fog reached back.

"What the hell, Daph?" Brenda jerked me to attention. "You just hit someone."

And I was proud of it. "They tried to touch her," I said. "Don't let them touch her."

Brenda dragged me beneath a sconce and looked me in the eye. "You realize you're protecting your self-proclaimed enemy, right?"

Someone had propped open the theater's front doors. The air was crisp here, chilling and uncorrupted.

"Sorry." I rubbed my head. My earworm-thoughts were still pounding against my skull, but I could fake refreshed. "That fan was a creep."

Brenda frowned. "The person with the blue-tinted glasses?"

"Yeah, the creepy fan. Like it's not dark enough in here."

"'Creepy'?" Brenda peered through the crowd. "That fan looks too chic to be 'creepy.'"

"Ted Bundy was a heartthrob, Bren, still a serial killer."

"I love their suit," Brenda said, not listening to me. And it was nice: perfectly gray, neither dark nor light, and just as androgynous as the person wearing it. Still—

"One whiff of it and you'll change your mind," I said, reliving the creepy fan's scent of lemony dumpster pork—and still not convincing Brenda. "Go ahead," I said. "Go listen to 'em taunt Fausten Cotter with how they warned her, too—"

"Warned her about what?"

"—making it all threatening and stuff, and then stand by while they try to touch her."

"Okay, yeah," Brenda said, "that is creepy."

The dome lights blinked, signaling the show was about to start. Brenda and I gamboled down the theater's center aisle and squeezed past a solo in the second row on the right, taking the two seats beside him. They were hard and tiny, but the view was good. Not one-hundred-and-thirty-two-dollars good, but good. The stage had two sets of stairs, one on either side, and to the far left, a burgundy drape hung over a doorway.

The lights dimmed. People shushed each other. The dark velour curtains creaked open, revealing a mic at center stage, and out of the wings sauntered a man in a burgundy sequined suit. The crowd clapped politely. The man paused midstride and looked us over…then grabbed the mic.

"*Ladies and gentlemen, boys and girls, and those of you who defy such labels—welcome to L'Aornum Theatre*!"

His baritone left my whole body resonating with its sound. But as I settled deeper into my seat, the thrum of resonance became the churn of anxiety. I hoped that Fausten Cotter would flop and prove that Andy's comment really had been just a joke. But I feared her performance on stage would be even better than the one in the lobby.

Other acts performed first: a juggler, a hula-hooper, a magician.

After intermission, the emcee asked us how we were doing and told us about an amateur night he was hosting next Friday.

"Now!" he said, "I can see from your many accoutrements"—he patted his top hat, and I chuckled along with the crowd, remembering all the white hats and my own stolen white flower—"that our headliner tonight needs no introduction. But let me offer one anyway.

"Coming to us from *mysterious* beginnings by way of the Orphic Starlight, our next act not only revives vaudeville—she reinvents it. A favorite of men and of women, this bold beauty combines the royal art of seduction with her own branded mix of séance and satsang—giving us her incomparable séatsang. Ahh, but tonight, she's changing things up a bit. Just for you. Ladies and gentlemen, boys and girls, and all the wild rest of you, I give you: the Pin-up Bride."

CHAPTER 5

DAPHNE

The lights went out. The theater rumbled, shaking my seat.

Onstage, a slant of light appeared, growing bigger and brighter as the floor opened, allowing something to rise from its depths. A platform. And on it lay a female silhouette.

My skin prickled with goosebumps.

The crowd roared with applause.

Shrouded in a dark cloth, the Pin-up Bride glowed. Concentric rings blazed around her, like a corona around the moon. Luminous fog seeped from her supine form over the edge of the platform and onto the stage, becoming viscous, almost solid, as its tendrils reached into the audience.

"Someone's exhausting the world's supply of dry ice," said the guy next to me, "and spiking it with quite a bit of laughing gas."

No joke. I'd tucked my nose into my scarf, but I couldn't help breathing in the scent of peaches. My shoulders relaxed and so did my chattering earworm. I began to feel euphoric, and the sound and feel of the rows behind me took on a similar tenor.

The audience was prepped for the show.

A spotlight clicked on, and a man in his twenties entered the stage. He had dark mad-scientist hair and a caped coat, like Sherlock Holmes—an inverness coat. It fluttered behind him in the mist, evoking a feel of early twentieth-century spiritualism. He pushed a cart of shiny tools.

A few people clapped for him.

Fausten Cotter had yet to move. She still lay on the platform, covered in cloth. Holmes approached her with an exaggerated frown. He seemed as confounded by her as I was.

"She sleeps," he told us in an accent matching his costume. "Perhaps..."

He unveiled her face—to a gasp from the crowd—and caressed a hand through her hair. The dark mass cascaded over the edge of the platform, flashing a streak of pink and mint green.

"Perhaps if I..."

He knelt beside her, and I leaned closer too. Her vitality gripped me. Everything about her, even the way she lay there as he touched his lips to hers.

Still as the dead.

"So much for true love's kiss," Holmes said. "Looks like I need help waking her." He paced the edge of the stage, shielding his eyes from the spotlight as he scanned the crowd. "Who'd like to come up?"

"Raise your hand," Brenda said.

"I don't wanna go up there."

Brenda lifted my elbow, forcing my arm into the air. But I was safe. The pink-suited guy in front of me was standing and waving his arms.

"You," Holmes said, pointing at him.

Pink Suit darted for the stairs.

"No, no. Sorry, old chap." Holmes visored his eyes and pointed at Pink Suit's empty chair, the one in front of me. I covered my face and ducked in my seat.

Behind me, hundreds of voices yelled for Holmes's attention.

"You," he said.

"You," said Brenda, pushing me toward the aisle. I ducked lower, but she pointed down at me from overhead. "You mean her, right?"

"You, you, plaid scarf and flower, you," Holmes said, and he moved on to select someone else with equal particularity.

Brenda pried me from my seat. "Get up."

"Fine." I squeezed past the solo and endeavored to climb the stairs, to level myself with the starlet I'd come to see, to study, to emulate. Six steps up, heart clenching the whole way, and there she was. I could touch her if I wanted.

An elderly woman in a straw hat with a black ribbon, a boy who kept waving at his mom, and a man who fidgeted like he, too, was onstage against his will stood in line with me behind Fausten Cotter's platform. Aside from my flower, none of us wore white: wouldn't want the volunteers upstaging the star.

"Now," Holmes said. "How should we wake her?"

"Shake her," said the boy.

Holmes summoned the boy to his side. "What's your name?"

"DeShawn."

"Go ahead, DeShawn, if you think she'll wake that easy."

DeShawn grabbed the PuB's shoulder and shook her with his whole body. She didn't move. She didn't even tense her eyelids. But she wasn't the most convincing sleeper. Her toes were pointed, not relaxed.

DeShawn's smile faded. Holmes gestured for him to step back in line.

"Any more ideas?" Holmes asked.

I didn't know about the others, but I couldn't brainstorm with all that light blinding me, all those eyes watching me.

We all shook our heads no.

Holmes nodded and asked DeShawn, "How'd she feel?"

"Fine."

"Was she warm? Cold?"

"I dunno."

"What about you?" Holmes said to me. "What's your name?"

"Daphne."

"And what do you do?"

"I go to SSU. Biology premed."

"Excellent. Come." He beckoned me closer to Fausten Cotter's platform, but I hesitated. "Come, come"—I did as he said—"Good. So, premed. Am I right you know how to check a pulse?"

Holmes uncovered Fausten Cotter's left arm, the one closest to the crowd. I leaned over the platform—over her—and pressed two fingers to the inside of her wrist. They slipped on her glistening skin, producing a scent like the lobby souvenirs, like peaches. I wiped her wrist with the cloth, but it took a vigorous scrub to create a dry spot.

She was wearing a ring. It was turned under, so I couldn't see the setting, but the silver filigree band was on the correct finger. Already engaged. Take that, Andy. I wondered to whom. This Holmes character, maybe? Nah. She could do better than him.

"Anything?" Holmes asked.

I jumped, reproaching myself for judging him rather than checking the PuB's pulse. I refocused, but all that slip on her wrist made it hard to find the artery. I moved around the platform to get a better grip, but I still didn't feel anything.

"Try her neck," Holmes said, tugging the dark cloth below her collarbones. They were prominent, of course, and perfectly straight. I rubbed my own puny, curved bones and shifted closer.

The audience fell silent as I felt for her carotid artery near the hollow of her throat. Her skin was drier here but still luminous. She'd enhanced her makeup since posing in the lobby. Plum lips and dark lashes. She was even more beautiful with color to her face—more beautiful than my mousy features could ever be—but beauty wasn't her secret. I knew this, because it was secondary; it hit you like an afterthought.

"Anything?"

I looked away from her face so I could concentrate. I closed my eyes. I felt, I pressed...

I frowned. "Nothing."

"Is she asleep?" Holmes asked the crowd. "Or is she something else?"

The crowd murmured awe as I backed away from Fausten Cotter to my place in line, next to the elderly woman.

"How about you, young lady?" Holmes said to her. "What's your name?"

"Gloria."

Holmes selected a piece of sparkling silver from the cart and handed it to Gloria. "Are you good with hand mirrors, Gloria? Would you say this is an ordinary hand mirror?"

Gloria looked at the silver mirror, front and back. It wasn't your average drugstore hand mirror, that's for sure, but it looked like it functioned the same. Gloria agreed it was ordinary.

"Good," Holmes said. "Would you mind holding it up to your mouth?" He positioned his palm a few inches from his lips to demonstrate. She did as he asked.

"See anything?"

"Just me."

"Anything else?"

Gloria's shoulders hiked up to her ears, and the lines in her skin deepened. I ran my finger along her reflection in the mirror, leaving a mark.

"Oh. Yes. I see it."

"Tell us what you see, Gloria."

"Fog? On the glass?"

Holmes turned to the crowd. "Gloria's alive and breathing, do you agree?" The crowd applauded. "Good. Now, Gloria, will you kindly hold the mirror up to Fausten's mouth?"

Gloria hobbled to the platform and positioned the mirror above Fausten Cotter's lips. I studied her torso for movement, but the dark cloth made it hard to tell. After some repartee with the crowd, Holmes asked Gloria if she saw anything on the mirror.

Gloria tested it with her finger. "No."

"She's holding her breath," said DeShawn.

"Smart boy," said Holmes. "Should we wait a little longer?"

Gloria gave him a pained look and rubbed her shoulder. I offered to take over the burden of holding the mirror, eager to be closer to Fausten Cotter.

Holmes said, "That's a lovely boater, Gloria. Are you using hatpins?"

She was. Holmes pulled a pin from Gloria's hat and held it high for all to see. He beckoned the last volunteer—Josh, he said his name was—to step forward. Holmes handed Josh the hatpin.

"Pierce her with it."

I dropped the mirror, then fumbled to reposition it before—

"That's enough," Holmes said, motioning me back into line. He took the mirror from me and showed it to the crowd. The glass was clear. No condensation. No breath from Fausten Cotter. The audience clapped. Holmes set the mirror on the cart.

Josh held the hatpin away from himself. Light glinted off its long, tapered tip, sharp enough to draw blood.

"You want me to *what*?" he said.

Holmes spoke to the crowd: "You want to see her perform, don't you?"

Their whistles and applause said they did, of course they did. And I did too. But nothing in her poster had suggested anything about blood.

"To see her perform, we have to revive her. If she's merely sleeping—or holding her breath"—Holmes stage-winked at DeShawn—"a poke should wake her."

Cold steam rose from Fausten Cotter's platform, renewing the mist all over the stage. Wind blew from nowhere, kicking up her hair. And...and something else. An eerie energy.

Josh darted wary glances around the stage, the rafters, the crowd. Like he sensed the eeriness too.

"Let's give Josh some encouragement," Holmes said.

The crowd applauded as Holmes pulled down the dark cloth, revealing the trim on Fausten Cotter's corset. He pointed at the swell of flesh just over her heart. "Go ahead, Josh."

Perhaps it was the opportunity to touch the Pin-up Bride's breast that compelled him, for Josh had no more qualms about positioning the hatpin.

The PuB's swell of flesh dimpled.

This was just a performance, no threat at play, just a show of Fausten Cotter's obvious physical control—paired with a collapsible pin. Sweet Gloria was a plant, a fake. She had to be. They wouldn't hurt their star. But would she bleed? I closed my eyes and hid my face in my shoulder. Fake or not, I—

"Don't," I whispered. I didn't want them to hurt her; I didn't want to see her bleed.

But I risked a peek. A surge of—I don't even know—energy?—clear, distorting energy flashed on the platform.

Josh howled in pain, and I flinched backward, hitting the cart. Tools crashed, scattering light, but I only saw the red of his blood.

Nope. I lunged for the stairs.

"Daphne!"

I heard Brenda calling my name, but I ran up the aisle, eyes trained on the doors. The theater rumbled. Lights flashed. The PuB's fans gasped and stood and pointed at the stage. But I couldn't stomach looking back. Not even when the audience roared with applause.

It must've all been part of the show, everything that had happened onstage, and captivating too, because Brenda never did follow me outside, and nobody else did either. I inhaled deeply, letting January's night air calm my blood-triggered nausea.

But nothing could calm my earworm: Fausten Cotter's superior appeal was obvious to me now, but her secret? It wasn't her beauty, it wasn't her style, it wasn't her moves. Well, it could be her moves, but *I'd* been too big a wuss to watch her whole act, to wait for that so-called séatsang. I hadn't seen her do anything.

And yet I'd felt it. Her secret. She'd just lain there, rendering herself mysterious, intriguing, desirable, and me dissatisfied with myself and that much more certain that I'd never be the kind of girl Andy would marry.

I crossed the street to the park, where I could kick benches and swat branches. Andy was out with the guys, but I called him anyway, betting all my hopes for our future on whether he answered. And why not? I had no other plan to secure his commitment.

But I would soon.

CHAPTER 6

FAUSTEN

So much for my big revival.

In the darkness following my act, Petty gripped my throne's armrests and rolled me backwards, off stage right, leaning into me with the effort. His gelled hair crunched against my cheek. Now that we had a job again, he was styling it in a high-maintenance blue ocean wave.

Petty picked me up and carried me through the crossover. Cloth backdrops dangled lifelessly overhead.

"You hear that, Faus?" he said.

To our right, on the other side of the backcloth, the emcee and our new boss, Conlin Washington, was onstage closing the show. We'd insisted he do so. And my fans were booing him for denying them my encore.

"Told you," Petty said.

My fans' exasperation was nice to hear. But not as nice as basking in their cheers, as taking the last bow myself.

Petty snuck me down the stairs to the dressing room hallway, then pinned me against the wall with the left side of his body, freeing his right hand to open the door to my prep room. He carried me inside and laid me on the massage table. Its cushion squeaked beneath me as he pulled on my limbs to straighten my body.

I heard the tickle of piano keys. Petty had turned on his motivational playlist. Up first was Evanescence, "Bring Me to Life."

"Okay, Faus, I'll make this quick as I can," Petty said. "Sorry."

I stared at the white speckled-tile ceiling, unable to even roll my eyes. Petty had designed my costumes for years, so even before my accident, he'd come into contact with every inch of me.

He undressed me in seconds. Everything I wore unsnapped all the way down now, like doll clothes. I heard the plunk of a sponge being dunked into water, and then Petty began scrubbing my arms. He'd reached my collarbones and was yelling, "Okay, Faus, chest time, sorry," over the Bee Gees singing "Stayin' Alive," when a new beat countered the music.

Stomp-foot, coming down the hall.

The prep room door banged open and in wafted the musk-and-mothball smell of my stage assistant's inverness coat. Guy plunked what was probably a box full of fan gifts on the floor and turned off the music. "Dammit, Fausten, I told you, don't be flash-bombing people. You could've hurt that guy."

"It's your own fault," Petty said.

So loyal. And so true. If Guy didn't want me influencing people to jab themselves with hatpins, then he shouldn't bring them onstage to assault my dignity. *He* was the one who'd told that guy to poke me. *He* was the one who'd turned my act into a freak show. I, on the other hand, had showed restraint in defending myself against the man with the hatpin. All I'd done was nudge his hand, a tiny push of my influence, when I could have done *this*.

I imagined Guy in just enough pain to remind him that my influence was strong and worked best against him. The energy wrapped around him, attacking him with what I envisioned as little pricks and pokes of hatpins. Millions of them. He groaned. I couldn't see him. None of my posters hung in the prep room. But I could hear him, and that helped me imagine. I imagined him writhing as he fought the pain, as he fought me. And so he writhed.

"What's she saying?" Petty asked.

No posters also meant I couldn't communicate. At least not with Petty.

Guy could hear me all the time.

"*She's mad...about...the show,*" he managed to say between labored breaths.

"As she should be," Petty said. "Those people you brought onstage weren't even real fans. That girl had a flower, I suppose, but it was obviously last-minute. Okay, Faus, doing the nether regions. Sorry."

"*Not...using fans...was the point,*" Guy said.

I let him go. He collapsed on my massage table, depressing the cushion beneath my feet.

"The point of what?" Petty asked. "Of maximizing the complete and utter humiliation?"

"Someone," Guy said, still catching his breath, "had to throw off Nechai."

Petty dropped his sponge with a wet splat. "She's here?"

Nechai was a fan. More than a fan. She'd seen my show a number of times, seen it at its best in LA.

So why come to an inferior show in Portland?

"She was in the lobby," Guy said, "admiring Aphrodite. Closely."

So closely I'd smelled the lemon soap she used, in vain, to mask the stench of her job.

"And she was wearing glasses," Guy continued, "tinted blue, like that wave on your head."

"Blue glasses?" Petty said. "Why blue? Okay, Faus, rolling you over."

Petty's cold hands grabbed my shoulders and Guy's warm ones took my hips. The boys tipped me onto my side, and the massage table's worn pleather snagged on my ring.

"No idea," Guy said. "But I bet her blue glasses are as innocent a fashion statement as that ugly-shit ring she gave Fausten. Turn that ugly shit around."

I loved my ring. Within weeks of receiving it, I'd started performing at a real theater.

The center stone in the backless bezel setting had been ugly back then, a yellowish brown with flecks of junk inside, something Nechai had called a...a *khawng-khlang*? A *khruang-pluk-sek*? I don't know, something Thai. She'd told me to just call it an amulet.

Regardless, Guy seemed more offended by my ring now, now that it was pretty, like a shimmery golden opal.

Pretty or not, Petty rotated the band around my finger, turning the stone under, and the boys flopped me onto my stomach. I stared at the scuffed linoleum, my face askew in the massage table's donut hole. I used to worry about wrinkles when this happened, but Petty said my skin improved daily. Turned out my accident had its benefits.

"Any chance Nechai came just to support the show?" Petty asked, his tone betraying his fear. "Or do you think she knows about..."

I could only assume Petty was pointing his lanky index finger at me, at my facedown body splayed bare on the massage table.

"That's why I brought people onstage," Guy said, "and not fans, because now Fausten's 'new skills' are just part of her act. People will think it's just another rumor—"

"You think Nechai's here to tell the media?!" Petty said.

"I was thinking the police, but sure, *the media*." Guy chuffed, gearing up for mockery.

"Don't say it," Petty said.

But Guy did, broadcaster style: "*New Skills or Scary Symptoms? Pin-up Bride Now Dubbed—*"

Petty's sponge splashed hard into the water, and he left the room, his footsteps fading down the hall as he repeated, "Don't say it, don't say it," so as not to hear Guy call me—

"*—the Flawless Carcass.*"

"Don't call her that," Petty yelled. "I hate when you call her that."

"She can't move, all vital signs point to dead, but she's not rotting," Guy yelled back. "What do you wanna call her? The Immaculate Mort? Our Lady Abra Cadaver? How about The Iffy But Spiffy Stiffy?"

Distant grumbling and stomping up the stairs to the stage was Petty's only reply.

"You know, they really do send people to prison for this *Weekend at Bernie's* shit."

Petty would never survive prison. He'd barely survived off-brand hair gel during our poor months, before we got this L'Aornum gig. But Guy wasn't only reminding Petty. He was also reminding me. Reminding me of what the all-powerful *They* would do to me.

The edge of my awareness flickered with amusement.

Schadenfreude.

She was listening.

The wraith, or whatever she was, had first made herself known to me the night of my accident. I'd nicknamed her Schadenfreude, after that *Avenue Q* song, because she'd enjoyed my suffering then, and she took pleasure in haunting me now. She flashed scenes in my awareness of all the different ways I might suffer at the hands of *They*. Oh, yes. And being buried or burned alive was just the anticlimactic finale.

Perhaps Guy hadn't let those people fondle me onstage just to mess with me after all. Our level of success was a privilege, one he knew he'd never have with anyone else. He might have humiliated me tonight, but he'd done it for the sake of our livelihoods, to cover our asses, to show we had no secrets. He'd done it to protect us. To protect me.

He'd always been a knight.

But the boys were wrong about Nechai. Nechai had once told me that nothing's more valuable than a secret and that secrets lose value with every telling. She would never breathe a word about my condition. She had already claimed my secret as her own.

She'd stood right in my line of sight tonight, perfectly positioned so that, even in my condition, I would see her, I would know that she had come.

But not to help me.

And that could mean only one thing. That angel of evil had known my accident would happen, what I would become, and had let it happen anyway.

She'd come here tonight to see its results for herself.

Heat and pressure built inside my body with no quick means of release.

If she had wanted me to suffer this fate, I confess I knew why. But our sins were hardly equal.

"Looks like Petty's not coming back," Guy said, and terry cloth alighted on my legs. He buffed me dry from hip to feet and toweled between my toes.

I sometimes wondered what might've happened to Petty and me these past eighteen months without Guy, without his twin vulnerabilities, misplaced guilt and duty.

If only the same, or any, weaknesses drove Nechai.

When I'd first seen Nechai in the lobby tonight, I'd felt relieved. I'd thought she'd come to do the right thing. If anyone could fix my condition, it would be her.

Her and her special ingredient.

My amulet had been made with her ingredient. Nechai had told me the ring would bring me success, fans, fame. And it had. Fast. I'd asked her then about the source of the amulet's power, but she'd told me I'd regret knowing the details, that everything about it was taboo. She'd actually thought she could keep her powerful ingredient and its mysterious source a secret from me.

She hadn't known me very well back then.

And apparently she still didn't know me now. Because I wasn't defeated just because she was refusing to help me. Nechai had eventually shown me how to perform the harvest.

I bet I could get the ingredient myself.

"No." Guy swatted my leg. "Don't hurt anyone else. Fix yourself by yourself. I know you can do it."

Yeah, yeah, and I would, I was. I just needed a little bit of ingredient. We'd have to keep watch for a Goldilocks source.

"No."

Yes. According to Nechai, an ingredient's power depended on its circumstances. To fix myself, I'd need a source that was powerful, but also...preparable.

We'd need a well-timed death.

"That's not what I—*meant...by 'no.'*"

Yes, well... I could either take control of my situation or stay trapped in my body forever. And I wasn't interested in finding out what might happen to me if something were to happen to my boys. And who knew? If harvesting the ingredient was easy, maybe we could start a side business.

"*No.*"

You're right. Let's not get ahead of ourselves. First we would need a source. Easy. Sooner or later someone would celebrate a special day at the theater. A birthday party. No, too common, too predictable. But something else, something relevant. A bachelor party, maybe. *Remember that night? The Orphic Starlight was hosting a bachelor party.*

"*No.*"

Okay, a bachelorette party.

"*Don't...you...dare.*"

Funny, I could have said the same thing about somebody's impromptu poke-'n'-prod-me bit tonight. Then again, maybe that somebody did me a favor. Maybe when that somebody called people onstage, he selected a source for me. And started the harvest.

"*I...did...not...*"

Maybe not, but can anyone but me really be sure? Petty hung my posters everywhere. And that means I am everywhere. Maybe I'm spying on your hand-selected sources right now. You know, I recognized one of your volunteers. The girl with the flower. The one who ran out. She tore down my poster last week. And she took it home with her. Flower Girl is desperately chasing an engagement. Now wouldn't that be a special day? The proposal could happen anytime, you know. It's possible I'm influencing Flower Girl through the poster right now, and within the week I'll have everything I need: her and her would-be fiancé enjoying their lives' next milestone moment at L'Aornum Theatre.

With me.

CHAPTER 7

DAPHNE

Out with the guys or not, Andy answered my call on the second ring, and ten minutes later I was climbing into his white Jeep Wrangler as he turned up the heat and aimed the vents my way.

Andy had a one-bedroom in Goose Hollow at the foot of the West Hills. The apartment wasn't high enough to see Mount Hood, but it was higher than I'd ever been. We sat on his hand-me-down couch, him lounging, me stiffly refreshing YouTube. Fausten Cotter's show had ended twenty minutes ago, at least, and still no one had posted a video. One forum said that she always used an electronics killer. Now that I thought about it, I couldn't recall anyone aiming their phone at her statue or the stage.

Or at me, running out scared. I couldn't be any less like Andy's ideal.

Andy laughed at one of the late-night Jimmys and put his arm around my shoulders, squeezing me closer and kissing my head. I slid the iPad between the cushion and the armrest and cuddled into him. He felt temporary.

We heard a knock at the door. I rose to answer, but Andy yelled, "Door's open."

Brenda barged in and whacked me in the stomach with my purse. "What happened? You missed the whole reason we went to the show."

"Hey, Bren," Andy called from the couch. "How was it?"

I tried to give Brenda a look. *Please don't tell him that I stalked the PuB, that I begged you to go with me. And please, please, don't tell him why I left early.*

Brenda grabbed a 7-Up from the fridge and popped it open on her way to the couch. She perched on the armrest and took a sip.

I sat in the club chair by the sliding glass door—in Brenda's eyeline but on the other side of Andy—and tried, again, to give her the look.

She finished sipping from the can. "It was amazing."

"Oh yeah?" Andy scoped her pink dress and looked a question at me. I quickly neutralized my face. "Wha'd you see again?" he asked.

"Fau—"

"A juggler, a magician," I said, cutting her off. "You know. The usual."

Andy's brows pinched. "You didn't see a movie?"

"Oh, no," I said, playing dumb. When I'd told Andy we were going to the theater, he'd assumed we were seeing a girly flick, and I'd never corrected him. "We tried that new theater on Park. It was a variety show." I made a face like it wasn't that great. He usually trusted my taste and was quick to drop pointless topics.

But his right eye squinted at me as his thumb tapped the remote. "You saw the Pin-up Bride?"

His tone was too neutral to read. Or maybe I just wanted it to be. My earworm expanded as I taunted myself with his likely thoughts: *You took Brenda and not me? Didn't we soothe your insecurities? Was she as gorgeous as ever?*

Andy chuckled. "I was wondering why you were all of a sudden interested in vaudeville." He tapped the iPad. All my queries must've come up as search suggestions. "Daph, I told you, I'm sorry. I was just kidding."

"Kidding about what?" Brenda asked.

I didn't answer. We all knew, or at least suspected, that I'd already told Brenda the details, and anyway, she wanted to hear the story from Andy. So did I. Words from Andy held more importance, more reality.

Andy plucked at the iPad, prying its blue cover off the magnet and letting it snap back into place. Between plucks, a phone alarm pinged. *Time for a change in subject.*

"It was stupid," he said. "I saw a Pin-up Bride poster one night and said I'd marry a girl like her."

My earworm buzzed with renewed reason to worry. My lungs contracted and pressure built within my tear ducts. I leaned my head back, trying to make room to breathe.

"Aww, Daph," Brenda said, and her bottom lip pushed out. She set her pop can on the coffee table, crossed the room, and leaned an arm around me. She hadn't understood when I'd told her over the phone, but hearing *him* say it...

"You know," she said, "this could work for you." She was whispering to me, but Andy still heard.

"Work how?" he asked.

Brenda pulled something out of her purse.

"What's that?" Andy asked.

It was a half sheet of fluorescent pink paper. Starbursts printed in the corners said, *Prizes Awarded!* I read it aloud.

Are you

Talented? Mysterious? **Just plain odd?**

Show us at

AMATEUR NIGHT!

8pm, Friday, January 17th

AT L'AORNUM THEATRE

All those disposed

TO AMUSE, ***AMAZE*** OR **ASTOUND**

the masses may enter.

Bill arrangement begins at 6

Doors open at 7

I frowned. "A talent show?"

Andy threw back his head and laughed. Something about the sound was foreign yet placeable. I'd suffered this laugh not even a week ago, amidst a moonlit fog and skeletal elms. So it was true. He wanted a girl like Fausten Cotter.

Brenda chucked a pillow at him. "What?" she said, playfully but still in my defense. "Why are you laughing?"

"Daph's got some great qualities," he said, still laughing, "but as far as I know they don't include stage talents."

Brenda nudged me.

"He's not wrong," I said.

"Did you take dance when you were little?"

"No."

"Gymnastics?"

I shook my head.

"Martial arts?"

More shaking.

"I know you don't play an instrument. You sing some."

"To myself. Not for something like this." I shook the flyer.

"No talents?"

I mussed my hair and twisted my torso as I looked over my shoulder, doing a seated version of Fausten's Aphrodite statue. "I can pose on a box as it rises from the stage."

"You can't do what the Pin-up Bride does."

Andy's words. The room stilled to let their clarity ring in my ears unchallenged. Brenda's fingers tightened on my shoulder, only deepening their damage.

Shouldn't copy her act. He just means I shouldn't copy her act. But a week of nurturing my earworm—of nurturing the thought that Andy would marry a girl like Fausten but not me—had left me sensitive to the subject, and so I heard in his words something far more disturbing.

I tried to flirt it away. "I can wear a miniskirt and corset and flaunt the goods." I shimmied my shoulders and pushed up my boobs.

"Now we're talkin'," Andy said.

"And I'm outta here." Brenda recycled her can in the kitchen and waved bye to Andy—but then she ran back and gave me a hug. "You'll show him," she said. "Show him you're even better than Fausten Cotter."

I nodded and drew my knees to my chest, tucking my chin as she left.

Still chuckling to himself, Andy patted the cushion next to him. I shook my head. He gave me a regretful smile and put on a funny show.

You can't do what the Pin-up Bride does.

Andy's words. I kept repeating them over and over, and every iteration only added to my earworm.

I'd never be as intriguing as Fausten Cotter. Not to Andy.

I'd never know her secret.

I'd never have her allure.

I'd never earn his commitment.

I reread the flyer, trying to rein in my expanding misinterpretation of Andy's words. What took its place was Brenda's suggestion.

Was performing what made Fausten Cotter so appealing? It didn't work for the juggler or the magician, but still...did I just have to put myself onstage?

Maybe. Look at how Andy had defended the PuB's still-life performance. Look at how he'd fidgeted just saying her name. And he'd just announced, again, that she was the kind of girl he could marry. *Would* marry. If I performed well, he couldn't deny me. But what were the chances? I had less than a week to polish a nonexistent talent.

I shook the flyer. "Does the offer still stand?"

CHAPTER 8

DAPHNE - 57 days left

I was up before my alarm, dancing a bit and humming "You Gotta Be" as I dressed in last night's clothes, found my boots, and sat on the bed to zip them.

Andy propped himself up on one elbow and rubbed the sleep from his eyes. "What are you doing?"

I leaned across the bed and kissed his lips. "Secret stuff."

"What kind of secret stuff?"

"The super-secret kind. You don't need to know."

"I'll show you super-secret." He grabbed my wrist and tried to pull me under the covers.

I swatted his hands. "Hey, I'm busy."

"Does it involve breakfast?"

"Nope." I grabbed my purse, then reconsidered and hunted through Andy's closet for his hiking backpack. I held it up—"I'm borrowing this"—and threw my purse inside.

"You're leaving me?"

I stopped at the doorway and glared back at him, at the concern in his copper eyes. A rare sighting. Andy could keep us together past graduation if he wanted, but regardless of his choice, I knew mine. My mom had instilled it within me. So until now I'd just been waiting for his decision, for the fallout either way. But his reply last night—it gave me something to *do*.

I blew him a kiss and let him realize he'd miss me.

I had less than a week to prepare.

I caught the Blue Line headed east. An hour later, I was in Gresham, halfway up the walk of a small single-story gray house. I stared at the black front door. I'd get in, get my stuff, and get out again before—

No. My day had been good to me so far. I'd behave as though she would be good to me too.

I started to ring the bell but then remembered that I hadn't called first. She wouldn't mind, but I didn't know about this new guy. I pulled out my phone, but the door opened.

"Daph?"

"Hi, Mom."

Mom had on yoga pants, a sports bra, and bright pink tennis shoes. She took her short blond ponytail in both hands and split the ends to tighten it. "What are you doing out here?"

"Sorry I didn't call." I held up my phone. "Out of minutes."

"That's okay. He's not here." Mom left the door open and retreated to the kitchen. "You staying long?"

"How long do I have?"

A pained expression crossed her face. "As long as you want."

I stepped over the square of linoleum that formed the entryway and onto the carpet. The floor creaked beneath me. The walls were beige and bare. Mom had pushed the coffee table up against the couch—blocking it and a side chair—to make room for the workout video she had paused on the TV. The only other chairs stood around a small dining table. I leaned against the wall.

Mom handed me a water bottle from the fridge, then unscrewed one for herself and chugged. I should've asked for my box while her mouth was busy, but my mom had always fascinated me to the point of distraction. The way she couldn't care less what others thought of her life. The way she'd achieved *four times*, effortlessly and with me as a hinderance, what I was struggling to accomplish once. The way she managed to look better than me in those yoga pants.

Mom finished the bottle with a satisfied *aah*. "So?" She put her heel on the coffee table and stretched her hamstring. "What do you need?"

I scowled. "Why do you think I need something?"

"College kids only visit when they need something."

I snorted but didn't deny it. And anyway, she was smiling when she said it. "Do you have my box?"

"Of course."

I straightened, waiting for her to point me in its direction. A sweat bead dripped from her bangs. She blotted it with her fingertips, then stretched the other leg.

"Where is it?" I asked.

"What do you need it for?"

I crossed my arms. "Where is it?"

She crossed hers too. "What do you need it for?"

I could've kept this up with her—I often did—but just being around my mom was draining my momentum-filled morning.

"Oh, honey, I'm just teasing you. It's in here."

I trudged after her, down the hall, to the first door on the right. Inside was a twin bed, the kind that used to be a crib, and a dresser that doubled as a changing table. Both were stripped of linens.

"Really, Mom?"

"I'm not interfering."

Riiight. After college, Mom had followed a boyfriend who wouldn't commit, tried to make him jealous and ended up with me, and then dragged me along on her never-ending cycle of husbands and homelessness, not to mention countless boyfriends of varying levels of seriousness. As for the who, where, when, and why of this new guy, her average predicted that he was a newly divorced workaholic that she'd met in the frozen dinner aisle about two months ago, and he'd quickly let her move in because she'd tidied up and made him breakfast the first time he'd brought her here. She'd be engaged or evicted by summer. Most likely evicted.

I would not be repeating her mistakes.

"So." Mom wiggled the fingers of her left hand. "Andy do the deed yet?"

I closed my eyes, blocking her out for a breath...then opened the closet. A single tiny outfit hung on the dowel and a huge pristine teddy bear sat on a twenty-five-gallon purple plastic storage bin labeled *Daphne* in thick black Sharpie. I set the teddy bear aside and pulled out the storage bin. I could've stored the bin at school with me, but Mom always said, *Home is where your kids' memories are.* Lucky for her, all my good ones fit in this super-portable box.

Mom said, "Maybe it's time for *you* to do the deed."

"And end up like you? No, thanks."

Mom strutted to the window to straighten the curtains, to flaunt for show what she'd never tell me out loud: that it wasn't so bad being her. Cute and coddled. Toned and taken care of. For today at least. To emphasize her point, she struck a pose against the wall, fluffing her ponytail and sucking in her already flat abs to create a hollow beneath her ribs.

"It's already January, Daph."

"I know."

"You graduate in what? Four, five months?"

"I *know.*"

"Life changes after that."

"I'm *aware.*"

More than she knew. After graduation, Andy was moving back to Woodburn. He had a job waiting for him. I hadn't told Mom yet because I didn't want her to worry, even though she had to know I'd never follow him without a commitment. And it wasn't like he was moving to New York. Woodburn, home to Oregon's premium outlet mall, was just outside Salem, only an hour away. I could still see Andy on the weekends. Maybe. But would that be enough? How would our relationship last, let alone progress, once he moved there? And what would I do if it didn't? Any relationship after Andy would be doomed from go by the memory of us.

"Then what's your plan?" she said. "By the time you get to med school, half your classmates will be taken."

"*Mom.*"

She stopped posing. "I'm just trying to make sure you're happy."

"I know," I said. "I'm trying to make sure too."

I took the lid off the purple box. Inside was a stuffed bear of my own, not nearly as big or as clean, but much more loved. I set the bear aside and dug through my treasures—colored pencils, sketchpads, my top-end box of oil pastels—*ah*, here it was. Letting everything else fall back into the box, I gently pulled the dress free and shook out the wrinkles.

"O*kay*," Mom said with approval. "Let's hear the plan."

Mom and I had found the wedding dress years ago at a thrift store. I'd been caressing the skirt's white satin ruffles when she'd come to find me. "That's it," she said, snatching the dress off the rack. She held it up to herself and step-touched toward the nearest mirrored column, humming the bridal march. "Daa dum da-dum, daa dum da-dum." But the mirror must've shown her something in my nine-year-old face, because after a moment, she turned around. "Why don't you keep this one?"

"Really?"

She nodded and held it out to me. "I'll find another."

And she did. Plus two more after that one, not to mention the one that had come before Harry. Mom knew how to get engaged. Which was why I didn't want to tell her my plan. She'd tell me I'd only embarrass myself. She'd kill my only idea.

But for this part of the plan, I needed her help.

"Andy told me he'd marry a showgirl."

Mom sat on the bed. "Like an actress?"

"No, like vaudeville or burlesque. Live shows."

"Kinky."

I gave her stink eye.

"Sorry." She put her hands in her lap like she was prim and prudish and not my meddling mother who knew from experience. "So? What's the plan?"

"You make it sound so manipulative."

"Love is manipulative. That's why we smile instead of complain. That's why we work out and shave daily and don't binge cookie dough at 2 a.m. in our Juicy pants. What's your plan?"

I shrugged. "There's no plan. I just think it might be fun."

Her nostrils flared as she sucked in air and forced it out again.

"There's this amateur night, talent show thing," I said.

Her bare abs flexed, but her face remained stoic. "A *what* show thing?"

"A talent show."

She nodded. She tried to contain it, she really did, but she soon cracked a smile, then busted with laughter.

"Forget it." I wadded up the dress and stuffed it in my backpack.

"Well, what are you gonna do?"

"Never mind."

"Daph." She put a hand on my arm. "Stop. What's the plan?"

I shrugged. "I figured I could recite a poem."

"Re-cite a po-em?"

"Like Anne of Green Gables. You know, 'The Highwayman.' Only not 'The Highwayman.'"

"Okay." She didn't look convinced. "What poem?"

"I don't know. I just heard about this last night."

"And you think Andy will propose if you...?"

Always. That's what he'd said last night when I'd asked him from the club chair, knees tucked to my chin, flyer gripped in my hand, if his offer still stood. He'd patted the couch cushion next to him. *Always.*

"He might," I said, and I smiled, remembering us brushing our teeth together, sharing the sink. I'd shaken the pink flyer. *So you'll come?* He'd choked on his toothpaste. *You're serious?*

"Yeah," I said to Mom. "I think he might."

Mom patted my hand, then pulled the crumpled dress from my backpack and held it up. "You'll probably want to see if you can practice onstage."

I looked at her.

"And we'll probably want to alter this dress. Shorten it up. Chop off the sleeves."

I hugged her. She smelled like warm, salty caramel.

"What's this for?" she said, slowly hugging me back.

"Nothing." Except my mom was going to help me. My way. "Let's get the scissors."

CHAPTER 9

DAPHNE - 51 days left

By Tuesday I'd selected a performance piece, and by Wednesday I'd memorized it, but by Friday morning, the morning of the amateur competition, my mom's harping about how performing on a public stage was different from performing in my private room had finally gotten to me. My right brain worried about blinding lights and heckling trolls while my left brain stressed that a good performance could secure my future with Andy.

I needed a real practice.

I left my studio at the usual time, but instead of following the hourly flow of students in earbuds and backpacks to my 9:00 chem lab, I walked upstream, to the Park Blocks. Most of the street's gray brick and stone buildings—museums, venues, and concert halls—faced each other on either side of the greenway, their entrances hidden away in courtyards and secret alcoves.

L'Aornum Theater's entrance toed the sidewalk at the corner of Park and Columbia. Its marquee was dark and its ticket booth curtained. I pulled on the main doors' handles. Locked. I walked around the corner, looking for another entrance.

The building was three or four stories high with windows at the top. Gray stones the size of boot boxes formed three of its walls, and the fourth wall was shared with the business next to it, on the right. I found a scuffed loading door but no people doors.

I returned to the front and banged on the main doors. "Hello?"

I heard a noise like creaky old hinges. I put my ear to the crack and pounded again. "Hello?"

No answer. But a Pin-up Bride poster hung to the right of the doors, and for a second it felt like she was watching me, pitying me from behind her veil. I'd spent all week detailing my costume, practicing my piece...and Andy had mentioned none of it, not my upcoming performance nor his tit-for-tat after. I was beginning to wonder if he'd even show up.

"Bet *you*'d never have to go through so much trouble," I told the PuB poster.

Resigned to hustle off to chem lab, I tried the doors one last time, as people do. This time they opened with ease.

"Hello?" I tried to prop open the door, to allow as much light as possible into the building, but the door wouldn't stay.

"I'm not afraid of the dark," I told myself, "and the only boogeyman who's not supposed to be in here right now is me."

I hope.

I stepped inside, letting the door close behind me with a trapping click. The cavernous space hummed silently and looked pitch black save for a tiny light shining from somewhere deep inside, a tiny dot of red.

"Hello?"

"Up here."

I stumbled backward and hit the door, my heart banging against my sternum.

"You're over an hour late, Miss Thing." Like the Great and Terrible Oz, the gruff baritone reverberated around me.

Focusing on the red dot, I pushed away from the door and held my hands out as I stepped slowly, carefully, through what I remembered was a small foyer and then the lobby.

"Where are you? Get up here."

I didn't respond. My eyes were slow to adjust, and I was too busy steadying myself against darkness vertigo. My fingers hit the corner of the bar. I followed it through the lobby. By the time I reached the other end, I could identify the source of the red light: an old manual fire alarm.

"If you can't be on time, we'll have to rethink your contract," said the gruff baritone. "I don't care how popular you think you are."

High on the wall, to the right of the fire alarm, a flashlight beam bobbed down the damask wallpaper in tempo with the footsteps of someone descending the grand staircase.

"Where are you already?" The beam swept over me, and a man's dark form stilled on the middle landing. "You're not Ms. Cotter."

I held up a hand to block the glare. "No, I—"

"How'd you get in here?"

"I just wanted to try out the stage. Before the contest?"

His flashlight ran the length of me. I'd topped my yoga wear with sweats, my peacoat, and my bulging backpack, and accessorized with a stocking hat, fingerless gloves, and my plaid scarf. I looked like someone seeking shelter rather than the stage.

He said, "You're here to rehearse?"

"If that's okay."

To my surprise, he smiled, his perfect teeth bright white in all the darkness. "If only the pros were as dedicated. Yes, my dear, let's get you to the stage."

His name was Conlin Washington. He owned and managed the theater. He was tall and lithe, graceful even, with a bald head, enviable brows, and those gleaming white teeth, none of which matched his gruff voice, which sounded familiar.

"Did you host the show last Friday?" I asked as I followed him up the stairs.

In answer he said, "*Ladies and gentlemen, boys and girls, and all the rowdy rest of you...*"

His voice gave me tingles. The way he used it, the way he controlled it. "How do you do that?" I asked.

"Practice," he said, and he did the voice thing again: "*So you're well on your way.*"

Upstairs, Conlin shined his flashlight around, showing me an empty ballroom with an L-shaped bar and balcony arches overlooking the stage. I followed him straight ahead, to a dark corner to the right of the arches. Conlin pulled back a curtain and brushed at the wall. A dim bulb lit overhead, offering just enough light to cast shadows down a steep and narrow staircase.

"Park!" Conlin's yell boomed in the stairwell and echoed into the dark depths below. "Help this young lady to the stage."

The only response was a strong wind creaking through the building like old hinges.

"Well, you'll find him," Conlin said, leaving me alone. "It's his show tonight."

I didn't like this stairwell. Each step swayed beneath my feet and there weren't any handrails. I kept both palms flat against the walls, just in case a stair collapsed beneath me, but it didn't keep me from tripping. I biffed it on the last step and landed hard on my knee. Pain shot up my thigh and into my gut. I rolled onto my back and held my knee and just lay there, whimpering.

Footsteps echoed across the wood floor, strong and steady, like the drumbeat of a one-man army. I looked toward the sound, but all I could see, floating toward me in all the darkness, was a glowing screen print of the Pin-up Bride.

Even though I was still on my back, I couldn't help snorting. "Nice shirt."

"Nice outfit."

I frowned and fidgeted with the ends of my scarf.

The PuB's biggest fan offered his hand to help me up. It was warm and a little grimy.

"Guy Vincent Park," he said.

"Really? Three names?"

Guy Vincent Park had thick dark hair, like a helmet, and he wore dirty coveralls, the top half unzipped and hanging around his legs, revealing that awesome glow-in-the-dark promotional shirt. Its screen-printed silhouette of the PuB fit him like an emblem of loyalty on a molded breastplate.

"It's a family name," he said. He grabbed a folding chair from against the wall and unfolded it for me.

Using the chair like a cane, I dusted myself off. "How very serial killer."

A loud click echoed from the building's depths, and all things electrical hummed to life.

"Riiight," I said. "*Now* you turn on the lights."

But the lights barely made it to dim. The hum was mostly furnace. Heated air hit cold, creating a vapor that clung to the rafters as if it were seeping through the wood from the floor above.

And the vapor glowed, eerie and unnatural.

But Guy Vincent Park seemed unconcerned as he fetched a clipboard from the top of a covered grand piano. "And you are?"

"Daphne."

"Daphne..." He scribbled on the clipboard. "Like Fred and Wilma?"

"Don't forget Shaggy and Scooby." Like I hadn't heard that one before. "I hope this isn't the highlight of your act."

"Nah, I'm not a comedian."

"Clearly."

Guy put on one of those insincere smiles people use when they're masking irritation and rubbed his scalp, making his helmet hair in serious need of a brush. "You do know we just met, right?"

"Sorry—"

"And that you want something from me?"

Right. I was just embarrassed that I'd fallen down the stairs. And annoyed by his shirt. And bitter that I was here, having to do any of this crap at all, just to convince my boyfriend, who supposedly loved me, to do so forever.

I took a deep breath and stood a little taller. "I just want to rehearse on the stage."

Guy leaned an elbow on the piano. "What's in the bag?"

I hitched my backpack up higher on my shoulder.

"Flamboyant costume?" he said. "Tap shoes? A prop? I'm thinking umbrella. *Singin' in the Rain*, maybe?"

I huffed through my nose and shifted my weight.

"I need to see it if I'm gonna clear your entry."

"What do you mean 'clear my entry'?" I said. "I thought anyone could enter. I thought I just had to show up at six."

Guy grunted and pointed his pen at my bag. "Show me."

My face grew hot. "Here?"

"You can take five steps that way if you want." He pointed to my left, in the direction of more darkness. "Fifteen if you'd like to stand center stage."

I didn't move. I didn't want him to watch.

"What?" he said. "Am I wrong about the tap shoes? Do you need a tumbling mat? A coatrack?" He flashed a grin, this one genuine. "A pole?"

"I need you to not be here."

He nodded. "Insecure, huh? How you gonna seduce a house full of strangers into voting you their favorite if you can't even dance for me?"

I chewed my lip and looked at the stage. The jackass had a point. And not just about the strangers. "Is there somewhere I can change?"

He made a show of turning his back to me, presumably to give me privacy. The best I would get, it seemed. I set my backpack on the chair and pulled down my sweats as I muttered to myself, "Fausten Cotter would never put up with this."

"What was that?"

I balanced on one leg and yanked at my sweatpants, trying to get the elastic over my shoe. "Will she be here tonight?"

"Who?"

"Fausten—"

Guy turned around so fast I flinched and lost my balance. I tried to hop back to stasis, but I hit the folding chair and fell to the ground, my feet still trapped in my sweatpants.

"*What?*" I said from the floor. "Dare I not speaketh thy starlet's name?"

Guy didn't answer, and he didn't offer to help me up. He focused all his attention on the rigging system in the rafters. Cloth backdrops swayed in the mist. Guy sniffed the air—and his jawline rippled.

The mist had thickened since the air had first come on, and it smelled like those souvenir vials, like peaches, but I didn't see how either of those things was a problem. Seemed to me someone was just testing the Pin-up Bride's fog machine.

"I thought I recognized you," Guy said, still looking at the ceiling. "Plaid scarf, white flower. You came to the show last week. You knocked over my cart."

"So?"

His jaw tensed. "You can't be here."

I tried to get up gracefully and failed. "But Conlin said I could practice."

Guy set his clipboard on the piano, but it fell off and rattled to the floor. He paid it no mind. His gaze remained on the rafters, on the mist.

"No," he said.

"No?" I yanked up my sweats. "What do you mean 'no'?"

"You're out of the competition."

Light flashed overhead, distracting me from asking him why, and for an instant I thought I saw what Guy must've been seeing.

But, no, the mist couldn't be that brilliant. It couldn't be expanding even as it condensed into haze, into smoke. It couldn't be swirling with energy, ready to engulf.

But the mist flashed again, proving it could.

"Shit," Guy said. He darted toward me, grabbing my bag and shoving it at me, forcing me up the stairs. But his effort stalled, like he battled more than just me. He groaned but couldn't push me any further. I yanked my arm, tried to pull myself out of his grip, but his fingers were a trap pinching my flesh. So tight I couldn't breathe to scream.

"*Daphne.*" His eyes were anguished, his face contorting like every spoken word sliced his tongue: "*Time...for you...to leave.*"

He let me go. I heard a thud, but I obeyed. Three stairs at a time. Misty fingers stung my ankles, icicles through my pants, but I didn't look back.

"*Don't...come...tonight.*" His voice was pain bellowing up the stairs. "*Please.*"

I flew across the ballroom, down the fancy stairs, and sprinted past the bar. I expected trouble from the main doors, but I burst through them, into the light of the white-gray sky.

CHAPTER 10

DAPHNE

I clung to a light pole in the park across the street from L'Aornum Theatre, and the more I sat there, hugging the cold metal, recovering my breath, the more certain I became that I'd just been duped.

It was like this: The mist had scared me good, I admit it, but if the mist had really been a threat, then Guy should've been trying to escape with me. And if he couldn't escape, then he should've been telling me to get help. But he hadn't. He'd just yelled at me not to come back. Yelled at me in a creepy stage voice like Conlin's, only not as good.

Guy had been acting. Probably trying out some fancy stage trick with the fog machine just to frighten me. Retaliation for my being a bitch to him, which, I admit, for a moment there, I had been.

My phone rang.

"Guess what?" Brenda said when I answered. "I met someone."

"Congrats," I said, lacking enthusiasm.

"He already asked me out and everything."

I shouldered my backpack and trudged back to campus. "Again, congrats."

"You okay?" Brenda asked.

I told her about trying to practice, only to be cut from the competition.

"I know the contest was my idea and all," she said, "but maybe that theater guy did you a favor."

My feet slapped the gum-covered sidewalk. "How's that?"

"Andy loves you—you know that, everyone knows that—and he said something stupid. It's not like it's his norm. Why drag it out?"

I pressed the phone to my ear so hard I crushed some cartilage. "Because if I don't do *something*, he'll never change his mind. He'll never ask me."

"Well, jeez, Daph, why don't you just trap him the old-fashioned way?"

"How's that?" I asked.

"You know: drain the ring, miss a few pills, take a needle to the condom."

"Right," I said. "'Cause *that* leads to a happy ending." It was like she was being dense on purpose.

I flopped on a bench and watched the joggers and the dog walkers. A little boy ran after the crows, waving his sippy cup like a net. *Hold still*, his mom said. *If you chase them they'll just keep—oh!* The kid fell and scraped his hands before she could finish what she'd been about to say.

"I want him to *choose* me, not be stuck with me," I said, then looked at the phone to see if it had disconnected. "Hello?"

"I was kidding," Brenda said. "And I still think you're just torturing yourself."

And torturing Brenda from the sounds of it. But she was right. I might never be enough. True emotion crept into my voice. "Then what should I do?"

"Aww, Daph, I don't know. Tell him the truth? Do something fun, just for him? I'm sure he'd like that better anyway."

I couldn't tell Andy the truth; it was too embarrassing. No one would ever oust a girl like Fausten Cotter, yet here I was, the biggest reject in variety theater. All I was missing was the scornful pull of a vaudeville hook.

We hung up. It was 10:30. I could still make it to the last ninety minutes of lab. Last hour if I went home and got my book first. If Andy asked about the show—and he hadn't all week, so why would he?—I'd just tell him I'd gotten the day wrong. There. A plan. I pushed off the bench, determined to salvage what had become of my life.

My phone rang. I sat down again and answered.

"Hey," Andy said, but then he covered the mic and spoke to someone else, someone with a flirty voice, and they both busted up with muffled laughter. I should've asked him who she was, but at that moment the gap in our relationship, between what I wanted and what I thought I could persuade him to give me, seemed too great for me to care.

"Sorry about that," he said to me. "Aren't you supposed to be in lab?"

"Then why are you calling?"

"I was gonna leave a message."

"Beeeeep."

He actually laughed at that. "Okay, I'll play: Hey, Daph, it's me. Just wanted to let you know I've got a surprise."

"What is it?"

He sang, "Anticipaaaation." It was one of his lamer jokes.

"Uh-huh. What is it really?"

"A *surprise,*" he said. "You'll know tonight."

"Like tonight happy hour or tonight bedtime?"

He chuckled. "We'll do it after your contest."

Yeah, now he asks. "About that, I got the—wait. What do you mean 'do it'? Like *it* it?" *Omigod-omigod.* "Where are you? Let's do it now."

His phone rustled, then, "We'll do it tonight. After you win."

"What if I lose?" *What if I don't perform at all?*

But he must've taken the phone away from his ear again, because he never answered. His distant, muffled voice talked to that flirty someone else.

"I gotta go," he told me. "I'll see you at the theater."

I took my time putting my phone away. It wasn't like Andy would withhold the surprise he got me. (*The ring he got me. Please be a ring.*) I mean, he couldn't really expect me to win. And it was too much effort to resize or buy or otherwise get me something just to abandon it in a drawer or return it after I lost. And losing was kind of like not performing at all, because, in either case, it wasn't a win. So, since he wouldn't withhold the surprise if I lost, chances were he also wouldn't withhold the surprise if I just didn't perform at all.

My self-talk was logical, but it didn't soothe me. Andy had gotten me a surprise thinking that I would perform. We'd kind of made a deal, an odd but apparently understood deal. He'd said he'd marry a performer, and I had offered to perform. Andy was honoring his part.

I was the one reneging.

"Oh, no, I'm not." I shot up from that bench so fast I scared the passersby. No matter. Andy was proposing. Tonight. The truth of it hit me with a full-body shiver that empowered me to my core.

I might have let Guy Vincent Park scare me and waste my morning, but I could not let him keep me from the stage.

CHAPTER 11

DAPHNE

I stood fifth in a line of about twenty, outside the entrance to L'Aornum Theatre. Rain drizzled from a blinding gray sky on my huge '80s glasses and black thrift-store wig. I scratched underneath it, triggering judgmental snickers from the girl behind me. Rude, but whatever. It was the best disguise I could find in the few hours I'd had to prepare it, and I'd just take it off if anyone other than Guy came out those doors.

Please be Conlin, please be Conlin, please be Conlin...

At 6:05, the doors opened. Our host came out hunched over, blocked from my view by the four contenders in front of me. He propped one door open, sticking it, somehow, to the wall, and then stood upright. He wore a pink-and-mint-green PuB shirt.

I puffed a sigh out my nose.

"Whoa, good turnout," Guy said, looking us over. At least two of my competitors were jugglers, probably from the club at Reed. I suspected some of the others were aerialists, acrobats, and pole dancers. Portland had several schools for each craft.

Guy reached inside the building for his clipboard. "Right, so when you get up here, I'll need your name, style, and music, so have it ready."

The line moved quickly. I couldn't hear the first few contenders, but the girl in front of me told Guy she was a break-dancer. Guy took her CD and waved her through with nary a look.

"Go ahead," he told her as he scribbled his notes. "Just follow the signs to the greenroom."

I blew out a calming force of air. I could do this; I could get past Guy and into the show. He'd never learned my performance details this morning, and I'd already selected a *nom de scène*.

As the break-dancer stepped inside, I took her place in front of Guy.

"Anne Gables," I said, silently congratulating myself on my steady voice. I waited on Guy with downcast eyes smiling behind my glasses. Tonight had the makings of an impressive engagement story: Andy proposes to the crafty "Anne Gables" the night of her debut. And then? Anne disappears—Poof!—Inexplicably!—just like Fausten Cotter.

Guy stopped writing but didn't ask me my style. He crossed his arms and hugged his clipboard to his chest. The girl behind me cleared her throat. I glanced up.

Guy said, "You mean 'Daphne,' right?"

Behind me, the line went silent, save for the brush of bodies shifting for a better view.

Guy plucked the glasses from my face and slotted them into my coat pocket. "Did you really think I wouldn't recognize you or just that I wasn't one hundred percent serious?"

"I'm sorry for this morn—"

"It doesn't matter."

"*Oh good.* Great. I'm doing a mon—"

"No, I mean I don't care about your apology. You're not doing the show." He looked over my shoulder. "Next?"

"You can't just cut me for no reason," I said.

"Sure he can," said the girl behind me. She must've had intel on the prizes, because she jabbed her elbow into my ribs and tried to push me out of the way. "Move yourself along."

I looked askance at Guy. He ignored me and asked the girl for her info. She elbowed me again—"Quit holding up the line. Some of us need time to prep"—but I held my ground.

"So what I'm hearing," I said, "is that this girl can be a bitch and still perform, but I can't?"

The girl's hand went to her hip and out popped her offending elbow. "Excuse me?"

"Hey," I said, "if you can't bear to hear the word, don't enact the definition."

Guy raised his palms—"Ladies, please"—but Elbows was already tugging at my bag. *Zip.* Out fell my makeup, my hair stuff, my shoes. Elbows snatched a black pump off the ground and held it in front of her mean, smirking face.

"No!" I tried to take it from her, but she took the toe in one hand, the heel in the other, and—*crack*—my shoe broke in two. Elbows raised the parts for all to see and then released them, a double clunk on the sidewalk.

"Ladies," Guy said, "this theater can only handle one prima donna, and we're already catering to her. Take it to LA."

Guy beckoned to the next person in line, who stepped forward and said he was an aerialist. The aerialist must've come with Elbows, because she started yapping her maw at him. He nodded along but wouldn't plead her case with Guy.

"You broke her shoes," he told her.

Guy took his music, and the aerialist stepped inside, giving Elbows a sorry smile and me a parting glare.

Mouth agape, Elbows rounded on me. I braced for her ire, but it didn't come. Her face crumbled into her hands, and she ran away. I picked up my stuff and hurried after her.

At the end of the building, she kept running, but I ducked around the corner. I hid there, peeking every so often, waiting for the line to dwindle. When the last contestant stepped through the door, I stepped up to face Guy.

"Please," I said. "Please, Guy, I need to perform."

"Need?" Guy unstuck the door and let it close against him like a shield. "Why would a premed student need to perform?"

I lifted my chin. I probably should've told him that it was a dare for my sorority, that preferential bathroom rights or a private corner bedroom were on the line. But all I had was the truth.

"So my boyfriend will propose."

His eyes bugged out of his ugly-ass head and he laughed this strange, maniacal laugh. The life or death of my relationship, my future, was in this asshole's control and he just laughed.

"Propose? Tonight? At the theater, prob'ly, too, right?"

My face burned. I pressed my lips together, trying to maintain my composure. All I could do was nod.

"Oh, man." He scratched his head, fluffing his helmet of hair, and looked away from me, at a poster of the Pin-up Bride. Captivated. "Yeah, you've gotta go. It's not—"

I lunged toward him, aiming for entry, but Guy slipped through the gap and yanked the door shut. The edges nipped my fingers. I reached for the handle, but it was gone. Nothing left but a couple of holes that might become a handle with the right tool.

I hit the door with my palm. I might've hit it a few times. People on the sidewalk veered wide to avoid me. By the time I'd finished raging, my scalp was sweating beneath my wig. Drips of perspiration ran down my temples, under my boobs. I took off my coat, my scarf. The wig too, screw it. The cold wind and the pummel of January rain felt deserved against my skin, and I stood there, languishing, as it pelted me in the face.

"The Pin-up Bride, huh?"

I startled. "What?"

A man with white hair stood next to me. He pointed at the wall I was facing, at the poster of the Pin-up Bride. "Has it sold out?"

"Doubt it. Tonight's just an—"

Easy solution. So simple I could've kissed the man. While I'd been standing here, feeling sorry for myself, more people had formed a line at the theater's doors. Not to perform, but to watch.

"It's a what?" the man asked.

"It's an amateur competition."

Ten minutes and fifteen dollars later, and I was inside the theater, the back of my hand stamped with approval.

CHAPTER 12

DAPHNE

I snuck up the fancy staircase, across the ballroom, and down the narrow, rickety stairs to the wing. Onstage, someone with thick dark hair and a mint-green shirt stood on a ladder, hanging silks from one of the beams. Guy.

Hugging the shadows, I tiptoed past him, following pink signs that pointed amateurs to the right, down a short set of stairs, and then to the left, down a hallway, to the greenroom.

A few amateurs waited in line for the bathroom, but the rest were in all states of dress, all too concerned with themselves to notice me. The quiet corners were taken, but I found an empty spot along the wall, next to the break-dancer.

I unzipped my bag, pulled out the old wedding dress, and gave it a shake to release the wrinkles. Mom had suggested we dye it a dark red—in a huge stockpot on her boyfriend's stove, no less. It had turned out great. The bodice had come straight from the '80s, so it already had a corseted look, and the skirt was shorter now, with extra frills and ruffles. It resembled Fausten Cotter's poster outfit. Only red.

I slipped the dress over my clothes and then used it for privacy to take them off. The hard linoleum floor chilled my fishnet-covered feet. I adjusted the bodice of my dress and reached behind my waist to zip myself.

Crap.

I couldn't reach the zipper. The only time I'd tried this on was at my mom's, and she had zipped it for me. I tried to reach over my shoulder, but it was no good. I scanned the room for a clothes rack with a cheap metal hanger, but all I found was a guy glaring at me from across the room: Elbows' friend, the aerialist.

I turned away and bumped into the break-dancer. "Sorry."

"No worries." She smiled and continued rolling the sleeve on her stretchy white button-up. She wore it with tuxedo track pants and a short purple tie.

"Would you mind zipping me up?" I asked. I pushed my hair aside and turned my back to her—and came face-to-face with trouble.

The aerialist wore nothing but a slinky pair of shimmer pants and a smattering of creatively placed tattoos. He was alone, but he must've told the whole room what he was about to do, because everyone was watching.

He crossed his arms low over his abdomen, probably so as not to disturb his nipple piercings. "Weren't you told to leave?"

"I'm here, aren't I?"

The aerialist turned and stalked away, his bare feet slapping the linoleum.

"Hey, James," the break-dancer called after him. "Just leave it." But the aerialist was already out the door.

"Drama, drama, drama," said the break-dancer. "I keep waiting for people to outgrow it."

"Where's he going?" I asked.

"To snitch." She sat on the floor and tied on her lime-green high-tops. "Don't know why he cares. It's not like anyone can beat him."

"He's going to tell Guy?"

I didn't wait for an answer. I shoved all my stuff into my backpack and looked for somewhere to hide, another exit, but there was only the one door.

I peeked down the hall. It was empty, save for six green doors on the same wall, back past the stairs. Probably dressing rooms. I hurried down the hall, moving silently thanks to Elbows breaking my shoes.

I reached the stairs and heard voices in the wing. The aerialist was talking to Guy—and blocking the only exit.

I tore to the nearest dressing room and tried the knob. Locked. I raced to the next. It was the same. I kept checking, and with every locked door, my temple throbbed. I winced at the pain, at the overhead lights—at the PuB poster at the end of the hall.

My earworm buzzed. What would Fausten Cotter do?

Not this. I flattened myself against the last door at the end of the hall. It was stupid, but it was all I could think of to do. I just hoped the door frame obscured enough of me, and that no one looked my way.

My red costume against the green doors and the off-white walls. *Riiight.*

Something cold slithered past my feet. Tendrils of fog were oozing from the crack beneath the door, thick and ticklish around my ankles. I moved to run, but Guy and the aerialist stepped down the stairs. I flattened myself in the doorway, shifting my feet to avoid the mist, but I couldn't keep it from snaking a chilly veil up my legs, my torso, my neck.

Guy looked my way. The peach-scented fog had almost completely shrouded me from his view, but I still gasped—and sucked in a lungful of haze.

And the fog began to clear.

"No, no, no." I needed it to hide me from Guy.

But the fog didn't listen, and six doors down, Guy Vincent Park stood with his clipboard in the doorway of the greenroom. He had his back to me, hadn't noticed me yet, but if I could see him, then he'd soon see me.

The stairs were too far away, but my only option was to get to them.

"Okay, you two, you're up," Guy said.

A girl in blue and the aerialist joined him in the hall. The aerialist clapped him on the back. "Saving the best for last, huh?"

I stumbled and caught myself on the wall. *Last?* What did he mean 'last'?

"Daphne." Guy stopped short of me and held an arm in front of the others as if shielding them from my presence.

"See?" said the aerialist. "I told you she got in."

"You guys go ahead," Guy said. He kept his eyes on me as his performers climbed the stairs. "You can't be here," he told me.

"I bought a ticket," I said.

"Then go to your seat."

"But I'm dressed, and I'm determined." I stepped toward him. "Please. Just let me perform."

"So your boyfriend will propose?"

I took his hand in both of mine, so grateful he understood. "It'll only take a second."

"That's all she needs." He seized my forearm and yanked me up the stairs. I put on the skids, bending my knees and gripping the steps with my toes. My fishnets snagged on the wood. I cried out, "Why do you even care?!"

"Quiet," hissed a gruff baritone. Conlin's baritone. Coming from the wing. I stopped resisting Guy's pull and fled past him up the stairs.

Conlin stood at the piano with a clipboard.

"Conlin!" I said, but he held up a silencing finger. Guy overtook me and pulled me toward the rickety staircase that led to the ballroom. I yanked back, trying to pry his fingers off my wrist. "Conlin," I whispered. "I was here this morning. I wanted to see—"

"I remember you," he said. "What's going on? Park, let the poor girl go."

Guy stopped pulling me, but he didn't let go. "She can't go on," he said. "She was late getting in."

"I was the first one here."

"I don't have her music."

"I don't need any."

Guy draped his free arm around Conlin's shoulder and tried to speak chummy in his ear. "Her act's not ready," he said. "Maybe if she'd gone on first we could've let her embarrass herself, but we can't let her go last."

"No, I'm ready. He cut me before I even got a chance. Please, Conlin? Please let me perform?"

The music stopped to polite applause. Conlin gestured for the girl in blue to exit back to the greenroom. "It's Guy's show tonight," he said. "If he says no..." And he swaggered onstage to introduce the aerialist, who was in the other wing, prepping his silks.

There was no one else to beg.

Guy tightened his grip on my arm. "Let's go."

I could do nothing more than tug back and dig in my heels, my nails, as Guy dragged me toward the stairs. I couldn't believe this was happening. Andy was in the audience and he had a ring. He might resent proposing if I didn't perform, and the stage was right there. *Right there.*

"Guy, please, just let me go on."

The stage curtain fluttered.

A breeze ruffled my skirt and chilled the backs of my legs.

Guy stopped pulling me and looked around with wary eyes. He sniffed the air—and his grip on my arm loosened. I yanked free and pushed him away.

The breeze must've pushed him too, because Guy slammed into the rickety steps, tumbling down them to the ground.

And like steam from the pavement after a warm spring rain, vapor rose from the stairs, from the walls, and wrapped Guy in a peach-scented haze. He writhed against it, yanking his useless arms and legs, but his misty captor only tightened its viscous manacles.

And as if all the attention I'd been paying it over the past two weeks had helped it develop its own point of view, its own mind, my earworm hummed with new clarity.

Neat trick.

Yes, it was. "Neat trick," I told him.

Guy's terrified eyes found mine. "*You've got. To leave,*" he said. But he couldn't make me. He couldn't even move. The best he could do was scream.

"*Leave!*"

I backed away from him, away from the haze, away from the blocked stairs. I turned around. Conlin and the aerialist to the left, dressing room stairs to the right, and straight ahead a covered piano blocking the darkness.

I darted straight ahead, past the piano and into the crossover that led behind the stage.

Light shone from an open freight elevator. I stopped short. My earworm hummed louder, encouraging me to enter. I hesitated, but I had nowhere else to go. I stepped inside. The doors shut before I could change my mind and opened one floor down, on a dark room.

My earworm pulsed, guiding me further beneath the stage, toward a soft glow of light. I weaved around wooden posts, stepping carefully across cold, gritty cement. The glow illuminated something on a platform. A pair of heels. Blue T-strap peep-toes.

My earworm nudged—

Put them on.

I scanned the dim room, looking for someone they could belong to, but I was alone beneath the stage.

I picked up the shoes. They were cute, in a shade of blue that complemented the red of my dress. And they looked about my size. I slid them on, buckled the straps, and climbed atop the platform, flat on my back, my backpack at my side.

The aerialist's music began, an aggressive classical piece that resonated with my nerves—but not as nervousness. Nervousness jitters the stomach; this energy jittered my limbs. Tingly, but not shaky, not weak. I felt stronger. Eager.

Quality wasn't part of my deal with Andy—all I had to do was perform—but to emulate his crush, my effort had to be controlled. Fausten Cotter wasn't perfect—her accident onstage proved that—but only because she compelled herself beyond who she currently was. She took risks. And maybe that was her secret.

When you aim beyond them, how can you not deserve your desires?

The aerialist's music stopped, and the audience replaced it with applause. Footsteps echoed above me, and then Conlin addressed the crowd, his voice muffled by the stage.

And the platform began to rise.

And my earworm began its crescendo, psyching us up for an inspired performance.

A hatch opened above me, and the platform pushed me through. I emerged from the stage to bright light, to a round of applause, to catcalls the Pin-up Bride wouldn't believe.

And my earworm reached the pitch of awe, soprano breaking glass.

I was ready. I pushed my backpack over the edge and scooted off the platform, catching my fishnets on the corner. I stumbled a little.

No matter. Keep going.

I righted myself and stood tall as the box lowered, the hatch closed, and the crowd roared with applause.

CHAPTER 13

DAPHNE

I'm sure there was bright light and darkness beyond, a deafening silence, but I felt too jazzed, too in the moment to notice such things. My only intention had been to finish "I Knew a Woman" by Theodore Roethke without flubbing the words.

But something more happened.

My voice teased, my body tantalized, warm and alight with the muse. My hips swayed in unchoreographed ways, hitting seductive angles, embodying a woman, thee woman, who could incite her man's adoration, his devotion.

I'd picked the poem in part for its shortness, and it was over too quickly. My senses began to refocus, taking in the stage and the silence of the audience like a good dream yielding to fearsome reality.

I squinted at the bright lights. Not even a cough, not even a fidget in the audience. I looked stage left for guidance. Conlin's mouth hung open. He blinked a few times, then crossed his arm over his abdomen and leaned forward.

"Bow," he mouthed to me.

I swept my leg behind me.

The theater erupted. Total strangers cheering for me. I scanned the crowd for Andy's proud face, his hummingbird applause, but I could barely see the first two rows.

Conlin joined me onstage, gesturing for something to happen stage right. Nothing did.

"Where's Park?" he said, looking around.

Last I'd seen him, Guy's crumpled body had been shackled by haze to the stairs in the left wing. But Conlin had just been watching my performance from there, so Guy had to be elsewhere. Safe and smug.

Conlin disappeared stage right and came back rolling a giant applausometer. He pushed it to the front of the stage and angled it toward the audience.

With microphone in hand, he was ready. "Ladies and gentlemen, boys and girls, and all you indefinables—did you enjoy the acts? Did you?"

The other performers filed onstage. I gathered my backpack and stepped back to join them, falling in line next to the break-dancer.

"Which was your favorite?" Conlin asked.

A handful of people in the front row called out for James, the aerialist. Somebody yelled for a juggler. But Andy and many others chanted for me: "Red, red, red..."

"What was that?" Conlin asked the crowd, holding a hand to his ear. "I can't quite hear you."

Someone came up behind me and shoved me aside, into the break-dancer.

The aerialist. He squeezed in next to me, posturing so that his right arm and shoulder eclipsed my whole left side. "I liked your monologue," he said, and a new chant challenged the one for me: "Silks, silks, silks..."

I ground my teeth. It was stupid. The participation award was plenty. Now that I'd performed, Andy was bound to propose. But what a story we could tell our kids if I actually won.

So I pushed back. I popped a knee, lifted my chin, my chest, my hem. The chant for *red* competed with *silks*.

The aerialist shifted his weight, the better to block me from the audience's view.

Conlin flashed his dazzling teeth and acquainted us with the applausometer. The half circle on its front was shaded from white to pink to red to burgundy to black. With all the chanting and clapping, the needle quivered at burgundy.

"Should we go through each contestant?" he asked. "Yes? Shall we?"

We all stepped forward to brave the crowd.

Conlin put his hand over the head of the girl to my farthest left. "The cellist," he said to a smattering of applause.

The needle didn't move past pink, despite some people still chanting *red* and *silks*.

"The chanters don't know they're helping you," Conlin told her, and they quieted as he moved down the line. He placed his hand above "the juggler," "the comedian," "the hooper," "the other juggler," "the magician." The applausometer vacillated between pink and red.

After "the singer," the audience anticipated the next amateur to be judged, and their chanting and staccato clapping resumed, spiking the needle to burgundy.

"Silks, silks, silks..."

Half a dozen amateurs, including me, would still need judging after the aerialist, but that didn't stop Conlin from making an early prediction. He sauntered past the aerialist (and me) to the other end of our line.

The aerialist crossed satisfied arms over his abdomen.

I fought the urge to tear out his nipple rings as my earworm pulsed with fury:

The aerialist can't win.

Conlin raised a hand over the rightmost amateur. The chanting of *silks* stopped.

And the peril began.

Fog started oozing from the light fixtures that skirted the stage. The thick haze crawled toward us, hugged our feet, crept up our legs.

Conlin shielded his eyes and looked into the back left corner of the house. "Hey, Vargas, could you turn off the fog and turn on the fan?"

The fan kicked on with a rumble, but the fog persisted.

The aerialist wheezed. He was standing right next to me, but the fog seemed thicker around him. He pitched forward, hands on knees. His face dropped into the haze.

"You okay, James?" Conlin asked.

"He needs his inhaler," said the singer, squirreling a shoulder under his arm. "We need to get him out of this smoke." She tried to hoist him offstage, but she was tiny. The aerialist needed someone else to help him. I could have been that someone. I should have been that someone.

But if I was still onstage at the end of judging and the aerialist wasn't...

"Vargas!" Conlin called.

The lanky guy with the ocean-wave fauxhawk came jogging down the left aisle. He ran up the stairs and got his shoulder under the aerialist's other arm. "I got it," he said, and the singer stepped back into line. As the lanky guy helped the aerialist exit the stage, Conlin waved in their direction (or at the fog, it was hard to tell) and said, "The aerialist," but the crowd's applause was muted by the confusion.

Conlin plastered a showbiz smile over his irritation, signaling to audience and contestants alike that the show would go on. "Well, that was exciting. Only two performers left." He put his hand over—"The break-dancer."

The rumbling fan had no effect on the smoke, but it held the applausometer idle at pink. With the audience's applause for the break-dancer, the meter moved into red, almost to burgundy.

Conlin put his hand above me. "The monologist."

Clapping and stomping and chants of "red" tried to push the needle to burgundy but could only tie me with the break-dancer. She nudged my hand and grinned. I gave her a tight-lipped smile, not feeling it at all.

But then a new noise arose, a rumble in the rafters that moved my needle to black. The crowd responded with a roar, and the break-dancer and I swapped expressions.

I'd won.

In the audience, someone stood and made their way to the aisle.

Andy? So much light in my eyes and yet all I could see was shadow. The guy had Andy's lean build and his thumbs on his phone, but Andy wouldn't make a call during my win...not unless he had last-minute details to confirm before proposing. Squee at the thought!

Conlin handed me a vase of bright daisies and carnations.

"From Andy?" I asked.

Conlin held the mic away from his mouth. "What? They're for winning. This too." He thrust an envelope at me and then closed the show with a sweep of his arm.

"One last round of applause for our amateurs."

For our winner. I bounced on my toes, ready to be dismissed. I couldn't wait to see how Andy proposed.

CHAPTER 14

DAPHNE

The curtain rattled to a close. My competitors filed down to the greenroom, but my eager blue heels clicked up the narrow stairs and across the ballroom to the grand staircase. I peeked over the railing at the lobby below.

A crowd had gathered behind a velvet rope that extended across the bottom of the stairs—but Andy wasn't among them. I bent lower, to peer through the balusters, and spotted him in one of the shallow alcoves that housed a Fausten Cotter poster.

He was talking on his phone. Disappointing, but I could make it work. I felt like I could do anything.

I skipped down to the middle landing and struck a pose.

"Andy."

Andy looked my way and his face made the best expression, a mixture of appreciation and guilt and seeing me anew.

"Nice job," he said, pocketing his phone as I descended the stairs. "Who knew you had it in you?"

"Me." *Not me.* All I could say was that, somehow, focusing my every intention on performing had put me in the zone to do just that: I'd felt inspired. I'd given a performance that was truly beginner's luck. Combine that with the typical bias of audiences expecting the best acts to go last and judging them accordingly when said expectation isn't obviously thwarted, and you get a winning debut.

At least that's what I was telling myself. And as for the fog and what it had done to me and to Guy and the aerialist, I couldn't explain it, but I was sure someone somewhere could. It had happened, so it had to be explainable. That's just how the world works.

But the whole thing still didn't sit well, so...I let it go. Life had taught me early on that it was best to ignore what I didn't like and couldn't change about it by hyperfocusing on what I did and could.

I snuggled into Andy as he gave me a side hug.

"Who's on the phone?" I asked.

"Just a recruiter."

"It's almost eleven."

He shrugged, took my backpack, and lifted the velvet rope. I ducked beneath it, careful not to tip the vase.

The lobby felt stifling. Someone had propped the exit doors open, but the night's winter breeze seemed to only help thicken the air. Andy palmed my lower back, steering me through the densening crowd, subtly pushing me to move faster. But the shuffling horde resisted and jostled us into an alcove.

Andy craned his neck, looking for the holdup, then shrugged at me and settled into the corner. "Well?" The alcove's acoustics made his voice so loud, it probably disturbed the PuB poster. "Let's see it."

I held up my winner's booty: my carnations and daisies and my envelope.

"Nice. How much did you get?"

I tore open the envelope. "Twenty bucks."

Andy laughed. "So it was worth it, then."

I puzzled at him, at his words. He knew why I'd done this, and it wasn't for money.

"So...?" I said. "I won...so...?"

"Right!" Andy grinned and turned his back to me, then pulled something from his pocket.

My stomach fluttered, anticipating his drop to one knee, his promise that graduation was just the beginning, that whatever happened after that, he wanted to do it with me. I set the vase on the floor and wiped my hands on my legs, making sure they were dry, my engagement finger ready.

Something popped, like the release of a pressurized seal.

Andy turned to face me, but he kept his hands behind his back. He said, "Good job, Daph," and he closed his eyes and leaned down for a kiss.

These weren't the classic steps of a proposal, but if anyone was the type to choreograph his own moves, it would be Andy. I rose on my toes to meet his lips—and heard the whistle of aerosol.

Sticky pink-and-mint-green wetness showered down on me, covering my head, my chest, my arms. Pastel lengths of silly string covered Andy too, but he was laughing about it.

I was not.

"It's like dumping the cooler on the coach after a win," he said.

I nodded absently and flicked at bits of string, wanting to sob or scream, but unwilling to do either in public. I focused on the poster of Fausten Cotter, feeling for the first time that the expression hidden behind her veil was rage.

"Your surprise has too many letters in it," I said. "You should've left off the S-T."

"This isn't my surprise," Andy said. "This was just for fun." He picked string off my bodice. "Fun for just me, I guess."

I made myself look at him. Andy should know better than to begin his proposal with a prank, but I could overlook his thoughtlessness if that's where this was headed. "There's still a surprise?"

"Well, yeah," he said, renewing my hope. "I'll tell you when we get home. If we ever get out of here."

"'Tell' me?" I said. "Don't you mean 'ask' me?"

His eyes made quick contact with mine, then darted away, over the crowd. The throng of people continued to bustle with stagnant energy, imprisoning us in this alcove.

Andy had understood my question, I knew he had. But he wasn't even going to acknowledge it, let alone reassure me. I closed my eyes and hugged my elbows. I was an idiot.

"Hey." He took me by the shoulders and bent down to face me. "I'm sorry about the string."

"What's the surprise?"

"I was gonna wait until we got home. You know, first we'd do your thing, then I'd tell you mine. I set the table. Wineglasses, candles—"

"Tell me now."

He straightened and rubbed his neck, forcing his lips into a smile that was too tight around the cheeks. "I got a job."

I frowned. "Where? I thought you liked Spencer's."

"This is for after graduation."

"After graduation?" He already had a job with his dad. *Unless*—"You mean you got a job in Portland? Oh my gosh." I hugged him. "What's the job? How's the pay?"

"Business analyst. Pay's good," he said, but then he rolled his neck and shoulders.

I knew that move. Worse, I knew what it meant.

"And what?" I asked.

My inner shields foresaw my pain and tried to protect me, tried to soften his confession.

A melody filled my ears. *Accept his news, Daphne.*

An ease calmed my mind. *Trust the process, Daphne.*

But something within me disagreed, and tonight it had expanded, taking up space in my brain.

My earworm. It fought my shields' attempt to comfort me, and I let it—I let it tamp them down. Its angry buzz mirrored my own, and I let it embalm me with fever. Let it amplify my inevitable disappointment until my entire body burned amidst Andy's words.

"The job's in Chicago."

CHAPTER 15

FAUSTEN

Well, this was disappointing.

Through the poster in the alcove, I watched Daphne cross her arms and blink back tears. She'd been so sure that if she performed tonight, her boyfriend would propose. And I'd outdone myself helping her too. Hiding her from Guy, getting her onto the stage, making her performance shine. But it had only made her boyfriend call to accept that job.

There would be no reviving my body tonight.

But there would be other opportunities to source the ingredient. Someone could come to the theater celebrating a promotion. Or news of remission. Or a couple could ask to propose during my act. Now that was an idea. By then my influence might be strong enough to harvest the ingredient onstage. I could revive my body *and* impress my fans, all while blinding the crowd to the more corruptive details. I should tell Petty to scout for couples.

I released the haze of my influence that was holding the lobby static, and the crowd flowed toward the exit.

Without looking at her boyfriend, Daphne picked up her backpack and flowers and pushed her way out of the alcove.

And something pulled at my chest.

Daphne stepped again, and I felt it again, a tugging sensation, like I was cumbersome luggage she dragged behind her.

Schadenfreude snickered at the edge of my awareness.

I ignored her and focused on Daphne. I'd released my influence on Daphne right after her performance, but I'd used a lot. I might have left some behind. I culled my influence and dissolved it all again, but Daphne continued toward the exit, and I continued to feel the tug.

It had a beat, like my silent heart used to have. But this pulse wasn't pumping life-giving blood through veins. This pulse delivered energy. I followed its wave through the air…into hair and bone and soft gray matter.

My influence was still in Daphne's head, rooted deep within her skull. I willed the root to rot.

It spread new shoots like fingers.

I yanked it, but my influence remained in Daphne's brain, and I couldn't—I yanked and yanked, but I couldn't get it free.

Daphne passed by a poster. I yanked harder and saw her wince and rub her head.

And something shimmered in her hair. An iridescent cord.

It reminded me of how my influence had looked in its early days, after my accident.

Back then I'd been capable of nothing beyond lying in bed, watching a water stain grow on the ceiling, and wishing that I could escape.

"You've got to stay focused," Petty would tell me, and he'd hung my posters above my bed to help me do that, to help me stay focused, but my posters only reminded me that I'd never be me again, not really, not the moving, flirting, rising star I'd been for far too short a time.

But if my eyes were open, I couldn't help but see and resent the girl on the glossy posters, and over time, I saw movement. An energy.

Tiny threads appeared.

Tiny, influential threads began to stretch between me and my posters.

They started out iridescent, but the longer I stared at them, dreaming of escape, the more solid and silver they appeared. And the more reliably they behaved.

If my physical eyes could see one poster, my energetic eyes could see through them all, whether hung on the walls of a theater or crumpled on the floor beneath someone's bed.

But it wasn't until I'd escaped through a poster that I'd known for sure. These silver threads were my will made manifest. My influence.

But not all threads were mine.

I yanked at the fledgling cord rooted in Daphne's skull, and the whole length of it shimmered. Its iridescence trailed from Daphne's hair, through the crowd, toward the ceiling.

Toward my room on the top floor.

I released my view from the alcove poster and entered the poster overlooking my bed.

The shimmering cord jutted up from the hardwoods and onto the mattress. It slunk up my leg and across my abdomen, to my chest, where it made a taut connection.

My influence threads conveyed only one intention. Mine. But this cord had a faint second feed.

Daphne admiring my posters on campus...tearing one down...stalking me online. Daphne taking my pulse onstage. Daphne in the dressing room hallway, wondering what I would do.

I influenced Guy all the time, and my will never stuck. But Guy fought me.

Daphne had let me right in.

I hadn't forged a connection with her tonight. I'd completed a connection that she had already started. It was weak. Like most people, she didn't know the power of her own attention. But tonight, together, we'd made the link stronger.

Schadenfreude cackled, confirming my fear.

Me and Daphne James were permanently connected.

I hurtled my influence through the lobby, halting the flow of traffic and shoving Daphne and her boyfriend into the last alcove before the doors. I couldn't let her leave. She had a piece of my influence, my *will.* If I was going to force an ingredient to do anything, let alone revive me, I needed my will. *All* of my will. Even complete, my will might not be enough. I had to take Daphne now. I had to retrieve that piece.

But could I? She wasn't freshly engaged, but she had enjoyed a milestone that would produce a decent enough ingredient. She'd performed in a talent competition. A first for her. And she'd won. She'd been thrilled. Surprised, even.

But I hadn't been surprised.

No, dammit, I couldn't take her now. But for my influence, Daphne would have bowed to an uncomfortable silence and the aerialist would've won.

No, without me, Daphne wouldn't have performed at all. Guy would've thrown her out on the street.

I'd made her special day happen.

I couldn't also be the cause of her death.

I'd rolled my eyes when Nechai had listed her nitpicky harvesting rules, but my condition was proof that failing to follow them had consequences and death was neutral territory. I couldn't risk ignoring any more of Nechai's warnings, and she'd warned me that details matter. There was a process. First, death on a special day, then the harvest, and then use. And the process had to contain some element of chance. One person couldn't be the cause of it all.

So if I was going to succeed in reviving myself without Nechai, if I was going to secure the source myself, harvest the ingredient myself, and use it on myself, then I needed a source that had come by its special day honestly. Anything too scheme-y and I would fail—I would never get back my piece of will, let alone my body and my life. And who knew what more I could lose.

I had to let Daphne go.

My influence quivered.

The crowd fidgeted.

Daphne sniffled.

The cord shimmered.

I couldn't do it. I couldn't let her go. She had a piece of me, and I might never see her again, let alone on a special day. To the death or the damned, this botched opportunity was the only chance I'd ever get to revive myself. I couldn't stay trapped like this forever, not forever-ever. I wanted to bow after my performances for as long as my fans kept cheering. I wanted to feel the heat of the sun on my sadly paling skin. I wanted to look with my own eyes upon something other than this wood-beamed ceiling. I wanted to laugh, I wanted to flirt. I wanted out of this goddamn bed.

I focused hard on Daphne, through the alcove poster.

She was leaning against the wall, hair hiding her face, arms hugging her flowers. There had to be something special about her, about today, that could salvage my only chance to revive my soul.

Daphne's boyfriend plucked a piece of silly string from her hair. "Oh, I get it," he said, "too many letters. String—ring."

Daphne snorted, refusing to look at him. She stared at my poster, giving me all of her attention but nothing I could use.

The boyfriend twisted the string's ends together, forming a loop. He pried Daphne's right hand from her crossed arms and rolled the silly-string ring onto her thumb.

"This isn't what I had in mind," she said.

"I know." He kissed her thumb and wrapped his arms around her, kissed the top of her head and laid his cheek on her hair. He hugged her close, and he closed his eyes, and his shoulders rose and fell with a sigh.

Okay. Maybe tonight wasn't my only chance to save myself. The boyfriend wasn't ready to propose today, but the way he held her, the way he considered her... He would propose to her soon enough. And I could be patient.

Well, maybe not patient, but I could be persuasive. And if I could help the talentless Daphne James win an amateur competition, then I could easily teach her the secrets that could help her snag her man.

I just needed him to propose before she found out about me, about my condition, about our connection. And his proposal needed to happen at the theater or near a poster, somewhere within the vicinity of my influence. According to Nechai's rules, once Daphne accepted, she'd have to die by the end of the day.

I'd feel safest if I claimed her on the spot.

But I was worrying for no reason. Thanks to my influence tonight, someone was already working on a way to keep Daphne close. Things, as always, were working out for me.

I took one last look at Daphne as she heaved a heavy sigh. I felt the same. But I would get another chance. And there would be no risk of me overinvolving myself this time. No matter what I might do to help Daphne get engaged, I couldn't force her boyfriend to propose. Obviously.

I released the energy that was holding people in place, and the crowd thinned. Daphne's boyfriend picked up her backpack, put his arm around her, and led her outside.

She took my piece of will with her. I felt its pull, slipping, further and further away.

I switched my focus to the poster hanging in my room so that I could see how Daphne's departure affected my end of our connection.

Petty was in my room, pacing through the shimmering cord at the foot of my bed and cursing about the not-so-amateur amateur.

I'd forgotten. I still had a consolation prize.

I could feel the aerialist's weight next to me on the bed, smell the beginnings of his decay.

It had been an accident. How was I supposed to know he couldn't tolerate much smoke?

Win, lose, or withdraw, performing hadn't been much of a milestone for our not-so-amateur amateur. So his ingredient wouldn't be potent enough to fix my body even if I weren't connected to Daphne.

But taking it would still be good practice.

Yes, *eau d'aerialiste* would do for now. Maybe Petty could mix it into his face cream. He'd like that.

CHAPTER 16

DAPHNE - 50 days left

I lay in Andy's queen-size bed, still wearing my costume. Light from passing cars loomed like specters on the wall. The TV heckled in the other room.

I should've fled to my studio, to get used to being alone. Seemed to be what Andy wanted. We'd graduate and I'd help him pack up his Jeep and he'd drive off to Chicago without me. I could see it now: him calling me from halfway there; me reassuring him that he hadn't forgotten anything important.

I curled my fingers around the sheet wrinkles on his side of the bed, missing him already. All that work, all that ruining of the wedding dress. I'd fulfilled my part of our deal and he still wouldn't commit. Not to me anyway.

But to a job?

He'd said his Chicago job was right in the Loop and that his company would help him find a place.

"Like an apartment?"

What about me?

"I don't know," he said. "Probably."

"When do you start?"

What about us?

"I don't know. Fall. Summer, maybe."

"When are you leaving?"

Can I come too?

“I don’t know. That’s it so far. They offered. I accepted. That’s it.”

Except it wasn’t. His offer required him to maintain a 3.6 grade point average. They wanted people who were driven, not people who coasted once they thought they’d arrived. Andy had said he couldn’t focus on the future of our relationship right now because he needed to secure the future of his career. As grating as this excuse was, it wasn’t new. His job merely spit shined his old I-wanna-focus-on-school reason for not proposing.

Yet.

I rubbed the silly string ring he’d made me. I’d lacquered it with clear nail polish from my costume emergency kit. I was determined to wear it until he replaced it. But I could no longer ignore the possibility that he might not. I had to re-up plan B. If Andy was going to focus on his career, then I had to focus on mine. I’d avoided classes with dissection so far. Maybe I could avoid anatomy in med school.

Ewgh. Cadavers. I’d never last a day organ hunting on Putrid Paul or Juicy Mama Lucy.

The apartment’s front door rustled open.

“Andy?”

“Yeah.”

I’d thought he’d been in the living room watching one of the late-night Jimmys. I got out of bed and was shifting my corset’s boning out of my armpit when he appeared at the bedroom doorway. He was wearing his navy-blue sweats and his winter parka. Messy hair. He hadn’t even put on socks.

He was hiding something behind his back.

He said, “Morning, Pro.”

Pro. Because I’d won last night. It was a lame joke—most of his jokes were—but it still made me smile. All I wanted was a life filled with his jokes. I held the short hem of my wrinkled red costume and curtsied. He brought his hand out from behind his back and handed me a rose. Make that two roses. Two perfectly coupled roses.

“What’s this for?” I asked.

He shrugged and unzipped his coat. He was bare-chested

underneath, like he'd gotten up all of a sudden, shoved his feet into the nearest shoes, grabbed his warmest coat, and left. Just to get me roses.

He threw his coat on the bed and said, "Have I ever told you about my parents?"

I went into the kitchen to add the roses to my winner's vase, but the carnations and daisies were already dying. I dumped them and gave the roses fresh water. "What about them?"

Andy grabbed my hand and pulled me to the couch. We sat facing each other, our inside knees touching. He blew out a big breath. "They divorced when I was ten."

"What? They live together."

"Aunt Pam says Mom was awesome—until they got married. Wouldn't go to McBride family functions. Didn't want us visiting my grandparents. Got really possessive of Dad's time. Our time." He glanced at me, probably thinking, as I was, of Christmas. "Real erratic, controlling behavior. And every year it just gets worse. She always has to get her way or there's drama."

"Okay," I said, wondering how the roses fit in, how I fit in.

"I thought Dad would leave once Jenny got to college, but he wanted to pay for our schooling, and then his company took a dive..."

"So now he can't afford to?"

Andy squeezed my hand. "I don't want to be like that."

I rubbed at the base of my skull...but then remembered how Andy's mom had started picking at her scalp before sending me home. I slid my hand beneath my thigh. "They're kind of an extreme case, though, don't you think?"

"I don't want to be like them in any case."

I squeezed his hand. Andy didn't want to end up like his folks. I could relate. I didn't want to end up like my mom either. But—"We're not like them."

He nodded. Sort of. It became a roll of his neck and shoulders.

Fine. I'd prove to him that we weren't like them. Andy was leaving for Chicago, maybe in the fall, maybe in the summer. By then I'd prove that I was nothing like his mom, that I was the kind of girl he could marry. I'd prove that I was worth the risk because I wasn't a risk at all.

An empty cereal bowl sat on the coffee table, but if I knew my Andy (and I did), he still had room for more.

"I was thinking of making an omelet. You want one?"

I said it nice and casual, because I just happened to be the kind of girl who did that kind of thing. Because someone lucky enough to be my spouse would be the constant beneficiary of such awesomeness. *Recognize, Andy. Recognize. Because if you're a lucky boy—and you are, Andy, you are—I just might cook in the buff.*

"Ham and cheese?" Andy asked.

My phone beeped. A text from Brenda. I left it for later and opened the fridge. *See, Andy? I prioritize you. Nothing like your folks.* "Yup. I can do onion, too."

"Yes, please."

I put the ingredients on the counter, chopped them up, and was turning on the stove to warm the omelet pan when my phone beeped a second time. Brenda again.

Did you do that amateur contest? said the first text, followed by, *Check your email.*

My dumbphone didn't have email, so I turned on Andy's laptop, which was sitting on the table. I whisked the eggs while it loaded.

My phone rang. I snatched the phone off the counter and answered it without looking at the caller ID. "I'm checking it now."

"Ms. James?"

The voice was a gruff baritone. Not Brenda. I glanced at the screen but didn't recognize the number.

"Yes?"

"It's Conlin Washington."

"Who?"

"Owner of L'Aornum. You broke in to practice. To great results I might add."

"Oh. Hi."

"Is now a good time? Vargas got me your number from the student directory. He says you're a med student. Very busy."

The computer finished booting. I sat at the table, logged into my email, and started weeding it of junk. "Now's fine."

"Good. Would you like a job?"

"What?"

"It's a theater hand to start. Selling tickets, ushering patrons, manning the lobby."

Smoke rose from the omelet pan. I got up and turned off the element. I'd never been offered a job before. I'd never even had a job before, at least not one that paid me. I supposed I could use some extra money, but I was more interested in the access. My performance hadn't gotten me a proposal (yet), but it had shifted something in Andy. The way he lingered when he looked at me. The way he'd gone out early this morning just to get me roses. If I worked at the theater, I could meet Fausten Cotter, become her friend, learn more of her Andy-attracting secrets.

Except a star like the Pin-up Bride probably wouldn't want to mentor a theater hand.

"What do you mean 'to start'?" I asked Conlin. "What's the growth potential?"

Conlin's chuckle said it was all sales puffery. "Let's just see how things go."

My inbox had an email from my scholarship people, probably telling me they'd disbursed my funds. About time. I'd spent the last of my money sprucing up my costume. I skipped the email for now and continued weeding the junk.

"I don't need a job," I told Conlin. "I'm on scholarship."

"Ah, beauty and brains."

I shot a glare at Andy, wondering when he would realize that. "Don't you already have a beauty?"

"Ah, yes. Quite gorgeous. Also quite flakey. Sure you don't want to think about it?"

A job would take time away from Andy. Not to mention time away from studying and applying to med school.

"I'm sure, but thank—"

"You were good last night," Conlin said. "Quite impressive really."

I *had* felt inspired. But I doubted I could recreate my performance. It had all been beginner's luck, I was sure of it.

Not that any of this mattered. Conlin wasn't looking for a performer. He wanted a grunt worker.

He hadn't mentioned pay yet, but judging by the looks of the theater and the twenty-dollar personal check he'd written me for winning, even minimum wage would stress his budget. And given the job description—tedious manual labor, maybe glimpsing the Pin-up Bride, most certainly dealing with Guy Vincent Park—no amount of money seemed enough.

"The theater wasn't really all I'd hoped it would be," I said, "but thanks anyway." I hit the end call button and tossed my phone on the table.

I finished cleaning my inbox, then scrolled to the email from Brenda. The subject said, *Can you believe this?!*

Inside was a link to a news article about the amateur contest. I grinned. Performing hadn't gotten me what I wanted from Andy (yet), but I'd enjoyed winning. I scanned the article for my name, hoping it was spelled correctly—ooh!—and used favorably in a sentence comparing me with Fausten Cotter!

The article mentioned the contest, but it was by no means the lead.

"Whoa," I said. "Hey, Andy, did you see this?"

"See what?"

"*Tragedy Strikes Amateur Contestant.*"

I read him the article.

> PORTLAND, Ore.—A Hillsboro man was found dead early Saturday morning in Portland's Cultural District.
>
> James Turner, 26, rode the MAX into Portland early on

Friday evening to perform an aerialist routine at the amateur vaudeville competition held Friday night at L'Aornum Theatre, according to Carrie Wainwright, Turner's fiancée. The pair had become engaged on New Year's Eve.

An anonymous tip led police to the South Park Blocks, where they found Turner's body. Cause of death has yet to be determined. Witnesses reported that Turner sustained severe trauma to his chin.

The proprietors of L'Aornum Theatre could not be reached for comment.

"His chin?" Andy scooted to the end of the couch and leaned over the armrest. "What do you think happened?"

I shrugged, imagining the aerialist falling on his face because he couldn't breathe, because I hadn't helped him.

"He's the guy who went on before you, right?"

I nodded.

"That's crazy. He was great. Someone said he's Fausten Cotter's understudy."

"Whaaat?"

"Padded bra and a wig."

Crazy indeed. I texted Brenda, saying as much.

"Just got engaged," Andy mused. I half expected him to add a marriage-pooh-poohing comment, like *that's what really killed him*, but he said, "That's rough," and he gave me this wistful look, like empathizing with James's mourning fiancée made him miss me. Even though I was sitting right here. Even though he could have me forever if he'd only ask.

In need of a pick-me-up, I opened my scholarship email. I liked seeing thousands of dollars with my name on it. Most of the money would immediately go to tuition and housing, but I still liked pretending for a moment that it was all mine to do with as I wished.

Pasted into the body of the email were photocopies of a letter and an envelope with *Return to Sender* scribbled across the front. Both had been addressed to my mom's old house.

> Dear Ms. James,
>
> We are in receipt of your grades for the autumn academic quarter, to wit, a 3.611 overall grade point average and a 3.533 science grade point average.
>
> As you know, a drop in academic standing below the grade point average indicated in your award letter results in revocation of the award for the following quarter. While we have overlooked your insufficient science grade in the past, a change in our circumstances requires that we now enforce this clause. Consequently, disbursement of your funds for winter quarter has been withheld.
>
> Please be advised that:
>
> (i) failure to achieve adequate academic standing this quarter will result in revocation of the remainder of your award, and
>
> (ii) failure to graduate this June will change the status of your four-year award from a scholarship to a loan.
>
> Please find attached a copy of your award letter with the relevant clauses highlighted. A copy of this letter has also been sent to your university.
>
> All the best,

"All the best?!" I jumped up, tipping over the chair, and backed away from the laptop.

"What?" Andy said. "What happened?"

"They canceled my scholarship."

"On a Saturday?"

They couldn't do this. I'd majored in biology instead of art history for this scholarship. I'd washed beakers for the last three summers, for *no pay*, because they'd promised me this scholarship. "And it says right there I got a 3.611. All I need to keep my scholarship is a 3.6."

I'd done everything they'd asked of me.

"Huh," Andy said, "I bet they wait until Friday, hoping you'll use the weekend to cool off before you call them on Monday. Smart. And rude."

This couldn't be right. I opened the PDF of my award letter. *Congratulations!* it began, but from there it was all business. I scrolled to page three, where a highlighted passage explained that if my GPA fell below 'Good Standing' they could withhold my funds. And even make me pay them back.

"Crap."

Andy got off the couch and hovered over my shoulder. I read him the definition of Good Standing, which made it all too clear I was the poster child for *screwed*.

"It says here, *You are in 'Good Standing' if your overall grade point average is 3.6 or higher, your quarterly grade point average is 3.6 or higher,* and *your science grade point average is 3.6 or higher.* I thought I just had to maintain a 3.6 overall. That's why I took that easy soc class. I knew physics would kick my ass. And look at this."

I read another highlighted clause.

"*In the event you fail to graduate with a bachelor of science degree from Stumptown State University within four years of your matriculation date, then the status of your award shall automatically convert from 'Scholarship' to 'Loan,' and we shall have the right to recover all monies disbursed to you plus interest at the rate of 5.25%.*"

I couldn't breathe. My heart pounded in my ears and out my eyes.

Andy wrapped his arms around me and squeezed me tight. "What are you gonna do?"

I had no idea. My scholarship was my sole support. Without it I wasn't just tuition-less.

I was homeless.

CHAPTER 17

DAPHNE - 48 days left

On Monday morning, I called my ex-stepdad to see if he could fix my scholarship problem, since his employer had provided the funds, but the shady microbiologist must've warned the receptionist that I might call, because, according to her, he'd been quarantined.

I had similar luck with my mom's current boyfriend. He worked at the local headquarters of a global shoe company. They hired paid interns every quarter, but I'd missed the latest round by a couple of weeks. Mom said her boyfriend was apologetic but unwilling to even pretend to ask the powers that be for an exception.

I talked to Financial Aid, but they said I should've applied for money last January, not this January. And I checked the want ads, but if Craigslist was any indication, I'd never get a job to cover groceries, let alone housing and my ridiculous tuition.

I was left with only one option.

Fortune-teller of doom.

That's what L'Aornum Theatre's ticket booth reminded me of, what with its burgundy curtains tied back and the glass globe blocking the pass-through hole. No soothsayers worked the counter, but the door was open, and a dim light shone from the sconces in the lobby.

I stepped up to the window and called through the speaker hole. "Hello?"

Guy poked his head of thick hair into the booth. His face, as grimy as his coveralls, scrunched into a scowl. "You can't take a hint, can you?"

"That you're an ass? Nah, I got it. Can I talk to Conlin, the emcee, owner person?"

"He's not here."

"Park!" boomed Conlin's gruff baritone. "Where's the bar key?"

I tapped the window. "Thought you said he wasn't here."

Conlin squeezed past Guy into the ticket booth and said, "Just got here. What can I do for—oh, Miss James. Here to see a black-and-white?"

"Um, no. I wanted to..." I glanced at Guy, then shielded my face to block him from the conversation. "Could we talk in private?"

Conlin's expressive eyebrows puzzled at me from beneath his pageboy hat, but he nodded for Guy to give us a minute.

"I'm manning the booth," Guy said. "Take your conversation elsewhere."

Conlin raised an eyebrow at Guy. "I own the place," he said. "You do know that, don't you?"

"And I bring the talent. What's your point?"

"I thought Fausten Cotter was the talent," I said.

Guy sneered and left the booth.

Conlin flipped through a top-bound spiral notebook. "Well?"

I wished Conlin had followed Guy's suggestion to take our conversation elsewhere. It was awkward standing on tiptoe to communicate through the window's metal speak-thru. "I was hoping to talk to you," I said, "about that job?"

"I thought we failed to meet your expectations."

"You caught me at a bad time. I'd just read that article about the aerialist."

Conlin's mouth contorted, but he didn't say anything.

"I really did have fun, though. Didn't it look like I was having fun? Isn't that why you called me?"

Conlin's gaze shifted to a middle distance somewhere over my left shoulder, giving me the impression that my performance hadn't been the main reason he'd called. But that didn't matter. Whatever his motive for wanting me specifically, he was thinking about it now, and that was my leverage. And I needed leverage, because I needed a real income, a salary, not just forty hours of minimum wage. But more than that, if I had to give up time with Andy, I wanted to gain time with Fausten Cotter. I wanted to learn the Fausten Cotter ways and steal her man-magnet tricks and maybe push her down the stairs like they did in *Showgirls*.

Nah, I wouldn't do that.

"This might be too soon"—too creepy, too morbid—"but I heard there might be an opening for an understudy."

Conlin looked blank, then laughed and covered his mouth. "I heard that one too," he said, morphing his laugh into a throat-clear. "You want to be Ms. Cotter's understudy?" He said it like it would never happen.

"You said I was good," I reminded him. "You said I was 'quite impressive.'"

His eyes drifted away again, to that middle distance, and he got this Mona Lisa smile. His head tilted. A nod of acknowledgment. "I called you for a theater hand," he said, "but you do have her charisma—at least you did onstage."

"Is that the secret of her appeal?"

"Ms. James, if I knew her secret, I'd get rid of her entirely and train someone reliable. But now that it's out there, she could use an understudy. You'd have to be ready for more than just illness or injury, though. She's...picky...about what she does."

"What do you mean 'picky'?" She'd posed naked within arm's reach of a crowd of strangers. How picky could she be?

"In fact, you might just become the lead for anything she..."

"Doesn't want to do?"

He was all teeth. "We understand each other."

"Okay. I can do that." I didn't know how, since I didn't know where the charisma had come from in the first place, but sure, I could do that.

"Good," Conlin said, and a light switched on inside him. He was all big hand gestures and big teeth as he told me about this show he wanted to produce. I deflated a little, realizing he wanted me to understudy a role in his new production, not the Pin-up Bride act, but at least I'd be in Fausten Cotter's proximity.

"Sounds neat," I said. "There's just one thing...um...compensation?"

"Ms. James, the experience alone is worth the world. It's priceless."

"You want me to do it for free?"

"There are plenty of other ladies who'd give us the enthusiastic yes, Yes, YES we're so used to hearing."

"I see. Well, please, Please, PLEASE—can you pay me?"

He snorted, more amused than annoyed, but I hadn't won him over yet. I whipped out a lie.

"It's just that I'll have to quit my job to make time for the show, since I'm also a student. Premed. Remember?"

"So money is assured you in the near future. And you have that scholarship, if I recall. Sounds to me like you're all set."

I'd found, in situations like this, that a patient smile spoke better than I. I offered the smile to Conlin. I could hold it forever, and if I actually had a talent, it might be the James Girls' all-purpose smile.

Conlin shrugged and turned to leave.

"Wait," I said. "What about that other job, the theater hand? What do you pay Guy?"

Guy stormed back into the ticket booth. "I'm not a hand." He whacked Conlin on the shoulder and gestured at me. "You can't be serious."

Conlin flipped through his notebook. "We need a hostess," he said, "an usherette, if you will. Maybe a bartender."

"No, we don't," said Guy.

Conlin appraised me. "Any customer service experience?"

My mouth hung open, too slack-jawed to speak. We'd gravely deviated from what I was trying to accomplish.

Conlin said, "Or is that beneath you?"

"No–no, that's fine," I said. "What does that pay?"

"How much do you need?"

I took a pen and an old receipt from my purse and wrote down the hourly rate I needed to cover tuition and living expenses, then flipped it over and slid it through the pass-through hole to Conlin. I stared at the gawking Guy as I did it. *None of your business, jackass.*

Conlin flipped up the paper's edge and peeked at the amount. His stomach quivered, and he actually grew a few inches in order to release the whole of his disbelief in one giant kapow of hysterical laughter. "Where do you work that pays you this? Are they hiring?"

To my dismay, he showed the number to Guy, who joined in on the funny.

I stuck my hand through the window's pass-through hole and tried to grab the paper, but I couldn't reach it.

"Good idea," Conlin said, passing it back to me. "You rethink that number."

I wanted to leave, but there was literally nothing else I could immediately do for money, nowhere else I could go. I did some mental subtraction. I had no idea how I'd pay for housing. Finding a new place could've been easy and convenient and just plain perfect if Andy would've offered to let me move in with him, but after I'd told him my current room was part of my scholarship, and therefore not mine anymore if I couldn't pay for it by February, he'd given me a hug—and that was it.

I could maybe live with my mom and her boyfriend, but that would leave me commuting an hour each way on the MAX. Which would leave me with zero time for Andy. Which would...*bleh.*

I was too shaky to calculate an hourly rate, so I wrote down the lump-sum cost of tuition. "This is what I need to get me through March."

Conlin pulled out one of those old calculators with a roll of paper attached and crunched some numbers.

"Okay," he said, "now we're getting somewhere."

Guy's smug look became dismay. "You're kidding, right? You're gonna pay her to do what? Babysit an empty theater during Monday films? Usher people to their seats when it's first-come-first-served?"

"If your girl wants to hide out until the final act, that's fine. She can play diva all she wants. And I can groom her replacement."

That sounded like Conlin still wanted me to be Fausten Cotter's understudy. I didn't have time to be a poorly paid theater hand and an unpaid understudy, but I let it slide for now. I tapped the paper to get Conlin's attention. "I need this by next week."

The phone rang. Conlin answered—"L'Aornum"—and shot me a look that said I shouldn't press my luck.

Guy heaved this great, dramatic sigh. What a wannabe actor. I stared at him with my own smug mug, hoping he'd leave, but he just shook his head and stared back at me, unfazed.

As Conlin listened to the caller, his eyes drifted to me. I shifted my weight.

"We can accommodate," he told the caller, and he hung up. "You start now."

"Now? But I have—"

"If you want this now"—he tapped the amount of money I needed—"then you start now."

Now was not good. I had physics next hour. Failing physics, so to speak, was how I'd lost my scholarship in the first place. If this term's grades weren't good enough to satisfy my scholarship people, they'd stiff me for spring term too.

But if I couldn't pay this term's tuition, I wouldn't get credit for it anyway, which meant I wouldn't graduate in June. Which meant I'd have to pay back my entire scholarship. With interest.

"Now's fine," I said.

Conlin left the booth. Seconds later the doors opened. Only the lobby's sconces were lit, and it made the hollow between them seem darker, more awake. Conlin waved me inside, but I stayed on the sidewalk.

"You're paid by the hour," Conlin said, "but you gotta come in first."

My earworm tapped a beat against my eardrum, coaxing me to step inside.

Behind Conlin, Guy's brooding eyes leveled on mine. *Go away*, they begged, like his glare alone could keep me on the sidewalk. But his posture...a guarded stance. It communicated a caution I noticed but dismissed. I needed this job.

I lifted my foot—and my earworm stretched. A fissure cracked in my cochlea. It was cold, colder than the average Portland winter, but the weather had nothing to do with the icy chill that rippled up my skin as I stepped across the threshold. As my earworm wiggled deeper.

I should've stayed on the sidewalk. My life trajectory took a decidedly sharp turn south that day. And there would be no recovery.

CHAPTER 18

DAPHNE

"So," I said, standing in the theater's dim foyer, "when do I meet Fausten Cotter?"

Guy laughed too loudly. Above us, the chandelier flickered, and he stopped mid-guffaw.

"See to the lights, will you, Park?"

Guy's chin tilted toward the chandelier, but his eyes looked left, toward a lobby alcove and its PuB poster. "Sure," he said, like Conlin's request was repetitive. And pointless.

"Not today, Ms. James," Conlin said, answering my question. "Ms. Cotter's barely here on the weekends."

The lights flickered again. Guy's jaw tensed.

"Besides," Conlin said, "you're here to *do* work, not network."

Guy asked about the caller, and Conlin said he was a motivational speaker, reserving the theater for tomorrow night.

"He only booked a day in advance?" I asked.

Conlin smiled. "Ladies and gentlemen, boys and girls, and those desperate for work and named Daphne—*this* is L'Aornum Theatre: our lights are shit, our equipment is old, and we take who we can when they're willing."

The lights flickered, then turned off altogether, for which I was grateful. "Got it."

"Good." Conlin held his flashlight under his chin, illuminating his bared teeth and casting eerie shadows over his face. He spookied his voice to match. "Then you'll fit right in." He backed away, affecting a slow-build cackle as he withdrew into the depths of the lobby.

Guy called after him. "So—what?—you hire her but she's my responsibility?"

The glow of Conlin's flashlight bounced on the walls as he bounded up the stairs. "Thank you!"

Great. I reported to Guy Jackass Park. I expected him to huff a big, chest-heaving sigh and toss his arms in rage against the world—much like I wanted to do myself—but he closed his eyes and rubbed his face with both hands.

The lights returned. Guy huffed and strode into the lobby. I hustled to catch up with him. He suddenly turned back around, and I smacked into his chest, releasing a whiff of grease and musk. He was solid under those coveralls, and he smelled as he looked, like a dirty, laboring guy.

The observation disturbed my earworm, and above us, the chandeliers buzzed with a low-grade menacing hum. Guy poked the butt of his flashlight into my chest and pushed me away, pushed until his arm was completely straight.

"Sorry," I said. *Ya weenie.*

When the chandeliers quieted down again, Guy dropped his arm.

"What is it you want?" he asked. "You already got your way. You performed, you won. You got a weird ring now, I see. Aren't you engaged?"

I shoved my hands into my pockets and shifted my weight.

"No, huh? Any chance lover boy will stop by and propose today?"

I sighed. Guy's people skills were astounding.

"No again? Okay-okay." He clasped his fingers in his hair, then let go with a sigh as if making a tough decision. "I'm gonna tell you something, okay? It's very important, and I need you to hear me this time." He bounced a little, like a champion preparing to fight, except instead of practicing his punches, he rubbed his face and scalp with both hands, helmeting his hair. "Okay," he said, and he took a deep breath. "Okay, here we go. You...should*n't*"—he pitched forward, like he'd taken a punch—"*be...here.*"

"Okay..."

"*Say it back to me.*"

"I shouldn't be here."

All the sconces, chandeliers, even the beer fluorescents behind the bar brightened to full light, illuminating worn Vegas-style carpet and the burgundy damask walls. The lights blinked, each in their own pattern. Guy never moved, never took his eyes off me. But he had to be doing this. Somehow, he had to be controlling these lights.

He kept talking, grimacing with each word. "*This isn't a good pl*-ugh—" He keeled over, like he'd been kicked in the nuts. Instinct told me to reach out to him, to make sure he was okay, but I stopped myself. I wasn't about to reward this farce.

He grabbed the edge of the bar and strained to look at me. "*Not...a good place...for you. Say it.*"

"This isn't a good place for me."

The lights went out. Wind roared through the walls. Fixtures crackled electric. Bottles clanged. Wood creaked.

And Guy screamed.

It was a good scream, an agony that rose above the racket. So good I almost believed him, almost cowered and called for help. But I wasn't about to let that turd know he was scaring me.

The noise crescendoed—then stopped, and the lights returned to dim.

Gasping for air, Guy grabbed the bar and struggled to stand up.

"Impressive theatrics, Guy. Really." I clapped to hide my trembling. "But next time, maybe get out the fog machine—ooh!—and that rumbler. Really shake the place."

He gaped at me, still hitching for breath. "You think I did that?"

"Aww, was I not fooled?"

He shook his head and reassembled a knocked-over straw dispenser, then brushed some nuts off the bar and back into their bowl. "You wanna get those?" He pointed at the floor behind me. White napkins littered the carpet, and several fifths of alcohol lay on their sides, their liquids sloshing inside the glass.

"How did—?" No. I would not be run out of a job, the income from which was already spent, by Guy Asshole Park. I crossed my arms and leaned against the bar. "Are you seriously trying to make me think this place is haunted?"

His eyes flashed. "Something like that."

"You want me gone that bad?"

"And never come back."

I gave him a catty little smile and patted his shoulder. "Well, it was a good try, but I'm not superstitious."

He shrugged me off. "This isn't voodoo. It's not like it can't manipulate you if you don't believe. This is gravity. She'll pull you down. She'll trap you whether you acknowledge she can or not."

"'She'?"

His eyes widened like I'd finally understood. His nod was almost imperceptible.

"The *building* will?" I said flatly.

The lights blinked. Guy scoffed and shook his head, like I'd willfully misunderstood him.

Maybe I had.

"Yeah. Sure," he said. "The building."

"Great. Got it: the theater is haunted. Anything else? 'Cause I'm not leaving. I can't afford to."

Guy deflated and looked away, at another poster in another alcove. He palmed the bar a few times and sighed. "It's not your birthday, is it?"

I frowned. "Not until July."

"Okay. And would you consider getting this job a significant milestone in your life?"

"A *significant milestone*?"

"So, no. That's good. And you're sure your boyfriend won't show up later today and propose?"

Right now I doubted he'd ever propose, but I wasn't about to say so.

"No again. Okay-okay." His eyes roamed in their sockets, no doubt in a futile search for thoughts. But they must've found one, because Guy suddenly smiled at me. As best he could.

"Okay," he said. "Let's go."

He crossed the lobby and yanked the house doors open, smacking them into the walls, then charged down the aisle, leaning forward as he strode.

"Slow down," I said.

He only walked faster. At the bottom of the aisle, he turned left, crossing in front of the seats, and pushed through the curtained doorway next to the stage. The curtain fluttered back into place.

"Thanks for holding that," I said.

I pushed the curtain aside, revealing a beige hallway. On the right, a railing kept people from falling out of the stage wing. At the far end, the hall opened onto a van and a loading bay door. And on the left, Guy stood halfway down the hall before the only people door.

"Storeroom," he said, pushing it open. "After you."

I couldn't do much ticket-taking or ushering or bartending back here, but maybe this was where Conlin kept the practice cash register. I peeked inside. Musty air tickled my nose. The storeroom looked small, maybe eight feet across, but it extended the whole length of the house. It stored everything—racks of old costumes, giant stage backgrounds, old movie reels, shelves of industrial cleaners, mops in buckets—all crammed so tight I couldn't move beyond the doorway.

Guy grunted and shoved past me. He climbed over an old sign that asked ladies to please remove their hats and disappeared behind a pile of cardboard boxes. Things clattered and clanged, echoing off the stone walls. Something scraped along the concrete floor. It might've been my pride.

Guy returned, shoving things out of the way of an ancient and barely rolling shop vac. One of its wheels was missing and another dangled uselessly. I sighed. Guy wasn't digging that thing out for nothing.

"You want me to vacuum?"

He said, "This is an upholstery cleaner. The speaker tomorrow needs full house lights."

He nudged the monstrosity toward me. It listed to the left and thudded into a plastic bin. The hose and cleaner head toppled off and rattled to the ground.

Guy disappeared deeper into the length of the storeroom. Unknown items crashed and thumped. He returned empty-handed, but he looked smug about something. He pushed past me, out the door.

I supposed I should follow him. I threw the hose over my shoulder and shuffled the upholstery thing down the hall. Guy pushed through the curtain, letting it flutter closed behind him.

"Thanks again," I muttered, untangling the fabric from the vac. "So kind of you to clear the way for us." I made it through and rolled the cleaner to the middle aisle.

"Ahhh," Guy said, as if breathing the great outdoors. He was standing onstage with his hands on his hips. "You smell that?"

I sniffed. A bit gross, but winter weakened the worst of the smell.

"That's the reek of five hundred seats steeped in alcohol and ass." He grinned. "Get to cleaning."

He hopped down and started up the aisle. "Oh, I almost forgot." He dug something out of his coveralls and tossed it to me. I sidestepped, and it hit the front of the stage. A green-handled tool with a head like a sharp metal spatula. Guy almost looked perky. "Don't forget to scrape the seats for gum and snot rockets."

Bile rose in my throat. "Seriously?"

"Yup." He strode up the aisle. "Be glad we show classics now and not porn."

It took a while to resign myself to the task. Then it took a couple trips to the storeroom, and the bathroom, to get the steamer working. You're supposed to add water and a solvent. Would've been nice if Guy could've mentioned that.

I started the first seat but then spent another hour searching the storeroom for gloves. I had to hold the seat cushions steady or they bounced when I scraped their bottoms of gunk. They were sticky, disgusting, and not what I'd signed up for. I'd thought I'd take tickets and hand out programs. I'd thought I'd at least be standing, not kneeling in filth.

Creak.

I stilled mid-scrape. The seats creaked and squeaked, but this noise was different, further away. I looked around. I didn't see anything, but every cell in my body took notice of something's presence. I felt it. Something was watching me.

Nah. It was just Guy's haunted-theater shenanigans getting to me, that was all. I shook off the feeling and went back to scraping at some purple gum that was too moist to pop off.

And, just in case, I raised my hand and gave whoever was watching me the finger.

But that only made me more sure: something was watching me. I closed my eyes, gauging the location of its stare. Behind me. Back left corner. Something was back there.

But this was stupid. Nothing was back there. And even if it was, it was *way* back there. Even if it decided to get me—which it wouldn't, because this was stupid—it would give me plenty of warning, banging the seats and making the creaky sound. I'd have plenty of time to get away. Which I wouldn't need to do, because this was stupid.

I dug into my work with gusto, scraping the crap out of the seats and whistling while I worked, like whatever was or was not back there was like a bear and I could scare it away if I made enough noise.

But then *it* made a noise.

Creak.

I grabbed the hose and whipped it around me, whacking all three hundred and sixty angles. My heart pounded; my skin burned with creeping chiggers. The hose hit stuff, me mostly, but nothing screamed in pain. I peered through the dim light of the house into the back corners. I tried to think of what rational thing might make a creaking noise, but I didn't see anything, not even shadows moving among the rows. Nothing but a couple of framed PuB posters.

Still… "Hello?"

Creak.

I froze. The noise was like old glass bracing against the wind, like fingernails raking my skin. I was standing. I was exposed. And the noise had come from the stage. Every hair on my body stood at attention.

"Guy, is that you?"

No answer. I peeked over my left shoulder.

Creak.

The sound came from my right. A flash of light. The hallway curtain fluttered.

"Guy?" My voice squeaked, but the thought of Guy trying to scare me into quitting helped me bring it back into normal range. I brandished the scraper and moved toward the aisle. "You're a real asshat, you know that?"

But even as I called his name, I doubted it was him, and my lips soon spoke another. Barely a whisper. No idea how it even got on my tongue.

"Fausten?"

The lights blinked twice and grew brighter. I winced and shielded my eyes, but the lights backlit my lids, blinding me like the sun. I couldn't see. But I knew it could see me. And it watched me.

Creak.

Came closer.

Creak.

It warmed me.

Creak.

It touched me.

"Fausten?!"

CHAPTER 19

DAPHNE

"She's not here."

I startled and glanced around the house. The lights softened into a dusty shade of pink before resuming their dreary dim setting. I didn't see anyone. "Hello?"

"Over here."

I whirled around, and there he was, standing in the shadows of the back left corner. I'd seen this guy before, at the amateur contest. The lanky guy with the blue ocean-wave fauxhawk.

"How long have you been here?" I asked.

"Not long. Just changing out the posters." He held up a cardboard tube. Above us, the lights shifted to mint green. "Sorry about the lights. We're testing them for the show."

I scurried to the edge of the seats and up the aisle. Sure enough, the wall next to him had a lighter rectangle, free of dust, where a frame had recently hung.

Creak.

"What's that noise?" I asked.

Creak—"That?" he said. "Just the tabs." He pointed out the little metal clips on the edges of the frame. "They hold the back on. They're kinda industrial"—*Creak*—"and old."

He picked up the frame and rehung it on the wall. Another white promotional of the Pin-up Bride. He wiped his hands on his black skinny jeans, leaving dust marks, then held one out to me. "I'm Petty Vargas."

"Daphne James," I said, shaking his hand.

"Daphne...the girl who won on Friday?"

I nodded.

He smiled strangely. He had full lips on an otherwise gaunt face; even his acne scars flattened against the bone.

"What?" I asked, fidgeting.

"You. This. Fausten will be pleased."

"You know her?" It sounded stupid as soon as I said it, but even though I'd seen her in person, touched her even, she was becoming a legend in my mind, a myth, nothing more than a fracture in my brain, an earworm wiggling in my imagination.

"I do her hair." He studied my reaction. "Her makeup."

I didn't disappoint. He associated with Fausten Cotter. How could I not be impressed? He knew her beauty secrets. That was almost as good as her inner secrets.

"Her wardrobe," he continued, adjusting his own boxy T-shirt. Black and blue with pops of red and splotches of pale yellow. Like a bruise. "Not that there's much styling to do anymore, now that her look's become so iconic. Like Marilyn. Or Audrey. You know?"

I didn't, but I wanted to. I nodded like I did.

His smile seemed so friendly. "Do you want to see her?"

Did I?

"Can't." I pointed the scraper at the attachment-tentacled monstrosity. "I have to clean the seats for tomorrow."

He raised a hard-angled brow. "We have a service that does that."

"What?"

"They come early morning. Conlin's got another task for you."

"What an ass."

"Guy? Yeah. This way." Petty skirted the seats and loped down the aisle to the stage.

I followed him. "I should put the steamer away."

"Guy'll get it."

Worked for me. I climbed the stairs and joined Petty onstage. He took the scraper from me and chucked it into the seats. It clanged somewhere near the steam cleaner. "Guy can get that too."

I followed Petty to the hallway that led to the greenroom, except Petty turned right, in the direction of the six locked doors.

"I hear you need a place to live," he said.

"Oh yeah?" I didn't remember revealing that to Conlin, but I supposed I could have.

"You'll think of something," Petty said. "Just being around Fausten is enough to inspire me. She always shows me exactly what I need to know."

He unlocked the second-to-last door. "You can come in."

Lush textures in shades of white decorated the room. I instinctively kicked off my shoes so as not to track dirt on the white shag carpet.

On the left wall, a huge PuB poster stretched floor to ceiling and the entire width of a sleek white love seat, dominating the room. The wall opposite the door was solid cinder block and held a glass shelving unit filled with accessories, memorabilia, homemade gifts from fans. I ran my fingers over drawings of the Pin-up Bride, dolls in white outfits, handmade scrapbooks. I touched several white hats, lingered over the velvet on a white French tam. The textures and colors said *Fausten Cotter*, but the styles weren't right. Neither was the bikini top on the dressmaker's form. Too many sequins for the Pin-up Bride, but the beadwork was nice. White and shades of white rolled beneath my fingers.

"Please don't touch." Petty stood at a glass desk, hunched over a laptop. He gestured to the love seat. "Sit."

I perched on the edge, for fear of ruining the white kidskin. "I love this space," I said, fussing with my jeans. They had a layer of grime that only worked itself in as I tried to rub it off. "Is this her dressing room?"

Petty tapped the keyboard. "This is my room."

"I thought I was meeting Fausten Cotter." Not that I was in any state to do so. I already felt like the veiled eyes of her giant poster were judging me. I pulled out my hairband and redid my ponytail, trying to smooth the flyaways.

"It'll just be a second." Petty pointed to a shoebox on a side table. "You can get started on the fan mail."

I picked up the box of letters. Most were flat white envelopes hand addressed to the Pin-up Bride, but some were pink or mint green or bubblewrap yellow and bulging with surprise. "This is Conlin's task for me?"

"The start of it." Next to the side table was a duffle bag of more letters and a sealed cardboard box. Petty pulled a box cutter from his back pocket and slit the tape. Inside were glossy photos. "Replying's a big part of how Fausten stays relevant."

I frowned. I didn't want photos to be the secret of her appeal. Andy already had pictures of me.

Petty misread my expression. "If you don't believe me, ask Conlin."

I'd believed Petty just fine until he said that, but any task was better than scraping seats of their snot globs. If Petty was lying about the cleaning service, I'd just tattle to Conlin. What did I care? My pride had died back in the storeroom.

I picked up a glossy photo. The Pin-up Bride had ordered reams of presigned images of herself in the same white poster outfit, the same kneeling pose.

"I love this dress," I said.

Petty's bony chest puffed with hubris. He pocketed his box cutter and returned to his laptop.

I studied the tilt of her veiled head, the arch of her back, the press of the bouquet into her fishnet lap. She had this way of drawing people in, of making them guess, without being too overt about it.

"Careful," Petty said. "Drool warps the paper. And you've only got a few hours."

"I'm supposed to answer all this today?"

"And read the letters. The fans usually tell her what they love about her. It'll help you become her." He straightened and closed the laptop. "That's what you want, isn't it?"

Petty Vargas, he of the ocean-wave fauxhawk, he of the gaunt cheeks and the gangly crossed arms—he had a sketchy vibe about him, a hint of the untrustworthy. I didn't like the upturned corner of his mouth or the mood in his inky eyes. I looked away first and rifled my shaky hands through the pile for stamps. "So where is she?"

"So eager," he said. "She'll like that."

He turned off the lights.

Above me, a projector whirled to life and lit up the wall opposite me with a bright square, a video prepped for play. Petty aimed a remote at his desk and the room filled with eerie music.

The video was dark, just the shadows of an empty stage and a circle of spotlight. The music built—and a white hat appeared in the spotlight.

I leaned toward it, rising off the couch.

The hat lifted, trailing a veiled face, a corset, a ruffled miniskirt with slightly longer bustle, great legs in wide-mesh fishnets—the Pin-up Bride in her poster outfit.

She stood with her head high, hands on hips, feet together with one knee popped.

I quit breathing.

Fausten Cotter swayed her hips to the beat of an applause so loud it drowned the music. Slowly, tantalizing me, she brushed her hands up the length of her body and over her head. She hit a high V.

And the video cut to static.

I collapsed on the couch, finally remembering to breathe. "That's it?"

"I know, right?" Petty turned on the lights.

"Where's the rest of it?"

"That's all there is. You can watch it on repeat if you want." Petty tossed me the remote on his way out of the room.

"Wait," I said. "I thought I was gonna meet her."

"*See* her," he corrected. "I asked if you wanted to see her." He pointed at the stack of photos. "Make sure those get in today's mail."

I usually had decent penmanship, but after hours of addressing envelopes to people like Buck Wilson in Imalone, Wisconsin, and Tennessee Hicks in Montana, my handwriting was unreadable. I laced my fingers and stretched my arms overhead, enjoying the feel of my joints popping.

It made no sense that these people had even heard of the PuB, let alone become fans. Fausten Cotter wasn't active on the internet, and I couldn't see her traveling to places I'd never heard of just to perform. But maybe they'd seen her while on vacation in LA and were instantly hooked—what did I know? However these admirers had come to write, there, on the white shag, sat a pile of Fausten Cotter's responses, pink and mint green and prepped for mailing.

I still hadn't touched the duffle bag.

This part of the theater had zero cell reception, but my phone had still searched for a signal until it died. I had no idea what time it was, but I was tired and hungry, and I doubted anyone would care if I continued this menial task at home.

I pushed off the couch and was gathering supplies when I heard a whistle. Long and low. I stilled, heart pounding.

But the whistle didn't care that I'd heard. It grew louder and higher until, finally, it petered away. I exhaled, recognizing the sound. Outside, the wind must've been blowing hard enough to force its way through the cracks in the building. No ghosts here; all was well.

Except I had that feeling again, that feeling of someone watching me. I looked up at the PuB poster. Those veiled eyes watched me all right, but that wasn't what I was sensing. Something else was—

No. I wasn't falling for that whole being-watched thing again. It had been nothing while I was cleaning the seats, and it was nothing now.

But I sensed more than just eyes on me. There was also a smell. I sniffed to be sure.

Yeah. Musk with a hint of peaches.

I sniff-inspected the room. It wasn't the stuff on the shelves. I sniffed the desk. Getting stronger. I opened the drawers. No smell here, nothing but office supplies and manila folders. Pink and mint green. One labeled *Trick—The Love Trap.*

I looked over my shoulder at the open door, at the dim and empty hallway. Hearing nothing, I pried the pink folder from the drawer. It contained a single sheet of white paper scrawled with eight words in four lines, each written with such elaborate flourishes I couldn't read them. I tried to identify each letter in the first word.

S-O-M-E-T-H-I... "'Something'?"

Bright light flashed twice in the hallway.

"Petty?" I crammed the folder between the others and quietly shut the drawer. The peach scent overwhelmed me. I covered my nose and moved toward the door. "Petty? Is that you?"

The door shuddered. I flinched away from it, my breath hitching, my heart pounding.

Just Guy hazing the new girl.

I rubbed my scalp, acquiescing to my earworm, because of course that's what it was. This was a theater, a place of magic tricks and sleight of hand. This shaky door, those flashing lights, it was probably just the work of Guy (the turd), but whoever had rigged it, I wasn't going to run screaming from the room just because the old hats were hazing the new girl.

Better yet, I'd have fun too. I narrowed my eyes at the door, challenging it to shudder again. Like it would.

But it did. It rattled the wall and creaked its hinges. The hall lights flashed like a strobe.

"You're a real assgape, Guy."

I sounded more confident than I felt. I didn't hear any flicking light switches. Didn't see anything wrong with the door. No contraptions. No wiring. There was no way anyone was shaking that door.

But shake it did.

I wanted out of here.

Now.

I lunged for the door. It slammed shut and rattled its latch. I looked around my cinderblock prison. No windows, let alone another exit. And nothing to open the rabid door from a distance. I flexed my fingers and reached for its gleaming silver knob.

The door shook so violently it cracked its frame.

"Stop it, Guy."

Silence. Stillness. For a moment, I didn't move. Then carefully, cautiously, I approached the closed door.

Bam! The door burst open, hurling me to the couch. I gasped, trying to sit up, but the air was thinning to nothing.

The light in the hallway dimmed, like someone's head blocking the sun.

Guy? His name wouldn't form at the back of my throat. It was barely in my head, and my head was a boulder on the couch.

A shadow darkened the doorway.

It wasn't Guy.

I tried to get up, get away. Couldn't breathe.

My head.

So heavy.

The shadow dipped beneath the jamb, creeping shade—

All the way inside. Its haze looming over me—

Thickening—condensing—

Its density pressing into me—

Bearing down.

Couch springs pricked my ankles...my calves... I tried to roll to the floor, but the weight of it—I couldn't move.

And it crept—

Crept—

Up the length of my legs.

I wheezed for air and it surged inside me, choking me with peaches, pinning me from the gut.

But it was my earworm that weighed most heavy. My cheek squished against the cushion as it forced me to face the wall.

As the motor above me whirred to life.

As another movie played.

Watch me, it said, *and learn.*

CHAPTER 20

DAPHNE

"How do I look?"

The female voice came from the speakers hanging in the corners of Petty's office. I didn't recognize the voice, and I couldn't see who was on-screen, because the lights were on.

The lights turned off.

On-screen, preening for the camera, a girl ran her fingers through her long black hair, fluffing the waves and splaying a pink-and-mint-green streak. She wore a short white dress—the same dress as the Pin-up Bride poster—but without the veiled hat.

I could see her face.

The voice that answered her came from behind the camera and sounded like Petty. "Stunning. Per the uszh."

She was, too. Even more captivating than her Aphrodite. There was life in her eyes, a mischief no one should admire.

But I did.

"Give it here," Fausten said.

She took something from the cameraman—a pink folder—then stepped away from the camera.

I could now see that she was in a white dressing room not unlike the one I was trapped in.

She said, "How about on the coffee table?"

"Sure," said the cameraman. "But I thought—"

"My ingredient isn't real, okay?" Fausten set the folder on the table. "And even if it was, Nechai's is better. She's got the highest grade there is around her neck."

"No, I mean, I thought Nechai already told you no," said the cameraman.

Fausten adjusted the folder just so and then set something else on top. A rectangular scrap of paper.

"No one tells me no," she said.

A knock came through the speakers.

Fausten singsonged, "This is my big niiight!" Then, "Keep that out of her face."

Rustling came through the speakers, as if the cameraman were putting the camera on a shelf, and the view of the room widened. On the right was a white couch and the dressing room door. On the left was a dainty white chair in front of a brightly lit vanity.

Fausten opened the door. "You made it. Come in, come in." She left the door open and crossed to the vanity. The camera focused on her, leaving the rest of the room slightly fuzzy.

A visitor stepped into the room. They were tall and slender, but I couldn't make out their features.

Through the mirror, Fausten flashed devious eyes—presumably at the cameraman, whom I still couldn't see—then spoke to the visitor. "Well, have a seat already."

The visitor shut the door and looked around the room. From what I could tell, they had short dark hair and wore a dark, fitted outfit. Pants. Rather than sit on the couch, they—

She, said my earworm. *Nechai Chaiprasit.*

She grabbed the edge of the white coffee table and dragged it closer to Fausten. The dragging sound strained the speakers. Onscreen, the pink folder vibrated to the edge of the table, threatening to fall off.

"Just sit on the couch," Fausten said.

Nechai stopped rearranging the furniture but didn't sit on the couch. She perched on the corner of the table, legs crossed at the thigh. Her foot bobbed—undulated—like she was trying to reach Fausten, trying to touch her with her toe.

Through the mirror, Fausten made can-you-believe-this-guy eyes at the cameraman, then plastered on a smile.

"Did you see the ticket?" she said. She opened a tube of mascara and began applying a coat. "It should be there, next to you."

Nechai looked over her shoulder, at the expanse of coffee table behind her, but she left the scrap of white paper and the pink folder where they lay.

The cameraman's lanky arm extended from the bottom-left corner of the screen and exchanged Fausten's mascara for a dark pencil. Fausten silently lined her lips. The lanky arm appeared again, exchanging the dark pencil for a red pencil, and Fausten filled in her lips. Another exchange, and she applied a bright shade to the center of her lips. By the time Fausten applied a light cream shimmer to her bottom lip, Nechai must've gotten bored, because she picked up the pink folder.

Through the mirror, Fausten glanced at the cameraman with an exalted smile on her not-quite-finished lips. His lanky arm handed her highlighter, which she dotted on her bottom lip, then lip balm, which added shine. Fausten leaned toward the mirror. *Mwah!*

Nechai held up the folder. And with a voice not unlike audio feedback coming through the speakers, she said, "What's this?"

"I'm doing it tonight," said Fausten. She picked up something the size of a small tube of lipstick, but given how much time she'd just spent on her lips, I doubted that's what it was. "Any advice for my debut?"

Nechai grabbed for the tubelike item, but Fausten held it away—and closer to the camera.

It was a vial. Not unlike the souvenir vials Petty sold in the lobby. Except the substance inside wasn't clear and glittery like PBP.

"Where'd you get that?" Nechai said.

Fausten tilted the vial. The contents sloshed from end to end, a dull and disturbing reddish brown.

Definitely not PBP.

"This isn't as good as the ingredient you could get me, but..." She lifted a shoulder.

Nechai said, "What more could you want, Fausten? Look at this place. You're the headliner at the Orphic Starlight. Isn't the *khawng-khlang* enough?"

"Told you," taunted the cameraman.

Fausten shot him a dirty look. She put her elbow on the vanity and admired her ring. Although I wasn't sure why. The center stone was kind of ugly, a speckled yellowish brown.

"The amulet was just your advertisement," she said to Nechai, wiggling her ring finger, "and *that*"—she pointed at the vial—"is just my opening act."

Nechai sat down again, crossing her arms and legs. Her toe bobbed frantically. "Don't do this. Not tonight."

"It has to be tonight. Guy's last show is tonight." Fausten turned in her chair to face Nechai, putting her back to the camera. "It'll work, won't it?"

Nechai scoffed in open-armed plea, then hugged herself and looked away from Fausten. "Who'd it come from? Do you even know? It's dangerous under perfect conditions. You could..." She glanced toward the cameraman, then looked pointedly at Fausten. "Just don't, okay? Not with that."

Fausten showed her profile to the cameraman. It must've been some kind of signal, because he crossed the camera's view and slipped silently out the door.

Fausten shook the vial. "I *have* to do it with this. *This* is all I have."

She set the vial on the vanity and picked up a blush palette. Behind her, Nechai's toe bobbed.

"I do hope you like the seats I got you." Fausten brushed a light pink blush onto her cheekbones. "I'm told they're best in house. I had to blow an old, fat season-ticket holder to get them for you." She smiled. "Just kidding. He wasn't that old."

Nechai huffed. "Keep your tickets."

Fausten tilted her head, admiring her face from all angles in the mirror. "I'm still glad you came tonight." She picked up the vial. "As you say, this—what do you call it?"

"*Nam man prai.*"

"That's right. As you said, using it is risky. This could be the last time you see me."

Still hugging herself, Nechai's left hand migrated from her elbow to her chest. She gripped at something beneath her blouse. Her toe bobbed faster.

Then stopped altogether.

Nechai sat up straight and reached her hands behind her neck.

Fausten leaned to her left, as if rifling for another beauty product, and looked directly into the camera. "Told *you*."

Nechai unlatched a necklace and pulled it from her blouse. She held it out to Fausten.

A vial like Fausten's dangled from the chain.

The pressure pinning me to Petty's sleek white couch dissipated, and, slowly, I was free again. I could move.

But I was tired. My earworm nodded against my levator muscles, tempting my eyelids to droop over my eyeballs. I popped them back open, but they fell again, melting my view into a haze of lashes. I rolled over and faced the back of the couch, adjusting until I found just the right spot, the coziness that would carry me off to...

CHAPTER 21

FAUSTEN

Sleep.

Just sleep, Daphne.

My influence had always been something I'd worked from the outside. Fog that hid or restrained Daphne, energy that halted Guy or pushed the hatpin. It was external. But this connection with Daphne was something new. It was internal. I could speak to her like I was a part of her.

But I could not make her act. That was clear from the way she'd hesitated before getting in the elevator or putting on the blue shoes. I couldn't force her to do anything. I was merely the...

Well, I knew I was no angel, and anyway, she already had a set of those. She called them her shields.

No, I was the other guy. I could distract her or hide a memory here and there, just the troublesome ones, just the ones of me that Daphne wouldn't miss and didn't want to recall anyway. I could suggest, persuade, cajole, although so far I'd never had to resort to those last two. In truth, I'd be nothing more to her than an ignored shrew, a disregarded nag, if Daphne wasn't interested in what I had to offer.

But she was. She'd never had ideas like mine before, and I could tell by the eager way she chose to act on them that she appreciated them.

She wanted more.

And I had more to give.

We'd start with the video. Daphne thought I was a private,

secretive star, unapproachable, untouchable, and she didn't know anything about Nechai. It worked best for me and the boys to keep it that way. So I would be hiding Daphne's memory of the video and probably the last few minutes in Petty's office before it had started too. When she awoke, the past hour would be nothing more than a new intuition for getting what she wanted from people, and the next time she saw him, she'd know how to handle her boyfriend.

She'd see results within the week.

I let the video play, watched it from the giant poster of me that Petty had hung in his office.

This was the night of my accident.

In the video, Nechai picked up the folder and took out the lone sheet of paper, the rhyme I would use with her ingredient. Her foot bounced as she read the page. But then she frowned and looked at the back. There was nothing on the back, but she flipped the paper again, front and back.

She said, "Is this your incantation?"

"Hmm?" video-me said.

She shook the page. "Your words. Isn't this an English wedding custom?"

"An *old* English wedding custom," video-me said. "'The better known the words, the greater their power.' Isn't that what you said?"

I probably sounded arrogant to anyone else, but I heard my uncertainty. I'd always been good at ignoring the naysayers, and they were many, but Nechai was different, harder to disregard. Sitting at that vanity, basking in the breakout of my success, I'd done a stellar job that night of not letting her faze me. I'd been fearless that night. In control.

So in control, I hadn't noticed how her frown had become a smile. Not quite satisfied, not quite relieved. A suffering smile. She set down the rhyme and turned away from the camera. Video-me had paid her no attention, but I was paying attention now. I saw her from the side, in the reflection of the mirror. She slid her hands into her trouser pockets. The faint rattle of change came through the speakers as she pulled them out again. She bowed her head over whatever she held. And her lips moved.

That sneaky bitch.

"So, where *is* Guy?" Nechai asked, returning to her perch at the edge of the table. She crossed her legs. And her toes stayed still.

"He'll be here," video-me said. *Just like you are*, I remembered thinking. Cockiness is an underappreciated asset. Though maybe not so much that night.

"I like your costume," she said. I'd rolled my eyes back then, at Nechai's attempt to make nice, but now I knew that she'd just been buying time. She had discerned her divine instructions and would now do sin to carry them out, like she was the brawn of a dispassionate brain. An angel resigned to evil.

"Same as the poster, yeah? *The Pin-up Bride.*" She flashed jazz hands. How had I not caught that? "It's cute. Catchy."

A ruckus came from the hall. Nechai turned toward the noise.

Guy burst through the door with Petty fretting behind him.

Guy tossed the boutonniere I'd wanted him to wear on the dressing table. "I don't want your gifts, Fausten. You. Your show. I'm done. After tonight? Done."

Video-me smiled as though I couldn't have cared less. Even now I almost believed myself. Guy had been kind to me once. He was still kind, all things considered, but there was a time when he'd been true, even after I'd broken out and he hadn't. He'd loved me, I thought. Until he'd discovered how I'd stolen the spotlight.

In the video, Guy groaned and rubbed his hair, making it stick out.

"Fix that before showtime," video-me said, handing Petty the boutonniere. He pinned the pink rose to Guy's lapel.

"Get through tonight," Guy muttered to himself. "You just have to get through tonight."

"I should go find my seat," Nechai said. She kissed video-me on the cheek and told Guy to break a leg. "Speaking of leg, your pants are... Here, let me."

And as Petty and video-me began discussing my hair like Nechai and Guy weren't even there, Nechai knelt at Guy's feet, out of the shot, presumably to do something helpful, like pull Guy's pantleg from his sock.

But I knew better now.

That sneaky fucking bitch.

The air in Petty's office rippled. The door yanked on its hinges and the lights flashed, berserk, but I couldn't help the negative energy coursing through my influence.

I'd always wanted to blame Nechai for my accident that night, to accuse her of giving me bad ingredient, but the blame had never stuck. Nechai's ingredient had been everything she'd promised. Something magical had happened onstage, just not what I had planned.

So instead of blaming Nechai, I'd been blaming myself. She'd once told me that it took a strong will to harvest the ingredient, and an even stronger will to use it. I'd assumed I just hadn't been strong enough to compel the ingredient to support me, but that's not what had happened. And even though I'd made a mistake with my incantation—Nechai's searching the paper for the rest of the rhyme had told me that—my use of the ingredient hadn't backfired either.

It had been defended.

Sabotaged.

Nechai did this to me.

She hadn't *known* my accident would happen. She'd *made* it happen. And all because I'd taken her sister's ingredient.

She'd deserved to lose it. She was a tease, Nechai was. She'd gotten me hooked on the ingredient with the amulet's single taste, only to deny me any more.

Schadenfreude chuckled, low and satisfied, and her chuckle confirmed my theory. Schadenfreude wanted her laugh to naysay me, to cripple me with further doubt that I'd ever revive my body, but it only strengthened my determination to try.

Why?

Because Nechai wouldn't bother sabotaging me unless she knew I was about to win.

My will had been strong enough then, and it was even stronger now. Schadenfreude's chuckle only made the fear about my ability to succeed give way to a certainty that I could not fail.

So fuck you too, Schadenfreude.

I just needed to be more vigilant this time. I needed to figure out how I'd messed up my incantation, and I needed to know what Nechai had done to sabotage me. Going forward, I would be careful about making any more mistakes. I would be careful about giving other wills a chance to corrupt my own.

But I would never again second-guess my need to make bold and hasty moves.

CHAPTER 22

DAPHNE

I woke with my cheek in a puddle of drool on the kidskin.

Kidskin?

I scrambled to standing and found myself in Petty's white office. *That's right.* I'd been answering fan mail. Must've fallen asleep from the tedium. I still had the duffle bag to do, but the responses I'd finished were gone. Petty must've taken them. He could've woken me while he was here, but I wasn't too mad that he hadn't. I felt good, like I'd just had a full-body massage followed by the best night's sleep.

The house and lobby were darker than dim as I weaved through the theater and out the main doors. The sun had set hours ago. I really had gotten a night's worth of sleep.

Back at my studio, I plugged in my dead phone. I'd missed several calls and texts from Andy, most of which asked if I was okay. I'd always appreciated Andy's show of concern, but tonight it prompted a new idea, a bold if foreign and nerve-racking idea.

Maybe I could use Andy's worry to my advantage.

I'm fine, I texted. *Just got home.*

He called back immediately, but I didn't answer. I'd never ghosted anyone in my life, but doing so now felt empowering. Maybe I *could* convince Andy to let me move in. I didn't see any downside to trying. I had to pack soon either way.

I skipped downstairs to the front desk and asked for a cardboard box.

I kept the door open as I readied my studio. The hallway was quiet. This late on a Monday, most people were studying. Or sleeping.

An hour after he called, Andy's shadow darkened my doorway. Right on time. He knocked on the wall.

"Hey," I said, managing more enthusiasm than I felt. I was super nervous. I crossed the room and rose on my toes to give him a quick kiss. Only our lips touched.

"Everything okay?" he asked. "I keep calling, but you're not answering."

I retreated into my studio, leaving the door open and him standing there. My clothes were strewn on the bed. I picked up a shirt, folded it precisely, and stuffed it into a top-load canvas duffle bag I'd salvaged from a lost and found.

"Sorry, I've just..." I sorted through my clothes like I was looking for something way more important to me than Andy. It was hard not to look at him. "I've just been really busy."

I didn't elaborate. He knew I'd been at the theater securing an income, that I still needed a place to live.

"Oh." He leaned against the doorjamb. "'Sokay."

Not the response I wanted. I moved my pretend search for the super-important item to my desk. I lifted Harry's crayon box and shifted my coffee bowl, trying to draw Andy's attention to the cardboard box stamped with bright orange letters, MOVING.

"Are you leaving?" He sounded worried. *Box did the trick.*

"Have to," I said. "Studio's part of the scholarship."

"Where are you moving to?"

"Mom's, I guess."

I kept my head down, meticulously organizing my highlighters. In the doorway, Andy rolled his shoulders, like he felt constricted, like my situation made him uncomfortable. Good.

But then he nodded, like he was coming to terms with my move, like he could accept me leaving campus if I were living with my mom. Not good. I didn't want his acceptance. I wanted him desperate.

So I said something I knew would make him feel bad.

"If my mom will have me." She wouldn't. "She lives with that new boyfriend now." So I wouldn't even ask. "Otherwise, I don't know. Probably a women's shelter."

The shelter was more than probable. If Andy didn't let me move in with him, then that's where I would go. I'd told him before about how my mom and I had spent time in shelters after Harry had died. No bed, just a mat on the polished concrete floor of a ten-by-ten room saved for women with kids—if we were lucky. It seemed like prison. Maybe worse, because it wasn't like we couldn't leave. We could. We could leave at any time. We just didn't because we had nowhere else to go.

Andy stopped nodding and skewed his face. A good sign. Any minute now he'd tell me I could live with him.

He stepped into the room, tiptoed his way through my mess, and pulled me in for a hug.

"She'll let you."

My heart stilled like a stone. Did he really prefer me homeless to living with him?

No. *No.* He probably just figured he could wait and see if that actually happened and *then* ask me. Well, too bad for him. I wasn't waiting until last minute to find a new home. And anyway, we weren't done here. I still had other tactics.

I put on a cheery smile and untangled myself from him. He picked up a shirt and folded it. He actually had the audacity to help me pack.

"Thanks," I said. "How about you get the stuff on the desk."

I'd left my schoolbooks on the corner. Underneath them was a clue for Andy. I thought he'd heave the whole stack in one go, but he picked up the books one by one, flipping through them before packing them into the box. His movements were absent. Pensive. Sloooow.

Finally, he picked up the clue: a trifold brochure.

"What's this?"

He knew what it was. It was a Trimet timetable. If I lived with my mom, I'd have to take the MAX to and from campus. Every day. I'd written on the timetable, in bright red marker for Andy's immediate understanding, just how long the trip would take me: a whopping hour and twenty minutes.

"Just preparing myself for the ride," I said.

Andy frowned at the timetable's front and then flipped it over and looked at the back. I'd also circled the times I'd have to catch the MAX after school.

"You'll leave campus by two thirty?" he said.

"Uh-huh."

"Why so early?"

Ha! I'd finally hit a nerve. Andy had class until late. Meaning most days, he wouldn't get to see me. Meaning most days he wouldn't get the perks that went along with seeing me.

"Gotta beat the rush." I rolled a pair of pants and put them in the duffle. "If I'm gonna be on the MAX for an hour, I at least want a seat so I can do my homework." Tone upbeat, all optimistic logic. It was a totally different approach for me.

And it was working. Andy nodded, but with a scowl. Awesome, because that little piece of logic—that I had a long commute—was only half of this particular tactic, and not even the most important half. Oh no, there was another, even more Andy-affecting fifty percent. I laid it on him.

"Hey," I said. Nonchalant. Keeping it cool. "Do you think when I'm done packing you could give me a ride out to my mom's?"

Andy's face shifted from confused to concerned as (I presumed) he remembered that I didn't have a car; as he realized that if it started taking me an hour longer to get to his place, I probably wouldn't be as agreeable as I used to be about coming over any old time he called; as it dawned on him that if he wanted to see me, he'd have to drive to Gresham.

And yet he folded the timetable and packed it in the box. "Sure," he said. "I can give you a ride."

I mumbled thanks and busied myself with my clothes. My hands shook. The moving box, the timetable—those were the extent of my plan. I didn't have anything else to convince him.

But maybe nothing ever would. Maybe Andy didn't fear commitment; he just preferred convenience. And maybe I just wasn't remarkable enough to change his mind.

I ducked into my closet so he couldn't see my face. I'd really thought he'd save us from a long-distance relationship. But if he wasn't willing to save me from Gresham, how could I hope he'd save me from Chicago?

He wouldn't. So maybe it was better that I was leaving now, that I was facing this now. Because the officialness of us ending was only a matter of graduating.

I sniffled. "Guess I should clean my stuff out at your place."

"What stuff?"

He said it like he wasn't really listening. I glanced at him. His shoulders were hunched, his head bowed over a framed photo he'd found on my desk. A candid shot of a group of us sitting in a big corner booth. Tyler, the birthday boy, was centered in the photo, wearing a sombrero—but Andy and I drew the focus. The way we were smiling at each other and laughing. Like we'd each be foolish to keep looking for someone better.

Andy ran his thumb along the glass.

"Toothbrush." I said it slowly, watching for a reaction. "Undies."

His forehead wrinkled like he didn't know what I was talking about. I couldn't help the snort. *That's right, Andy. I practically live there already and you don't even notice, let alone mind.*

"Omelet pan."

His jaw clenched.

"Pillow."

He glanced at me.

I turned back to the closet.

Footsteps echoed in the hall. A female voice and male laughter. A rustle of keys and a door clicking shut. *Bet that guy wouldn't need this much convincing.*

"It can stay."

"What?"

"You don't have to clean out your stuff."

His words swelled my heart, but the hope they gave was false. His words weren't enough. His words only made it worse. *Your stuff can stay, Daph, but not you,* they said. *I don't want you.*

I rubbed my temples to calm my fuming earworm. Fausten Cotter would never have this much trouble getting what she wanted.

"Thanks," I said. And just that morning I wouldn't have said more. But I felt myself drawing in breath, realizing that there was more that I could say—and that Andy was someone who would hear me. And my response, though not my norm, came effortlessly: "But it probably won't get much use there anymore. I might as well give you back your space."

"But you're always at my place."

"Yeah, now. It's a twelve-minute walk from here. But when I'm at my mom's..."

I let him fill in the rest. Judging by his face, he was coming up with terrible scenarios.

He set the picture frame in the box and gestured about the room, at my schoolbag and books, my pens and my clothes. "Is this all you have?"

"Pretty much. Plus my shower caddy."

He nodded and his gaze wandered. I chewed my nail so as not to interrupt. His fingers played absently with the scarf on the back of my chair. When he finally looked up, he focused on me with the most vulnerable eyes he'd ever revealed.

"Would you want to live with me?"

A jolt of triumph ran through me, but I didn't dare move toward him. A distraction could break the spell. "Really?"

"Yeah." He tossed my scarf at my duffle. "You kind of live there already."

Yes. I. Do. And isn't it your pleasure. Thank you for finally realizing. "Okay."

I stepped toward him. Calm, careful, mindful that his offer still felt tenuous. But then he smiled his cockeyed smile. I crossed the room at a run. He dropped into the chair, and I dropped into his lap, wrapped my arms around his neck. I couldn't believe this was real, that this had actually worked.

I moved to Andy's that weekend. I had zero furniture and not much else, so it only took one trip in his Jeep.

He was quiet in the elevator, leaning against the wall, carrying the cardboard box. When the doors opened, he let me go first and lagged behind me in the hall. I stepped aside so he could unlock the door, but he stayed behind me.

"What's up?" I said, fearing he'd changed his mind.

He balanced the box on his hip and reached into his back pocket. "Here." He handed me something small and metal and warm from being in his jeans. A key. He'd already made me a key. It was pink with tiny rhinestones that spelled *home*. I hugged him so tightly my arms ached.

"Try it out," he said, laughing. "This box is heavy."

I put the key in the lock, but it stuck.

"You gotta lift up on it."

I did and let us in. Andy set the box on the counter, then hung back while I put my bag in his room. Our room. The top two drawers of his dresser were open and empty, save for a few pieces of clothing I'd already been keeping at his place. The closet was open too, and all his clothes were pushed to one side. In the bathroom I found a new shower tower.

"For all your girly stuff," he said.

He watched me discover all of this while keeping a shy stance, his hands stuffed in his pockets, his body angled toward escape.

"Thank you," I said, respecting his distance.

He shrugged, hands still in his pockets. "You're welcome."

I bit my lip, not sure if I should move, not sure where I could be. I'd always made myself quite at home before, but my usual spots felt off-limits.

But then Andy opened his arms. I went to him and buried myself in his chest, and when he kissed the top of my head and rested his cheek on my hair, I exhaled completely, releasing my muscles' every tension and my mind's every concern.

Maybe Petty was right. I still hadn't met Fausten Cotter, but maybe just being around her costume rejects and fan mail was enough to absorb her secrets. It had certainly inspired ideas and attitudes in me that had gotten me out of my tiny studio and into a bigger and better place with the man I loved—and *he'd* asked *me*.

My muse: a few more weeks with her, and I'd have Andy down on one knee for sure.

Until then, working at L'Aornum Theatre wasn't so bad. On performance nights, I took tickets and manned the lobby, and on black-and-white Mondays, when the theater was open but nobody came, I worked off my advance doing homework in the ticket booth.

Guy still didn't want me around. Every day, first thing, he'd ask me if I'd gotten engaged, and when I told him that he was a jerk, he'd ask if I expected Andy to come by later to propose. Fortunately, I could just ignore him completely, because Conlin stripped him of his Daphne management duties. My guess was that Petty had told Conlin that Guy was assigning me tasks the theater paid other people to do. Guy was still a grumpy ass, just not one I had to obey.

But he still managed to cause me trouble.

CHAPTER 23

DAPHNE - 30 days left

A few weeks into my stint at L'Aornum, Conlin called as I was walking home (to Andy's!) from class. "Can you come in early?" he said. "I need you to run sound and lights."

"Doesn't Guy do that?"

"Park's out tonight."

"Guy's shirking a Friday?"

"Be here by four thirty."

"But I don't know the show."

In fact, I had yet to see the rest of Fausten's act. My job during performances—especially during her performance, with her heavy use of strobes and fog—was to sit in the lobby (which raised another question: who was gonna sit in the lobby?) in case any of the patrons came out feeling nauseous. No one ever did, but there I sat, readin' physics and gettin' paid. Every night, I considered peeking in at Fausten's performance, but opening the doors would distract people. (Okay, really, when I considered peeking, I'd remember that hatpin poised to make her bleed, and as curious as I was about her and the rest of her show, I just couldn't stomach that again.)

Conlin wasn't concerned about my newbieness. He said the lobby would be fine without me and that sound and lights was easy.

L'Aornum Theatre's control booth was a tiny dark room hidden in the house's back-right corner. Conlin unlocked the door, sat in the seventies-orange desk chair, and rolled himself into position in front of an old gray console and a tinted window that overlooked the stage. The console had two matching sets of sliding levers that controlled the sound and lights—a preset board, Conlin called it. Sitting on top was a spreadsheet.

"This is the cue sheet," Conlin said, and he explained the gist of the job. I'd set the top row of sliding levers according to the light settings on the cue sheet for the first act. While that act performed, I'd set the cues for the next act on the bottom row. Between acts, I'd slide the crossfader to switch between settings. Reset and repeat.

"But since I go on between each act, one row is always my preset." Conlin slid the levers on the bottom row to his liking without referencing the cue sheet. "So, really, you'll only change the cues on the top row and only while I'm onstage."

Simple enough, but Conlin still reviewed each act with me. I matched the levers to the numbers on the cue sheet and slid the crossfader. Ta-da! The lights changed. As for music, Guy already had it cued and all I had to do was push play. The recordings would end on their own and the next song cued automatically. All was well and good until—

"Piss." Conlin flipped over the spreadsheet. The back was blank. He rolled backward in the chair and looked under the console.

"What's wrong?" I asked.

"The last act's not on here."

"Fausten Cotter's act?"

Conlin slid some levers. Lights and sounds turned on and off, but Conlin just shook his head. "I don't know Ms. Cotter's settings. Park designs them and he's already gone."

Something thudded in the lobby. I thought it might be Fausten getting ready for the living statue act, but after that creepy fan had said creepy things and tried to touch her with their creepy hand, the crew had decided that the Pin-up Bride would no longer pose every night; she'd pose occasionally, at random, to deter the weirdos.

Tonight was not a posing night, not with Guy absent.

I peered out the house doors into the lobby.

Petty stood at the bar, opening a box of delicately clinking glass with his box cutter. He noticed me peeking out at him, and his face brightened. "Hey, Daphne. How's your day going?"

We'd never reviewed the fan mail task he'd assigned me, but he must've been satisfied with my work, because every time he saw me he was friendly.

We exchanged pleasantries as he pulled tiny vials with pink-and-mint-green labels from the box and readied them for sale. I hadn't seen this souvenir since the night I'd come to the show with Brenda, but I remembered the sales guy—Petty—saying that the clear and glittery Pin-up Bride pheromones brought luck. His spiel had seemed woo-woo at the time, but the vials had sold out that night, and people kept asking when we'd get more.

"Does Fausten use that stuff?" I asked.

"*Use* it?" Petty gave me an odd smile, and I noticed his acne scars had faded. His skin looked smoother, more evenly toned. "I wouldn't say she *uses* it."

"Do you?"

"Is that Vargas?" Conlin came into the lobby. "Vargas, Ms. Cotter's presets—do you know 'em? They're not on the cue sheet."

Petty waved away the question. "They're a trade secret."

"Of course they are." Conlin handed me the cue sheet and headed toward the stairs. "Please show Ms. James the settings."

"What? Why? Where's Guy?"

Conlin smacked his palm on the railing. "Park's out tonight. Do you know Ms. Cotter's presets or not?"

Petty looked between Conlin and me. I didn't know him well enough to interpret his expression, but it wasn't encouraging.

Conlin bared his teeth. "Do you?"

"I'll come by tonight and set them."

"Fine," Conlin said, and he pounded up the grand staircase to get ready for the show.

But something about this wasn't fine. I didn't have enough experience with the control booth to know what, exactly, was wrong, but something about it wasn't fine.

All by myself in the control booth. Five minutes to curtain. I dimmed the house lights, prompting everyone to take their seats. When the clock struck the hour, I turned on Conlin's lights.

"Crap."

Conlin's settings were on the bottom row and I'd just turned on the top. But a slide of the crossfader fixed it fast. *Phew.* Not a promising start, but not a disaster either, and other than that, the show's first half went well. Hula-hooper, juggler, singer, contortionist. At intermission, Conlin came to check on things. By then I'd figured out what was bothering me.

But Conlin had other concerns.

"Vargas come set the lights?" he asked.

"Not yet."

"*Trade secret.*" Conlin scoffed and wiped his bald head with a towel. "He'll probably try to kick you out before he sets them. Don't let him. I want those cues. I want you to write 'em down before you switch 'em back to me. I'll close the show, and then there's the finale lights, like I showed you—"

"And then the house lights," I said.

"Right. Okay, then." He checked his watch. "I gotta get back."

"Wait," I said, wanting to ask about the thing that had been bothering me. "Isn't Guy onstage during Fausten's act?"

"I'm filling in."

"Okay, but how does he do her lights?"

Conlin shrugged. "He runs really fast?" He clapped the doorjamb. "Gotta go."

I watched the clock until the precise moment when I was supposed to dim the lights to signal the last five minutes of intermission. I hoped the dimming would also remind Petty that he needed to set Fausten's lights, but those five minutes passed with no sign of him.

It was time for Fausten's act.

I made sure the crossfader was set to Conlin's row and turned on his lights.

Conlin strolled to center stage and asked the audience if they were having fun. They obliged him with polite clapping. Conlin asked if they were ready for the headliner, and the clapping tripled in volume.

My feet and fingers twitched. The audience was ready, but I was not. If the Pin-up Bride's lights weren't right, the audience would be pissed, Conlin would be pissed, Fausten Cotter would be oh so pissed. Conlin would probably blame Petty, but the crowd wouldn't understand. The crowd would blame the dumb girl in the control booth.

The control booth's door burst open.

"There you are," I said. "How do I—?"

Petty's appearance stopped me. His gradient-blue hair was slicked back with sweat, and he was dressed from head to toe in matte black.

I tried not to laugh. "Nice spandex."

"I need the chair," he said.

I relinquished the throne to Petty. Instead of adjusting the levers, he leaned back and crossed his arms. The white tips of his hair dripped sweat onto his hood.

"Why aren't you setting the cues?" I asked.

"'Cause you're still here."

"I have to switch them back when she's done so Conlin can close the show." I whacked his skinny arm. "Come on, Petty. Show me how you guys make Fausten's act so eerie and magical."

I heard banging under the console. Petty's black-slippered foot was tapping the desk leg.

"Oh, are you nervous?" It was almost endearing. "Is this your first time too?"

Petty cut his eyes at me and his foot stilled. But his fingers picked up where his toes left off, tapping his skinny matte-black-covered arms.

The house erupted in applause, drawing our attention to the window. Conlin had finished announcing the Pin-up Bride. He was exiting the stage.

Petty hit the master switch, turning off every light except the aisle runners. The stage went pitch black.

The theater rumbled. It was cinematic, like an action-film soundtrack. Except Fausten didn't have any music on the player.

"Is that her lift making all that noise?" I didn't think so. I wasn't even sure the lift had started. Petty hadn't pushed any buttons.

Petty didn't answer.

The floor at center stage opened, and fog billowed from the hole, seeping into the audience and illuminating the house.

"Petty," I said, "where's the fog coming from?"

"The fog machine."

"But you didn't turn it on."

"It's on a timer, same as the lift."

"And the lights?"

Petty didn't answer.

Lying on the lift, Fausten Cotter rose from the stage with her long dark hair hanging over the side of the platform. This was the same entrance I'd seen opening night. The memory turned my stomach.

"If Guy's not here, will people still go onstage to inspect her?" I asked.

Petty shot me an offended look. But then his face lost all attitude as it took on an expression I could only interpret as *oh shit*. He launched out of the chair and out the door, saying, "Don't. Touch. Anything."

Moments later, a strobe light flashed.

But I hadn't touched anything.

I checked the preset board. All the lights were off except the runners. And yet the fog was blinking brightly. I stood and peered out the window, up at the light rack that held the big lamps. No light beams shone from the rack. The strobe light had to be coming from the stage...from where Fausten Cotter was still just lying on the box. I hoped she wasn't waiting for some prompt from the control booth.

Shadows shifted on the stage, becoming darkest just behind her. She started to rise, her movements slow and jerky in the flashing strobe. She swung her legs over the side of the platform and stood, raising her arms into a high V.

The crowd roared with applause.

At least *they* were happy.

An elaborate chair glided downstage, and Fausten Cotter sat. The strobe light stopped and the forestage lights brightened.

What the...? I hadn't touched anything. And yet the lights had changed. They couldn't all be on a timer. If they were, Petty would've just said so. If they were, he wouldn't have rushed in here before her act. He wouldn't have been so nervous.

"Can we get a volunteer?"

It was Conlin speaking, but I couldn't see him. He wasn't onstage.

A spotlight turned on, illuminating him in the aisle.

My skin prickled with goosebumps. I hadn't turned on the spotlight. I couldn't explain the spotlight.

I had to figure out the spotlight.

I checked the buttons to the right of the preset levers. Conlin hadn't reviewed them with me, but one of the switches said *Spotlight 2.* It was switched off. Everything was switched off.

Conlin selected a volunteer and chatted with the audience as she made her way to the aisle. Onstage, in a blur of brilliant fog, Fausten Cotter sat completely still.

I touched Spotlight 2's skinny silver knob—and my earworm stretched, tickling my brain's pleasure center. I didn't know what flipping the switch would solve, but the worst that could happen was I'd turn on a second spotlight.

And so what?

No big deal. I'd just turn it off again before Conlin could glare at me.

I pressed my thumb against the switch. It resisted, so I pressed harder—*click*.

KABOOM.

Speakers screeched with feedback. Spotlight bulbs exploded.

And the house showered the audience with glinting shards of glass.

CHAPTER 24

DAPHNE

After making sure the audience was okay and giving them free passes in apology, I returned to the house to see what Conlin wanted me to do next. Hopefully nothing. I wanted to get out of here before he could ask me why the lights had exploded.

The house was dark except for the aisle runners and Conlin's headlamp. He handed me a dustpan and pointed at some glass he'd swept up. I positioned the dustpan near the pile. Glass clinked against Conlin's broom. He didn't say anything. He had yet to say anything.

The groan of an opening garage door and the chirping of something mechanical came from backstage. Moments later, Guy pushed through the hallway curtain, saying, "I got your message. Did Faus..."

He looked around, covering his nose against the smell of smoke and fried electronics. A red-and-white takeout bag hung from his hand. The contents looked heavy but too small to be leftovers.

"What happened?" he asked.

Conlin leaned on his broom. "The lamps blew."

Guy skirted the stage, crunching glass with every step. "Anyone hurt?"

"No," said Conlin. "Most of the glass landed in the aisles."

Guy snorted. "Course it did. I'll get the ladder. Bulbs in the storeroom?"

"Not the bulbs," Conlin said. "The lamps. They all blew. Except the runners."

"What?"

"Speakers too."

"Do we have insurance?"

Conlin's laugh was too loud for the situation.

"Is that a no?"

"Oh, they take their money every month, but the deductible's claim-prohibitive."

"Well, it's been a good month, right? Do we have enough money to rent equipment for tomorrow?"

The light on Conlin's headlamp bobbed. "That'll get expensive, though. They need replacing."

Footsteps echoed on the stage. It was Petty collecting Fausten's black sheet. He wore a clean T-shirt and skinny jeans, and he'd restyled his hair into its complicated wave. How nice of him to groom while we picked up the mess.

Petty shielded his eyes from the glare of Conlin's headlamp. "Don't look at me. I told you not to let Daphne do lights."

"*Daphne* did lights?" Guy said. "You told me you'd get a student."

"And I did," said Conlin.

"I did the first half perfectly," I said. "Petty's the one who was all secretive about Fausten's settings."

"I told you: they're on a timer."

"No, you said the *fog* was on a timer."

"And I told you not to touch anything. But *you* flipped Spotlight 2."

In the bright light of Conlin's headlamp, Petty sneered at me. He wasn't guessing. He was tattling. "Yeah, good job," he said. "You overloaded the circuit."

My mouth moved, wanting to defend myself, but I didn't have a comeback. Petty was right. I'd flipped the switch.

This was my fault.

"Well, there's your money answer," Guy said. "Fire Daphne. That'll pay for new lights."

"What?!" The glass in my dustpan chinkled to the ground, a total waste—I should've launched it at Guy.

He grinned...but not at me. He was looking at his takeout bag, as if impressed with its heft.

"The money does need to come from somewhere," Conlin said. "And you did break the lights."

"I'm still paying off my advance," I said. "How am I supposed to pay for lights?"

Conlin asked the boys, "Am I correct in assuming Ms. Cotter's still not making extra appearances?"

"Don't put this on Fausten," Petty said. "You can't fire us anyway; we're within contract." He jumped down from the stage and came at us, his bony finger pointing at me. "This is *her* fault."

Conlin batted at Petty's hand. "No one's getting fired," he said, "but we do have the benefit for *Love, Inc.* coming up. Theater patrons. Wealthy donors." Conlin rounded on me, all teeth. "You'll work the benefit," he said. "As the Pin-up Bride."

"NO!"

"Well, look at that," Conlin said over the ring of Petty and Guy's voices. "You two *can* agree."

"No way," Petty said. "She can't go out as Fausten."

He was right. I couldn't. Fausten Cotter was a presence, a force, a magnet that could capture anyone's attention. Me, I could barely capture Andy's. I couldn't be Fausten Cotter. Never mind fundraise a benefit.

"I didn't say she'd work as Ms. Cotter," said Conlin. "I said she'd work as the Pin-up Bride."

Petty threw up his hands. "They're one and the same."

"No, the Pin-up Bride is a fiction, a character. Ms. Cotter puts her on and takes her off again."

"Fine," Petty said, "but Fausten's the only one who's ever going to put her on."

"If Ms. Cotter doesn't want her understudy stepping in for her, then maybe she should get out of bed. Until then, Ms. James can be the Pin-up Bride."

Petty sought reinforcements. "Guy?"

"Someone should work the benefit," he said, sounding resigned. "Even without needing new lights, her fans, the donors—they'll want to see the star."

Petty huffed and crossed his arms.

Despite my reservations, I felt myself grinning. I didn't know how to convince benefactors that I was the Pin-up Bride, much less to pull out their checkbooks and pay for new equipment in addition to Conlin's new show, but I was more than willing to try. Conlin had said it: this would officially make me Fausten Cotter's understudy. Me. I could use the night to show Andy that, oh yes, I could be like his crush, the magnificent Fausten Cotter. And not only could I be *like* her—I could be her in fact.

I could replace her.

I breathed in deep, solidifying the affirming feeling that everything was coming together for me. Somehow I'd managed to ruin the theater's sound and lights, and yet I was closer than ever to securing my future. I would be the Pin-up Bride. I would be everything in her that Andy thought he wanted plus everything in me that he actually needed. I would be the Pin-up Bride, and then Andy would propose. He'd have to.

How could he resist?

"I can work the benefit." I'd have to figure out later what, exactly, that meant. "Can I borrow one of Fausten's costumes?"

"NO!" Once again, Guy and Petty agreed.

"Of course. Get her an outfit." Conlin waved a hand, assigning the task to Petty.

"Hold up," Guy said. "You just want Petty to find her something white, right?"

Conlin's tone warned that he was losing patience. "Get her an outfit."

"It's fine," Petty said, holding his hands waist high, wrists extended, as if collecting himself. "The benefit isn't for weeks. I can get her something that'll work by then."

Conlin shined his headlamp on Petty's face, making him wince, and his baritone rang with a menace no one could ignore. "The last time I let you wait until last minute, the lights and speakers blew. And I don't want something that'll work, Vargas, I want the Pin-up Bride. Now—get her an outfit."

CHAPTER 25

DAPHNE

Petty mumbled obscenities as he led me backstage, into the crossover, where a thick black fabric covered the back wall to muffle sounds. Petty pushed the draping aside, revealing a hidden elevator. Hidden, but familiar. This was the elevator I'd taken to the trap room the night of the amateur competition.

Petty pushed the call button. The door slid open, and I followed him inside. He pulled a key card from his pocket and swiped it on the control panel. The panel allowed for three floors: zero, one, and three. Petty pushed three.

"What's with the key?" I asked as the elevator rose. "Costumes can't require that much security."

Petty leaned against the elevator's quilted gray padding and crossed his arms, refusing eye contact. "Keep quiet when we get there," he said. "She's sleeping."

My body warmed, realizing the significance of what he'd said before I did. I had only ever seen Fausten Cotter in character, and even then only a couple of times. "She'll be there?"

"Sleeping."

The elevator opened onto a square hall. Petty unlocked the door to the right and led me into a spacious room. The overhead lights were off, but light from streetlamps and passing cars filtered through two walls' worth of windows that overlooked the park.

Gauzy netting hung from the ceiling over a king-sized bed, its white bedspread molded over a human-sized lump. If she were anyone else, I wouldn't have given her a second glance, but I was drawn to Fausten Cotter. I wanted to know if she wore an eye mask, if she used sulfur on her acne, if she even had acne. I wanted to know if she slept on her side or on her stomach.

Behold: she was the rare sleeper who lies royally on her back.

And look at her skin: so flawless, so luminous, even through the netting.

"That's close enough," Petty said.

I was up against the mattress, face pressed against the gauze. I straightened, fixed the draping, and looked around the room. Four poster-sized frames hung on the wall, alongside the door. All four displayed images of Fausten Cotter.

Petty gestured to the first three images, which weren't posters but blown-up photographs. "I took those."

And judging by his voice, he was proud. He crossed his lanky arms behind his back and puffed his skinny chest like he could wait on me all night, so long as I admired his work.

The leftmost photo's color palette was all wrong. Fausten was wearing a garish, puffy dress covered in hot pink and forest-green sequins. She looked not so much young as inexperienced, standing, hands on hips, in front of a tavern called the Rusty Duck. Several lights were burnt out on the D.

"We all start somewhere," Petty said. "I have more photos in the scrapbook, but these are my favorite. Even though *he's* in that one."

Petty pointed to the second photo. Fausten posed with someone who had an arm around her, his hand gripping her low on the hip. It looked like Guy, except the guy in the photo looked happy; the Guy I knew wasn't acquainted with that emotion.

Fausten had one knee popped and her arms stretched wide. Big smile. They stood in front of Milo's, a club with faux candles in the windows and darkness beyond. The ground-level readerboard said the headliner was Hank and the Happys. I'd never heard of them, so I didn't know if their name was spelled right.

"You don't have any other nice-bar photos of just her?" Hard to believe, considering all the scrapbooks lying about.

"She broke out too fast." Petty gestured to all four frames. "These photos are all from two summers ago."

"All of them?" It didn't seem possible.

"This show was a couple weeks later."

He pointed at the third photo, a wide shot of Fausten standing by herself under the marquee of the Orphic Starlight. Behind her, two men were rolling out the red carpet. Fausten, in white, had one knee popped and her arms in a high V. Her smile was cheeky, that coy yet elusive pout she'd become known for. The theater's digital readerboards displayed the same thing on all three panels: *Tonight at 8 — THE PIN-UP BRIDE.*

"And this was its poster." Petty pointed at the last image. "They had to rush it. I remember we were running late for the shoot. They were not happy. But she gave them *that* in the first click of the camera. I didn't even have time to try the fruit platter."

The rightmost frame held the Pin-up Bride poster, the one of her kneeling, sitting back on her heels with her back arched and her bouquet pressed into her lap. Her white hat veiled her face, but it still felt like she was watching me, understanding me in a way no one else ever would.

"Spectacular, isn't she?"

I could only nod. Had to nod. I didn't want to admit it, not ever, not even to Petty, her biggest fan, but she was. She was.

"All four in about a month." Petty watched me, waiting for me to put together what the timing of these photos meant, to feel both astonished and intimidated that Fausten Cotter had gone from wannabe to somebody in the amount of time it had taken me to lose a scholarship and ruin the theater's sound and lights. His eyes challenged me to compete with her—now, at the benefit, for Andy—but I couldn't. We both knew I couldn't.

The best I could do was leave the lanky prick feeling just a little bit miffed.

"The Orphic Starlight," I said. "Isn't that where she had that accident?"

Petty slowly turned his head toward me, his eyes narrowing into a glare. "Let's get you that costume."

No objections here.

Petty opened a set of french doors opposite the bed and strode into the largest walk-in closet I'd ever seen in person. The smell of powder and peaches tickled my nose. Racks of costumes filled the wall opposite the door with a color explosion, which surprised me since the Pin-up Bride mostly if not always wore white. Metal hangers screeched along the rack as Petty rejected garments with a bored *no* and pushed them aside. I thought the sound would irritate Fausten, but she didn't say anything.

Petty considered a totally wrong blue-and-yellow jumper. "No." *Screech.*

Behind him stood an entire rack of appropriate costumes done in white and shades of white with hints of pink and mint green. He had to know that, and yet he considered a black-and-red bodycon.

"No." *Screech.* "She's curvier than you, but I guess we could get you some shapewear."

Screw you too, Petty.

I inched toward the rack of white. I savored the scents of lavender and peaches, the care with which each costume had been pinned so delicately to stuffed hangers. My fingertips tingled, caressing all the fabrics. Satin and silk, brocade and velvet. Even the lace felt soft and luxurious. One costume stood out, and I pushed aside the other garments. The hangers screeched along the rack.

"What are you doing?" Petty held a costume even worse than that garish hot-pink-and-forest-green one from the photo. It was so revolting I had to look away.

I hugged the white clothes, comforted myself in the rack of softness. Petty pulled me away and fussed with the hangers until all the white garments were once again spaced evenly along the rack. "Go stand somewhere else."

I obeyed, but I knew which costume I wanted. The top was corseted with flounced off-the-shoulder straps, and the skirt was fitted with thin tiers of ruffles in all textures and shades of white, the back a little longer and fuller than the flat, short front. It was thee Pin-up Bride dress, the one she wore in the poster.

"Come here." Petty held his choice up against me.

No way. Fausten Cotter might've dressed cowgirl once upon a time, but she'd never do it now. The fabric was this disgusting scratchy polyester bleh in blotchy pinks and browns that smelled of mothballs and cigarettes. I nearly gagged.

"This'll work." Petty grabbed a black garment bag from a pink storage box and stuffed the dress inside.

"You're kidding, ri—*urgch.*" I heaved and covered my mouth. Not even a thorough dry-cleaning could make cowgirl work. "Out of this entire wardrobe, *that's* what you think I should wear? It's not even white."

"You can wear your own dingy white underwear for all I care." Petty pushed the dress's hanger through the hole at the top of the garment bag, zipped it shut, and held it out to me.

"Fausten would never wear underwear," I said, "just like she'd never wear that. It's old—"

"It's vintage."

"—it's brown, and there's a hole in the armpit."

"Whine all you want, but we've worked too hard to get Fausten to where she is to give you one of her whites." Petty's voice held a sadness that surprised me, an uncomfortable honesty I stepped away from. But he saved me from pitying him when he puffed his chest and reclaimed his Diva's Asshole Assistant attitude. "I'm not letting some reckless hack play dress-up with Fausten's image."

"But you heard Conlin. I have to stand in for her, pretend to be her, convince those people that I am her. It's my job."

"No, it's your punishment." He wagged the bag at me. "So take it."

But I couldn't. Seriously. I'd bleach the red out of the '80s wedding dress I'd worn for the amateur contest before wearing that cowgirl costume.

Petty sighed. He set the garment bag on the dresser next to me and dug a step stool out from under the clothes. "What size shoe do you wear?"

"Seven."

"Good. Find your own shoes. Now all you need is a hat."

Oh goody. A cowgirl hat to go with my cowgirl dress. My back hit the doorway. My body was subconsciously retreating from the room, from that outfit. I couldn't wear it. I wouldn't. It wouldn't fool anyone into thinking I was the Pin-up Bride. It wouldn't convince anyone of anything, except that I was a hack playing dress-up, just like Petty said. And the worst part? The best outfit ever was right there. Right there wanting to be worn, if Petty would just let me wear it. If Petty would just—

Give Daphne the outfit.

"Faus?" Petty was off the stool, pushing past me, lifting the gauze on Fausten's bed. I thought she was sleeping, but I heard him whispering to her.

I wasted no time. I was at the rack, soundlessly picking through the whites for my dress. The worst that could happen was Petty'd get mad, but what could he do? Refuse to do my makeup? He'd probably do a poor job on purpose anyway. And besides, the Pin-up Bride wore a veil. I'd have to find a veiled hat, but I'd sooner fashion one from meat mesh and a styrofoam cup than wear that cowboy crap.

I found the outfit. Power and rightness surged through my fingertips, up my arms, and into my core, releasing all my doubts with a shiver of tingles. Surely this dress would impress Andy. Persuade him. Drop him to one knee. And while I was making peace with theft by hoping it resulted in a proposal, let's not forget that this all started because I'd been ordered to raise money. People would fund Fausten Cotter, and hopefully they'd fund her properly dressed understudy, but no one would ever fund Daphne James, the ugly-ass cowgirl.

A rustling sound came from the other room. Petty doing something for Fausten, no doubt. I unzipped the garment bag, took out Petty's nasty choice, and stashed it behind the door. I unracked the poster outfit. So beautiful. So exciting. I hooked the hanger through the garment bag's hole and tucked the dress inside.

"Borrow it, if you want."

I startled, my shaking hand still holding the pull on the unzipped garment bag.

Petty crossed his arms and rose to full height, almost reaching the top of the doorway. "But it doesn't leave the theater."

I didn't move. I didn't trust Petty's permission. I waited for him to change his mind.

He looked down at the garment bag, at the unzipped gap and the shades of white inside.

"Fausten's not just an outfit," he said, "I don't care what Conlin says. He's an idiot if he thinks you can pass for her." He shook his head. "Not in a fog. Not in the same dress. Not even with this to hide your face."

He held out a hat, the white one with the pink and mint-green accents and the white mesh veil.

Petty could say whatever. I knew I'd look perfect.

CHAPTER 26

DAPHNE - 29 days left

The next morning came straight out of my matrimonial daydreams. I woke to the smell of something baking and the sight of Andy tending the stove in nothing but his navy-blue sweats.

I came up behind him and circled my arms around his waist. "I thought you didn't like blueberry pancakes."

Andy shrugged, flipped a pancake onto a plate, and handed me a fork. "You do."

We ate breakfast at the coffee table. He'd set out our textbooks—finance for him, physics for me—but we didn't study much. When I was with Andy, I tended to forget about my life's crap trajectory, so content to just stay in, snuggled on the couch with the comforter pulled from the bed. I savored the moment of life finally going my way.

We were interrupted when Conlin called to ask if I could come help Guy.

I opened the theater's house doors. Guy was on the stage sorting through some boxes, and the first thing out of his mouth was, "Andy propose yet?"

He was such an ass.

I traipsed down the aisle. "Any day now, Guy. Any day."

"But not today, right?"

Maybe. Andy's proposal was imminent, I could feel it. And it was more than mere hopefulness. It was becoming a certainty again, a certainty that had me smiling as I climbed the stairs to the stage.

"Right?" Guy asked again.

I threw him some eye daggers. They slayed his curiosity.

Hours later we were still onstage, installing the equipment Guy had rented to temporarily replace the equipment I had ruined.

Well, Guy was installing equipment. I was playing tool-grabber.

"Grab me the wrench," Guy said from midway up the thirty-foot ladder. He reached down to exchange the pliers I'd just handed him.

The wrench was on top, but I rooted through the toolbox anyway, making the sound of metal grating on metal echo throughout the house. My phone rang. I answered with a grin. "Yes, Andy?"

"What are you doing?"

"Same thing."

"Still?"

"Wrench," Guy said.

I maneuvered up the ladder, using my left wrist and right elbow, to make the exchange. "Still," I told Andy.

Guy strained to reach me. "You're gonna have to come up higher," he said.

"I gotta go," I told Andy. "Was there something you needed?"

"Just you."

Yes, Andy was a keeper. He never said so outright, but he liked us living together. And he'd like the stability of commitment, too, I knew he would. He just needed help, a little push, to overcome his resistance.

I ended the call with Andy and took the pliers from Guy. "You know, we'd get done faster if you kept both tools with you," I said, "stuck one in a pocket while you weren't using it." He'd filled the front pocket of his coveralls with what looked like a red-and-white plastic takeout bag. "What do you have in there, anyway? Trash?"

He ignored me. "Andy again, huh?"

I held up the wrench, but Guy's fingers had gone lax. I tapped them with the wrench. "So?"

Before he could respond, the house doors opened and Conlin's baritone boomed down the aisle. "Park! It's almost two. Should I call an installer?"

"I'm good," Guy said, "but we'd get done faster if you took Daphne's phone."

Such an ass.

Conlin said he had to go to the prop shop. "If we need an installer, I can call one," he said as he left. "I want you groomed for tonight."

"I will be," Guy said.

I choked on some disbelief. "Did Conlin just order you to manscape?"

"Begged me," Guy said. "That was Conlin still begging."

"Riiight. What's the occasion? Fausten tired of your grungy Sherlock Holmes?"

"I wouldn't want to ruin the surprise. And Daphne?" He waited for me to look past the dirty smears on his forehead to his smug eyes and his smug confidence. He accepted the wrench. "Fausten loves my grunge."

I mimed gagging. "If that's true, then why'd she dump you?"

The utility lamp flickered. So did Guy's eyes. "What?"

"I saw the photo of you two hanging in her room, the one where you're beaming at her." I pressed my knuckles under my chin and mocked him with lovesick eyes. "Like you's witnessin' an angel."

"Just so you know," he said, "I left her."

Outside, wind gusted against the theater, shrieking through its cracks, but the sound wasn't nearly as loud as me busting a gut.

Guy? Dumped Fausten Cotter? "*Oh*, okay."

Guy laid a protective hand over his bulging pocket of trash and eyed the ceiling.

A heater had kicked on. Warm air was meeting cold wind and filling the rafters with mist. Guy's dark hair ruffled in the peach-scented breeze.

He twitched a smile and climbed back up the ladder.

"And she wanted me back," he said.

The ladder wobbled.

"I take it back," he said. "She dumped me."

"Whatever you say, Guy. I really don't care." *Just quit it with the ladder.*

The ladder kept shaking. Guy hunched his back and clung to the rails. I planted a foot on the ladder's bottom rung to steady it for him, even though I knew he had to be doing some balancing trick to scare me. I'd been working here for a few weeks now, and doing a good job too, I thought, but Guy still took every opportunity to scare me or chafe me or gross me into quitting.

"She dumped me," he yelled toward the ceiling. "Crushed me like a stampede and all that sad, broken shit. Happy?"

The wind subsided and the ladder stilled. Guy's body relaxed, but his face did not. He glowered down at me and told me to hand him a light case. I did, then sat on the bottom rung to hold the ladder steady.

"What's her story anyway?" I asked.

"No more Fausten talk." Guy flashed me a tortured smile. "The theater doesn't like it."

"Riiight, the haunted theater." *Please.* "Last night, when we were getting the costume, Petty and I were a little loud and she was trying to sleep. I thought she'd go all diva on us, but she didn't say anything. Is she shy or just above speaking to the likes of me?"

Wind howled through the building, chilling my neck.

"See?" Guy said. "The theater doesn't like it."

I scratched at a chip in the ladder and decided that the wind was just a coincidence. "Do you think I could talk to her?"

Guy leaned away from the ladder to leverage the wrench. He grunted as he did it but was otherwise as silent as a sleeping Fausten Cotter.

"She really broke out that summer, huh?" My mind still boggled at the timing of her success. Her changes in appearance seemed years apart rather than weeks.

Guy pulled a tool from his back pocket and focused all his attention on stripping and twisting some wires.

"How'd she do it?" I asked.

He stripped another wire.

"What's her secret?"

"Is this about you getting engaged?" he asked.

My turn to play deaf. I thumbed my silly-string ring. The nail-polish coating wouldn't preserve it much longer.

"He seems into you," Guy said. "Why don't you just relax? Get a hobby?"

"I work here."

"No, I mean find something to do for itself," he said, "not as a strategy."

I scraped at some gunk on the stage floor. Collecting wayward crayons entertained me well enough, but I otherwise felt undeserving of my goals when I did frivolous things that couldn't support them.

Guy said, "You know what kind of girl I'd be interested in?"

I didn't, but I thought now might be a good time to stick these screwdrivers in my ears.

"I'd be interested in someone confident, secure...and relaxed."

"Someone like that wouldn't need assurance," I said. "Someone like that wouldn't need anyone."

"You're right," he said. "Leaves you free to just appreciate someone."

"You don't get it."

"Oh, but I do. You're clinging so tight to the signpost that you can't see which way leads to happy, even though all you have to do is let go and lift your head."

The lamp flickered.

"Yay," I said, celebrating one light closer to done (and the change in subject).

But Guy swore and his wire strippers fell to the stage. He shook his hand and scowled at the lamp.

The empty lamp.

Guy hadn't installed the bulb, just the fixture. The flickering hadn't been light. It was sparks.

He'd been shocked.

"Are you okay?"

Guy clenched and flexed his fingers. "Hand me a bulb and unbox the rest of the fixtures," he said, avoiding my eyes. "Then it's time for you to go."

The ladder rocked.

Guy lost his balance and almost fell off, but he scrambled to hug the top step.

The ladder continued to rock.

"Go," Guy told me.

I stared at him, at his tense arms gripping the top step. Those microflexes were probably causing the instability that had him *appearing* so precariously perched atop the ladder—which made this whole display just another scare tactic, the turd. He was right: I should just go. And why not? I'd been ready to go home for hours now, and the turd was telling me that I could.

But his wide, fearful eyes begged the opposite. And I couldn't be sure they were just an act.

I grabbed the ladder, trying to steady him, but the ladder teetered and rapped the stage. Faster. Louder. Pounding like a drumroll.

"*Go.*"

I backed away. "Come down," I told him. But the ladder was too shaky. So loud. The rafters crackled. And the mist—

"Guy, watch out."

The mist struck and the ladder folded, becoming a trap that crushed him vertically against the prompt corner. His eyes widened and closed. His head lolled against the rail.

I grabbed a rung and tried to pull the ladder away, but it wouldn't give. I yanked harder. Harder. "Guy?!"

He groaned, lifting his head, and the burdened sound morphed into a battle cry as he strained to push the ladder away. We couldn't get it off him.

The mist condensed into haze, into smoke, into thick, intelligent fog.

A flash of it struck the ladder.

I gasped and backed away, my fingers stinging, bitten with cold—and the ladder tipped forward. Guy fell like a severed marionette as it toppled off the stage and rattled to the ground.

I crawled to Guy. His eyes were on mine, cautious like mine. Had he seen our attacker? Thick and white. Sharp and exact. I didn't ask. If he said no, I'd be crazy. If he said yes, he'd fuel this fear.

And the sparks, the haze—surely it all had a rational explanation. Maybe Guy had forgotten to turn off the electricity. Maybe there was insufficient grounding. Terrible insulation. It was an old, decrepit building. It was just some mist.

Guy winced as he sat up. "You okay?" he asked.

I checked my fingers. The tips felt tender but looked fine. I nodded. "You?"

His voice was high. "I could use a towel."

He lifted his hand. His knuckles were covered in streaks of something dark. I sucked in a breath, trying to hold down the bile, and told myself it was just dirt, which got easier to believe because Guy wasn't concerned about his hand.

He touched his thigh and hissed through his teeth. Then he tugged the fabric above his knee and raised a mass of flesh.

I barely made it to the lobby bathroom before upchucking my blueberry pancakes. I gargled some sink water and got a bucket of ice and a clean towel from the bar. Guy put the torn piece of pant-covered flesh in the bucket, and we limped backstage to where the theater parked its van.

Guy climbed into the passenger seat and hugged the bucket of ice to his chest. I couldn't think about what was in it without gagging, and it didn't help that the van reeked of motor oil and greasy fries. The van started just fine, but it made an embarrassing chirping sound the entire five-minute drive to urgent care. By the time we got there, Guy's blood had soaked the towel.

"Get the wheelchair," he said.

"Huh?"

Guy waved toward the back of the van. I opened the rear doors and, sure enough, found a blanket and a wheelchair. Guy sat in the chair and wheeled himself through the clinic's sliding doors. I followed, leaving the van parked cockeyed at the curb.

When the nurse called Guy's name, I stood, but Guy didn't want me going with him. Worked for me. I grabbed a magazine off the table and settled in for the wait. But my mind wouldn't relax. Was I really blaming his ladder accident on *mist*? Mist that rushed so fast it turned opaque? Mist that struck so fast it *stripped off skin*?

No. He must've cut himself on the ladder.

I squirmed in my chair and flipped the glossy pages, hoping to find distraction in an article about how too much stimulation can interfere with an introvert's memory. I kept replaying the look on Guy's face, the look in his eyes when he'd told me to leave. Like he was scared. Like he was scared for me even though he was the one who'd been shocked.

I'd thought he was just terrorizing me as usual, still trying to get me to leave the theater and never come back. I'd thought he just didn't like me because, well, because not everyone likes everyone—or because I'd been a bitch to him when we'd first met, whatever—but now? The theater couldn't be haunted, that was just silly, but after what had happened with the sound and lights, and now the ladder...

I meant to ask Guy if the ladder had been a prank gone wrong, but when he returned, his appearance cleared my mind of all other concerns. His coveralls were now cutoffs, and his shirt was draped over the collapsed wheelchair, which he pushed like a rolling cane. White bandages covered his shoulder, his hands, his thigh. He walked gingerly, blood already spotting the bandages. He said he got forty-two stitches on his hands and shoulder. I stopped him before he could tell me what was necessary to fix his thigh.

"Well," he said, when we were back in the van, "so much for Conlin's big surprise."

I put the van in drive and looked over my shoulder for traffic. "What big surprise?"

"For the fans," he said. "To get people back into the theater after last night."

I sank a little in my seat, the blowup last night being my fault and all, but Guy wasn't trying to goad me.

"Conlin's been teasing it on social media," he said. "Fausten's posing tonight. With a guest."

My nose wrinkled. None of the regular performers were physically comparable, let alone someone I thought the reclusive starlet would let near her. "Who?"

Guy didn't answer.

I was watching traffic, but in my periphery I saw him looking at me. "What?"

The corner of his mouth rose.

I stopped at a red light and stared back at him. "What?" But then I got it. "You?"

His smile widened. He shrugged.

Consider me dumbfounded.

I'd only ever seen Guy in dingy coveralls or some weird-ass costume, which wasn't a fair assessment, I suppose, but the thought of Guy posing naked with Fausten Cotter made my upper lip curl.

"What's that look for?" he said.

I didn't think it was possible to offend Guy Vincent Park, but he had a hint of hurt in his voice that made me look at him anew. His head was decent enough, I guess, so long as it wasn't speaking. He had his shirt off, was only wearing shorts, but all I'd really noticed was his bandages. I relaxed my eyes and let my vision adjust until it downplayed the white gauze and revealed Guy's—*Oh.*

I see.

Consider me corrected.

But he was still Guy, and he had me circling back to this nugget of truth when he popped his pecs at me. I flinched and he grinned. The turd. My bad for lingering, I suppose, but thankfully, the light turned green, traffic flowed, and I was saved from having to respond to the smug look on his face.

But the turd's big surprise was sparking my earworm. I sensed it fiddling in my imagination, scraping together a crazy idea. Potentially fun. Definitely scary.

Too intriguing to ignore.

"So," I said, "who do you think'll pose with Fausten now?"

"Don't know. The other acts won't have time to get all the paint off before they have to go on."

"Petty?"

Guy laughed, probably imagining Petty shedding his skinny jeans, missing an ass, not knowing what to do with his lanky arms if he wasn't allowed to cross them. "I don't think he'll ask Petty."

I nodded, and my bold idea expanded, becoming an excited churn in my gut. It was risky. It made me nervous. But I'd just ask Conlin and see what happened. Probably nothing.

But maybe everything.

This could be the final push Andy needed.

CHAPTER 27

DAPHNE

"No way," Petty said. He, Conlin, Guy, and I had gathered in the theater's dim lobby ninety minutes before the show. "If he breaks character, Fausten won't be happy."

My earworm wiggled in my memory, inspiring a response. "Andy won't break. He can hold warrior pose for a really long time." He could, too. And drunk. He'd won an impromptu yoga challenge at a party one night.

"For what?" Guy said. "Five minutes? An hour of posing like a statue doesn't seem that long, but it is. It takes training to keep from getting distracted. I was practicing in malls when I was seven." Guy jutted his chin at Petty. "When did Fausten start?"

"Fausten's a natural."

Guy made a long-suffering face.

"Well, you've got to start somewhere," I told Conlin.

"That's true," he said, but he flipped back to the beginning of his binder and took another look through the photos of all his previous performers.

Petty crossed his arms. "We don't even know what her boyfriend looks like. He could be skinny fat." He shuddered at the horror.

Conlin turned a skeptical expression toward the theater's main doors, where I'd left Andy standing outside in the cold.

I pulled out Andy's phone and showed Conlin a picture of the two of us taken two summers ago, at Long Beach. Me in a tankini, standing next to Andy in board shorts, showing off his naturally sculpted torso.

Arms crossed, Petty peeked at the photo…and rolled his eyes. "No need to gloat."

I grinned wider. Andy could totally hold his own as Ares, God of War, next to Fausten's Aphrodite.

"I don't know," Guy said, and his chest flexed beneath his PuB shirt. "He's a little skinny for Ares."

"No, he's not. Shut up." I flipped to another picture, this one a headshot. "Please," I said to Conlin. "He's not a barrel chest, like Guy, but I know he can do it."

Guy eyed me. "Why do you want your boyfriend to pose naked with another girl so bad?"

Guy's question poked at my biggest problem with this plan, but I ignored him. I held the phone out so Conlin could see that Andy had the right build for the part. "Please?"

Conlin took the phone and flipped through the pictures. "He is a little too skinny for Ares, isn't he?"

I swallowed against the ice block growing in my stomach. Andy had said he didn't want to pose in the living statue act at first, but I'd convinced him that it would be fun, a lifetime opportunity, especially for a soon-to-be Chicago business analyst. I'd also conveyed that if he stuck with me, our life together would be exciting, that I was confident and playful and nothing like his mother. But if I'd gotten his hopes up for nothing, if I'd made him ditch his study group only to disappoint him for my own secret purpose, I'd be exactly like his mother.

I stopped Conlin's swiping on a candid shot. Andy was always attractive to me, but more people agreed with me when they saw him smile.

"Handsome," Conlin said, resuming his swiping. "Just not an Ares."

"It's been a while since Fausten posed," Guy said. "I'm sure the fans will be happy with just her."

"They'd prefer it," Petty said.

"I'm sure they would," said Conlin, still swiping. "He's not an Ares, but he'd make a good Adonis."

"Hah!" I poked Guy in the chest. "Take that, you turd. And PS, Adonis was hotter."

"I don't know about that," Conlin said, stealing the oomph from my triumph. "Patrons like the Ares props. But the statues are similar. Adonis will work." He handed back the phone. "But if things go poorly..."

"Fausten won't like this," Petty said.

"Then she should've offered her own solution," said Conlin.

"I might have a remedy for that too," I said. And my nerves started jittering. I hadn't expected to get this far.

"A way to mollify Ms. Cotter?" Conlin said. "This should be good."

"Well," I started to say, but I was so scared about what might happen in the next two hours as a result of my crazy question that my teeth started to chatter. That tankini at Long Beach? I'd only managed to sport it because my relationship with Andy had been too new for me to say no. I didn't know if I could follow through on what I was about to ask, but I was willing to leave the comfort zone for the crazy naked zone if it got me Andy's commitment.

"I know Fausten works really hard and could probably use a break, and so I thought that I could, you know, that I could maybe...pose for her?"

Petty hooted.

Guy said, "Oh, I get it."

And Conlin smiled down at me like I was a clumsy street urchin failing to con him.

"Please, Conlin? Consider it understudy practice."

"No," Petty said. "The dress, the benefit, the posing boyfriend. Daphne's gotten plenty."

Conlin said, "That's kind of you, Ms. James—"

"*No*," Petty said, "I'm not letting some amateur nobody interlope Fausten's success."

"But aside from her act," Conlin continued, looking pointedly at Petty, "posing is all Ms. Cotter's contract requires her to do, and we've already limited her appearances. She's not getting out of this one."

"Finally," Petty said, "a good decision." He marched past the bar to the stairs, where he paused to scowl back at us before drawing a curtain across the width of the lobby to block the far end. Fausten liked to enter unseen and then have the curtain pulled back, unveiling her perfect, statuesque form. No one ever saw her prepping. It helped maintain her mystique. Or so Petty claimed.

Conlin sighed and waved a hand toward the front doors. "Well, get him in here."

"Right." I moved toward the door, not entirely relieved that I didn't have to pose tonight. All the progress I'd made with Andy in the last month could evaporate when he pressed his naked body against the perfect body of the Pin-up Bride.

But if posing naked with him myself proved my confidence, then arranging for him to pose naked with his crush proved me the saint of confidence. Plus, I'd get credit for my willingness to pose without actually having to get nude.

I lifted my chin, straightened my shoulders, and opened the doors, affecting an air like everything had gone according to plan and wasn't I the coolest girlfriend ever for getting Andy this gig. It's how Fausten Cotter would play it. And she was a pro. Nothing bad would happen.

"Sorry," Andy said for the third time from behind the curtain. Petty had insisted he wear a blindfold while they set up the pose. "Don't you ever talk?"

"She's in character," Petty said. "Like you should be."

"Doors in one minute," Conlin said.

Normally I'd take tickets, but Conlin had recruited one of tonight's performers to take my place so I could keep watch over

Andy. I stood by the bar, shifting from foot to foot and fidgeting with my scarf. My boyfriend was about to pose naked to naked, buff to buff, with Fausten Cotter. I wanted Andy's commitment, but this could get me dumped.

Petty pulled the cord, drawing open the curtain and revealing the platform.

My stomach rolled.

Fausten stood, still as could be, gazing up at Andy. Her right forearm rested on his shoulder, her left caressed his cheek. She wore nothing but a gauzy shawl knotted well below her belly button and draped to look like it had slipped from her hips, down to her thighs, her luminous skin on full display.

And Andy… His half of the statue didn't ease my second thoughts; it made hackles rise up my spine. He wore nothing, literally nothing, but a strategically placed fig leaf that challenged gravity. Iridescent glitter dotted the green felt—as if the shock of green alone wouldn't draw enough attention.

But worse than Andy's non-outfit was the way he curled his arm around Fausten's tiny waist and beheld her with this look of adoration.

I tried to remember if he'd ever looked at me that way.

The front doors opened. Conlin's booming baritone welcomed the cold air and excited patrons. People chattered and clutched each other as they scurried through the lobby toward the statue. Andy glanced at them, then looked at me and grinned.

"Hold still," I mouthed, but I had to smile. His grin for me was lifetimes better than the look he'd been giving Fausten.

"How's it going?" Conlin asked on his way upstairs to get changed.

"He keeps moving," Petty said.

As if on cue, Andy wiggled a little, like he had an itch. Not entirely statuesque perhaps, but more endearing than awkward, I thought.

"He looks okay," Conlin said, and my chin rose with pride. "At the very least, his presence should deter the grabbier fans."

And it did for a while. Andy kept glancing at his audience, which wasn't ideal, certainly not as skillful as the stoic Fausten Cotter, but Petty tolerated it, only shaking his head every time Andy snuck a peek. But then Andy did more than sneak a peek. He beamed a smile into the crowd.

"Quit moving," Petty said.

I scanned the crowd, looking for friends we knew, but all I saw was unfamiliar theatergoers admiring the living statue, getting drinks at the bar, perusing the night's program. I figured he hadn't seen anyone in particular, just a funny shirt or a contagious grin, but then he waved.

"*Tchht,*" Petty hissed, motioning for Andy to quit. Andy dropped his hand, but instead of gazing fondly at Fausten, he grinned at the gathering crowd.

Tipsy-toeing girls our age were pushing their way to the front. They stepped right up to the velvet ropes, then whispered and giggled at the full, sexy nakedness of my boyfriend. One of them must've felt my annoyance, because she looked around and made eye contact. I smiled and fluttered my fingers. *That's right, girlfriend present.*

"He's not taking it seriously," Petty said. "If he doesn't take it seriously, neither will they."

And they didn't. I couldn't tell if they were doing it on purpose, but as they giggled and gawked, they nudged the velvet rope stands, shrinking the buffer that protected Andy and Fausten. I could've told them to stop, but I didn't want to detract from the act, and I certainly didn't want to be the bad guy. Andy was having fun. He'd give me major appreciation for getting him this opportunity, but he'd resent me if I embarrassed him. If the girls became a problem, Petty would say something.

One of the girls held up a dollar. Something about her. She wore a pink scarf, and she had thick dark hair, like Fausten Cotter's. And a flirty voice. "Does he dance?" she said.

Andy grinned, but it was his smiling-while-uncomfortable grin. I glanced at Petty, waiting for him to stop this, but he seemed determined to wait and see.

The girl reached her dollar over the velvet rope. Andy stilled, his ab muscles flexing, his attention finally focusing on Fausten.

Petty grunted. "At least they're keeping him in line."

Not the response I'd expected, but if Petty could keep his cool, then so could I.

And I would have, if the dark-haired girl would've just dropped her money at Andy's feet.

She tucked it in his fig leaf.

"Hey." I waved to get her attention. "Back off."

She couldn't hear me. Or she pretended not to. She and her friends squealed and bounced and hid their giggling faces in each other's shoulders. The dark-haired girl pulled out another dollar.

Poof! A squirt of smoke erupted from the platform and blew at the girls. They shrieked and jumped out of the way. Two of them collided, and one struggled to regain her balance. She tripped on the velvet rope and crashed, headfirst, into Fausten.

Fausten knocked into Andy and the living statue tipped. Andy righted himself quickly enough, but Fausten fell from the platform like a bumped mannequin, landing hard on her elbow.

Crunch.

"Faus!" Petty lunged toward her, trying to forge his way through the crowd. I tried to follow, but the crowd shuffled, holding me in place. People pushed toward the exit; others pushed toward the act. A couple people jumped the velvet rope and rushed the platform. I thought they'd help Fausten, but they yanked the gauze from her legs and fought over the souvenir.

"Move!" Petty broke through and dropped to his knees next to Fausten. He gingerly touched her left hand, still positioned like she was caressing Andy's cheek. Andy stood next to them, coughing and waving at the haze.

"Andy." Petty snapped his fingers to get his attention. "Where's Guy?"

Andy shook his head, then stumbled back as the crowd closed in. I lost sight of him. But he was a big boy. He could take care of himself. He was at least standing, unlike Fausten Cotter.

Petty rolled Fausten onto her back. She continued to hold her arms as if one hand was on someone's shoulder, the other caressing someone's cheek, like she was still posed as Aphrodite.

"Is she okay?" someone asked.

Petty looked around in horror and spotted me, still trying to break through. "Get the curtain."

Good idea. The drawstring was on the wall, between the bar and the stairs, back the way I'd come. I shifted directions, but a big guy, stunned immobile by the downed and naked star, blocked my path.

Light flashed, blinding and quick, like an old-fashioned flashbulb. The big guy jerked back—and the crowd retaliated, pushing us forward and driving me down to the floor. I sprawled across the velvet rope, pulling down more stands and conking myself on the head.

"*Ahhww.*" The back of my head throbbed. I tried to push myself up but couldn't. Too dizzy. Someone rolled me over. "Ow." My head hurt. Too tender to rest it on the floor.

"Where's Andy?" Guy said. I tried to look toward his voice, but dark and white spots dotted my eyes.

"Leave her," Petty said. "Get the curtain."

"Andy," Guy called.

Someone got an arm beneath my back, another beneath my knees. My head lolled against his chest as he picked me up. Not Andy. Too brawny to be Andy.

"Take her home," Guy said, and for a second there were extra arms beneath me. I was being passed off. My head lolled to the other side, against a wool coat, a T-shirt that smelled like peppermint gum. This—this was Andy.

CHAPTER 28

DAPHNE

Andy set me on the sidewalk, beneath the ticket-booth window. He had beige paint on his forehead. Take-charge concern filled his eyes. He brushed my hair from my face and pulled my coat tighter against the chill.

"You gonna be okay here for a second?" he asked.

I nodded and he walked away, disappearing around the side of the building.

So much for tonight being the final push Andy needed. I'd be lucky if he continued to notice me at all after the attention he'd gotten from the girl with the Fausten Cotter hair and the mad money-tucking skills.

My head spun like my earworm was whirling on a merry-go-round. I closed my eyes and rested my head against the stone wall. Conlin's voice boomed inside the theater, inviting everyone to take their seats, but the front doors opened and a few people left. I hoped Guy and Petty didn't try to blame tonight on me too. I couldn't afford any more of Conlin's punishments. Andy hadn't been the best statue, but falling wasn't his fault. Falling was the fault of that girl. She and her friends, they were the rowdy ones. They were the ones who had knocked into Fausten Cotter.

But I couldn't blame them for Fausten holding her pose instead of catching herself. Andy had managed to catch himself. Fausten had tipped like a tree.

Andy's white Jeep pulled to the curb. I pushed up the wall and held on to it as I stepped away, testing my balance. So far so good. But when Andy came around the front of his Jeep, I got dizzy again and fell against the wall.

"You okay?" he asked.

His body was blurry. Nothing else in my vision was blurry, just Andy. I blinked, but he was still muted, still pixelated with fuzzy edges.

I nodded anyway.

Andy opened the passenger door and helped me into my seat, then went around front to the driver's side. I rolled down the window for air. My arm felt dead.

"Bye, Andy," said a flirty voice.

I looked out the window. A gaggle of girls were huddled beneath the awning, out of the rain. They had their hoods up, so I couldn't tell if they were the same ones. Andy got in, buckled his seat belt, and put the Jeep in gear like he hadn't heard anyone calling him.

She must've been calling some other Andy.

I watched the girls as we pulled away from the curb. One of them waved something green and glittery.

The walls inside Andy's apartment flickered with shadows. Candles lit the kitchen table—wavy, blurry candles with wavy, blurry flames.

Andy went into the bedroom, but the kitchen table was as far as I could manage. I grabbed the back of a chair. My hand felt heavy and numb, like it wasn't moving, but the chair slid out. I sat and rested my elbow on the table, my cheek in my hand.

Andy reemerged from the bedroom with my PJs in hand. He really was the best. A true nice guy. Some people find that boring. They don't realize how important kindness is until they've failed a few jerks. I'd watched my mom fail enough that I didn't need any more convincing. Andy helped me out of my coat and pulled up my shirt, lifting my arms overhead. I tried to keep them up while he slid them through the sleeves, but the best I could do was lay them on my head. I was so tired.

My earworm was not. It had abandoned the merry-go-round and was now spinning itself in place, into a chrysalis, tighter and tighter, faster and faster.

Andy sat in the chair next to mine and took my hand. He was blurry again. I blinked. I rubbed my eyes. Still blurry.

He slipped off the edge of his chair and came down on one blurry knee. He held something crisp in his blurry hand, pinched between his blurry fingers.

I looked at his blurry face, his cockeyed smile. His eyebrows popped with question.

Wait, was it Thee Question? Did he ask me? Did I miss it?

There was no way I would miss it.

But maybe I had. I nodded, just in case. *Yes. Of course, yes.* I hugged him, but he pulled away. Maybe I'd misunderstood. But no—he still had it. A ring. Shiny and crisp between his blurry thumb and forefinger. He took my left hand and slid the ring into place.

The gem was like nothing I'd wished for. It wasn't a diamond. It wasn't cut into any of the faceted styles I'd coveted in magazines. It wasn't cut at all. It was a cabochon, a shimmery golden opalescent cabochon.

And it was perfect.

Andy opened his arms. I leaned into him, inhaling his scent and reveling in the way he held me, like making this decision had finally allowed him to release his fears. He held me tightly.

Too tightly.

He squeezed me hard, bruising my arms and crushing my back. I couldn't breathe.

My eyes flashed open.

My body felt tingly, alert to the moment, like it did during a rise and retreat of my shields. Except I didn't feel the shields themselves.

I was lying on my back in a dark room, in the bed I shared with Andy.

Andy?

I looked for him next to me. Or tried to. My neck muscles tensed, but my head wouldn't move. I couldn't move.

But the dark at my feet moved.

Fight or flight! But I'd froze. Adrenaline surged inside me, accomplishing nothing but strain. I wanted to move. I struggled to move. I could not move.

But I could marvel. Darkness had never been more than just that, but this darkness wanted exception.

It rippled to life.

Get up! Not even my fingers obeyed. *Get up! Get up!*

The darkness came closer, a substance in the shadows, and I couldn't stop it. I couldn't even scream.

Wake up!

I backed away from it—but only within the trappings of my body. The forming figure could get as close to me as it wanted. And it did. It did. So close I couldn't see the ceiling, just its head.

It had no face, but it touched its coldness to mine. Tickled my nose. Caressed my left hand.

Ow!

My ring finger zinged, bitten with cold. My whole left side went numb. I burned with tingles I could not shake.

WakeupWakeupWakeup!

The darkness rose and drifted off the bed. It backed into the corner. It cocked its head at me. It watched me, and I watched it.

I watched it as my body seethed, as it picked its nails—as if it had nails to pick.

I watched it as my heartbeat slowed, as the darkness brightened to crisp, white smoke.

I watched it past fatigue, as the smoke retreated down the wall.

I watched until my fingers moved, until the ghost wasn't there anymore.

CHAPTER 29

FAUSTEN

The shadowy haze of my influence drained to the corner of Daphne's room and back into the poster she'd torn down weeks ago.

The girl who'd wagged her money at Daphne's boyfriend while he was posing as my Adonis had caused a lot of chaos. But I'd made use of it. I'd added to the confusion. And tonight, for the first time ever, I'd accomplished two new skills.

First, I'd altered Daphne's experience in real time. Just a little, sure. Just enough to blur the shift from reality to dream. But it had been enough, I was sure of it.

And even more impressive? I'd accomplished this blurring before I'd made our bond even stronger with my second skill.

What could I say? *I'm amazing.*

And that second skill? I'd been pushing my influence through my posters for months, but tonight, while Daphne had been dreaming blissfully, I'd pushed through something solid.

Something real.

Daphne was in for some fun.

I rolled the poster back beneath Daphne's bed and released it from my influence.

And something snapped.

I jerked back to my body with a jolt that surged the room's electrical bits. The lights flickered and a bulb burst.

"Faus? Was that you?" Petty leaned over me, his dark eyes worried. "Are you back?"

The room was bright. White speckled tiles covered the ceiling beyond him. The boys must've moved me to my prep room while I was visiting Daphne. Losing sight of my posters might have caused the snap. But my body felt off. There was a tightness in my chest. I hadn't breathed in over a year, but I'd still felt full, like I was holding my breath.

I felt empty now, like I'd exhaled and needed to inhale, desperately needed to inhale, but couldn't.

"Is she saying anything?" Petty's voice echoed in the hallway as he called out to Guy. "Was that her or a power outage?"

Guy didn't answer.

Petty rubbed my arm, then rubbed it again. "Something's not right," he muttered. "This isn't... Guy!"

"What?"

"Get in here."

In the next room, Guy huffed and a couch cushion drew in air. He stomped down the hall, and his shadow appeared on the ceiling, merging with Petty's.

Petty said, "Does she look normal to you?"

"As normal as she can."

"Her skin doesn't look dull to you, a little ashy?"

Guy's warm hand rubbed my leg. "It's a little dry. I guess."

"It's *flaking*."

Schadenfreude perked to attention, ruffling the edge of my awareness.

"It's probably just the weather," Guy said. "It dropped to the teens last night."

"*Hmph.*" Petty rifled through something to my right. "Maybe this'll help."

Plastic grated plastic as Petty opened one of his cosmetics, filling the room with a putrid smell. The scent of death.

Good thinking, Petty.

"What *is* that?" Guy asked.

Globs of oily cream landed on my cheeks, my chest, my thighs. Petty's cold hands massaged it in. "What do you think? Is it working?"

Guy's warm fingertip rubbed my shin. My arm. My cheek. My shin again.

Say something.

"I guess it's working," he said. "Some."

Petty's cold hands massaged the length of my body, his bony finger scraping my skin to spread the goo. "We need more."

"What is it?" Guy said. "I'll run over to Rite Aid."

"The cream's just a carrier. I made it special with aerialist—"

"*Gah*—no," Guy said, shoving my massage table. My skin was so dry, I slid around on the pleather as it tipped and tottered back into place.

"I told you," Guy said, "I don't want to know about that shit."

"You see this?" Petty tapped something made of glass. It rang small and hollow. The vial we'd stored the aerialist's ingredient in was empty.

"I don't care." Guy's footsteps pounded toward the door. I imagined him halting, as if hitting a glass wall—and he did, crying out in pain, then breathing heavy. He didn't have his protective jar.

"This is it," Petty said. He took his hands off me, probably to flash Guy his oily palms. "This is the last of that stuff."

"*Not. My. Problem.*"

"Well, it will be your problem when it takes me longer to get her ready because I have to use foundation." Petty rubbed my arm like he was buffing a car. Poor Petty. So bad at handling stress. But he'd helped me harvest the aerialist. He could help me harvest someone else. We could think of it as more practice for the eventual harvest of Daphne. We'd get her engaged, and we'd fix me. The boys and I, we'd be okay. We were always okay.

"Oh no." Petty grabbed my left hand and sniffed my fingers. "*Ewf.* Guy, look." He pulled my arm and wagged my hand. "Look, Guy, look. LOOK. That's not good, is it?"

I couldn't see what Petty saw. No posters hung in the prep room. But he had Schadenfreude's attention, all of it aimed at my left hand.

My influence hid, tight and coiled, in my stomach.

Guy's body heat moved to my left hip. "*Ewgh*," he said, taking my hand from Petty. "Must've happened when she fell."

"More like when she was *trampled*. You should've been helping her instead of doting on Daphne."

But no one had trampled me. Whatever was wrong with me, it wasn't because anyone had trampled me. People had touched me, taken my clothes, but nobody had harmed me. Someone could've hurt me, but Petty had taken care of me.

I prayed that Petty could take care of this too.

"This isn't from being stepped on," Guy said. "This is more... I don't know. It looks infected."

"Already?"

"It looks past infected."

"Does it hurt her?"

Not physically. I hadn't felt pain since the night Nechai had caused my accident.

"I don't think so," Guy said.

"Shhh," Petty said. "Do you hear that?"

The room stilled. All was silent except for a soft crackling noise, like tiny pops of bubblewrap.

And a single fly's interested buzz.

Schadenfreude cackled like something she'd long desired but couldn't control had finally come to pass.

"Will it heal?" Petty whimpered. "This is the hand she holds up in her act."

"I don't know," Guy said.

But I did. My body was screaming its truth as loud as it could. The breathless feeling, my lackluster skin, the blemish the boys had found on my hand. They all had the same cause.

The amulet. Its power had given me allure, beauty, success. But the amulet was gone now, and so were its effects, all of it transferred to Daphne.

But this was okay. This, in fact, was the plan. I hadn't expected it to feel like this, but that didn't mean something was wrong. Whatever my body's condition, my will was strong enough to revive it once I had Daphne's ingredient, and I would take it as soon as she got engaged, which was far more likely to happen now that she had my amulet. The amulet would make her irresistible to Andy. To everyone really, but Andy was the one who mattered. The amulet would draw his proposal.

Until then, Daphne worked at the theater during every performance, so the amulet's effects should still draw me an audience and empower my show.

And Petty was a makeup master. He could fix my skin.

But my self-reassurance only made the tense coil in my stomach tremble. Who was I kidding? Petty's worry, Schadenfreude's laugh, Guy's hesitance. They all confirmed I'd made a mistake.

I'd meant to give Daphne the source of my success, but I must've given her something more.

Something vital.

And my hand wouldn't heal until I got it back.

It might not heal anyway.

Schadenfreude cackled, loving where that would lead. She showed me images of my truly dead and decaying body.

But I couldn't worry about that. I couldn't worry that I was already too late to fix myself. Hope is for the weak, and I wasn't about to make an exception for the rotting.

I told Guy to take me upstairs. As soon as I saw my posters, I'd send my influence back to Daphne's room and retake my amulet.

Schadenfreude snickered, making me wonder if I'd overlooked something. She tickled one of my threads.

And my other threads shuddered.

The thread she'd singled out was no influence thread. It wasn't silver. It wasn't even iridescent.

It was gold.

And it was severed.

Schadenfreude tugged, and the golden stump frayed, becoming dust, a pile of death in my hand. My left hand.

I told Guy, again, to take me upstairs to my posters, but he ignored me. My influence could halt him but it couldn't make him move.

I felt for the length of iridescent cord in my chest, the one still too new to be silver that connected me to Daphne. I expected to follow it inch by inch, but giving her my amulet had changed our bond.

One touch of the cord and our connection pulled me in. I saw with Daphne's eyes, watching the corner of her room. I heard with Daphne's ears, listening for a ghost.

And just like with my posters, I pushed my influence through her eyes. And now I saw things Daphne couldn't.

The rest of the golden cord lay frayed and dying on Daphne's bed, its other end encircling a finger on Daphne's left hand.

"Hold up," Guy said, back in my prep room, and he grabbed my left hand. "Where's Fausten's ring?"

Petty rescued my hand and placed it on the massage table.

"Tell me you have it," Guy said to Petty. "Please tell me you hid it somewhere."

"I don't have it," Petty said as haughtily as he could. He knew where my ring was. And he still trusted that I had everything under control. "Maybe someone snatched it when she fell. I told you: you should've been helping her, not Daphne."

"No way," Guy said. "She would've noticed if it was missing. She would've told me." He grabbed my head and squeezed as he leaned into me, his face inches from mine. "What are you up to, Fausten?"

"Let her go!" Petty tried to wedge his fingers under Guy's, but Guy held me tight. He crushed my temples, his eyes searching mine. He'd hated me lately, but all I felt now was his fear. He channeled it into shaking me.

And I let him.

I hadn't been the only one to change after my accident. My ring had changed too. The ugly yellowish brown had become a beautiful, shimmering opal.

An opal of gold.

"Fausten! What did you do?!"

I didn't know.

What was that golden opalness?

What had I done by giving it away?

CHAPTER 30

DAPHNE - 28 days left

Just a dream, then?

I blew out a big breath. Just a fantastic, terrible dream. Just a nightmare. But I'd been awake for part of it. I knew I'd been awake, because I never went back to sleep. My wide eyes still watched the corner of the room where the smoky apparition had disappeared.

I patted the left side of the bed, looking for Andy but only finding cold and wrinkled sheets—and a light flashed on the wall. I flinched, but the rainbow light remained. It danced on the wall, in sync with the movement of my left hand.

I rubbed my thumb against the crease between my palm and ring finger—and discovered cold, carved metal.

A rush of realization warmed my arms, my legs, and I closed my eyes as my heart swelled with the fulfillment I had hoped for only every second of the past two years.

But where was Andy?

The fan in the kitchen hummed over the sizzle of something dropped onto a hot pan. Andy was cooking breakfast. As if this ring weren't enough. I flipped back the covers and scrambled out of bed, ran to the kitchen, and wrapped my arms around him.

"Hot grease here," he said, but then he set down the spatula and hugged me back. I pressed my face to his chest and squeezed him as tight as I could.

"What's this for?" he asked.

"Thank you," I said, my lips brushing his warm skin.

"You're welcome." He let go of me and returned to the bacon. "It's not like I'd leave you at the theater."

I swatted him playfully—"No, not for that"—then kneaded his lower back with my knuckles, working my way up his spine. He hunched his back, helping me hit the good spots. When I reached his neck, I jutted my left hand over his shoulder, in front of his face. "For this!"

It was so beautiful. I loved how it sparkled despite the smooth cabochon cut. Like it was alive inside.

The setting was simple and elegant, a golden, pearlescent stone bezel-wrapped on a band of filigree-cut metal in a whitish shade of silver. Did that make it platinum?

Squee at the thought!

Andy said, "What? That bruise on your hand? I didn't do that."

"No—this, this!" I wiggled my fingers.

He grabbed my hand to keep it from shaking. "What? I don't see anything."

"Shut up, you do too." I pulled my hand back and admired my ring. Giggled a little. Did a little jig. Squeeehehe!

Andy hip-checked me. "What's funny?"

I grabbed the dish towel off the counter and held it up to my face, like a veil, like I was shy about it. I was, a little. I couldn't believe it had finally happened. But that didn't stop me from throwing my arms into the air, victory style, and proclaiming for everyone who could hear me that "I'm getting married!"

"What?" Andy pressed the bacon, making it smoke. "Who you marrying?"

"Shut up." I held up my left hand and pointed to the ring on my engagement finger. "Hehe."

Andy didn't look at the ring. He looked at my face, his copper eyes puzzled, his head cocked to one side. "Are you doing something different? You look...even prettier than usual."

What could I say? Engagement suited me. I wiggled my fingers.

Andy grabbed my hand and inspected the stone. His forehead creased. A look less approving than confused.

"Nice ring." He dropped my hand and turned back to the stove. "Your fiancé has interesting taste."

I swatted his shoulder. "So, whaddaya think? This summer? Next summer? How about this summer?"

"For what?"

"Come on now." I ripped a stretch of paper towel off the roll and slapped it onto a plate.

Andy glanced at my ring. "It's not from me."

I gaped at him.

He grinned, undercutting his words. He transferred the cooked bacon to the plate and patted the oil with a fresh paper towel. "Want one?"

Forget the beige apartment-kitchen setting, the dull roar of the range fan, the acrid smell of crispy bacon. Forget that I was wearing threadbare pajamas, that Andy had grease at the corner of his mouth, that we both had bedhead. Where was Andy's enthusiasm? The sparkle in his eye? The obvious, smitten love? Where was our giddy celebration?

"What about last night?" I asked.

Andy took a bite of bacon and nodded. But he was looking at the bacon. It was a nod of satisfaction, not concession. I could've strangled him. I settled for widening my eyes. *Answer me now.*

Andy took his bacon to the couch. I followed him as far as the kitchen table. Out came his marketing book, on went the TV. Wile E. Coyote chased the Road Runner—over a cliff.

I squeezed the back of a kitchen chair. My other hand made its point on my hip. I might have stamped my foot a little. "Well?"

"Last night?" In went another piece of bacon. "You got hit in the head with a rope stand and I brought you home."

I held up my left hand, knuckles out. "And this?"

He glanced at me, then back to the TV. *Meep, meep.* He turned a page in his book.

I tapped the gem of my ring against the table. *Clink, clink.* I mean, it wasn't like I was making this up. The ring was on my finger, solid and real. *Clink, clink.* I loved the sound it made. *Clink, clink.*

"Could you stop doing that." Andy picked up the remote and changed the channel to something noisier, a commercial for a vacation resort, a montage of happy couples—newlyweds—frolicking on the beach, dining in their finery, luxuriating in their suites to a tune meant to remind us just how good, great, beautiful... He flipped the channel again, and again. He flipped it with such force I thought the remote might crack from the pressure.

"Well?" I said.

His lips moved, but I couldn't hear him.

"What did you say?" I also couldn't keep the anger from my voice. Hopefully it was masked by the TV.

Andy muted the volume—"It's not from me"—then turned it back up.

"So..." The words—his words—he kept saying them, but my brain refused to let them make sense. "So...what? You changed your mind?"

Andy rolled his neck and shoulders. "What do you want me to say?"

"How about 'yes, this summer'?"

He gave me the dirtiest look he'd ever given me. A scowl of distaste. A glare of contempt. He closed his eyes and rubbed his forehead, apparently trying to calm himself, but when he looked at me again, his expression hadn't softened a bit. It stayed just as hard as his tone as he slowly enunciated each word. "It's *not*. From. Me."

He flipped pages, pretending to read while he toggled between a romantic comedy and a murder mystery, finally deciding on one of those shows that dare its viewers not to feel superior to its guests. This one featured a man who wanted back living expenses from his ex-boyfriend because he'd faked an illness to force their relationship. Andy tried too hard to enjoy the spectacle. He guffawed too loudly. His shoulders shook too much.

"So...what, then? You want it back?"

"*IT'SNOTFROMME.*"

CHAPTER 31

DAPHNE

"Fine," I said. "My mistake." *Yeah, right. Andy gave me this ring. He did. Last night. We got home; he got me dressed; he got on one knee; he—*

He'd hugged me so tight I couldn't breathe.

My breath caught now, reliving the nightmare, the ghost, how it had frozen me in my bed. It had touched my hand...but that was just a dream, just a shadow of Andy's real proposal. Andy had given me this ring. It couldn't have happened any other way.

But two unbidden thoughts said:

(yes, it could)

But only if you're crazy.

The first thought felt like my shields, except they didn't rise with their usual sensations. Their guidance was faint and now forgotten, as if stifled by a ring of parentheses.

They'd been overpowered by the second thought.

The second thought was my earworm, only stronger now, transformed overnight from larva to pupa, from softly offered suggestions to bold-faced, taunting words. Those words forged an impression, indentations in my brain. I rubbed my head, trying to soothe it all away, but the earworm cocooned itself, pink and mint green, in the dent.

Lesion.

Huh-uh.

Insane.

No. It only feels like my brain has been dented; I do not have brain lesions making me crazy. And I could prove it. I got out my laptop and sat at the kitchen counter, putting my back to Andy. As my computer warmed up, so did I: deep breath in, slow exhale out.

Okay, so: I had a new ring on my finger. *How did it get there?*

I typed the question into a word processing program and worked it backwards: Before noticing the ring on my finger, I'd experienced a ghost standing over my immobile body. Scary as hell, and, if I was being honest, reminiscent of that shock-induced hallucination I'd had after Andy had said he'd marry a girl like Fausten. The postergeist. That was probably the inspiration for last night's dream. And last night had to be just a dream, because there's no such thing as ghosts. Hallucinations, maybe. No ghosts. And hallucinations, if induced, didn't make me crazy. I could live with that.

I typed *hallucinations* into my list.

And I typed *ghosts*, what the hell.

So, before all of *that*, I'd been at the theater, where I'd apparently fainted from getting hit on the head. Could last night have been a bonk-induced hallucination? Maybe so, maybe so. A little delayed, but maybe so. The rope stand had conked me pretty good when I'd fallen. And why had I fallen? I'd fallen after Fausten—

(made you fall)

"What are you doing?"

Andy's question startled me, and I lost the thought. I reached for it, but it was gone, everything about it except a feeling that it had been a flash of insight, a gift from my shields.

See? Mind working just fine.

"Nothing," I said, holding back the what-do-you-care? words if not the tone. And to think I'd gotten him a naked hour with Fausten—*right*, Fausten: she'd fallen. But she hadn't braced herself. She hadn't even tried. I'd once seen a girl fall on her face because she'd tripped with her hands in her pockets and couldn't get them out in time—but she'd tried. It's Survival 101. People brace themselves for a fall.

Or was Fausten's strange fall another part of my dream?

(in a way)

Couldn't be.

No, it couldn't be. I'd gotten hit in the head *after* Fausten had fallen.

(like a mannequin)

Like a pro.

And she'd stayed that way, down and still posed. Almost like she was *paralyzed* or *comatose*.

(or dead)

I typed the additions to my list.

Dishes clanged.

"You're jumpy," Andy said, putting his plate in the sink. "You gotta be doing something."

"Just schoolwork." I shook my head, mourning my fleeting thoughts. I read my list, trying to catch the cognitive train. *Hallucinations, Ghosts, Paralyzed, Com... Com*atose. (I finished typing the word.) Yeah, comatose. That's kind of how I'd felt when I'd woken frozen. I added *waking frozen* to the list.

Across the counter, Andy watched me through the space beneath the cabinets. Our eyes met. He smiled, but it was weird. I frowned at him, and his weird smile grew bigger. Like Fausten Cotter's fans after a show. I had no idea how to respond nicely to that smile, so I returned to my work.

I typed variations of the words on my list into a search engine. According to the internet, migraines could cause hallucinations. I had headaches sometimes. Like now. The earworm was pulsing, but just enough for me to notice. I wouldn't call it a migraine.

I kept searching. After a few more misses, I found a couple hits. The first was locked-in syndrome, a chronic condition where you can't talk or move any part of your body, except for maybe your eyes. It could last for years, even for life. I was fine now, so locked-in syndrome didn't apply to me, but having spent what was probably only a few horrifying seconds in such a state, I could appreciate not being stuck like that for—

(a year and a half?)

"Done yet?"

"Why, Andy? We going somewhere?" I wished he would go somewhere. I couldn't think or remember anything with him staring at me.

He leaned over the counter and rested his chin on my screen. His eyes flicked to my left hand—my ring—then back to my face. "Hi."

I stared at him. He had just denied proposing like he never intended to, ever, and now he wouldn't leave me alone.

I clicked the next hit: sleep paralysis. The page called sleep paralysis a *phenomenon*—not a *condition* or an *affliction* or some other term suggesting scientific acceptance, but a *phenomenon*. The page said this *phenomenon* is when a person can't move or speak or react during their transition between asleep and awake.

Huh. Phenomenon or not—

Sounds right.

(but you were awake alread—)

Sounds. Right.

—it sounded like what I'd experienced. The page said sleep paralysis was temporary but could last for several minutes to an hour. (Yikes.) It could also include hallucinations.

Well, how about that?

A search for *sleep paralysis* returned twenty million hits, and I had myself a good laugh. I wasn't the only person who'd suffered from it, scary hallucinated demon included. One page said sleep paralysis is linked to the mythology of incubi and succubi. There's even some famous art depicting their attacks. I found that comforting. I sat back and relaxed in the relief that I was no less sane than twenty million crazy people.

Something encircled my waist. I jumped, not realizing Andy had come around the counter. I was still mad, but I couldn't help leaning into him and closing my eyes.

He hugged me tighter. "You talking to your fiancé?"

"What?" He sounded dejected, like he was jealous. Was he jealous?

I wriggled enough to turn around and see his face. His expression was still weird...like he was jealous, now that I'd pinpointed it, like he felt threatened.

He peered at my computer screen. "Incubi, huh?" He snuggled my neck. "I'll be your incubus." He *was* jealous. The confident Andy McBride was jealous. Over me. "Why are you looking up incubi?"

"No reason. Just a dream I had."

He backed away from me, frowning at the ring. "When?"

"Why's it matter?"

We stared at each other. I expected him to drop the subject, but he braced a hand against the bedroom door frame. "You know how Mom"—he rolled his neck and shoulders—"how she sent you home for Christmas?"

"Yeah."

"I only went along with that because Dad thought she was about to have an episode."

"'An episode'?" I had no idea what he was talking about. "And did she?"

He nodded. "Ran around the house blocking all the doors and windows, swearing Santa was coming to kill her."

"Whaaat? That's—"

"Crazy? Yeah. That's exactly what it is. Good times, let me tell you. Be glad you left."

I reached for his hand. He let me take it, and I pulled myself in for a hug.

"Really, I'm surprised she let you guys visit at all," he said. "In high school, she wouldn't let our friends come over. And she was still mostly normal then. Unstable and controlling, but normal. The erratic stuff came later. The paranoia mixed with delusions of grandeur."

"Why are you telling me this?"

He watched me with wary eyes, then looked at the laptop screen. I'd left it on an old painting of the incubus myth, a red demon floating above a sleeping girl.

"It was just a dream?"

I didn't even need to close my eyes to relive how the darkness had rippled. How its cold had zinged my knuckle. How it had floated off the bed and faded down the wall. I'd been just as awake then—watching it, feeling it, fearing it—as I was now.

But of course it was just a dream. Andy would never commit to someone who reminded him of his mom. And as for the ring, maybe I'd found it on the sidewalk beneath the ticket booth while Andy was fetching his Jeep.

"Don't worry, Andy. I'm not crazy."

His shoulders relaxed and he hugged me tighter.

We were still hugging when his phone rang. He answered, and a flirty female voice spoke on the other end. "Yeah, okay," he told the caller as he pulled out of our hug. "Yeah, I'll be right there."

He mumbled something to me, got dressed, and left the apartment. I was still standing there, staring at the closed front door, when I finally realized the gist of what he'd said.

He had to study.

For midterms.

I'd completely forgotten.

CHAPTER 32

DAPHNE - 24 days left

I came out of my last midterm in a mental fog, just clear enough to notice my fellow students giving me double-take glances as we passed each other in the halls.

Yes, people, I am the long-running poster child for screwed.

My first midterm had been biology, multiple choice. It should've been easy, but instead of selecting his own questions from the material he'd actually assigned, Professor Gordon had used a random question generator. Halfway through the test I'd closed my eyes...

And something else had offered to take over.

> ***There, there, Daphne. Check out for an hour. Let autopilot handle this one.***

I'd accepted.

I'd accepted on chemistry and physics, too. I doubted autopilot would improve my grades enough to reactivate my scholarship; I just hoped it didn't retro-activate it into a loan.

Conlin had offered me time off to study, but I couldn't afford to take it unpaid, so I'd popped popcorn for a birthday party on Sunday, strolled the aisles of the near-empty theater on black-and-white Monday, and cleaned the lobby on Tuesday and the house on Wednesday. Only after I'd vacuumed the aisles had he told me not to come in today, Thursday, because he hadn't booked any events all week. So frustrating. Not that I would've studied if I'd had the time off. The peace I'd found in being one of millions who suffered from sleep-paralysis hallucinations wasn't lasting. I'd witnessed other strange things at least four other times. All at the theater. And all in the presence of Guy.

"You mean the mist?" he'd said when I'd asked him about it. We'd been preparing for the birthday party. He was blowing up balloons, and my hands were covered in papier-mâché. I shrugged, even though the mist was exactly what I'd meant. It seemed to have capabilities far beyond that of a mere fog machine. "Why? You scared?" he said. "Done blaming a faulty HVAC?" He blew up another balloon. "I've tried to tell you we're haunted."

His surlier-than-usual answer had soothed me more than he'd meant it to, but not enough. The faulty heating system probably had produced some of the unsettling effects I'd seen, but I feared my faulty mind had created the rest.

They say only sane people question their sanity, but questioning my sanity wasn't making me feel sane. So I'd been trying not to think about any of it—the hallucinations, the ring, my grades, Andy leaving—and all that left me to think about was Fausten.

Tip—crunch.

Her performance with Andy still bothered me, but at least her issues had nothing to do with mine.

"She's fine," Petty had said when I'd asked about her. We'd been shoving old junk away from the left side of the storeroom's door to make room for the rack he wanted installed to hold Fausten's Aphrodite platform. "Just needs rest."

Tip—crunch.

"What about her arm?" I asked, rubbing my own elbow. "Did she break it?"

"Bruised it some. Just needs rest."

"Why didn't she brace herself?"

The once-pocked skin around Petty's now-smooth nose hiked up on one side. He'd given every dusty item he'd had to touch the same contemptuous look, but this time he gave it to me.

"When she fell," I said. "She just tipped"—*crunch*—"like a mannequin."

"No, like a *statue*. As was her character. She stayed in character. Like a professional."

That answer might've made perfectly good sense to an actor, but to a biology major it was just stupid.

So I was trying not to think about anything. Which just made it easier for my crazy to come to the fore.

More and more of my thoughts were feeling foreign to me. Some had an urgency that gave me anxiety even though I couldn't remember their message. Others had a disturbing boldness in their clarity.

And so it was, inside my head, when, after my last midterm, I found myself trudging across campus in pursuit of—

(secrets)

Trouble.

—a risky yet irresistible urge to ask a certain instructor about...

(secrets)

Trouble.

I wasn't sure. But I felt like it was in my best interest to go.

I tiptoed down the dark and empty corridor to Sullivan's office.

Part of me hoped she wouldn't be here. The last time I'd seen her, she'd cut me, rudely, from her Biology of Paranormal Phenomena seminar. But a light shone through the crack beneath her door. I rubbed my mittened hands together. Then I knocked.

"Come in."

I tried the knob, but it was locked. After a rustling inside, the door opened.

"Daphne?" Sullivan let the unspoken *What are you doing here?* hang in the silence, allowing me to interpret her expression as *confusion* about my being here rather than *irritation* at my presence.

"Sorry," I said. "I'm sure you're busy, but I was hoping you could, um, could you help me? With something?"

Now she looked confused. "Help you?"

I bit the corner of my mouth and nodded, hoping Sullivan could explain my hallucinations in a way that would let me consider myself sane.

Sullivan's expression softened. She pulled the door open and backed into the room, scooting around a large suitcase.

"Taking a trip?" I asked.

She sat in the chair behind her desk. "Flight's in"—she looked at her phone—"five hours. And I have to finish grading midterms before then. Can we make this quick?"

I closed the door and perched on the edge of the chair across from her. My fingers gripped my knees. The sun shined off and on through the window behind her desk.

"So…?" she said.

"So, I was wondering…um." I took a deep breath and, looking everywhere but at her, I rambled: "Do you know of any biological paranormal phenomena where…um…" I noticed a glossy sheet of paper under a pile of exams on her desk. The lettering was pink and mint green.

Sullivan unearthed the Pin-up Bride and slid her toward me. "It's a show in town. You were saying?"

Even out of place, among drab wood furniture and biology books, Fausten's two-dimensional presence demanded attention, and it distracted me from—or maybe focused me toward—why I'd really come here. "Are there any phenomena where a person doesn't…move?"

"Sure. Coma."

"Yeah, but not hospitalized."

Sullivan leaned back in her chair and looked off to the side. "Well, there's locked-in syndrome. That's where—"

"You can't move or communicate, yeah, but they're all—"

Sullivan gave me a pointed look. "I'm busy, Daphne, and it sounds like you don't need my help."

She stood, and I rose too, reaching for her hand to keep her from showing me out. "No, I do. I'm just...I'm trying to understand. Please. I'm sorry."

She hesitated. Then sat and gestured for me to continue.

I said, "Don't people with locked-in syndrome—don't their hands and feet usually curl in on themselves?"

She nodded. "Almost always."

"Is there anything like that where you don't curl? Where the body is completely fine?"

"The body needs to move to be completely fine," she said. "If it doesn't move, it'll get bed sores, at the very least. Except..." She frowned, her thumb tapping her keyboard.

"Except what?" I asked.

Sullivan tilted her head, squinting at me like she was judging whether the exception was worth mentioning. Whether I was open-minded enough to hear it. "There's the incorruptibles."

Goosebumps rippled over my shoulders and settled in the small of my back. I shifted, trying to get away from them. "The what?"

Sullivan typed on her keyboard. "Incorrupt corpses. It's when the body doesn't decompose."

"Decompose?" Talk about off topic. "Wouldn't that make you dead?"

"*Doesn't* decompose. And yes. It's a condition usually attributed to Catholic sainthood, though other religions have their cases too. After a period of years, they exhume the body to see if it's still as fresh as the day it died."

She swiveled her monitor, showing me a picture of a young woman's face, eyes closed, hands in prayer beneath her chin. Her skin was dewy and luminescent. Beautiful.

"This is actually a mask," Sullivan said. "Most of the incorruptibles are so old and emaciated when they die, their skin is like wrinkled leather. So they cover it."

"What about her hands?"

"Mask."

"Do you..." I hesitated, the words jumbled in my mouth, in my brain, as if the earworm was thwarting connections my mind was trying to make. "Do you know of any cases that don't need a mask?"

"Don't *need* a mask? There are incorruptibles that don't *have* a mask, but if you're asking if they look this good"—she tapped the image of the beautiful incorruptible—"no. It's not like Sleeping Beauty."

(yes, it is)

Just a fairy tale.

I leaned an elbow on the desk and bit my thumbnail. Mask or no mask, Fausten was just as dewy and luminous as this lady. And, from what I'd seen of her act, Fausten just sat there or lay there like this lady too, like—

A skilled professional.

—like Sleeping Beauty, now that Sullivan had mentioned it.

But Fausten wasn't always still.

(no?)

"Can incorruptibles move?"

Fausten moved. It was jerky and stylized in her act, but she moved.

"Move?" Sullivan laughed. "Not on their own. They do tend to stay supple enough to be moved, you know, by others. Supple, warm to the touch, sometimes presenting a nimbus, secretions, the odor of sanctity."

I shook my head. "Sorry, odor of what?"

"Sanctity. Instead of smelling dead, the body smells fresh—sweet, like flowers or fruit."

(or peaches)

I shivered. The theater smelled of—

Popcorn.

—peaches. But it more often smelled like popcorn and stale beer.

"And the...secretions?"

"Tears, blood. Viscous mucus sometimes, like egg whites. But usually just clear oils that seep from the pores."

I wiped my hand on my pants, remembering how my fingers had slipped along Fausten's skin when I'd been called onstage to check her pulse.

(no pulse)

LOTION.

She'd probably slathered herself in lotion. That was probably the key to the trick.

Sullivan said, "Secretions can seep from other orifices too: ears, nose, eyes. They say the secretions bring good fortune. In the old days, people in power would collect it—"

(in vials)

"—and use it like perfume."

The vials of pheromones Petty sold in the lobby were used by Fausten's fans like perfume. They smelled nice, like—

JUNK.

But those vials were just a junky souvenir, one Petty had admitted Fausten never used.

"And what's a nimbus?" The only nimbus I knew of was Harry Potter's broom.

"A halo," Sullivan said. "Or sometimes a full-body glow."

"So an incorrupt corpse is a warm, rot-resistant dead body that glistens, glows, and smells nice?" Talk about way off topic.

"That's just the basics," Sullivan said. "Some cases produce phenomena. One corpse in New Mexico shook the earth and came up through the ground of its old church."

"The *corpse* shook the earth?"

"Twice," she said. "Once twenty years after death—that's how they discovered it—and again, forty years later, after they reburied it. And neither incident occurred during an earthquake."

I nodded like doing so might rattle my brain's marbles back into the slots where they'd be useful, but my mind still tried to liken ground shaking in New Mexico to mist striking or electricity surging in L'Aornum Theatre.

RUMORS.

But even if the New Mexico corpse story were true, I couldn't attribute the theater's phenomena to a similar cause. There weren't even rumors of dead bodies buried at L'Aornum.

Sullivan typed on her keyboard. "In some cases less than the full body is incorrupt. You might find just a perfect finger or a perfect nose. Or a ringsel."

She brought up an image, a bowl of light-colored beads.

"These are ringsels," she said. "They're gems, more or less, like pearls or crystals. They're sometimes found in the remains of monks, although I've heard of secretions congealing into ringsels."

I glanced at my ring and saw its opalescent shimmer with shocking vividness, as if a second pair of eyes were studying the gem with me.

The ring's golden cabochon looked a lot like these ringsels.

I buried the ring beneath my thigh. "So ascetics have pretty gallstones, so what?"

She ignored my tone. "According to legend, ringsels contain a person's crystalized essence."

I suppressed a snort. "O*kay*."

Sullivan sighed. "This might be too esoteric for you."

"No, I'm listening." And I was. Closely. Despite my disbelief, I felt hyperfocused. As if a second pair of ears were listening with me.

"Ringsels are crystalized life force itself," Sullivan said, gauging my reaction, "at least according to contemporary collectors: ringsels are the golden bowl of the Bible."

"Um. I'm not familiar..."

"The silver cord and the golden bowl. Two aspects of the same thing, really: an ethereal umbilical cord."

"Okay." She was right. This was woo-woo.

"The silver cord is best known," she said. "It's the cord people see in near-death experiences, the one that connects the soul to the body.

Although"—her brows rose with interest—"there are reports that strong emotion can make the silver cord sprout additional strands, strands that forge connections with the person, place, or thing that elicited the emotion."

"Creepy," I said, rubbing the back of my head. "Or should I say *spooky*?"

Sullivan smiled at my Einstein reference. "You're saying additional strands sounds like quantum entanglement? Only dubious?" She shrugged. "It's a fringe theory. Anyway, the golden half of the cord is how...God? The Universe? Source?"

"Whatever."

"It's how Whatever empowers the soul."

I suppressed another snort. "So this cord is basically the life thread, like the three Fates in Greek mythology: they spin, measure, and cut the thread of life?"

Sullivan tilted her head. "Not exactly. The golden cord flows eternal life from Source to soul. The silver cord flows consciousness from soul to body. And when the silver cord severs, you die—at least in theory—because your soul can no longer return to the body."

"So an incorrupt corpse is—what?—a trapped soul?"

(yes)

I sat upright, squirming in my seat, my own question having taken me aback. Part of me felt spot-on in my understanding of what Sullivan was saying, but another part—the part that seemed to sense with its own eyes and ears—felt numbed, like it had just received an untreatable diagnosis.

Sullivan frowned at my conclusion about incorrupt corpses being trapped souls. But I knew I was right.

"That's what you're saying, isn't it? You start to rot once your consciousness leaves. But an incorruptible's body isn't rotting—meaning it's still got some life, some trapped life. So an incorrupt corpse is a trapped soul."

(yes)

Her brows pinched. "I wouldn't put it that way. I wouldn't call a trapped soul a miracle."

This time I couldn't help the snort. "Skin so gross after death it requires a mask is a miracle?"

Sullivan gave me another pointed look. "I'd call the phenomenon *preserved life force*. With incorruptibles the cord doesn't snap and pull away; it dissolves. At least that's the theory. It dissolves and releases the soul—"

(not always)

"—but it leaves behind a residue."

"A life force residue?"

"The golden bowl," Sullivan confirmed, her eyes excited. She loved this stuff. "With incorrupt corpses, the so-called bowl remains intact, preserving some residual life force within the body—as a ringsel."

She tapped the image of the beads.

I shivered. "So ringsels are powerful."

"Very."

"Like a harnessed piece of God or whatever."

Sullivan nodded. "These relics—the corpses, fingers, ringsels, what have you—they have rejuvenating properties. They can keep their collectors young and beautiful, prosperous even." Sullivan cocked her head and looked at me strangely. "Is this helping?"

Good question. I'd come here to shore up my sanity, to rationalize away my dream, the ghost, the mist, the haunted theater, but this conversation… I picked up the flyer for Fausten's show. I still hadn't seen her act in full, nor had I ever talked to her myself. For all I knew, Fausten Cotter could be one of these incorrupt corpses.

(yes)

But that was stupid. And not just because Sullivan's incorrupt corpse theory was stupid. Fausten performed for hundreds of people every week, and Guy, Conlin, and Petty talked to her every day. I set her flyer back on the desk, pushing it away from me.

Sullivan said, "I can maybe help you more if you give me more to work with." She grabbed a pen and paper from the corner of her desk and knocked something into a roll. I caught it before it reached the edge and set it back on the desk—then snatched it up again. It looked like one of those quarter-ounce vials of pheromones Petty sold at Fausten's show, except this vial's substance wasn't glittery, nor was its label pink and mint green.

This vial held a reddish-brown oil and its white-and-gray label had an unfamiliar brand name: NEC.

I held it up. "Where'd you get this?"

Sullivan glanced up. "That? A visiting professor."

I didn't know why, but I felt oddly livid, like those second eyes and ears were fuming. I pointed at the vial's label, where it identified the contents.

(don't—)

Ask.

"A visiting professor gave you *romantic oil*?"

"They were gifts for the seminar students," Sullivan said. "We had a guest lecture on Thai healing practices from Dr. Chaipra—"

"*Ah!*" I yelped, cutting her off as something shoved me in the back. I pitched forward, dropping the vial and catching myself on the desk. I looked behind me. Nothing there but the closed door. I looked a question at Sullivan, unsure of what had happened or why part of me was feeling far more angry about it than scared or surprised.

Sullivan folded her hands and gave me an odd smile. "I suppose you could also call it Thai *magical* practices," she said.

Spooky indeed. I scanned Sullivan's desk for the dropped vial and found it on top of Fausten's flyer.

Curls of smoke were rising from the paper.

I scrambled out of my chair and backed against the door.

Sullivan looked at me like I was loony, like it was completely commonplace for things on her desk to smolder.

Or like she couldn't see the smoke.

But then her expression changed, and she sniffed the air. "Do you smell that?" she asked. She sniffed around her desktop and closed in on the vial. She picked it up and sniffed the lid. "Mmm," she said, "reminds me of home. I love the smell of peaches."

I smelled peaches all right, ripe peaches at that—but the vial wasn't the source. The vial wasn't smoking. It was the flyer. The glossy image of Fausten Cotter was oozing tendrils of gaseous plasma. They spread across the desk like long, bony fingers reaching for the vial.

(or preparing to source a new one)

I flattened against the door, heart pounding, mittened fingers fumbling for the knob.

Like a dancing cobra, the thick, hunting vapor rose into the air.

Swaying—deciding—

And Sullivan just sat there.

I cowered. "You don't see that?!"

"See wha-*chk*—" The smoke struck her in the face. Sullivan jerked away from it, rolling her chair into the credenza, but the smoke circled her, thick and silver, tight and trapping. She waved at it with panicked hands, tried to speak, but could only heave and gag.

I pushed away from the safety of the door and grabbed for her flailing arms, but the smoke surged toward me, forcing me away.

Sullivan slid out of her chair and hunched low to the ground. It was quick thinking. Smoke rises after all.

But not this smoke. It dropped with her, streaming into her ears and up her nose. My own lungs burned as it crept into hers, taking hold.

Taking over.

A ray of sun broke through the clouds and came through the window, brightening the room—and giving me an idea. I held my breath and hugged the wall as I skirted the smoke to get to the window. I yanked the handle.

Painted shut.

Sullivan grabbed the back of my pants, but I jumped out of the way, and she couldn't hold on. Her hands returned to her face, clawed at the smoke searing her bulging eyes. She reached for me again and knocked over her suitcase. Her face blistered. Her lips turned blue. Veins popped in her sclera, darkening her eyes to blood red.

My stomach lurched. I clapped a hand over my mouth and backed away, hitting the desk, knocking exams, pens, and her phone to the floor.

Her phone. I pressed its lone button. The screen asked me to enter a passcode. I didn't know it, but I didn't need it to make this call. I touched *Emergency*.

The phone didn't respond.

Something crashed. Sullivan had knocked over a pile of books. She tried to climb up onto her chair, out of the smoke, but it swirled unrelenting around her head.

I yanked off a mitten and hit *Emergency* with my knuckle. Success. I knuckle-hit 9-1-1.

"I'm sorry," I said as I opened the door. Sullivan's arms dangled lifelessly at her sides. "I'm so sorry."

Something pushed me into the hall and slammed the door behind me. I didn't argue. I ran toward the green exit sign. I took the stairs so fast I should've tripped, but I pushed myself to go faster. My footsteps clanged in the stairwell, jackhammers mirroring the pounding in my head, but I didn't dare draw breath, not until I burst through the door, into daylight, and felt the cold winter air smacking me in the face.

CHAPTER 33

DAPHNE

I sprinted aboard the MAX and hunkered down in the nearest plastic seat. The doors took forever to close. Once they did, I exhaled and hung my head between my legs. This was crazy, and worse than *hallucination* crazy. This was *superstitious* crazy. *Crazy* crazy. Something beyond the realms of normal had—

No. I got up and tried to get away from the thought I'd been about to think. I didn't want to nurture the crazy. I feigned looking for the perfect seat. Anything to move, to not sit there with the image of Sullivan—

No. I dropped into another seat. I wanted to be home, in the safety of Andy's apartment, but I didn't want to be alone, not even for a second. With shaky hands, I dug through my bag for my phone and called Andy. It rang and rang. I considered calling Brenda, but with me working, studying, and Andying, and her seeing some new guy, we hadn't talked in a few weeks, and I didn't want to renew our friendship with a favor—or have to explain why I couldn't just walk.

Andy finally answered.

"Thank gawd!" My voice came out loud and delirious. "Can you pick me up?"

"I'm out at the Engine 8." An old fire station that was now an entertainment venue about twenty minutes away. "I'd come get you, but I drove us all out here to celebrate."

"Done with midterms!" declared a flirty voice in the background. Andy chuckled.

"Who's that?" I asked.

"Ericka?"

He said it like a question. Did that make him enamored, annoyed, or indifferent? Something told me it wasn't the last two.

"Who else is there?" I said, but instead of an answer I heard a beep. "Hello?"

I looked at my phone. It still had power but was out of minutes. I groaned and jerked my arms and legs, dancing the jig of the jilted.

I looked around the MAX car for someone who might loan me their phone. Most people were staring out the window, but two guys at the back of the car grinned at me, then whispered to themselves like they'd just spotted a famous person doing everyday things like a regular person.

I made eye contact. They sat up straighter and waved. I waved back. The sun caught my ring and made prismatic rainbows on the ceiling. One of the guys beamed. He stood and pointed at me, then pointed at his mint-green T-shirt, at its pink screen-printed silhouette of the Pin-up Bride.

It was smoldering.

Forget the phone. I got up and found a plastic seat at the far end of the other car. I even went all two-year-old and turned my back to Fausten's crazy fans. 'Cause if I couldn't see them, then maybe they and their smoking shirts wouldn't see me. By then, the MAX had rolled past Union Station and was lurching across the river. That decided my next move.

I transferred at the Rose Quarter and took the Blue Line out to my mom's. I'd be safe at my mom's. If she let me stay with her.

I knocked, but no one was home. I found a spare house key in the backyard, taped to the bird feeder, and let myself inside. They had the heater on high. I peeled off my backpack and my peacoat and stashed them beside the couch.

A wineglass sat on the coffee table. I found another in the sink and an empty champagne bottle on the counter.

"You've got to be kidding me."

It must've happened last night.

I sank into the couch and turned on the TV. I checked the local channels, but it was too early for the news.

I must've been exhausted, because a couple hours later I woke to a rattle of keys at the front door. I stretched out of the ball I'd curled myself into and straightened the pillows. Mom pushed open the door and walked past me into the kitchen, set a bag on the counter.

"Hi," I said.

She startled and clutched her chest.

"Sorry," I said.

"Daph? Everything all right?"

I nodded.

"What are you doing here?"

I lifted a shoulder.

She eyed me, then nodded and unpacked the groceries. She wasn't dumb. She knew something was up. But she was willing to give me a moment to tell her on my own before nagging me. "Are you staying?"

"Can I?"

"I'm sure it's fine for the night. Hungry?"

I got off the couch and trudged to the kitchen, scuffing my toes along the carpet.

She pulled a plastic tub out of the grocery bag. "Yogurt?"

I nodded but didn't move any closer. She waited a beat, then opened her arms, inviting me in for a hug. I was there in an instant.

"I don't think I did so well on midterms," I told her. She deserved something.

"How much is it worth?"

"Fifteen percent in physics, but forty in chemistry. I wish I'd never elected premed."

Premed had done nothing to help me save Sullivan. I hoped the medics got to her in time. I didn't recall seeing their trucks or hearing their sirens.

Mom stroked my hair. "You're not there to be top of the class, honey. You're there to become a doctor's wife."

"I still have to pass. No med student wants to pay off two sets of loans."

She pulled away from me. "You have a scholarship."

"Only if I pass."

"*Psh.*" She swished her hand, magically wizarding it all away. "You want to help?"

I put away the cold stuff. "You do know I'm paying for this term out of pocket, right?"

"I'm sure you'll be fine."

I nodded. It was easiest. "What's with the champagne?"

She clasped her hands behind her back, and a huge grin spread across her face. "You'll never guess."

Nope, never. "Already?"

She flashed her left hand. A little diamond sparkled on a little gold band.

I snorted a laugh. Mostly out of disgust with myself. "Congratulations," I said. "At least someone's getting married."

She wiggled her fingers and admired her ring. It was nowhere near as glittery as my cabochon, but she only had eyes for her own. "Andy still holding out?"

"He's got a *new friend*," I said, fingering air quotes. "Her name's Ericka." At least I assumed the flirty voice I'd been hearing through Andy's phone—from the day of the amateur contest to the reminder about studying for midterms to just now, on the MAX—had always been Ericka's.

"Well, at least you won't be blindsided. Use protection."

"Ew, Mom. Gross."

"Well..."

"I don't think it's that bad."

"Yet?"

I shrugged. "She's in his study group. She's not the only one in his study group, but it sure feels like it."

Mom looked at her ring. "I'm sure it'll all work out. Things usually do. You're pretty and fun and smart, and someone fabulous and rich will love you."

I looked around the entirety of Mom's fifth fiancé's tiny house. "Yup."

"And you could always do what I did."

"No, thanks. No offense."

"Worked out for me. You're the best part of my life."

"Uh-huh." I didn't want to talk about this. I found a spoon in the drying rack and took my yogurt to the couch. I opened my textbook and scanned the local channels again. Still no news. Mom disappeared down the hall for a bit and came back in her cozy clothes. We sat on the couch in silence—me pretending to read my physics book, Mom reading her fashion mag—until the news started.

"Everything all right?" Mom asked.

My breath had shortened to shallow gasps. I tried to deepen the inhale and slow the exhale. "Uh-huh."

I turned a page in my book but kept my eyes on the TV. The lead story was about bike theft. I didn't usually watch the news. Maybe they gave viewers time to settle in before hitting them with the day's doozy. The next story was about this being our driest winter in decades. The talking heads closed the hour without mentioning a single mysterious death.

The next day, Friday, was Valentine's Day. I'd asked Conlin for the night off a long time ago, but Andy and I had been too busy with work and midterms to make plans.

Mom had plans. She spent most of the day getting ready for dinner with her fiancé, who was still at work. I sat cross-legged on the couch with my books and watched her bustle around the house. She paused mid-prep, between the hallway and the kitchen, and looked at me funny.

"Aren't you going out with Andy tonight?"

I swirled my lacquered silly-string ring around my thumb. Andy might have denied giving me the cabochon, but he had given me this. We'd been together for two years. Plans or no plans, Valentine's Day was a given.

"I think so."

"Shouldn't you be getting ready?"

"I have time." I'd have forty-five minutes or so once Andy called. *And he'd better call.*

Mom's fiancé came home with two dozen roses. She gushed of course. She kissed him. She put them in a vase. He was in and out of the shower by the time Andy called.

"It's Valentine's Day," he said.

"I know."

"When you coming home?"

"When you pick me up."

"I'm not driving out to Gresham."

"You drove out to the Engine 8."

"I wasn't sick then."

"Please. You're not sick."

"I am, though."

"It's probably just guilt."

"Guilt?" he said. "What am I guilty of?"

Mom and her fiancé walked into the living room, pulling on their coats. Mom said, "Is that Andy?"

I nodded.

"Ask him when he's gonna propose."

"Mom says hi."

"I heard. So I thought we could just watch a movie or something."

"If you don't pick me up, you're watching it by yourself." Lamest V-Day ever. "Hello?"

My phone was dead. I'd bought more minutes last night, but the charger was at Andy's. I could've called him back with my mom's phone, but I didn't want to put in that much effort. I wanted Andy to make the effort. That, and I didn't want to return to campus alone. If I was going to be alone, I felt safer in Gresham.

An hour later, Andy showed up at the house. His face was blotchy. His hair was a mess. His clothes looked like he'd slept in them all day. He handed me a movie, slumped onto the couch, and pulled the afghan off the back. By the time I had the disc in the machine and the input setting adjusted, he'd fallen asleep.

Okay, so maybe he was sick. And yet he'd driven out here anyway, to spend even a lame Valentine's Day with me. I sent him some mental love. Then I got a better blanket from the closet, swapped out the afghan, and settled in beside him. I turned on the movie, but at ten, I paused it to watch the news. The night's top story was a burglary at an old folks' home, then politics. Nobody dead.

When Andy awoke, I drove us back to his apartment. He didn't say much. I thought he was quiet because he was sick, but it was just a twenty-four-hour bug, and we didn't talk much the whole rest of the weekend. I was supposed to work, of course, but Andy's sickness had given me an idea. Maybe not the boldest idea I'd had lately, but I liked it. I called the theater every day when no one was there and left a message for Conlin that I was ill.

Mentally, at any rate.

And it was the theater's fault. Not because the theater was haunted—it wasn't; there was nothing supernatural at work here, no matter what Guy said—but that didn't mean the theater wasn't to blame. The theater was my trigger. All this craziness had started when Andy had said he'd marry a girl like the one on the poster for the theater. And it had gotten worse when, wanting to become that kind of girl, I'd performed at the theater. And it had worsened further when I'd agreed to work, daily, at the theater.

I didn't know if staying away from the theater would make the hallucinating stop, but just the thought of never returning felt like relief. And that decided it. I would no longer work at the theater. I still wanted Andy to propose, and I still wanted to learn Fausten's secrets, but not if it meant becoming crazy.

I spent the time I would've been at work scanning Craigslist for new work and trying not to stress that I still had to pay off my advance and that every day I missed put me further in debt to Conlin.

Mom called a lot. She said she just enjoyed having me over and wanted to keep in touch better, but I think her motherly instincts knew something was wrong.

"I just need a job that pays more and has friendlier hours," I told her.

"Mmm," was all she said. She didn't like talking about work or money. I didn't think I'd hear from her after that, but early Friday morning she called again.

"What are you doing around five?" she asked.

I didn't know what Andy had in mind, but we hadn't made plans. "Nothing."

"Can you make it to Beaverton?"

"Why?"

"Chris got you an interview. They're deciding today, but he said they can squeeze you in. Can you make it?"

"Yeah. What's the job?"

Mom wasn't sure, something administrative or maybe retail. Not that it mattered. Anything was better than being near the theater and its hallucination-triggering fog and flyers.

I got my interview outfit ready while I watched the morning news.

Andy got out of the shower and padded into the bedroom. He came back half-dressed, socks and shirt in hand. "News again, huh?"

I shrugged.

"Everything okay?"

"Yeah, why?"

"I don't know. Zombied through midterms. Suddenly addicted to the news. Not going to work anymore. More interested in twisting that ring around your finger and glancing behind you for who knows what than studying." He finished putting on his socks and stood, hands on hips. "That's not the Daphne I know."

And prefer. He didn't say it, but I heard it.

I turned the TV to a late-night-Jimmy repeat, pulled down my sleeve so that Andy couldn't see the cabochon, and packed up my books for the library. "The theater's taking up too much of my time," I said, "and the stress is starting to get to me. So I was just watching the news for job prospects. But don't worry. I have an interview today and should have a new job by next week."

"So everything's okay?"

"Better if I get this job, but yeah"—I smiled—"everything's fine."

"Good. 'Cause I like my confident, capable girlfriend." He kissed my forehead and went back to his morning routine. I needed to shore up his opinion of me, but he seemed pacified for now.

I, however, was more concerned for myself than ever. The morning news had opened with a visit to a cupcake store. Here we were, a week later, and still no breaking story about the mysterious on-campus death of a Stumptown State University PhD student. Sullivan should've been found by now. A dead body would start to stink.

So maybe I'd hallucinated *everything* that had happened in Sullivan's office and not just the flyer's smoke. Maybe Sullivan was okay. *I* wasn't okay, but maybe she was. She'd said she was taking a trip. Maybe she was on a beach somewhere, oblivious to my worry.

Never thought I'd be happy to consider myself a hallucinator, but it was better than being that other kind of crazy, that superstitious, paranormal kind of crazy. Because if I was *that* kind of crazy, it meant that a supernatural ectoplasmic smoke had killed Sullivan and nobody had noticed.

Because the smoke had taken her body.

CHAPTER 34

FAUSTEN

Several flies buzzed around my body.

Guy had pushed the bed netting aside, the better to yell at me about what I had done. Every few words, he sprayed me with spit and shook my new vial of ingredient in my face. He never liked it when I had new ingredient, but he hadn't seen Daphne in over a week, so he was particularly anxious about this ingredient.

He demanded I name its source. He'd take anybody, anybody but one particular, off-limits source.

I refused to ease his mind. Call me childish, but the information he sought felt like the last thing over which I had control, and I wasn't giving it up.

My amulet should've gotten Daphne engaged by now. Instead, it had created a rift in her relationship. It had raised her suspicions, leaving me to do damage control that had ultimately scared her away.

I was rotting for nothing.

It was almost funny. I was trapped in my body for eternity, and yet I no longer had the luxury of time. I had to get Daphne engaged and her ingredient harvested before my body decayed beyond repair. Whenever that was. If I was too late, which might have already happened, I'd revive myself into a sentient and mobile, yet still rotting corpse.

I could hear Conlin now. *Ladies and gentlemen, boys and girls, BEHOLD! A real-life zombie!*

But wait! There's more!

If I was too-too late, I'd fail to revive myself at all. I'd be trapped in a rotten body the boys couldn't work with. We'd lose our livelihood, and I'd lose my stardom. Again. This time for good.

But I'd get back the luxury of time. I'd get to mourn forever the life I'd almost lived.

Guy's warmth moved away from my body. He threatened to open the vial and dump the ingredient on my bedroom floor.

But his threats were lies. Not even Guy would waste the only thing keeping our show alive.

"Tell me," he said. "Tell me whose this is, or I pour."

He made a racket of twisting the lid.

And the vial screamed.

It was a frustrated sound, the kind I used to make myself in the privacy of my car, back when I had one. But it wasn't at all the same. It had an unearthly quality. A quality I'd heard once before.

Hearing it again now, amidst Guy's ranting, reminded me of something Nechai had said a few nights before my accident, the night I'd discovered the truth about her secret ingredient.

I had just performed at Resonance, a club in Los Angeles with black decor, round tables, and a platform stage. It was standing-room-only in early August. My stardom was on the rise and it was all thanks to Nechai.

"You were wonderful," she said, cornering me in the hallway between the stage and the bathrooms. She backed me into a nostalgic pay phone nook graffitied with phone numbers and stooped to kiss the edge of my mouth, then offered more compliments in that gravelly voice of hers. I basked in her praise until it petered out on its own. I loved nothing better.

"I'm impressed," she said. "I've never seen an amulet take so well."

I admired my ring. She'd given me the amulet-ring the week before. Its face had been darker back then, like tiny trinkets encased in amber.

But I knew it wasn't amber. I knew it was something far more powerful.

"Can you use amulets for other things?" I asked.

"Sure."

"Love?" My voice cracked. It had sounded pathetic in my mind. Out loud was even worse.

Nechai laughed.

"It's not funny."

She stopped laughing but kept smirking as she assessed me. Not like she was admiring my new whites, but like she could see my darker parts. And maybe she could. Because even though I spoke of love, this part of me was darkest.

"Why would someone like you need help with love?" she said. She brushed my hair from my forehead. "Aren't you with that stagehand?"

"He's not a hand," I said. "But, yes, him. Guy." My skin warmed all over just saying his name. "But we're not together, not anymore."

"No? He seems devoted to you."

I shrugged and leaned into the hallway, scanning the crowd, the bar, the front door. He'd left without me. I'd tried to convince him that I was being good, but we both knew I wasn't. He'd put out word that he was looking for a new theater to call home, a new troupe to call family.

"You could apologize," she said.

I don't do apologies.

"If he's devoted, then an amulet should be easy," I said. "It wouldn't even need to be that strong."

Nechai said, "Love is simpler, and therefore too complicated for an amulet. Amulets can influence anything, but love isn't a thing. As far as amulets are concerned, love isn't even a concept, like the entertainment you give or the success you get in return."

She gestured at the venue and its paying fans. I still couldn't believe I'd headlined my own show. At a one-off stage, perhaps, but still. It wasn't a dive bar.

"Love's not a noun at all," she continued. She took my hand and ran her thumb over my ring. "Love is something you do, not something you take."

"But you must know something we could try. You're brilliant. If not an amulet, then something."

She narrowed her eyes. "Does that technique really work for you?"

If flattery didn't work, flirting usually did. I hooked her arm with mine and said, coquettish, "I'm just curious."

"It's too risky." She patted my hands, her fingers lingering on mine. "Too risky for *you*, the wielder, not just for the subject."

I waited for her to go on, but she didn't, and a passing group of sequined performers threatened to steal her attention.

"What do you mean the wielder?" I caressed her bracelet, her wrist. "What exactly is it you're wielding?"

She narrowed her eyes at me again. Less playful this time. She wasn't falling for my act, but she wasn't angry about it either. So I kept performing it.

"Please?" I gave her my biggest endearing grin. "It's not like I could wield whatever it is myself. Not without your guidance."

She rolled her eyes, but her face softened. She couldn't help it. Little by little, I was winning her over.

I could win anyone over.

"You're basically overcoming another's free will," she said, "so you need something direct, like an enchantment."

"What's the enchantment?"

"You mean the words?"

Shrug. Big, sweet grin. "I don't know. Do I?"

She sighed, but her amused smile said she was enjoying my attention. "The words are the easy part. And before you ask what the words are, you can use any words. I've found that using someone else's words can make an enchantment stronger. The better known the words, the better the results."

"It sounds like there's a *but*."

She nodded. "Other people's words are strangely easy to mess up.

Making up your own words may not add any power, but it's one less thing to go wrong."

"What happens if something does?"

"Depends." Her gaze lowered. "I knew someone, once, who performed a will-taking enchantment." Her pupils shrank, her lids squinting in spasm, as if reliving something horrid. "Others reduced him to ashes and told me to heed the warning."

I shivered and tightened my grip on her arm to mask the tremors.

She patted my hand. "I never did learn what had them so afraid."

"So what's the hard part?" I asked after a moment.

"The hard part?"

"You said the enchantment's words are the easy part," I said. "What's the hard part?"

Nechai extracted herself from my grasp and checked her waistline, retucked her blouse. She didn't want to say, and she didn't want to succumb to my tricks. Fine. I didn't need tricks. Nechai liked me and she wanted me to like her, and that was trick enough. I leaned into the hall, checking the line at the bathroom, and made an excuse to leave. Other people to meet.

"Everything," she said, pulling me back into her confidence. "The hard part is that everything—amulets, enchantments—pretty much everything takes this one type of..."

She touched her chest, pinching the material of her blouse as she chose her words.

"Let's call it an *ingredient*. It takes a special ingredient to affect anything, but you need a certain...a certain *grade* for love. It's risky. Not just procuring the higher grade, though that's risky too, but *using* the higher grade. I'm oversimplifying, but higher grades—they're more powerful, but they're also more...temperamental."

She lowered her gaze again, remembering something, pulling absently at whatever was beneath her blouse.

"What do you mean 'temperamental'?" I asked. "Like you can make it mad?" I chuckled at the absurdity.

"The ingredient is already hostile," she said, growing somewhat hostile herself. I was demanding to learn in a few minutes something she had studied her whole life, and I wasn't even bothering to treat it seriously. "You've harnessed its will, after all. The ingredient can still be helpful if it wants to be, but it's less inclined when there's…ill intent. If an ingredient has to be used, it wants to be used for good—"

"What's better than love?"

"—and it can get downright nasty if you try to take another person's will."

Ah. "But you can?"

"I'm sure it's possible if you have a strong enough ingredient. But your own will better be stronger, and your enchantment best be perfect. Mistakes allow the ingredient to challenge your intent. And to punish you for it."

"It's an ingredient," I said, picturing sugar and spice despite knowing it must be something else entirely. "How can it punish?"

"Haunt you, make you a vessel, make you a beacon for trouble. Whatever it wants, if it wants." She shrugged. "No one knows, really. It's happened so rarely. Until I learn the ingredient's secrets, I figure it's best to show it respect."

"I could win it over." I flashed her my winning smile and slid my fingers beneath the hand she still held pressed to her blouse. The silk hid a small cylinder. "You have some around your neck, don't you, this 'highest grade'?"

Nechai touched the pendant again but didn't draw it out. "A gift from my sister."

I smiled, still hopeful.

"She was pregnant when she drank the pesticide. This is all I have of hers."

I muttered my condolences. It had been worth a shot. "So where do you get this mysterious ingredient?"

"Walgreens."

I laughed but gave her a look that said I wasn't fooled. She would give me the answer.

She held my gaze, looking burdened but also proud. Still my friend but threatening as if my enemy.

"I'm not a middleman, Fausten."

My shoulders broke out in chills. "You make it?"

"In a sense."

I looked at my ring, at this venue. Whatever the ingredient was, it was powerful. And whoever could make the ingredient had to be even more powerful. For the first time in my life, I looked up at someone without raising my head. My eyes strained against my lowered brow, but I couldn't look at her directly. I was afraid. I was afraid of Nechai.

"Does anyone else make it?" I asked.

"Sure, but there aren't many masters on this continent. And I don't really make it so much as I...procure it."

My stomach rolled, warning me that I would regret learning how she *procured* it. But I was too curious.

"From where?"

She stepped closer, too close, even for touchy-feely me. So I stepped closer too. Her words teased me as her fingers wound themselves in the tie that bound the front of my corset.

"I could show you."

"And you'll get me some?"

She was too close to step any closer, but that didn't stop her from trying. Her body was warm against mine, full of the power I feared she possessed.

She said, "But you'll have to do something for me."

"That would be new, wouldn't it?" I meant to lighten the mood, to rebalance the shift in power, but the statement was too true to be funny, and she stood too close for it to cut through.

"Once I start the process, you can't leave," she said, "and you can't stop me. No matter what happens."

No, Nechai was not a middleman. And that truth had my whole body trembling. But I didn't want to deal with middlemen either. I wanted to *know*. I wanted to be as powerful as Nechai. I wanted the power to make something so powerful.

Desire lifted my chin and defied my anxieties.

"Okay," I said.

Nechai buttoned her jacket. "Let's go."

"Now?"

"The timing is right, the source is ready. You're driving."

"And you'll get me some?"

She shook her head. "I don't have the grade you want. We'll do this for another order."

I got the sense she wouldn't fill my order in any case. Dissatisfying, but if she showed me how it was done, I could *procure* the ingredient myself. "So where do we do this?"

Nechai gave me directions to the university where she worked.

Motion-sensor lighting clicked on and off, section by section, as we walked the carpet-inlayed tile halls to her office. She went to her desk and unlocked the bottom left-hand drawer, took out a box and unlocked that too. Out came a black wrap that looked like something Petty might use to store makeup brushes. Nechai untied the wrap and unrolled it on the desk. The wrap held things that might need security, but she took only a long silver lighter and an empty vial.

I don't know why I'd thought we'd find the ingredient in a garden or some pampered windowsill pot, but I found myself increasingly unnerved as I followed Nechai through the university's halls to the gross lab.

Nechai taught anatomy. On actual dead people.

"We're going in there?"

"The ingredient is an oil," Nechai said. "It comes from a woman who's taken her own life and that of her unborn child."

She cut her eyes at me, regarding me as if she expected me to squirm.

I kept my eyes from widening, my hands from shaking, but I didn't trust my voice. I nodded for her to continue.

"That's the traditional source anyway. My grandfather's soul might be raging right now, but working in the lab has let me experiment with other sources and simpler rituals. With some success."

I nodded like a bobblehead, lest she test me again. The rest of my body was numb.

"It helps for a corpse to have died by violence, you see. Violence makes the oil more powerful. Accident can work for some things. Natural death is generally worthless. But I've found that even the quietest of causes will work so long as death happened on a meaningful day or in a meaningful way. Even better if that meaning is relevant."

She let the words hover, knowing I didn't understand, signaling that if I wanted to, I'd have to participate.

I deepened my voice to keep from squeaking. "Relevant?"

"Say you want success as a performer," she said, humor brightening her eyes. "A lesser oil could be potent enough if sourced from, say, an actor who died onstage."

I thumbed my amulet, remembering a trapeze artist who'd fallen to his death less than a month ago, during a matinee in Vegas. My shoulders rippled with chills. Vegas wasn't that far from here.

Nechai dug out her lab keys and reached for the lock on the door. Her coat brushed my elbow, making me flinch.

"Jumpy," she said. "It's unlike you. Sure you want to do this?"

I looked at my ring, at the amulet's face. Its trinkets sparkled amidst the amber-colored goo. I'd had it less than a week, but on the drive here, Petty had called. He'd said we'd booked the Orphic Starlight.

They'd called us.

"Absolutely."

Nechai opened the door to the gross lab and handed her lighter to me.

A week later, Nechai had given me her sister's vial of oil, and when I'd tried to use it on Guy, I'd heard a scream. It had sounded unearthly. But I'd assumed it must've been someone in the audience, because I'd never heard such a scream before or since.

Until now.

A similar scream was coming from the vial Guy had opened at the foot of my bed. It had the same unearthly quality but conveyed a different emotion. The vial in Guy's hand was angry.

The scream the night of my accident had been giddy.

Schadenfreude. That first scream had been Schadenfreude. She wasn't just a bored wraith haunting me. Hers was the will that had empowered the oil that had trapped me in my body.

She had trapped me in my body.

I hadn't realized she was such an idiot.

Sure, she'd been strong enough to win her challenge against my ill intent, but the punishment she'd chosen for me required her to join me in my immobile body. Forever.

Why didn't you just put in a little more effort and push me the fuck out?

"That's it, Fausten," Guy said, and at the foot of my bed, the stench of death flared. Guy had removed my new vial's cap. He was no longer just threatening me. He was taking action to dump the screaming oil.

And I knew now what that scream meant. It meant that the oil believed Guy's threats. It considered them an incantation, one backed by ill intent. One he was butchering with mistakes. The scream was the oil's warning that if Guy dumped the oil, it would challenge Guy's will.

And Guy would lose. He didn't seem to hear the scream. He didn't know anything was wrong. And he'd never believe me if I told him what was happening.

Please. I flooded the room with my influence, my thoughts, my pleas. I let the oil know that even though an angry, misguided fool was taking a risk he refused to understand, his intended victim—me—welcomed the use of its will. I let the oil know that its power could still be used for good.

So long as Guy poured it where I needed it.

I imagined the oil floating toward me, using my influence to pull the vial, still in Guy's grip, toward my left hand. Doing so was surprisingly easy compared to disposing of the professor's harvested body or trying now to ease what was left of her mind.

"Stop it, Fausten." Guy steeled himself against the bed, depressing the mattress near my feet. The vial stopped moving.

Pour it on my hand.

"No. You're done using people."

He tipped the vial. Drops of oil splattered the floor. I yanked his arm with my influence, willing at least a sprinkle of that powerful oil to land on my rotting hand.

Droplets showered my legs with sharp, then tender surprise, like the burning of boiling water.

And the screaming grew louder.

Wait! I wrapped my influence around my body, letting it film my skin. I imagined it forming tiny channels, channels that would coax the burning oil to move. I'd never done it before, so I didn't know if it would work. But I begged those tiny channels to guide the powerful drops of oil toward the rot on my left hand.

The screaming stopped.

"I hate you, Fausten."

And Guy seemed fine. I asked him if the oil had done my hand any good. I'd never felt such pain with Petty's oil-infused cream.

"Promise me this oil wasn't hers and that you won't go after her, that you won't...*harvest* her."

So easy. Promises are meaningless. Only actions are real. I told him I promised, I wouldn't go after Daphne.

Not for her oil anyway. My body was a loss. I still wanted to hear it from Guy, but I knew this was true. I could feel its emptiness, its silence, its sloth. There was no point in using Daphne to revive my body now.

But I couldn't forget her entirely. She had my amulet on her finger, a speck of my will in her brain, and my vitality, or what was left of it, in that golden-opal ringsel. There was no *me* without her.

"The crackling's quieter," Guy said, not trusting my promises. "But it isn't getting any better. The decay has spread past your knuckles."

Schadenfreude's giddy snickers taunted me. Not from the edge of my awareness, but from the rot on my left hand. She amplified the sensations. I could feel the cells liquefying, the mushing as it spread.

My beautiful body... I wouldn't be able to perform much longer in this condition.

But things were always working out for me. Thanks to the screaming vial of oil, and to the broken lamps and speakers, and to Petty discovering how Nechai had caused my accident, and to Conlin, even now, finding a way to return Daphne to me by showtime, I already knew exactly how to fix myself.

It would take a very specific ingredient.

And harvesting this ingredient would take a very strong will.

Where was Petty? We needed to prepare a room. I'd have my ingredient by the end of the night.

Poor Daphne. She wasn't going to like my new plan.

CHAPTER 35

DAPHNE - 16 days left

The MAX to Beaverton was so packed I had to reach between people to hold the stability pole. The trip would take fifteen minutes plus a fifteen-minute bus ride. Assuming no traffic, I'd make it to my interview right on time.

My phone rang. I didn't recognize the number, but it was probably the interviewer calling to confirm. I put on a cheerful, professional air. I was someone to hire.

"This is Daphne," I whispered, trying not to disturb the people around me.

"Oh good, you're not sick."

I knew that baritone. I coughed for good measure. "Hi, Conlin."

"No. No more hooky. I need you at the theater in half an hour."

"Can't. I have a meeting."

"You're meeting someone all right, but unless your guy loves theater, the Pin-up Bride, and gifting big checks, your meeting's at L'Aornum."

The benefit. I was supposed to raise money for replacement sound and lights.

Conlin said, "You can charm Dr. Chaiprasit into writing me a check or you can write me a check. Either way, I'm easy. But tonight, someone writes me a check."

"I have to go," I said, but my trembling fingers failed to disconnect the call, and Conlin's baritone boomed through the phone: "You're here in thirty or you get the bill."

I closed the phone and clutched it to my chest. I was already a week behind in paying back my advance. I couldn't afford to add to the debt.

I called the number that had arranged my interview and asked for Mr. Tanner.

"One moment, please."

It rang and rang. Our meeting was in twenty minutes, and I was almost to the bus station. I should probably just hang up, go to the interview, and arrive late—

"Ken Tanner."

"Hi, Mr. Tanner. This is Daphne James. I'm meeting with you—"

"Is there a problem?"

"No, no. It's just—"

"There's a problem?"

"An emergency. Sort of."

"I understand."

My whole body relaxed. "Thank you, you don't know—"

"Best of luck to you, Ms. James."

"Wait—can't we reschedule?" We had to reschedule. I'd skipped chemistry to finish the application, to translate my menial theater tasks into skills a real business could appreciate. I needed this job.

"We've seen enough applicants," he said. "Frankly, your résumé suggests you're not up to the challenge."

"No, I am. I'll show you."

The MAX stopped at the transit center. I pushed the emergency button to get the doors open faster and sputtered into the phone that I'd be there, that I was transferring to the bus now.

I shouldn't have bothered. Mr. Tanner disconnected with a loud, dismissive click, and when I got to the front desk, the receptionist said, "He's left for the day. Did you have an appointment?"

Back on the MAX, I slouched in a seat to myself, dreading my future. With Andy in my life, I could see myself—us—doing enjoyable work while making the house payment and taking the occasional weekend trip to the beach. Without him, I saw myself either in scrubs, tending to bloody wounds while trying to hold down my blueberry-less pancakes, or else in Juicy pants, plastering a permasmile over dwindling resources and mounting complaints—in either case, struggling to survive.

My phone rang but I didn't answer. Seeing Conlin's number was reminder enough that my crappy life could still get worse.

I arrived at L'Aornum Theatre on high alert for smoke-oozing posters, but fear of hallucinating soon gave way to fear of Conlin. He was waiting for me out on the sidewalk with crossed arms and one foot holding the door open. "You're late."

"I know. Just let me get the dress."

"Not yet. Go put this on."

He handed me what looked like a wad of gauze. I shook it out and held it up. *Hmm.* Bandeau top or skimpy sarong, but not both. Not enough fabric for both.

Conlin snatched it from my hands and tied it on me. "It goes around your waist."

Except it didn't, not really. The knot sat just above my lady business and the draping hung off my ass.

"Why would I wear..." But then I recognized it, and nerves I never knew existed said *hello*. "I'm posing for Fausten?"

Conlin opened the door and pushed me inside. "Go. You're on in fifteen."

"Why isn't Fausten posing?"

Conlin laughed without humor. "We'll be lucky if she does the workshop."

I wondered why, but right now I faced bigger issues. My knees were buckling and my feet wouldn't move. I bit the corner of my mouth.

"Yes...?" Conlin said.

"I can't do topless."

"No? You were keen a couple weeks ago. Begging, if I remember." Conlin ducked into the ticket booth and came back with his garment bag. He smiled like he had me. "Well, weren't you?"

"Yeah, but..." I would've been posing with Andy. Andy would've helped me feel comfortable. Andy would've helped me hide my tiny boobs. If any of the benefactors saw my tiny boobs, they'd know for certain I wasn't the real Pin-up Bride.

Conlin swatted me with his garment bag. "Go. People could arrive any minute."

I sighed and trudged to my doom, my feet dragging like tombstones.

Something scraped and thumped at the other end of the lobby. Petty was setting up the platform.

Petty. He'd freak when he learned I was posing for Fausten. I undid the knot at my waist and waved the gauze. "Petty! Is this the right outfit for Aphrodite?" I modeled the fabric so he could see the whole horrible effect and put a stop to this.

"Yeah. Paint's on the bar. And hurry up. Fausten's never late." He dusted off the platform and vanished into the house.

Conlin put an arm around my shoulders. "Aww, did that not go your way? Who did you think canceled for Ms. Cotter?"

I sighed and continued my trudge of doom.

"Good. Ares and Aphrodite—go. I gotta get ready myself." Conlin jogged past the bar and up the stairs, garment bag in hand. I stared after him, my comprehension process slower than my feet.

Ares and Aphrodite?

"Wait! Who'm I posing with?!"

CHAPTER 36

DAPHNE

I ducked behind the bar and stripped off my suit, my shirt, my undies.

The house doors squeaked.

I covered my boobs with my suit jacket and peered over the bar.

Oh, gawd. Avoiding debt was not worth such horror.

Guy sauntered toward me with nothing but a pink towel around his waist and a paint can in his hand. He clunked the can on the counter, leaned over the edge, and, upon seeing me—cowering in the corner, frantically covering my girly bits—he grinned.

"Go away!" I said.

He grinned wider and held out a brush. When I didn't take it, he poked my shoulder with its bristles.

"Just leave it!"

He chuckled, set the brush on the bar, and backed away. I waited until it sounded like he was painting himself, then grabbed the brush.

My arms and legs turned into marble easily enough (although, I noted, not as luminescent as Fausten's), but I worried about painting my face.

A beer mirror hung behind the bar. I wrapped the gauze around my hips for maximum coverage, crossed my arms over my chest, and checked to make sure Guy was occupied.

Gah! Boy, was he—bent at the waist and painting the tops of his feet. I blinked, trying to cancel that mental image before it stuck with me for life.

Breathe. Just breathe. I faced the mirror and ran a streak of paint down my nose, hoping it wouldn't clog my pores.

"So," Guy said. "Why isn't Andy posing?"

I glanced at Guy through the mirror, but he was hidden by the bar. "What do you mean?"

"I figured you'd ask Conlin if Andy could pose with you."

I dipped the brush into the paint can, wishing I'd asked Conlin if Andy could pose with me. "I didn't know I was posing until I got here," I said. "Why isn't Fausten posing?"

As if in answer, Guy straightened and came around the bar.

"What are you doing?" I backed into the corner, hunching my shoulders and using my paintbrush for privacy. Guy, however, had no such shame. Feet wide, arms wide, fig leaf already in place. His scars looked puffy beneath the paint, especially that nasty jag on his thigh. He didn't stop coming toward me until he stood within arm's reach.

He said, "You keep holding yourself like that you're gonna rub all the paint off."

I squeezed my boobs tighter.

"Already did on your..." He wagged his finger at my underboob. "Want me to get it?"

"I want you to go away."

He held out his brush. When I didn't move, except to cower more, he shook it. "Do me."

"You mean 'paint' you?"

"Just the spots I can't reach." He showed me his unpainted back. I would've protested, but we'd soon be canoodling more or less naked. Seemed a little late to establish boundaries.

I had my own brush, but on second thought, I didn't want to mix use. Keeping one arm over my breasts, I exchanged my brush for Guy's and painted his neck beige. He flinched at the first stroke, then relaxed.

"So?" I prompted.

Guy glanced back at me. "'So' what?"

His willful stupidity made me want to jab paint in his ear. I settled for painting his shoulder with rougher strokes, hoping they hurt. The brushes suited walls better than skin.

"So, why isn't she posing?"

Guy looked over his shoulder, grimacing as he ignored my question and watched me paint.

When I reached his scapula, the beer mirror's fluorescent light hit my ring, making it sparkle, and a look of recognition flashed on Guy's face. He grabbed my hand. He probably could've kept hold of it too, had I not been naked, but when he turned to face me, necessity made me strong. I yanked and got my hand back—just as he jerked away from me, howling in pain.

He stuck his hand, paint and all, in his mouth. "How'd you get that?" he asked around his fingers.

"Get what?!" I tried to cross my arms over my chest, but I was hindered by the paintbrush. I burrowed it into my armpit. The cabochon on my ring felt warm and tingly against my skin.

Someone pounded on the theater's front doors.

"They're here," I said. "Turn around so I can finish."

Guy didn't move. He stared at me, his eyes teetering back and forth between mine.

I hunched my shoulders. "*What?*"

Guy started to speak, but Conlin's footsteps thundered overhead, and he reluctantly turned around. I grabbed the second brush and painted Guy's back in a hurry, T. rex style, my triceps pressed against my boobs.

Guy studied me in the mirror, his brow creasing over troubled eyes. "I tried to warn you," he said.

"About what?"

"Come on, come on," Conlin said, taking the stairs two at a time. He wore a classic tailored suit. "We can't make them wait much longer."

"Done." I dropped the brushes into the can.

Guy turned to face me and stepped closer. I shoved my hands into my armpits and backed away. "What are you—?"

"Let him paint you, Ms. James. And pull up your hair."

I cowed at Conlin's tone and let Guy swing me around. As I tied up my hair, cold wet paint tickled my back. I tucked my pelvis to minimize my butt—but had to relax it again when Conlin squeezed past me and crouched low to sift through the bar's bottom shelves. He was lucky the paint dried quickly; his hip kept bumping my legs. I was trapped between Guy's fig leaf and Conlin's tailored ass. If I didn't get more personal space, I'd explode.

"Done." Guy dropped the brush in the can, and the scratchy sensation on my back yielded to a drafty chill. I exhaled a long-held breath and pressed my chest into the counter while I undid my hair.

"Put your hair back up," Conlin said.

"But Fausten..."

Conlin plunked a cardboard box on the bar. "'Fausten' what?"

Fausten covered her boobs with her hair. Weren't they gonna let me cover my boobs with my hair?

Nope. Conlin dug in the box and pulled out what looked like a dead beige cat. He forced it on my head and topped it with Aphrodite's gold crown. My head itched, but the wig matched the paint and hid the fact that I didn't have glossy black hair nor a pink-and-mint-green streak, so I really couldn't complain. He handed me a gold armlet. I carefully slid the plastic bangle onto my arm.

"Left bicep," Guy said, correcting me. He hefted a red-plumed helmet from the box and stuck it on his head.

I carefully switched the bangle to my other arm and then stood there, covering myself, not looking at anyone, feeling all sorts of uncomfortable.

Not Guy. Unflappable physical confidence, that was his secret. I'd be out of luck if it was Fausten's secret too.

But it wasn't, at least not the secret of her appeal: the public had never heard of Guy Vincent Park.

Guy scooched around me (pressing his chest against my back on purpose, I just knew it) and went to twirl in a slow, exposed circle in the brightest part of the lobby, wearing nothing but his helmet, bits of gold, and his green fig leaf.

"Check my paint."

"You're good." I didn't look. I'd seen enough of Guy. Carved, smooth marble worthy of Michelangelo, yet—dare I think it—sexier than *David*.

Such a turd.

"Just a touch-up here," Conlin said. He did some quick work on Guy, then turned the brush on me. I flinched and made myself as small as possible. Conlin worked around my cowering without comment.

It took both of them to drag me onto the platform, Guy pulling my elbow, Conlin pushing me from the back. I didn't see Petty come in, but suddenly he was there, handing Guy a spear.

"You can't wear that," Petty said to me, taking my silly-string ring but saying nothing about the cabochon. I told him to save it behind the bar, but it broke in his hand and he threw it in the trash.

Guy took position beside me on the platform: weight on his left foot, right hand holding the spear. He opened his left arm wide, ready to hold me.

Still covering my boobs, I stepped into position, close enough to feel Guy's heat.

"Closer, Ms. James, closer. I said *closer*."

I closed my eyes and did as Conlin said, and my mons pubis hit something bony. I cringed. *Please be Guy's hip.*

"Right leg over left." Conlin jerked my right foot until my posture matched the original Canova statue. Then he critiqued the gauze. "This isn't how Fausten wears this."

Of course it wasn't. I'd tied it modestly. Or as modestly as one could tie a four-foot square of fabric. Conlin loosened the knot and the gauze draped lower on my hips.

"Is this really necessary?" I said, trying to stay the fabric with an elbow.

Petty said, "Fausten is nothing if not authentic."

I tried to stop the gauze anyway. "I doubt anyone'll notice the difference."

Conlin swatted my elbow. "Leave it," he said. He positioned the gauze to his liking, shared a silent conversation with Petty, probably telling him to keep a watch on me, then strode to the front doors.

"Wait," I said. "Where are the ropes?" Velvet ropes always kept distance between Fausten and her fans just in case they got grabby.

"Not tonight," Conlin said. "The benefactors get a little something extra."

Ew. "Is that why she's not posing?"

"If only," Guy muttered.

I was not happy. Not only was the gauze now draped oh-so-fashionably over my knee, leaving the hip closest to the fans bare to midthigh, but also—there were no ropes.

Petty crossed his arms and tilted his head. "Your arm's wrong."

"Aren't I supposed to drape it on his shoulder?" I whacked Guy in the chin to show Petty just how correctly I'd placed it.

Petty said, "They're both supposed to be draped," and he tugged at my left arm.

But I was using it. I pressed it tighter against my chest, pushing up the flesh of my minimal bosom.

"What's wrong?" Guy whispered.

Duh. I so wanted to answer with sarcasm, but I was too overwhelmed to think of a lie. I told him the truth. "I don't want to show my boobs."

"Why not?"

Truth again: "They're not as nice as Fausten's."

"Let me see."

I glared at him and clutched myself tighter.

Petty huffed and gave up the fight.

"They're nice enough," Guy said, but I heard something more, and my body warmed, warmed to the idea that maybe they were enough, that maybe the person they were attached to was enough too. "Just step closer until they're pressed against me."

I shook my head. Enough or not, Andy's girlfriend was already so close to Guy Charming Park that she could see a tiny dimple on his cheekbone.

"Yes." He tightened his hold on my lower back, pulling me closer. "I'll hide them, so you don't have to."

It was a sound plan, but I still couldn't willingly remove my arm from my chest.

Petty tugged on my arm again, and this time I let him take it. I pressed closer to Guy until both my breasts felt covered. A quick check confirmed that they were indeed both hidden, pressed firmly against Guy's massive lat.

And immediately—and despite the cold and my shivering nerves—our points of contact began to drip.

I sighed. "Fausten doesn't sweat, does she?"

I meant to say it so only Guy could hear, but Petty said, "*Ew*, gross, of course not."

"It happens," Guy said.

"I blame you." Guy was hot—*temperature* hot. I rubbed my thumb in his neck sweat.

"I blame *you*." He rubbed his thumb in my lower back sweat.

My eyes bulged. How dare he?! I wiggled under his hand. "Okay, that's enough."

He grinned and relaxed his hand, then licked his lips and relaxed his face. His chest expanded and contracted. "Breathe," he told me.

Good idea.

Inhale. Exhale. So what if Fausten never perspired? She probably lived in the nude and didn't need reminders to breathe, either. Inhale. Exhale. What was crazy was that I didn't care. In this moment I felt confident. That rejection-happy job interview guy had been wrong about me: I could too handle a challenge. And I could thrive. And why would I want to work for someone like him anyway when I could work here and become a star?

Like Fausten Cotter.

Conlin opened the front doors and a freezing gust of air chilled my skin. He welcomed the benefactors in a loud voice meant to warn us that Ares and Aphrodite were on. I took one last deep breath and lifted my chin to look at Guy and complete the pose.

Guy was already looking at me, but when our gazes met, a smile crinkled his eyes. "It's only an hour," he said.

"Shhhh." I might have been faking the rest of Aphrodite's pose, but the fond look she gave Ares felt genuine. "No talking."

CHAPTER 37

DAPHNE

Smoke billowed up from the platform and covered my feet. My muscles tensed. Despite being in the theater's lobby, surrounded by posters in every alcove, I hadn't experienced any hallucinations since the incident in Sullivan's office, and I liked it that way. But this billowing smoke was not a hallucination. (*...not a hallucination...*) This was just the fog machine doing its job. Smoke hugged the platform like we stood in a cloud.

The benefactors oohed and aahed just as they would've for Fausten Cotter. Without the ropes, they could get close to us—and they did, mostly with their eyes, leaning forward from the waist with their hands behind their backs, as if studying the real sculpture. If they lingered too long, though, the smoke thickened until they stepped away. They oohed and aahed at that too.

I trembled. The last thickening smoke I'd seen had become murderous smoke.

Guy rubbed my back with his thumb. "We're okay."

I exhaled, trying to relax, but Guy's muscles flexed like he, too, was worried. He winked at me with the eye no one else could see. I twitched a smile and tried not to think about the people or the smoke.

I focused on Guy's face. He'd painted his dark hair beige but had missed a spot at his temple. Both ears were pierced, but I'd never seen him wear earrings. A tiny scar marred his brow and another underlined his lip. He had a divot in the tip of his nose and a dimple in his cheek. He was cute if I forgot who I was looking at.

Eventually the benefactors meandered upstairs and Conlin dismissed us. Spell broken, I covered my chest, hiked up the gauze, and hurried toward the bar to get dressed.

"No time for that," Conlin said. "Where's your outfit?"

Guy handed me his pink towel. I wrapped it around myself, then gathered my clothes and slipped on my flats.

"In the storeroom," I said. I'd hidden it there just in case Petty changed his mind about me borrowing it.

"Good," Conlin said. "I need you upstairs in twenty."

I cleaned up in the bathroom—the paint peeled off fairly easily—then hurried to the storeroom. My heart fluttered the whole way. I was about to don the outfit of the Pin-up Bride. I was about to simper and flirt with her fans. I was about to be her stand-in for real.

And afterwards, I'd play the role for Andy.

I retrieved the garment bag from a rack of old costumes and unzipped the plastic. Layers of fabric glowed white inside. I ran my fingers across the textures of satin and velvet and lace. I squeed. I did the giddy dance. I dropped the towel and found my underwear. I toed off my flats—

"Crap."

I didn't have the blue heels.

Fausten had plenty of shoes, but I'd never forget Petty's face when he'd asked me my size and then told me to get my own.

I found shoes on the shelves, but they were basic theater shoes, black with a stubby heel and a strap that buckled across the arch. They weren't ugly; they just weren't something Fausten Cotter would wear.

I pulled out my phone to call Andy, but it showed no reception. I dressed in my pants and blouse and snuck outside to make the call. It took him four rings to answer.

"Hey," he said, "how'd your interview go?"

"Oh—it was canceled."

"How come?"

"I dunno. Can you do me a favor?"

He took an uncharacteristic second to think about it. "Probably."

"Can you bring me my shoes, the blue T-strap peep-toes?"

"Only if you promise to wear them for me, and nothing else."

"I could do that, but I've got an outfit even better."

"Yeah? Okay. Bring them where?"

"The theater?"

"I thought it caused you stress."

"Still does. Can you bring them?"

He took another long second to think about it. "Yeah, I'm headed that way anyway. Be there in a bit."

I waited for Andy as far away from the Pin-up Bride poster as I could get while staying under the awning, out of the rain. I kept a wary watch on the poster, but it seemed my tendency to hallucinate had passed. And without Andy ever suspecting. Thank goodness.

It took less than five minutes to drive to campus from Andy's apartment, but twenty minutes later, I was still waiting. *Oh well.* I could deal with complaints about my tardiness, but without the right shoes I'd be worthless.

I thumbed my ring and scanned the sidewalks. The poster continued to behave, but the passersby did not. They looked at Fausten's poster, then looked at me. Looked at her. Looked at me. One of them came a little too close for my liking and pointed at the poster. "Are you...?"

I gaped at him. "You think I'm *her*?"

He flinched and wandered away with slumped shoulders, like I'd hurt his feelings. It probably wasn't how the PuB would've handled it, but I was starting to panic. Andy should've been here by now. What was he doing—showering first?

A white Jeep drove by. I started to wave, but there were two people up front. I checked my phone. Ten past seven.

The Jeep drove by again and found a parking spot. A dark-haired girl got out on the passenger side. I glanced the other way, still checking for Andy, then glanced back. The girl was jogging toward me, hunching against the rain and clutching something she'd wrapped in the ends of her pink scarf. As she slowed to a walk, the fabric slipped, revealing a pair of blue shoes.

Behind her, Andy hustled to catch up.

"What the—?"

(it's not what it seems)

It's worse.

The muscles in my cheeks tensed into a smile. I was late for work and Andy picked up some girl first?

Worse.

Their approach slow-motioned as I tried to understand. Andy was leaving for Chicago, still hadn't asked me to go with him, and now what—this girl? I mean, he was letting her hold my shoes.

What else of ours had she held?

I looked at my feet, trying to calm myself. The staples I'd used to hem my pants had come loose and the fabric was dragging beneath my flats. I looked like the failed dress-for-success that I was, and she, with her curvy figure and her wavy dark hair and those mint-green flowers on her pink scarf—she looked like a before-she-was-famous version of the Pin-up Bride. On a date.

Worse.

A midstage date. The stage where they're still trying to impress each other but plan to end the night the right way.

Even Worse.

"Sorry we took so long." I had a hard time hearing anything Andy said after the word *we*...until he used it again. "We're in the same study group. Ericka, this is my *girlfriend*."

He emphasized the last word, but not like he was proud. He said it like he was making a point, like he knew that I was pissed and thought clarifying our connection would make me happy.

It made the PuB poster shimmer.

"Hi." Ericka held out her hand. Behind her, the PuB poster extended one too.

I didn't take either. I couldn't move.

Ericka frowned and unwrapped her scarf from my shoes.

Behind her, the poster oozed out a smoky head, a torso the same color as the cloud-gray sky. A shade stepped out of the poster.

Ericka handed me the T-straps. "Great shoes."

"Thanks," I said, but I couldn't meet her eyes. The shade was slinking closer, hovering just behind her.

"Where'd you get them?" she asked. "I've never heard of that brand."

The shade curled itself around her body, like a snake seeking her chin.

I looked down, pretending to look for the brand, and closed my eyes. I didn't want to see postergeists anymore. I didn't want to be a girl who hallucinated.

I blew out a breath and opened my eyes.

The shade waved its fingers.

Ericka looked over her shoulder, then frowned at me and glanced up at Andy, like she couldn't believe he would date someone so crazy.

He wouldn't.

She couldn't see what I saw. Couldn't see the ghost just behind her. Didn't feel its fingers in her hair, gripping her temples like her head was a pumpkin ready to pluck.

"O*kay,*" she said. "Well, anyway, they're pretty."

She smiled, complacent as the shade used her to provoke me. She didn't notice its hand beneath her chin. Didn't feel the heat as it summoned—

Flame.

I hurled my arm out to smother the fire.

Ericka shrieked and covered her head. Behind her, my blue T-strap landed with a thud on the sidewalk.

I'd thrown my shoe.

"What the hell, Daph?" Andy rubbed Ericka's back. "You okay?"

She nodded but made herself small and meek. Andy squeezed her shoulder.

"We should go," he told her. "Good luck tonight," he told me, but he was shaking his head and scowling. He looked disgusted with me.

I watched them walk away, whispering sorry when they were too far away to hear, my boyfriend with another girl. A girl like Fausten Cotter.

She looked up at him. He leaned down to hear her, and his shoulders scrunched around his ears. He did that when he laughed. She was making him laugh.

About me?

I hurried away from the thought; hurried to collect my shoe, then hurried back under the awning and yanked the door open. But not fast enough.

"Nice meeting you," Ericka called with a wave of her fingers. It wasn't politeness. I didn't deserve any, but it wasn't politeness. Her smile warned that if she'd had any misgivings about her intentions for Andy, they were all gone now.

I wished my shoe had hit her in the face; she'd be less glib with no teeth.

But chucking it at her hadn't done me any favors. Andy never once looked back.

CHAPTER 38

DAPHNE

Jealousy makes for ugly. I didn't want to be ugly, but, lucky me, I got the two-for-one jealousy special: it made me both ugly and crazy.

The theater wasn't triggering my hallucinations. The theater and its star merely triggered my jealousy, and *that* triggered my hallucinations. The first time I'd seen the postergeist, Andy had just told me that he'd marry a girl like the Pin-up Bride. And the night I'd hallucinated the ghost in our room, Andy had just posed with Fausten in that fig leaf, and those girls, the one wagging the money...

Had that been Ericka?

My heart smoldered in my throat. Andy's declaration about marrying the PuB had sparked the flame, and working at the theater had stoked it, but Ericka...she was real. She was in his study group. She looked like the PuB, and—

Worse.

—she wanted him.

But I couldn't let myself become any more ugly. Andy wouldn't propose, adamantly denied giving me this ring, and now this girl, this Ericka girl. But I couldn't let this spark become a blaze.

"Ms. James?" Conlin's voice boomed from somewhere in the house, reminding me that I was actually triple lucky: I was ugly, crazy, and poor. I still had to raise money for lights.

I put on Fausten's poster dress with dead limbs and no enthusiasm, but as I looked at myself in a cracked mirror I'd found leaning against the shelves, my mood brightened considerably. I couldn't believe Petty had made this costume, but if he had, he had my compliments. My legs, clad in tan fishnets, were already my best feature, but this short ruffled skirt made them pop. The boned corset gave my otherwise sad décolleté just the right amount of oomph, and the flounces around my biceps softened the look with a touch of romance.

"Ms. James?" Getting closer.

I applied bronzer on my arms, which got me closer to Fausten's complexion, but I still wasn't satisfied. The biggest problem? My hair. Forget the pink-and-mint-green streak. I had light hair. Fausten did not. The hat and its veil covered enough of my face, but not enough of my hair. I searched the shelves and found a tin of black shoe polish. The product was dry and cracked when I pressed it, but my finger came away dark and greasy.

"*Ms. James.*" Getting angrier. And no wonder: I was seriously late. He'd forgive me if I looked good, but as it was...

"Coming!"

I left the safety of the storeroom and headed into the house.

Conlin waited at the top of the aisle with a two-gallon cylindrical box.

"The patrons are getting impatient."

I pulled up the corset and tugged down the skirt. I adjusted the hat, but it was no use. "I can't do this," I told him. "They'll never think I'm Fausten."

Conlin's frown became a half-moon of white teeth. "You're not impersonating Ms. Cotter," he said. "You're playing the part of the Pin-up Bride. Even Ms. Cotter has to make an effort to become the Pin-up Bride."

I glanced around the house, at the half dozen Pin-up Bride posters hanging on the walls. It felt dangerous to even listen to such claims in their presence—insulting what you aspire to be tempts insanity—but Conlin had a point. The Pin-up Bride was an act. It wasn't Fausten; it was Fausten in an outfit. And I was wearing the outfit.

"But what about my hair?" I yanked at the light strands. "No one's gonna believe Fausten changed her hair to dishwater bleh."

"The hair is a problem," he said. "But fixable. Like the lights, hmm?"

I held up the tin. "Shoe polish?"

"Come with me."

I followed Conlin into the lobby, then into the girl's bathroom. He set the cylindrical box in the middle sink and took off the lid. Tissue paper concealed his surprise.

"What is it?" I asked.

He reached in and came out with a handful of squeaky styrofoam. The tissue paper fell to the floor, giving me instant tingles.

"Omigod, are you serious?"

"Of course," he said. "And just between you and me, I think she wears one too."

I could've kissed him. "You got me a wig."

"Well, actually, Vargas got it," he said, "but I paid for it, and Ms. Cotter approved."

"She's okay with me doing this?"

"You'll be fine."

I grabbed the wig—so soft, like real hair—but Conlin stopped me. "There should be a wig cap in the box."

There was. My fingers fumbled to rip open the plastic, to unfold the cap, to un-Daphne myself and to become Fausten Cotter.

No, no—to become the Pin-up Bride.

"Someone's excited."

I was. There was magic to be had in completing the look, and my hands shook, wanting to possess it. I bounced on my toes as I tucked all my hair beneath the wig cap. I faced Conlin. "Wig me."

"With pleasure." He lifted the wig like a crown and set it on my head—*zap*.

"*Ah!*" I batted at the wig, at the cap. They fell to the tile floor, landing with a soft *floof*.

"What are you doing?" Conlin said. "It looks good."

Hallucinating? I wasn't sure. I massaged my head, but the sharp sensation lingered, like the wig had electrocuted me. But I couldn't tell Conlin that. It sounded too crazy.

"Did it shock you?"

How did...?

Conlin pointed at the mirror, at the reflection of every strand of my long, light hair standing on end.

"Static electricity," he said. "We haven't had much rain this winter. Your hair's probably dry."

I bit my lip. The electric jolt had felt too strong, too lasting for mere static electricity to have been the cause, but the explanation was better than mine. And I couldn't go upstairs without the wig. I could either suffer the wig for an hour or owe the theater money.

I picked up the cap and put it back on.

Conlin picked up the wig. "Ready?"

I nodded and braced myself for pain. But it didn't sting. It tingled. From head to toe I tingled.

Conlin was all teeth as he styled me. "We may just get that new equipment yet."

Yes. We. May. Pink and mint green streaked a wave of black at the corner of my eye. My transformation was complete. I could feel it.

Conlin helped me don the hat and secure it with pins, then pulled down the veil. "Have a look-see."

I turned toward the mirror, but slowly, slow enough to close my eyes. I laughed at myself, but I wasn't ready to look, not yet.

Conlin knew what I needed. He whispered in my ear, sending shivers down my arms.

"Ladies and gentlemen, boys and girls, and all the wild rest of you, I give you—"

"The Pin-up Bride."

CHAPTER 39

DAPHNE

Conlin held the bathroom door open for me, and I slinked into the lobby. Being all made up like this, channeling the full glory of the Pin-up Bride—it put me in a daze, almost like a dreamscape. I wanted this. And not just to prove to Andy that I deserved his marital intentions. I wanted this for me.

We met a fancy-dressed couple on the grand staircase. The woman saw me—"The Pin-up Bride!"—and hurried down the last few steps. She took my hands and peered at me through my veil. I tried to back away—I could see powder dust on her nose, so I figured she could see me too—but Conlin's hand on my spine kept me in place. I held my breath.

"We love your show," the woman gushed, and I relaxed, suddenly certain I could pull this off—and I loved it. I loved this feeling of confidence, of control.

"Eerie. Enlightening. Love it," she said. "How do you do that thing with the mist?"

"Uh..."

"Trade secret," Conlin said. "Sorry to hurry by, but we're late to entertain." He leaned into the couple and stage-whispered, "We need new equipment ASAP. You understand."

"Right, we heard about that," said the man. "Lights exploded, glass everywhere, but no one was hurt." He pointed at me, his eyes sparkling with wonder. "That was you, too, wasn't it? Another trade secret?"

"Um—"

"Nothing markets better than word of mouth," Conlin said. "You're staying for the workshop, yes?"

"Can't wait," said the woman. She squeezed my hands. "Anything special planned for tonight?"

"Uh—"

"Ah, the thrill of anticipation," Conlin said. "Theater's closed to the public tonight. You know how to take advantage." He flashed them his toothy grin and prodded me up the stairs, whispering, "Looks go a long way, Ms. James, but to raise money, you'll need to use your words."

"I can't do this," I said. "I don't know anything about Fausten's show."

"You wouldn't divulge even if you did. Part of maintaining her mystique is maintaining the mystery. Or so Vargas tells me."

"Where is Petty?" I asked as we reached the middle landing and the first few tables came into view.

"Probably playing gofer or massaging her feet. Ah, there she is." Conlin pointed his pinky into the crowd. "That's who we need to sell."

I followed the line of his finger to where Guy served three people at the bar. Two of them had their backs to me, but the third—

"No way." I backed away and my foot slid off the tread. I lurched for the rail and hotfooted it down the steps to the middle landing, where I cowered behind the banister.

The real Pin-up Bride would not be proud.

Conlin sighed and followed me down the stairs. "Now what's wrong?"

I pointed in the direction of the problem. "That's the creepy fan."

"Creepy?"

The creepy fan wore a peach dress, one-shouldered with a long drape down the back. It wasn't her usual androgynous look, but it was her. "She's always here," I said, "always poking around, peeking behind curtains, trying to get close to Fausten. Guy says she's been doing it since LA." I didn't know what would be worse: the creepy fan thinking I was Fausten or the creepy fan knowing for certain that I wasn't. "Do I have to get the money from her? What about everyone else?"

Conlin flashed a big smile toward the top of the stairs—toward any potential benefactors who might've heard my crass question—then bowed his head to mine. "All money is good money, Ms. James, but she's the only one here with big money."

"Ninety thousand is a lot."

"Oh, good, you understand that. I was beginning to wonder." He adjusted my wig. "Her pocket or yours."

"Fine." We were in public. I'd be fine. I pulled down the skirt and pushed up the boobs. "Let's do this."

"*Determined* isn't quite the Pin-up Bride look," Conlin said. "Tease. Play coy. There you go."

Core tight. Shoulders back. I turned on my flirty walk as Conlin escorted me back upstairs and past all the patrons. Some stood in groups; some sat at tiny tables; but all responded to my arrival with a chorus of murmurs, and the closest ones reached for my hand. I kept it limp, flowing it through their fingers. Patrons further away from me waved, but I didn't wave back. Waving didn't seem like Fausten Cotter. I simpered and popped a flirty shoulder. It felt weird, but the wavers grinned, like I'd surpassed their expectations. It was surreal.

Conlin pushed me toward the bar. "Dr. Chaiprasit—"

"Nechai," said the creepy fan. She flipped her hair and the short, glossy black strands fell to the right, revealing the shaved left side.

"Nechai," Conlin amended. "May I present the Pin-up Bride."

Nechai peered at me through her blue-tinted glasses, then over the tops of their black frames. Her lips formed a smile quite different from those of the other patrons. She wasn't fooled.

With my elbow tucked to my ribs to keep from shaking, I held out my left hand, palm down, as if expecting a knuckle kiss rather than a handshake. It seemed like the Fausten Cotter thing to do.

The creepy fan's vigilant eyes narrowed to suspicious slits. Palm-down was probably a mistake, but Fausten Cotter wouldn't second-guess. I lifted my chin, and I waited.

Nechai smirked and took my hand. "All things come to those at ease," she said.

I glanced at Conlin to see if he understood. He patted my shoulder—"I'll let you two mingle"—and wandered into the tables.

The creepy fan pressed her lips, warm and smooth, against my knuckles. Breath from her nose puffed against my skin. "Beautiful ring," she said. She lifted her eyes and assessed me over her glasses. "What sort of stone is this?"

"Opal?"

Wavy, skeptical lines appeared in the skin of her forehead. She dipped her head, and the tip of her tongue slithered, cold and moist, along my finger. The sensation crept like chiggers up my arm and down my back.

"I don't think so," she said, and she released my hand. All I wanted to do was wipe it on the pale peach fabric that hung from her shoulder, but I set my forearm on the bar and let my hand hover, hoping my tickly wet skin would dry quickly.

Nechai smirked and crossed her legs, revealing a long hidden slit in the sheath of her dress. She rested an elbow on the back of the barstool and signaled the bartender.

Guy served us two tumblers without looking at me. I couldn't tell if his lack of eye contact was due to the creepy fan or because posing naked together had made things awkward. I hoped it was the creepy fan.

She looked regal as she sipped her drink, like tonight was her night, and like she couldn't wait for everyone to know why.

She pointed at my glass. "Aren't you drinking?"

I wasn't planning to, but I couldn't exactly deny the requests of the person I was hoping would agree to my own ninety-thousand-dollar demand. And considering how anxious *that* thought made me feel—how would I even broach the topic?—maybe drinking was a good idea. The liquid in front of me was clear and on ice. Gin? Vodka? I didn't like either. I took a sip.

Water.

"Mm," I said, pretending it was strong. I sipped again and glanced at Guy. He still wouldn't look at me, but I sent him some silent appreciation all the same.

"I told you it would backfire."

"What?"

Nechai nodded at Guy. "Your plan for him. You must've done it wrong."

I sipped my water. I'd thought Nechai knew I wasn't Fausten, but maybe she didn't. I rolled my glass in my hands, buying myself time. What was that improv rule Guy had taught me? Act as if? Always say yes?

"Why do you say that?" I asked.

She bobbed her finger at me. "You know what it was? It was your incantation." I frowned and she waved it away. "Your magic words. You borrowed them, giving them strength, but you didn't say them correctly. You didn't say the whole thing."

"It wasn't me." The response came so quickly it felt foreign. But I knew it was true. Fausten wasn't the type who screwed up. Fausten was the type who laid blame. "It was you."

Nechai laughed so loudly I looked behind me to see who we'd disturbed.

Everyone. Everyone was watching us. I smiled and popped an apologetic shoulder—*Sorry we're loud but I'm Fausten Cotter so it's okay*—and turned back to Nechai.

"My ingredient worked," she said. "It always works. Look at this." She gestured to our surroundings, to the theater and the adoring patrons behind us. “Look at you. You’re a literal overnight success. It’s miraculous, really.” She leaned toward me, bringing the scent of lemon, rot, and ammonia. My shoulders twitched. Her lips touched my ear. “Tonight, even *you* are a star.”

“Rumors,” I said, sitting up straight and forcing Nechai from my space. I’d read about that rumor in the Fausten Cotter fan forums, heard it again from those eavesdropping girls the night of Fausten’s first show: the rumor that she’d risen to fame overnight, only to disappear just as quickly after botching a trick. A magic trick.

Nechai held her glass in salute. “All the better to stoke the fame.”

“No.” I sipped my drink, channeling Fausten’s cool demeanor. “Those rumors are mean. I worked for this. I worked hard for all of this.”

Nechai laughed out loud with real amusement. “Did you?” She set down her glass and twisted in her seat to face the rest of the room. “Show me.”

I grabbed her shoulder and tried to turn her around.

“Your fans are restless,” she said. “Do something fun for them. The third bit.” She held up her hands and called for everyone’s attention. “Wouldn’t you all like to see the Pin-up Bride’s third bit?”

They clapped their approval. Of course they would.

I smiled and waved them off. “The workshop’s soon. In fact”—I looked around for a clock—“I should be getting ready.”

“Come now. The Pin-up Bride doesn’t disappoint her fans. Just do the finale, then. That little bow you do.”

A nasal female voice yelled, “That’s not—”

“*Chchch.*” Nechai popped off her stool, pulling me with her and silencing the room. Sixty expectant pairs of eyes focused on me. “What about the opening?” Nechai said. “You can do the opening, can’t you?”

Maybe. I tried to remember the move Brenda had taught me opening night. I thought I could do it. But if I did, would that satisfy Nechai?

It had to, because really, what more could she ask of me?

I held out my arms, prompting Nechai to give me space. I'd do the opening, and then I'd ask for the money, and then I'd get myself out of here.

The patrons clapped, and I admit, a big smile spread across my face. The genuine appreciation—from total strangers—this was why she did it. This was why Fausten put up with the likes of Nechai.

I bent my knees, trying to keep them together and as ladylike as possible as I crouched to the floor. I crossed one foot over the other and slowly swirled to standing, undulating my arms and moving my hips. My balance was a little off, but hopefully everyone would blame that on inebriation and not the fact that I'd only ever done this once before. I finished with my arms in a high V.

The patrons stared in silence.

Oh, right. I popped my knee and said, "Shuhga."

Nechai clapped, slowly and alone.

"That's not the opening," said the nasal voice. "That hasn't been the opening in years."

I dropped my arms and scanned the room. None of the faces were friendly. I looked for Conlin, for a rescue, but he was gone, and Guy just stood behind the bar, biting his thumb and looking sorry for me. And Nechai. Shoulders back. Chin high. Her face held a dash of pity but mostly offered a vindicated smirk.

I ran for the stairs.

"Wait." It was Nechai, but I was done making a fool of myself to please her.

"Wait." Louder this time. Closer. She caught up to me on the stairs.

"You're messing with me," I said. "You knew I wasn't her."

"I had to be sure. And it was so funny the first time you performed it, out on the sidewalk, for that scalper."

I huffed and continued down the stairs.

"Stop."

Oh-okay—not gonna happen.

"I know what you want."

I kept going, but slower.

"I was here the night the lights burst. I know they blamed you."

That stopped me. Her choice of words. She knew they *blamed* me. Meaning she didn't think it was my fault. Meaning she, too, thought there was something abnormal about those lights.

Shoulders back, chin up, I put on my best Fausten Cotter as I looked back at her. She stood on the middle landing, tall and knowing in her peach dress.

"We need ninety thousand dollars to replace the sound and lights," I said.

She stepped toward me, down the stairs. "I'll make sure they're fixed for you."

"Thank you." I skipped down the rest of the way, already undoing my corset.

"But you have to do something for me."

I stopped, but I didn't look back. She had to know that I, Daphne James, had nothing to offer.

"I want to see Fausten."

"She's not here." I gestured to my outfit. "Why do you think I'm doing this?"

She shook her head, stepping closer. "That's not why."

"Then why?"

Nechai had an energy about her that I didn't want to be alone with, but I held my ground as she stepped closer, closer. She showed me her hand, her empty palm, and then, slowly, she lifted my veil.

She said, "It's impressive, really."

"What is?"

She took off her blue-tinted glasses, and I flinched. Her eyes were so light green they were practically yellow.

(angel—)

Demon's eyes.

I shivered and tried to step back, but she gripped me by the chin and turned my head from side to side. "Your glamour."

For a second I thought she meant something akin to fairy glamour—

(she does)

—but she must've meant that my makeup looked glamorous, because nothing else made sense.

Except I wasn't wearing makeup. Not really, not like Petty did Fausten's. I didn't know how, not to mention I couldn't afford it. I could barely afford food.

Ninety grand...

"Tell you what," I said. "Tell Conlin you'll pay for the lights, and I'll give you a tour backstage."

Nechai shook her head. "Tour first."

"But I already told you: Fausten's not here."

"Oh, she's here," said the creepy fan. "She's never not here. If I'm wrong, you'll still get what you need. But tour first."

CHAPTER 40

DAPHNE

I yelled up the stairs for Guy. A second later, he popped his head over the banister.

"Nechai wants a tour," I said.

Guy started to speak but stopped, like something had stolen his breath. Then, with effort, "*Okay.*"

"You okay?" I asked.

He nodded and stepped out of view.

I didn't know what to make of that exchange. Nechai looked like she didn't know what to make of it either, and our shared puzzlement made her slightly less creepy. I figured I'd be okay alone with her. Besides, alone with the creepy fan or not, a ten-minute tour was bound to be the easiest ninety grand I'd ever make.

We pulled open the house doors and followed my flashlight beam down the aisle to the stage.

"So," I said. "What do you want to see?"

I admit, I wanted to find Fausten. I wanted to see her out of character, absorb more of her secrets, ask her how she managed to hold her pose when she fell. But as Nechai brushed past me, making my arm tingle with creeps, I hoped for Fausten's sake she wasn't here.

Nechai climbed the stairs to the stage and veered right, into the wing. The walls whispered beneath her fingers.

"If you're looking for a light switch, they don't work." I'd offered her a flashlight, but she'd declined it, and she insisted on wearing those blue-tinted glasses.

A light switch clicked.

And down in the hall of dressing rooms, a glow flickered to life.

"She's this way," Nechai said, and she descended the steps to the hallway.

"There's nothing down there but Petty's office," I said, remaining on the stage. The stage was safe. The stage was viewable from the ballroom by the benefactors. "The rest of the building's pretty boring, really. Want to go back?"

At the bottom of the stairs, Nechai looked left, toward the greenroom, then right, toward the six dressing rooms.

I said, "You can check the greenroom if you want, but I don't have keys to the dressing rooms." Conlin unlocked them only upon hefty deposit. Refundable, to inhibit vandalism.

Nechai walked toward the dressing rooms. When she didn't come back, I descended the stairs just enough to peek into the hallway.

Its overhead lights dimmed and brightened in a languid slither, their filaments hissing with unnatural energy.

Nechai was standing before the third dressing room door. She had her hand splayed as if feeling for heat, and she was mumbling something, her tone disarming. Like she was luring a nuisance animal with a poisoned morsel.

After a moment, her hand relaxed and she walked to the fourth door, her steps slow and deliberate.

I stayed on the stairs. No way was anything coming between me and the only exit. Nechai probably wouldn't try anything—I'd told Guy about the tour—but I wasn't chancing it. Rich guys usually got off scot-free. A rich gal probably wouldn't get charged at all.

Nechai splayed her palm, checking the fourth door. When her hand relaxed, I told her the next room was Petty's, hoping she'd speed up her process, but she checked it anyway. Whatever. One more door and we could go.

Nechai splayed her fingers, checking the last door. I counted ten Mississippis, waiting for… I don't know. A twitch in her fingers? A hitch in her voice?

"She in there?" I asked, knowing she wasn't. If Fausten were anywhere, she'd be in her room upstairs.

Not that I'd share that information with Nechai.

Nechai grabbed the knob.

And the door opened.

A dozen flies buzzed out and hovered in a figure eight between the room and the hallway's last overhead light.

Nechai surveyed the doorway like the room might be booby-trapped, then looked back at me and smirked.

"She's in there?" I said. If she was, I had to know. I bounded down the stairs and met Nechai at the end of the hall.

"After you," she said.

The doorway looked safe enough to me. I peeked my head in.

The room was mostly dark, but tea lights on a massage table gave it a glow. And an energy. I stepped one foot inside.

Placed among the tea lights was a box of vials similar to the ones Petty sold in the lobby, except they were empty and unlabeled. With another step, I was fully in the room.

Pop.

I jumped. "What was that?"

Standing beyond the doorway, beyond the edge of candlelight, Nechai raised an eyebrow in a satisfied smirk. She nodded at something behind me.

A love seat.

Someone was sitting on that love seat.

Someone with long dark hair and a short white dress.

"Fausten?"

Fausten Cotter sat on the couch with her hands in her lap. One hand held an empty vial; the other, a long, flickering candle. I blew it out. She didn't object.

"Fausten?"

I touched her shoulder. She tipped onto her side, and her arm jutted out at an awkward angle. I grabbed her hand to check her pulse. Her skin looked ashy and dull, and it had too much give. My fingers dug into something slimy.

"*Ewgh.*"

Noxious vapors rose, thick and putrid, from the wound. I held my hand to my nose and leaned closer. Fausten's hand was—*Oh, wow.*

Inflamed skin surrounded an oil slick of violets, beiges, and blacks. Purple blotches mixed with pus and blisters. Something like bacteria popped and cracked as it dined on Fausten's skin, a lot of it already black with death.

My stomach queased, and yet I watched a finger—mine—press down and deep within her wound. The necrosis oozed, discharging a rancid fluid. Like dirty water. Dripping.

But no blood. Just viscous, oozing, peeling...flaking...

I passed out and fell forward, coming to as my mouth bumped Fausten's ulcer. I dropped her hand and heaved, but I could still taste it. Its sweet, pungent smell lingered on my tongue. I had kissed her hand. I had kissed Fausten Cotter's rotting abscess.

"How was it?" Nechai asked from the doorway.

I backed away from the smell and tried to leave the room, but my head—the earworm—it took on the weight of my brain's mass in gold. I lurched for the doorway and stumbled into the jamb. I leaned against the frame. My head. So heavy. I slid down the wood until my forehead smacked the ground.

Nechai stepped over me and into the room. "Amateur, Fausten. Like you didn't even try."

Fausten Cotter still lay on her side. She didn't respond. She didn't even move.

Nechai knelt before her and propped her upright, brushed the hair from her face.

"Look at you. Were you hoping to take *my* ingredient?" She took Fausten's vial and candle. "I brought my own supplies, but I do like these." She sniffed the candle. "Beeswax. You *were* listening."

Nechai set the items aside and picked up Fausten's hand. She inspected it closely.

"Is this why you gave Daphne the amulet?" she said. "You're decomposing, so you give it away? Or are you decomposing *because* you gave it away, because of what's on it now? What *is* on it now? And why give it to her?"

Nechai glanced over her fabric-draped shoulder at me, at my cheek still pressed to the linoleum, my arms buried beneath me.

"You know, I used to feel sorry for people in your situation," she said to me, her tone revealing that she still did, "people who probably wouldn't stay on their current path if they could see where it was taking them. But I've learned that even when I warn people about something they're obsessed with doing, they keep doing it. They think that since they're now aware of the problem, they'll avoid it. And sometimes they do. But even then they always encounter something else that's just as undesirable."

I glanced at Fausten, still motionless on the couch, seemingly staring at the tip of her own nose.

"Because potential consequences aren't even a reliable destination, never mind a reliable compass," Nechai continued. "The true compass is the immediate emotional feedback. In your case, I'm guessing you've been feeling a lack of control. That's a tough one to navigate. But you should know that if you act from that place, you'll feel even less control later."

She sighed a rueful snort. "But you won't remember this conversation, will you?"

I wasn't sure I was experiencing it now. The earworm didn't just hold me down; it veiled my eyes and clouded my mind. The scene had a haze, like a movie's dream sequence.

Not that I would be walking away from all the progress I'd made and could still make with Andy, with my life, even if I did happen to remember Nechai's advice. She was probably right about that.

"No," Nechai said, answering her own question. "She wouldn't want you to remember her like this, not like this. She wouldn't want you remembering me either." She smirked—then narrowed her eyes. "But you're here because Fausten wants you here. Why?"

She turned her gaze back to Fausten. "You stopped Guy from interfering. And Petty—was he too weak-willed to help? Was Daphne supposed to fill in for him? So where's Petty now? Waiting next door for us to finish?"

Nechai stilled, as if listening for something other than the soft crackle of the microbial ecosystem thriving on Fausten's hand.

"Or did you just make another mistake?" Nechai smirked and taunted her. "Damn those who force guarantees."

Nechai stood, then looked down at me again. "Good luck, Daphne. But whatever happens, don't feel too bad about it. We're all still learning to use the compass, and no one arrives without hitting a few surprises along the way, bad and good." She faced Fausten and sighed. "Not even me."

Nechai pulled up the skirt of her dress and unvelcroed something black from around her thigh. She unrolled it—a wrap, the kind that holds art brushes—and selected three items.

First, a small electronic device. She set it on the couch, next to Fausten, and pushed a button.

"Friday, February twenty-first, nine forty-two p.m. Basement of L'Aornum Theatre. Twenty-five-year-old female. Incorrupt corpse."

Second, an empty vial. She removed the lid and set it aside.

"Decomposition centers at the knuckle of her left ring finger, about three inches in diameter. Believe her ringsel became external to the body at an unknown time and was recently removed, likely within the last two weeks."

Third, something long, slender, and silver. She touched its tip to a candle and set the torch aflame.

"Am attempting to release the subject's oil," Nechai said, "and my sister."

Nechai began to chant. With the vial in one hand and the torch in the other, she raised her arms, and she chanted, her refrain growing louder with every repeat.

And the room stirred.

The earworm slept in the folds of my brain, but when something stirred, it cracked its cocoon.

Something stirred, and Fausten stirred, too. Her head tipped back, and her jaw fell open, and smoke rose from the gape of her mouth: it was sentient and silver like my hallucinated ghost, only denser, brighter—

Madder.

It flashed with light and writhed as if trapped. It didn't want to come, but Nechai didn't care. The ghost thinned and stretched and filled itself in, filled up the room, as Nechai forced it to rise, forced it to rise with her chant.

Nechai's words never made sense, but when the roar came, I understood. The ghost roared, but not to life. It roared from death. It roared with protest. It roared in revolt.

"YRAAAH!"

And Nechai chanted louder.

The ghost kept screaming, and I screamed too, at a knifing pain in my skull. Like metal to a magnet, the earworm had been summoned—but it bellowed against bone. It was trapped.

The ghost, filled out now, towered above us. A piece of its haze flashed bright.

"I see you," Nechai cried. "I see you, but where's the rest of her? How is she hiding the rest?"

The piece broke free, and Nechai's chanting hitched.

Like a firefly, the piece swirled around her, flashing to the beat of her now-whispered chant. Nechai closed her eyes and pressed her cheek to her own shoulder, as if cuddling the dimming light, embracing it until it faded, until it was gone.

"Goodbye," she said.

The smoke-ghost started to shrink.

"You're not fighting!" Nechai said, and she renewed the force of her chant. "You have to resist me, Fausten! You have to rage!"

The smoke-ghost drained with leisurely control back into

Fausten's mouth. Her mouth closed—and the weakened earworm stopped struggling. Its bold-faced bravado was gone now, I could tell, and it was tired. I was tired.

"Subject's oil suspected to be incomplete," Nechai said, sounding disappointed, "but still revealing"—she knelt at Fausten's feet—"and still gratifying to take."

She tipped the torch to Fausten's chin.

The flame flickered, lapping at Fausten's jawline as Nechai rolled the flame...rolled the flame...charring Fausten's skin.

I couldn't trust my eyes, but when the stench came, my nostrils flared. The stench burned, flavoring the air with a metallic tang, like long-dead liver barbecuing over copper coins. Sizzling.

Drip.

"Oh, yes." Nechai sniffed the vial. I couldn't fathom why. I held my breath, and still the stench of burning flesh and rancid oil permeated my pores.

"These days I only get what comes in," she said. "Worthless disease usually. Sometimes an accident. Never anything this potent."

Drip.

She sniffed again. I thought I would hurl. "Mmmm. It's got a certain auspicious zest to it. The secretions appear glittery, almost luminous. Maybe even better than a pregnant suicide."

Drip.

She inhaled and sighed. "Yes. The hint of peaches cutting through the typical odor. I'll know for certain with further testing."

Fausten sat there, saying nothing, letting Nechai roll the flame against her black and blistering chin.

Back and forth, back and forth.

Drip.

Drip.

Drip.

CHAPTER 41

DAPHNE

Someone shook my shoulder. "Ms. James?"

I lifted my head. Saliva crusted the corner of my mouth and coated my hand.

Conlin's baritone said, "You feelin' okay?"

I stretched out the stiffness and rubbed my face. There were sleep creases on my cheeks.

I was in the ballroom, sitting at a table for two. My side hurt where the edge had pressed into my ribs.

But wasn't I just with someone? Yeah, they'd wanted a tour. I'd taken her backstage, and then… "How'd I get here?"

Conlin set a glass of water in front of me. "Vargas found you in one of the dressing rooms."

That's right. The last one was open. There were candles. I'd stepped inside, and then…

"He said his manicure chemicals spilled," Conlin continued, "that the fumes must've knocked you out. Dr. Chaiprasit came to right away, but you—"

"Have been snoring for an hour."

I knew that voice and yet I didn't recognize it. It had never before criticized me without a note that said it was joking. That note was missing now.

Sitting two tables away from me, Andy held my suit, flats, and backpack in his lap. He finished his drink and stood. "What do I owe you?"

Conlin waved him off, but Andy's question made my heart pound. I sat up. "Where's Nechai?"

"Gone," Conlin said, dismantling a table. "Show finished twenty minutes ago."

"Did she pay for the lights?"

Conlin pulled a piece of paper from his inside pocket and tugged the ends, unfolding it with a pop. It was a check.

"Ninety grand?" I asked.

"Not quite."

"But she said she'd pay for the lights," I said, reaching for it. "How am I supposed to come up with the rest?"

Conlin slid the check toward me. A spidery hand had written it out to L'Aornum Theatre in the amount of $90,600.00. I grimaced. Ninety thousand would pay for the lights, but that left—"Only six hundred for the show?"

"The show got its own check. Checksss," Conlin said, all teeth. "We can start casting soon."

The show got its own check? The amount of *this* check was more than we needed for equipment. I read the check again, this time noticing the memo: *for lights and the stand-in*.

Conlin grabbed the check and put it back in his pocket. "Should cover your sick days, hmm?"

My whole body relaxed against the chair, except for my cheeks, which tightened into a grin. I was balanced again in the money department. Hallelujah.

"So, can we go?" Andy asked. He picked up my stuff and held out a hand, offering to help me up.

Conlin squeezed my shoulder. "You did good tonight, Ms. James. Go home. Get some rest."

I took Andy's hand. He pulled away from me and flicked his fingers. "Gross. What's on you? Drool?"

"Probably," I said with a laugh, too relieved by the check to feel offended by Andy's tone. I wiped my hand on the tablecloth, but whatever was on me, it wasn't drool. It left a brownish-red stain. An image of something—

(rotten)

—flashed in my mind, but it vanished before I could put my finger on it.

Or was it—

(fausten)

—on my finger?

"What about Fausten?" I asked, grasping at the fleeting thought.

"She did *Strings*," Conlin said. "I've never seen a good marionette performance—I was thinking we'd do aerial rope or Spanish web—but this..." He shook his head in awe, a reluctant acknowledgment that as much trouble as his star caused him, she was worth it.

But my fleeting thought had left behind a nagging feeling, and Conlin's answer wasn't helping it go away. I had the sense that only one thing would.

"Can I see her?" I asked.

Conlin puzzled his brows at me as he rolled a cart of folded tables into their closet. Fausten insisted on retiring to her bedroom immediately following each performance, and she never received visitors. I knew that. By now, everybody knew that. Still—

"I want to see her."

"Then don't be sick tomorrow," he said. "You still owe me the rest of your advance."

Not a problem. I wanted to check on Fausten. Out of concern more than jealousy, so there was probably no threat of me hallucinating. I should be fine. I'd be here tomorrow.

Outside, Andy helped me into the passenger seat of his Jeep, slammed the door behind me, and stalked around the back. When the driver-side door opened, the air wasn't the only chilly thing that got in.

"What's wrong?" I asked.

"Nothing."

He slammed the door and jammed his key in the ignition, turning it too far for too long, making the starter grind. He flipped a bitch, and my head slammed against the window.

No, nothing. Nothing at all. Just that he'd brought Ericka to deliver my shoes, and now he seemed mad about having to pick me up. He'd never before complained about having to pick me up.

I smoothed my short skirt. I was still wearing Fausten's poster dress, and I wasn't the only one who thought my legs were my best feature. I crossed them and gave Andy my best inviting stare. "So? What do you think?"

"Cute." His tone was off, but at a stoplight, he flipped the ruffles, and the corner of his mouth rose. Good enough smile for me. I leaned toward him for a makeup hug, but he pushed me forward, pressing my chest to the dash, and tugged at something beneath me. I shifted to one hip. He pulled the item out from under me and tossed it in the back.

I frowned at him. "What was that?"

Andy tapped the steering wheel and checked his side mirror.

I leaned through the seats and felt around—*there*. I held it up to the streetlights passing by the window. It was a pink scarf. Mint-green flowers decorated the ends.

We arrived at our apartment building, but instead of turning right, into the parking garage, Andy pulled alongside the front entrance. He kept the engine running and his eyes on the road.

"What are we doing?" I asked.

"I have to take it back."

"Tonight?"

He rolled his shoulders and rubbed his neck. Then he flared. "Sometime. What do you want me to do?" He snatched the scarf from me and flung it into the back cargo space, then looked out his window and sighed.

I opened the door and hopped out. He was gone before I'd cleared the awning.

Upstairs, I tried to sleep, but I kept wondering where she lived, this Ericka. Would Andy just drop off her stuff or would he stay awhile?

I got up and tried to busy myself to keep from picturing them together. I spaced the chairs around the kitchen table and pushed them in. I recycled the cans and put the glasses in the dishwasher. I checked for expired stuff in the fridge and made a grocery list.

And I did the math. Andy and I would graduate in fifteen weeks. I had just under four months to get him to propose and invite me to Chicago.

I folded the blanket on the couch and fluffed the pillows. I found all the remotes and lined them up on the end table. I scrubbed the toilet. I cleaned the mirror.

Four months. A lot could happen in four months. A little less than four months, but still, it was enough. It had to be. I could convince him in four months.

I picked up his socks and tossed them in the hamper. I put his shoes in the closet. I pushed in his dresser drawers. I picked up his books and put them in his backpack.

And that's where I found it. It was in his backpack, sticking out of the pocket meant for airline tickets. Appropriate really.

It was a letter. The envelope had been opened with a letter opener instead of a finger. Andy and I didn't have a letter opener. I didn't want to know where Andy had found a letter opener. The letter itself was a single sheet of paper, the thick kind with fabric threads. The letterhead read, in embossed silver: *Grahame Tucker Consulting*.

Dear Mr. McBride,

We are pleased to offer you an internship with Grahame Tucker Consulting for the spring quarter.

While this internship is unpaid, we will work with you to obtain academic credit through your university and provide

> a stipend to assist with living expenses. We hope your experience this spring will help you select the department you'd like to work with permanently before you begin your new, full-time position next fall.
>
> To accept this internship, please complete the enclosed form and return it to the address above by March 10.

Enclosed form? I rubbed the thick piece of paper between my fingers, willing it to become two sheets. It didn't. I checked the envelope. Empty. I riffled through Andy's backpack. Nothing but notebook paper.

I sat on my heels and stared at the offensive letter. It was dated February 1. Andy had received this internship offer three weeks ago. And yet he'd never mentioned that even though he'd already committed to leaving for Chicago after graduation, Grahame Tucker wanted him to leave me even sooner, at the end of winter term. In a month.

The front doorknob rattled. I took a deep breath and stood. The door creaked open. Footsteps padded on the carpet. I stayed where I was, watching the bedroom door and waiting.

Andy pushed the door open and threw his coat on the bed. He noticed me and jumped.

"You scared me," he said.

"Not as much as you're scaring me."

His brow furrowed, and his gaze traveled down my arm, to my hand. I held up the letter.

He sighed and sat on the bed. I faced him but remained standing. Chin high, shoulders back. My ankle shook. He looked everywhere but at me. He was probably waiting for me to lay into him, to yell, to scream. Not this time. I licked my lips. I relaxed my jaw. I blew out calming breaths.

Andy's toes wiggled, creating waves in the fabric of his Nikes. He was nervous. I didn't know if that was good for me or bad.

"I don't even know if I'm taking it," he said.

And so it began. Deep breath in, calm voice out. "Why wouldn't you?"

I wanted him to say because he didn't want to leave me. Because he might not be sure about marriage, but he was sure about me. I wanted him to mention me. To mention us.

"I'd have to start four days after finals," he said. "If I don't do the internship, I'd start in the fall. I'd have the whole summer off."

Rational, but unsatisfactory. Deep breath in. Slow breath out.

He half smiled. "Plus, Sturdivant is doing his seminar spring term."

I bit the fleshy nob at the corner of my mouth—it always made me look pissed, but that was too bad—and waited for him to say more. But Andy relaxed, like he'd gotten out everything he'd wanted to say.

"So you just want to goof off for another six months?" It came out more hostile than I'd intended, but it was useful. All Andy did was shrug. A concession. He didn't want to fight with me. "So you're not taking the internship?"

"I don't know yet."

"They want your response by March tenth. That's two weeks away. You'd leave in four, Andy. *Four weeks.*"

He winced and rubbed his neck.

"Where's the form?"

He got off the bed like he was grateful for a reason to move. He opened his marketing book, took out the form, and handed it to me. Andy's tiny capital print covered the page in blue ink.

"Looks to me like you want to go."

He shrugged and kept his voice down. "There's only two internships. I'd get a head start against the other hires."

I set the form on the nightstand. "So you're taking it?"

"I told you: I don't know."

He shifted his weight, then sat on the bed and wiped his palms on his knees. His jeans had an ink spot. By the time I asked my next question, the ink had blurred, becoming two separate spots.

"What about me?"

"You?"

I choked on my stupidity. "Forget it." I hugged my arms, but I wasn't enough. I grabbed a pillow off the bed and fled to the living room.

Andy followed me out. "Is this the marriage thing again?"

I flopped on the couch and hugged the pillow. Still not enough. I wrapped myself up in the couch blanket.

"I told you, Daph. It's got nothing to do with you."

"Yeah, nothing."

"Yeah. Nothing. I don't want to get married because I don't want to get divorced. We're not married now and things are fine. Usually."

"But you're leaving."

"I don't know that yet."

"I do."

He leaned against the wall and fidgeted with the lampshade. The light blinked out. He twisted the bulb, turning it back on.

"Answer me this," I said. "If you leave..."

But I couldn't finish the question. Andy sat next to me, picking up my feet and setting them on his lap. He had to know what I wanted to hear even if I couldn't bring myself to beg for it. I wanted to know that he wanted me with him. I wanted to know that I meant something to him, that my presence in his life mattered. He had to know that I wanted his reassurance.

"'If I leave' what?"

But he wasn't going to give it.

I pulled my knees to my chest. I didn't want anyone so willing to watch me, to *make* me, break touching my feet.

We sat like that for a long time. I thought he'd fallen asleep, but then the couch cushion shifted. Andy turned on the TV, found a rerun of my favorite sitcom, and set the remote beside me. Then he walked into the bedroom and shut the door.

CHAPTER 42

DAPHNE - 15 days left

Andy was up when I got up, but other than grunting acknowledgments at each other, we didn't talk. I futzed around the apartment getting ready for work.

Conlin had an event booked that afternoon. He had success renting the theater for birthday parties. He'd play whatever movie you wanted so long as you brought it with you. Marvel and DC and Pixar, oh my. I corralled kids, served pizza, and made popcorn—activities just challenging enough to keep my mind and mood off Andy—while Guy wowed the kids with magic tricks and Petty made balloon animals. After the party, Guy prepped the stage for the show and Petty and I prepped the lobby.

I still hadn't seen Fausten, but it seemed my concern for her had replaced my jealousy. I hadn't hallucinated (or even had any bold thoughts) since the Ericka-shoe incident—and I wasn't dreading that I would. My mind was preoccupied with something else, a word that made my nose wrinkle.

"...festering."

"What?" My heart pounded in my ears. *That's the word.*

"I said she's resting." Petty put down the red paper he'd been cutting into fourths and crossed his arms, daring me to say something snide about Fausten always resting.

I eyed his pile of cut paper. Teaser flyers for the next show. They remained static, producing no smoke nor any other scary business.

Good deal. I resumed cleaning the popcorn machine. "She's performing tonight, though, right?"

"Doesn't she always?"

I asked Conlin if I could watch the show. It had occurred to me last night, when I was too sad to sleep, that it hadn't been me that had gotten the smile out of Andy; it had been the PuB's skirt. And it hadn't been just any smile he'd given me either; it had been the look he'd given the PuB's poster the night he'd told me he'd marry a girl like Fausten.

She still held his interest. And I still hadn't seen her perform.

I needed to see her. Even if it meant sitting in the back with a barf bag, I needed to see her show.

Conlin couldn't believe I'd never seen it, but he still said no.

"There's no one else to man the lobby." It was something he'd insisted upon ever since the sound and lights had blown.

"How about next week?" I asked. "Can I watch her next week?"

"We'll see."

I settled for seeing Fausten in the lobby, but she didn't do Aphrodite. I asked Conlin why not.

"Vargas says the clamshell's busted."

So I decided to risk peeking in at Fausten's act. I spent most of the first half of the show figuring out how to turn off all the lobby lights so that no one would notice when I opened the doors. But after intermission, my head felt like the earworm was shooting cannonballs from my eye sockets. I spent the whole of Fausten's act lying on a bench with a damp paper towel on my forehead.

My head cleared as the house erupted in applause. The doors burst open, and Fausten's fans poured out, sporting huge grins and wowed expressions. As they filed out onto the sidewalk, I handed them the red teaser flyers and asked about Fausten's act.

"She's so good. All that stuff she does with the smoke."

"It's uncanny. For an hour I'm in a fugue."

"It's like a dream."

"She changed her costume," said a girl.

I grabbed her tiny shoulder. Her parents continued outside, unaware that I'd taken hold of their child. She gave me a stranger-danger look.

"What did she change?" I asked.

The girl's wary expression became a gap-toothed grin, and she spirited her fingers. "Gloves," she said. "White ones with pink and mint green."

"What about her face?"

"What do you mean?"

I rubbed my chin. I didn't know. "Did it...did it look okay?"

"Yeah." Her tone said I was crazy for suggesting otherwise, and her mother reclaimed her before I could ask her anything else.

After the last patron left, Petty and I swept the house. I asked him about Fausten's costume addition.

"She's reinventing herself," he said. "Like Madonna."

"A pair of gloves does not a reinvention make," I said, but I did wonder if reinvention was her secret.

Petty exaggerated a sigh. "She's known as the Pin-up Bride," he said. "She's reinventing herself within the context of her image. Okay?"

"What's wrong with her hands?"

Petty reached his lanky arms between the seats to remove an elusive piece of trash. "Nothing."

"I saw it."

(festering)

I looked at my own hand, remembering the goo that had covered it after the benefit.

"Did you?" Petty tossed the cup in the garbage. "Then you tell me. What's wrong with her hand?"

(festering)

The word expanded in my mind, becoming pus and rotting flesh.

Petty maneuvered the broom. "I'm waiting."

"A sore." I swallowed.

Petty stopped sweeping and glowered at me. "A sore?"

"A big one. On her"—I twisted the cabochon ring with my thumb—"on her hand."

"And you saw this when—last night? You mean the night you stood in for Fausten because she was running late, as in *not here for you to see*? Wasn't this the same night you *passed out* due to fumes and I had to carry your weak ass upstairs? Is *that* when you saw this so-called sore?"

I stared at him, trying to remember. I'd given Nechai a tour...entered a dressing room, the last one. There were candles and... "Is there furniture in the last dressing room?"

"How should I know?"

I thought I remembered seeing a couch or maybe a massage table, but seeing Fausten was still at best a feeling and not a memory. The last memory I had of her was from the night she'd posed with Andy, all stunning and incomparable. It was like my earworm, my belief that Andy wanted someone like Fausten because she was the perfect ideal, had been nurtured to a point that any contrary information about her couldn't break through the barrier between subconscious and conscious.

Petty continued sweeping. "She's a brat," he said. "Is that what you want to hear? She's wearing gloves and not cleaning these seats because she's a spoiled theater brat who does what she wants. Happy?"

I scratched my chin. "Is her face okay?"

"Fine, Daphne, beautiful as always. Why do you ask?"

"Can I see her?"

"She's—"

"Resting. Right."

Before I left for the night, I asked Conlin if I could see inside the dressing rooms. They each had a dressing table and a vanity chair, the last room no different from the first four. No signs of candles, no signs of use.

On the way to return Conlin's key, I went backstage to the elevator, thinking I'd sneak up to Fausten's room. I'd forgotten the elevator took a key card, but it didn't matter. The slider had been replaced with a keypad. Fausten's third floor now required an access code.

When I got home, Andy was out somewhere. I missed him but figured I should get used to an empty apartment. Andy would take the internship; I knew he would. And even if he asked me to go with him, I'd still have to stay here during spring term to fulfill the requirements of my scholarship so that it didn't become a loan. But that was okay. We could survive a few months. What we couldn't survive was Andy accepting the internship while deferring his decision about me for another day.

If Andy accepted the internship without deciding about me, then I would decide for him.

Lights off, eyes closed, ears open. I was long in bed, organizing Harry's box of mishmash crayons, when Andy got home. I turned out the light and pulled the blanket over my head. He banged around the living room for a while, then tiptoed into the bedroom. His pants flumped to the floor. He slid under the covers and stretched out on his stomach. His foot hit mine. He pulled it back, crossed his arms under his pillow, and turned away from me.

But at least he wasn't sleeping on the couch.

CHAPTER 43

DAPHNE - 14 days left

The next morning, I woke with an idea. An oldie, but a goodie. Maybe not as good as those bolder ideas I'd had four or five weeks ago, the kind that had gotten me moved in with Andy, but still. It was something to *do*.

I hopped in the shower, shaved, moisturized, styled, preened. I put on Andy's favorite blue top and jeans. I looked pretty, but not like I was trying too hard. A natural beauty. Effortless. Like Fausten Cotter.

And then I made bacon. Andy couldn't resist bacon. He padded out of the bedroom like he hadn't slept well.

"I made breakfast." Tone sweet. Smile in place. "You want some?"

He never looked up from the carpet, but he bobbed his head on the way to the bathroom. Good enough for me. I made up two plates and sat at the table. A few moments later, Andy pulled out a chair and sat with me. So far so good.

I let him eat in peace. This was only morning one of my idea: Operation Perfect Fiancée. I had approximately twelve more mornings to go—fifteen if Andy PDF'd his internship acceptance form, instead of mailing it. I could pace myself. Things would go better if I paced myself.

When I finished eating, I washed my plate, put it away, and cleaned the cooking mess I'd made. See? Wouldn't I make a good life partner?

Andy rinsed his plate and left it in the sink. "Thank you," he said.

"You're welcome." *Ha!*

I made a show of gathering my backpack, purse, and keys.

"You leaving?" he asked.

"I was gonna study at the library."

He nodded. I waited for him to say more, but it looked like I'd have to carry this one. I kept it simple.

"I don't work tonight. Conlin's having the new sound and lights installed. You want to watch a movie?"

"Yeah. I'll get one."

We still hadn't looked at each other, not really, not in the eye. He looked at me now, and he smiled the sheepish version of his cockeyed smile. I dropped my stuff, crossed the room, and buried my head in his chest.

I was pacing my strategy, not my affection.

Andy wrapped his arms around me, kissed the top of my head, and rested his cheek on my hair. I could've stayed this way forever...but I made sure I pulled away first.

That night, along with a movie, Andy brought home Thai food. I love Thai food; Andy, not so much. Another score for Operation Perfect Fiancée. But I couldn't savor the success. Andy still hadn't said anything about taking the internship. Or me.

We started the movie with a foot of couch between us, but after getting up multiple times for remotes, napkins, drinks, we were thigh by thigh, me leaning into him, him draping his arm around my shoulders.

I don't remember what we watched. I closed my eyes and rode the rise and fall of his chest, listening to him breathe, memorizing the feel of his arm around me, the side of his body warming mine. He was real now, but in two weeks he could be nothing more than a memory.

CHAPTER 44

DAPHNE - 8 days left

It was Saturday again. Already.

OPF had started out well, but Day One had been a Sunday, not real life. On Monday, real life had continued. I'd spent all week going to class, going to work, and trying to study in between. Andy had wanted to study too, so at night we'd sit on the couch and read our respective textbooks in companionable silence. It was nice, but I didn't feel any closer to receiving his commitment.

I missed those bolder ideas.

I stood at the bathroom sink, taking my anxiety out on my teeth. Six days gone and nothing to show for it; six (maybe nine) days left. And I had to waste yet another night going to work.

I asked Andy if he wanted to come to the show.

"Fausten's got a new costume." I hubba-hubba'd my eyebrows. If Andy came, Conlin might finally let me watch Fausten's act.

Andy gave me stink eye. Now that I thought about it, he hadn't mentioned his crush since before the amateur contest. Guess I shouldn't have mentioned her either. Minus one point for Operation Perfect Fiancée.

"Sorry," I said. "I just wanted to hang out together. I might lose you in a few weeks."

Andy's acceptance form still lay on the nightstand. At some point in the next six to nine days he'd turn it in or throw it away. But he'd turn it in, of course he'd turn it in. And that was fine. I didn't care which path he chose. I just wanted his decision to include me.

Either way, I would know in six to nine days.

"I can't tonight," he said, letting my comment slide. He knew he was delaying his decision unnecessarily. Another score for Operation Perfect Fiancée. "It's Tyler's bachelor party."

This was news to me. I'd thought Tyler and Madison weren't getting married until June, but I hadn't been keeping up with our friends very well. Maybe they'd changed the date. I played it cool, the perfect fiancée. "Right, the bachelor party. And where do the night's dalliances begin?"

Andy hunched his shoulders and made this super endearing, embarrassed face. "The Boobie Trap."

"Niiice," I said. "Just don't come back with glitter in your pants."

Work was work. Fausten didn't pose, and Conlin didn't get anyone to fill in for me, so I sat in the lobby while she performed.

I got another headache. Seemed the stress of Andy's indecision was putting a new twist on my Fausten Cotter earworm. I must've moped around looking pitiful about it too, because Conlin dismissed me before it was time to clean.

When I got home, the door was ajar. I peeked inside. Andy stood at the table, looking at his phone. I resisted the urge to ambush him with a hug and instead merely pushed the door open. He jumped at the squeak, then saw me and smiled.

"What are you doing here?" I asked. "Aren't there boobs to be seen?"

He shrugged. "I've seen nicer."

"Mm-hmm." Not true, not at this boob show at least, but I appreciated the implication. "Who you calling?"

He shrugged. "Thought you might want a ride."

"I got off early."

"I see that."

Andy set his phone on the table and stepped toward me, dragging his hand along the counter, smiling his cockeyed smile.

Maybe I don't need those bolder ideas.

I wanted to go to him, to meet him halfway, but this was a major score for Operation Perfect Fiancée.

I let him come all the way to me.

CHAPTER 45

DAPHNE - 5 days left

On Tuesday, I sat in Biology, listening to Professor Gordon click through slides. Midterm grades would post in fifteen minutes.

I wasn't worried anymore about my scholarship converting to a loan. Winter term was paid for and I could continue working at L'Aornum to pay for spring. I'd rethink this plan if I started hallucinating again, but so far I felt on the mend. As long as I received passing grades I'd graduate as scheduled and without a loan. And thank goodness.

That said, passing grades weren't enough. My grades had to shine, or I'd still face three problems.

First, my theater income only covered tuition. Andy bought almost everything else. I could probably live on oatmeal, theater birthday-party leftovers, and the free-food events they had on campus, but if my grades weren't good enough to reinstate my scholarship and the housing allowance that came with it, I'd be homeless in three weeks, assuming Andy accepted the internship. He still hadn't said either way, but he would. I knew he would.

I'd already started planning for it. Conlin had asked me to clean out the storeroom, but he hadn't specified how, and judging by the absence of Conlin-sized footprints in the decades-thick dust that covered everything (and only the one set of Guy's prints from when he'd rolled out the steam cleaner and which I had been stepping in myself to keep from kicking up said dust), no one knew what was in the storeroom, just that everything needed to go.

I didn't think Conlin would ever suspect I was selling it all. He'd watched in amused silence as I'd hefted garbage bags of old props to the van before, as far as he knew, driving around town to leave a deposit in all the local dumpsters. (I'd taken the lot to a prop house. They'd given me pennies per item, but what did I care?) On black-and-white-movie Monday, I'd taken pictures of some of the neater crap in the storeroom and posted it on Craigslist. Someone had already emailed me about the double-reel film projector. Goodbye oatmeal, hello rice and beans.

My second problem was that if my grades weren't good enough to rescue my scholarship, then they also wouldn't be good enough to dust off plan B and get me into med school. (Never mind that I wanted less than ever to go to med school.)

But the worst thing about bad grades? Andy's disappointment. We always shared our grades and supported each other, usually with a celebration because we did so well. Bad grades would validate Andy's concerns that I didn't have my shit together and might become like one of our moms.

The clock struck 9:30. With trembling fingers, I entered my ID and password into the student portal page and waited for my grades to load. And there they—*wait a minute.*

I thumbed my ring and squinted at the screen. Right name, right classes. This was undeniably my account. Guess those were my grades.

Maybe I'd use that Craigslist money for shoes.

Andy walked into the apartment just after I did, with a spring in his step.

"I take it you did well?" I said.

He dumped his bag on the kitchen counter like he was in a hurry.

"Average in accounting was a ninety-one, but Keiting still graded on a curve. Bastard." He opened the fridge and pulled out condiments. "You want a sandwich?"

I shook my head. The closer we got to his internship deadline, the less I wanted to eat. Grahame Tucker wanted Andy's acceptance by Monday. Andy would have to mail the form by Friday. Three days. Unless he PDF'd it the day it was due, then six days. But I had a feeling he'd decide sooner.

"Maybe half a sandwich." I leaned on the counter, expecting to hear about Andy's other classes and then be asked about mine. I couldn't wait. My grades would put to rest any concerns he had about me becoming a crazy flake.

I thumbed my ring, making rainbows on the wall. I liked this ring. This ring had appeared the weekend before midterms, and in addition to testing well, I'd raised ninety grand, gotten caught up in repaying Conlin my advance, lost some weight. My skin even had a dewy glow, and it was winter. The timing of the ring's arrival was mere coincidence, of course. Correlation, not causation. Still, I liked it. Fausten had her secrets; I liked pretending that this ring was—

(hers)

—mine.

Andy flipped the lid on the ketchup, looked at it funny, then put it back in the fridge and took out the mustard. He'd done the same thing with hot sauce and mayo.

"Something up?" I asked.

"What? No." He squirted mustard over the mayo, spread it evenly on the bread.

"O*kay*. So, how'd your other midterms go?"

"Good. Fine." He cut the lunch meat diagonally and placed the pieces precisely, edge to crusty edge.

"O*kay*. Well, aren't you gonna ask me how I did?"

He gave me a look of pity. "You sure you want me to?"

"Why wouldn't I?"

"Well..." His phone vibrated. He snatched it off the counter, looking relieved, and walked into the living room, turning his back to me to answer.

"I'm ready," he said. "See you then."

He hung up and came back into the kitchen. We met eyes. I quirked an eyebrow but didn't nag. The perfect fiancée.

He started toward the bathroom, then stopped and turned back to me. His arms hung limp at his sides.

"I'm going to a meeting," he said.

"Okay. What kind of meeting?"

"Informational." He rolled his neck and shoulders. "About internships."

My heart filled my throat. I swallowed it back down. "You decided to go."

"No, it's an informational meeting," he said. "I'm going to get information."

"So you can decide to go?"

He sighed and shut himself in the bathroom. We'd had a good weekend. Nothing forced, no special date. Just stayed in, relaxed, enjoyed our time together. Like an old married couple. I'd been hoping my good grades could segue into finalizing our plans. *Our* plans. Chicago had several med schools. If I continued to do this well, I could get into one. Or at least let Andy think so. We could move what we had going on in Portland to Chicago.

But not only was Andy leaning toward taking the internship, he apparently was so certain that I'd become a failure that he wasn't even going to ask me about my midterms. Like if he didn't ask me, then he wouldn't have to console me. Like he didn't want to care right now. Or ever. And definitely not forever-ever.

I pounded on the bathroom door. "You want information, Andy? I got a ninety-two in physics, a ninety-four in chemistry, and I aced biology."

He flushed and ran the water.

I backed against the counter, clutching my elbows.

The bathroom door opened. "Good job," he said, but he had that look again, that piteous look, and he walked past me to his sandwich. I squeezed my elbows, hugging myself, because Andy might never again.

He cut the sandwich and pushed half toward me, then leaned against the counter and took a quiet bite.

I couldn't eat mine. "Don't you need to go?"

His eyes flashed to me, then refocused on his sandwich. "I'm getting a ride."

"From who?"

"Ericka? You met her. The girl—"

"I know who she is." And I remembered how Andy had once said his internship was one of two. I laughed, but nothing was funny. "She got the other internship, didn't she?"

"What?" He swallowed. "No, not with Grahame Tucker. A different one." He took another bite.

I snorted. "But it's still in Chicago?"

"She just wants me to go so she'll know someone."

The intercom buzzed, announcing Chicago-bound Ericka's arrival, but Andy didn't move. He watched me, like he was waiting for my permission.

I said, "Better not keep us both waiting."

"She's just from marketing group."

"If you say so. Go," I added when he still hadn't moved.

He finished the last of his sandwich. I slid him my half, and he ate that too, then put the sandwich fixings away and went to brush his teeth.

The intercom buzzed again.

I said, "You want me to ask her up? No, better to meet her downstairs and keep us separated. Hurry up, then."

He came out of the bathroom wearing a pained look. He rifled through his backpack.

"Oh, I see. Making girls wait is part of your charm. Niiice. 'Cause that's not rude at all."

My phone rang. It was Brenda. I answered with a flirty tone, hoping to raise Andy's curiosity. "Hey, I was just thinking about you."

"Daphne?"

I giggled. "You're so funny. How *are* you?"

Andy slung his backpack over his shoulder and left the apartment without looking at me. I picked up the remote control and chucked it at the couch.

Brenda rambled in my ear about the happenings since I'd last talked to her, which had been forever ago, but I couldn't pay attention. I kept seeing Andy turning away from me to talk to Ericka. Andy brushing his teeth for Ericka. Andy going to Chicago with Ericka.

I went out to the balcony to see if I could watch Andy leave for a meeting with Ericka.

"Anyway." Brenda singsonged the word, interrupting my obsession. "I would've called sooner, but we've just been so busy."

"'We'? Oh, right. That guy you're seeing."

"Lame excuse, I know, but, Daph, there's something I need to tell you."

I gasped. I didn't actually think I'd see them together, but there they were: Andy climbed into a pink Bug with mint-green flowers on the hood.

I backed away from the rail and hit the sliding glass door. "Word of advice, Bren: treat plan B like it's plan A. Plan A is for spinsters." I threw myself on the couch and dug my nails into the cushion. "Hello?"

"So anyway," she said, "I hear you've been busy too, with the theater. That's why I called. The girls want to start the party at the theater."

"What party?"

Brenda sighed. "Madison's bachelorette party."

She said it like I should've already known. And maybe I should have, Tyler's party having happened the previous week and all.

"Why are they doing them so early?" I said. "I thought they weren't getting married until June."

"They're not. She's going to Italy next term."

"What about Tyler?"

Brenda grunted like I should've known this one, too, only now my ignorance was irritating. "He's graduating this term," she said. "He's going with her. Didn't Andy tell you?"

No, Andy had never told me about Tyler's romantic gesture. Or that his best friend would be abroad next term. Or that this development gave him yet another reason to spend spring in Chicago.

"So can you?" Brenda asked.

"Can I what?" Convince Andy to commit? Didn't seem like it. "Hello? Bren?"

I checked my phone. It still had power and minutes, but the call had disconnected. I thought Brenda would call right back, but she didn't. She emailed me the next day, asking me to book L'Aornum's ballroom for Friday.

I was throwing Madison a bachelorette party.

CHAPTER 46

DAPHNE - 2 days left

Friday night at L'Aornum. Guy and I stood in the ticket booth, peeking through the curtained window at the bachelorette and her party girls. They were huddled beneath the awning, shivering in their coats and heels. I'd get a thank-you, at most, for my hosting efforts tonight, but if Madison didn't have a good time, she'd complain to Tyler, who'd complain to Andy, which wouldn't be good for OPF. And OPF needed...something.

Despite our fight, Andy had come home within the hour. He'd set a handful of internship pamphlets on the kitchen table—where they remained, untouched—and sat on the couch to study. I was already on the couch, so it was all very encouraging. I handed him the remote so he could pick the background noise, and he said thanks. Score steady for OPF.

But now it was three days later, and our communication hadn't grown beyond gestures and one-word sentences. The only multiword sentence I'd kind of received was this afternoon, when he'd taken a call from Grahame Tucker's HR department on speaker. The recruiter had asked if Andy's form had gotten lost in the mail.

"I'll let you know by Monday," Andy said.

I had three more days.

"What's the holdup?" asked the recruiter, making no attempt to mask his irritation, which felt good. Really good. I might not have convinced Andy to stay (yet), but Ericka still hadn't convinced him to go, and not even his future employers could force his mind.

"The more you pressure me," Andy said, which surprised me—he was blunt sometimes, but not usually with professionals—"the less I'm ready to answer."

He looked up from his phone and we met eyes. I tried not to frown at him—he wasn't frowning at me; he looked tired at worst—but if his decision to go wasn't an easy yes, then by default it should be an easy no. That's just good life management.

Guy elbowed me and pointed through the crack in the ticket booth's curtain, at the bachelorette and her party of eight. "What about that one?" he said.

I glared at him. He'd groomed for the party. Instead of his grungy coveralls or musty Sherlock Holmes costume, he had on jeans that fit. They were clean too. So was his shirt. And he'd done something to make his head cuter.

"No," I said. "They're all taken except Sasha, the one in the blue, and she won't like you either."

Guy made a face like Blue would not only do, she'd change her mind. "So, you gonna let them in?"

Outside, Madison linked arms with Hannah and Jade. They, too, were engaged, and I didn't think that was a coincidence. Nor was her positioning under the awning. Its overhead light spotlit the night's leading lady, tightly flanked by her supporting cast and fawned over by her ensemble.

"Do I have to?" I said.

"I'll do it."

"No." I squeezed past Guy, into the foyer, and pushed open the front door. The squeeing started immediately. As did the stumbling and giggling. Great. They'd prefunked. I backed away, so they'd have one less thing to trip over, and tried to boost my mood to the level of squee. It was not easy.

"Ladies." Guy opened his arms wide. "Welcome to L'Aornum. Your party is in the ballroom upstairs. If you will just follow me."

"Anywhere," Jade whispered. The rest giggled and followed him closely. I brought up the rear, wondering if excessive eye-rolling counted as jealousy, 'cause if so, I was in danger of triggering a relapse. I still hadn't hallucinated since the Ericka-shoe incident, but having the girls here, having to host this party, this *bachelorette* party…

Madison was already testing my trigger.

"I'm the bride," she said. The girls had bypassed the party favors and torn straight for the costume racks we'd set up in the ballroom's back corner. Madison was now yanking at a purple dress also held by Sasha, who let go. The bachelorette stumbled backward, but she came up smiling, clutching the dress to her chest. "Where can we change?"

I started to point out the bathroom, but Guy said, "How about right there?"

Madison shrugged and took off her coat, flinging it at me, like it was my job to hang it for her. "So," she said, "is Fausten Cotter here yet?"

"Probably," I said.

"I can't wait to see her show," said Jade. The girls voiced their agreement. I secretly hoped to see it too, but Conlin still hadn't given me permission.

"You should go get her," Madison said, "She should hang out with us."

"No can do," Guy said from the bar. "She's got a pre-show routine."

Madison pouted, but Guy walked out from behind the bar with the froofiest drink I'd ever seen, and she perked right up. She took the glass from his tray and slurped down half of the pink-and-mint-green liquid through the straw. "You guys." She licked her lips and pointed at her drink, not caring much when it sloshed on her costume. "You have to try this."

Guy returned to the bar to make more drinks. I followed him.

"You want one?" he asked.

I shook my head.

"You want a water?"

I nodded, reluctantly grateful that he'd offered to help. He would keep the girls happy, but it would still be a long night.

"Daphne, I need you."

I tried to smile instead of roll my eyes, but it was near impossible. Madison needed help with her zipper. She could've asked any of the other girls, all of whom were closer, but she reserved the honor for me. I then zipped up Raquel and Piper and got Madison another drink. Once all the girls were dressed and dining on the penis cookies Aja had made, Madison decided that she needed me in costume. I donned this multimetallic lamé number that had been left on the floor. Jade cured its stench of mildew and mothballs with a spritz of perfume, but there was nothing to be done about the muddy footprints covering the front. *Ah well.* Given my role tonight, they seemed appropriate.

"Daphne, time for presents."

Yay. I moved the chairs into a tight circle, then restacked the presents to Madison's liking in the center. Sometime after the third pair of crotchless edible handcuffs, the bachelorette impressed us with her regard for details.

"Luckily, I found out in time to have the mail clerk dig the invitations out of the drop box. *Tyler.*" She looked skyward and shook her head, then sighed. "But I love him. So, the next day we drove to Bridal Veil to have the invitations properly mailed."

She scanned our faces expectantly but was ultimately disappointed. We'd all received our invitations within the last few days, but not even Madison's fellow engaged had noticed the cancellation stamp of her carefully selected post office. We'd all missed the extra, braggadocious detail that her wedding invitations had come from not just anywhere, but from *Bridal Veil.*

Madison grabbed Brenda's hands, as if speaking specifically to her. "Still, it's the little things, you know? You should go."

"Oh. My. Gawd." Sasha launched out of her chair and grabbed Brenda's hand. "What is this?"

Brenda looked embarrassed. She gave Madison an apologetic frown, but Madison's smile said she'd known what she'd been doing.

The girls gathered around Brenda, and I did too, trying to see over them, trying to see what was going on.

"When did you get this?" Sasha held up Brenda's left hand—and its sparkle shocked me. I jostled my drink, spilling it on my dress. The blessing let me escape the squee-filled circle to get a towel from the bar.

"I think I'll take that drink now," I said.

Guy set one on the counter. "Not good to drink in envy."

"Quit knowing me," I said, and I pouted into the clear and bubbly. 7-Up.

Behind me, the girls squeed over Brenda, but I couldn't bear to listen. I stayed back, apart, away. I hid among the costume racks, rescuing castoffs from the floor and reuniting them with their hangers, earning my place among the rejects. Brenda had never seemed interested in getting married, and she'd barely dated the guy a minute. How was she, of all people, engaged? But she was hardly the only one. Madison. Hannah. Jade. *Mom.* Everyone. Everyone but me.

I found a clean, if gaudy, green-and-gold dress and held it up to me in front of the mirror. Brenda's eyes met mine in the reflection. She left the gaggle of girls and walked over.

I eked up the corners of my mouth. "Congratulations."

"Thanks." She flexed her left hand and adjusted the solitaire. It was a self-conscious movement, not bragging. Brenda wasn't like Madison. "I'm sorry I didn't say anything on the phone," she said. "I tried. It's just—"

"I wasn't in a great mood, I know. I'm sorry." I squeezed her hand. Her diamond gouged my palm. "Are you sure, though? I mean, it's only been—what?—like two months, max?"

Brenda pulled her hand away and rose to full height. A smoldering glow brightened her face. Radiant eyes. Happy smile. She was sure.

It wasn't fair.

"You guys." Raquel waved us back over. While I'd been envying Brenda, Madison had decided we should all gather in a circle with our hands in the center, seven-year-old-soccer style, and call, "One, two, three, bachelorette party!"

No, she wasn't kidding.

"Left hands, ladies."

The girls gathered around her and stuck out their hands.

Brenda gave me a sheepish shrug and joined the circle.

"Daphne, we need you."

I hung up the green-and-gold costume and plastered on a smile. "Coming." I skipped to the group and slapped my hand on top.

"Daphne, your left hand."

"Right, sorry." I switched hands.

"Oh. My. Gawd," said Sasha, and the girls squeed. Corrine grabbed for my hand.

"What?" I said, yanking it back.

Sasha wiggled her left ring finger. Behind my back, I thumbed at the cabochon's band, uncertain what to do. I'd been wearing the ring for weeks now, but aside from Nechai, no one had noticed.

Jade, standing next to me, took my elbow and lifted my hand high for all to see.

"Well?" Raquel asked.

The cabochon shimmered on the faces of my friends. Their brows high, their eyes bright. As soon as they heard the truth, their expressions would change. Brenda's to pity. Sasha's to relief. Madison's to superiority. What could I say to avoid answering?

I bit my lip—

And they all squeed.

"You're engaged?" Madison said. "Andy actually proposed?"

"Why didn't you tell me?" Brenda said.

"When did this happen?"

"Details, details."

I didn't know what to say. I shook my head, no, but the attention they gave me—the admiration, the validation, the celebration—the shaking came with a grin.

"Oh. My. Gawd!"

"You're keeping it secret? That's so romantic."

"Tyler said Andy would never propose."

The girls crowded around me, hugging me their kudos, wanting to see the ring, praising its uniqueness and Andy's great taste. I was fussed into a chair and handed a fresh drink. Had we set a date yet? Did I want a big wedding or private? Traditional or less so? I got caught up in their questions. I had answers. I gave them.

Madison sat next to me and linked her arm with mine. "We still can't believe Andy let you move in," she said, and she pulled her phone from her costume. "You think the guys are at the movie yet? Tyler's gonna give Andy *hell.*"

CHAPTER 47

DAPHNE - 46 hours left

Shit. My brain was buzzing: the earworm was going crazy.

I'd just let the girls think I was engaged, and now they were gonna tell Andy. My hand flexed, wanting to snatch the phone from Madison, but she'd ask me why, and I wasn't ready to say. I didn't ever want to say.

Madison sent a message and put her phone back in her costume. Cell service worked up here, but it was spotty. There was a chance I could intercept that text.

"A toast," Madison said.

"Wait." Jade held up her empty glass. "We need more drinks."

"I'll get them." I elbowed my way out of the circle before the girls could object and hurried toward the bar. Guy was gunning cola into a glass, but his tense eyes tracked me as I slipped behind the counter and searched for a napkin and a pen. I had to warn Andy before he heard it from Tyler. And I had to do it without sounding like a sociopath. I crouched low, behind the bar, to compose my message in secret.

When I finished, I got my phone from my purse, but it had died in a futile hunt for reception. "Hey." I showed my blank screen to Guy. "Can I borrow your phone?"

Guy glanced at the girls, my ring, my face, and filled another glass with cola. "Why?"

I glared at him, the heartless turd. He didn't even have the potential to understand.

He made a give-it-here gesture. "Read it to me."

I bit the corner of my mouth.

"Trust me," he said, "you need a second opinion."

And I couldn't get one from the girls.

Still crouched behind the bar, I duck-walked closer to Guy and read the napkin at a quick whisper.

"Funny thing just happened. The girls think I'm engaged, and I didn't correct them. I couldn't. But I will. Tomorrow. If I have to. Just wanted to let you know in case word gets back to you."

I sucked in a breath, having rambled the whole speech in one exhale, and looked up at Guy. He was frowning at me. I held out the napkin just in case he was a visual rather than auditory learner and not just an idiot.

His frown morphed into a judgmental grin. "I thought that's what happened over there."

"You're an ass."

"Yeah, okay," he said, like he was just a kettle, whereas I was a big-ass pot. "If Andy hasn't proposed by now, that's not gonna help."

Maybe not. But Andy had a good sense of humor. And he liked me, loved me even. Maybe even enough to propose and save me the embarrassment of having to confess my silent lie.

Either way, his internship form was due Monday.

I hid the napkin down my dress. "I think it's fine. Where's your phone?"

Guy gunned another glass with cola. "Don't have one."

I rubbed my growing headache. "You don't have a phone behind the bar?"

"N—" The soda gun dropped to the floor, and Guy stiffened liked his shirt had been filled with ice. He gripped the edge of the bar with both hands, arms tense, veins straining. The tips of his fingers turned white. His wide eyes met mine, but he wasn't looking at me; he was concentrating, using me as a point of focus.

I wagged my finger at his schooled expression. "What's going on with—"

"*Go use the phone in the ticket booth.*" He heaved a sigh and his body relaxed.

"Are you okay?" I asked.

He picked up the soda gun. "Just go," he said, sounding defeated. "I'll watch the girls for you."

Streetlight stretched through the ticket-booth window and lit up a Pin-up Bride poster.

Pin-up Bride poster? There hadn't been any posters hanging in the ticket booth when Guy and I were waiting for the girls to arrive, and as far as I knew, Petty was out running errands, so I had no idea who'd hung it. My stomach tightened. I glanced behind me and listened. All I heard was the girls upstairs, but I still didn't feel at ease.

The poster had a strange new dimensionality. I thought I could see Fausten's eyes behind her veil, staring at me no matter where I stood in the room. Her lips looked glossy and her flowers velvety soft. Textured. Like if I ran my finger along her thigh, I'd feel her fishnets.

Nope. Just smooth glass. I blew out a breath. It was better this way.

The black rotary dial sat in the corner of the ticket booth's desk. I picked up the receiver. White vapor flowed from the holes. I stilled, muscles tense, as the vapor spread throughout the booth and vanished into the air.

I told myself it was just trapped moisture finally released. (*...not a hallucination, not a hallucination...*) I checked the holes. Sniffed them to be sure. Finding them empty, if smelling a little like peaches, I held the phone to my ear.

A low buzz hummed in the earpiece, loud but distant. I dialed Andy's number, cranking the rotary to the right and letting it tick back into place. After the last number, I couldn't tell if the silent phone was working.

"Hello?" I said.

"Hello."

I dropped the phone, but the voice repeated in my mind, so confident and controlled I didn't know whether to be scared or intrigued. But then I laughed. It had probably been my own voice echoing in the silence.

Had to have been.

I picked up the receiver and dialed again. This time the line rang. Andy's voicemail answered. I'd expected this—all the guys had gone to the movies—but it was still a relief. I read the napkin and disconnected.

And I felt better. I knew I shouldn't have succumbed to the girls' excitement (and guaranteed judgment had I told them the truth), but their fawning over me had felt so good. Andy would understand. And if he didn't, I'd fix it. I'd confess everything to everyone. They'd laugh. They'd call me pathetic. But everything would be okay. I'd do anything for Andy. Tomorrow.

But not tonight. Tonight I would keep for myself. Just one perfect night with people who believed Andy had decided to share his life with me. That I had earned his commitment. Tonight I would enjoy the thrill of being engaged.

And of seeing the Pin-up Bride.

CHAPTER 48

DAPHNE - 45 hours left

Conlin couldn't say no to pleading girls clad in sequins and lamé. He made me man the lobby during the show's first half, but at intermission the juggler relieved me. I headed into the house, and Piper and Raquel waved me down to the front row, where they were guarding the other girls' seats.

"Brenda says you've never seen the Pin-up Bride," said Piper. "Is that true?" I confessed it was. "You're in for a thrill," she said. "I've never seen anything like it."

Well after the five-minute warning, the rest of the girls tipsy-toed down the aisle, sloshing their drinks on the floor and demonstrating in sticky detail why I worked late most nights.

Madison had two drinks. She held one out to me, crinkling her nose with the effort to keep it steady.

So she hadn't heard back from Tyler yet. I took the drink with a shimmy and a smile and tried not to worry about how her niceties would end once she learned I'd lied about getting engaged.

The spotlight came on as we settled in—Madison on my right, Brenda on my left—and Conlin sauntered out of the wing to center stage.

"Desired the world over," he said, his sequined suit glittering purple and royal blue, "our next act has made L'Aornum Theatre a destination for those who like their auspicions served with mystery.

Intrigued? You should be. Her secret eludes us all, but she'll be sharing it tonight. Bringing you her unique blend of séance and satsang, her unparalleled séatsang, ladies and gentlemen, boys and girls, and all the sassy rest of you, here she is: the Pin-up Bride."

The lights extinguished. The theater rumbled, and the crowd erupted with deafening applause. My temples throbbed with the beginnings of a headache, but I'd come prepared. I set my beer on the floor, dug some aspirin out of my bra, and nudged Brenda for a sip of water.

The stage floor cracked open, and a beam of light shot to the rafters, followed by something that looked like a swarm of flies. But they couldn't be flies. There were too many. Hundreds. They had to be something else. But as Fausten Cotter rose from the stage—lying beneath her dark sheet, emitting her glowing mist—I breathed in her peach scent and relaxed in my chair, no longer caring about the flies.

A strobe light flashed. I didn't recall a strobe light flashing at Fausten's opening-night performance, but the change was effective. Fausten sat up, and so did the hairs on my neck.

She swung her legs over the side of the platform and stood, raising her arms and hitting a high V as the dark sheet dropped.

The audience roared.

I put my concerns about her well-being to rest. She looked good. Maybe not as luminous as the first few times I'd seen her, but that was probably just the novelty wearing off. Her thick mesh veil curled beneath her chin, so I couldn't see her face, but I also didn't see any fluids oozing through the fabric of her over-the-elbow gloves. They and her thigh-high boots weren't the reinvention choices I would've made, but she made them look good. She exuded confidence. Control.

And perfect timing. A throne glided forward, and she sat just as it reached her.

At that, the strobe light turned off. I expected Fausten to glow with her usual full-body halo, with that light that seemed sourced from within, but the entire stage remained dark. It was several moments before a lamp clicked on above her, illuminating her in a circle of light.

A second spotlight shone down from the light rack, and Fausten's assistant entered the stage.

Guy received catcalls of his own, mainly from us rowdy girls in the front row. He wasn't wearing his usual Sherlock Holmes–inspired duds. No, indeed. For tonight, he'd chosen black tuxedo pants, a pink-and-mint-green bow tie, and shirtless cuffs. For tonight—for the girls up front, mayhaps?—he'd dressed as a pin-up groom.

Madison leaned into me. "Where have you been hiding him?"

I shook my head. "He's going back when this is over."

Guy raised his palms to silence the crowd. "By a show of hands, who *hasn't* seen Fausten's show before?"

Just me from the looks of it, and my hand only made it chest high.

"Let's do it, then," he said. "Who's first?"

"Pick me!" people yelled.

Guy visored his eyes, looking far and wide for the perfect volunteer. The girls pointed at Madison and hollered for him to pick the bachelorette. She ducked her head into my shoulder, like she was embarrassed—"No, someone else go"—then snuck peeks to make sure she still had everyone's attention.

She didn't have Guy's. He seemed determined to pick someone from the back corner.

But a wisp of pink smoke slithered out from beneath the Pin-up Bride's throne and reached for Madison, lifting her chin from my shoulder and tempting her out of her seat.

The crowd applauded. Guy dropped his visoring hand and looked at Madison, then at the Pin-up Bride. An un-showman-like expression flashed on his face, but he recovered his smile quickly and continued to play his role.

He knelt at the edge of the stage and held a hand out to Madison.

Our bachelorette swooned. *Bleh.* Hannah helped her stumble forward to take Guy's hand. He assisted her to the stage, walking on his knees around the edge of the apron, then standing as she climbed the stairs.

Guy said, "It's Madison, right?"

Madison nodded. She tried to step closer to Fausten, but Guy held her back. One misstep and she'd tumble off the stage.

Guy said, "What's your question, Madison?"

"Umm." She looked at the first row for guidance. The girls cheered for her. "Um," she said with more vigor. "I want to know...how do I guarantee a happy married life?"

The crowd applauded her question, and she beamed at us, bringing fists to shoulders in a bouncy pop of squee.

The strobe light flashed.

With a flourish, Fausten raised her left hand, palm up, as if holding an imaginary tray.

And smoke oozed from her fingers.

It trickled to the floor, gaining height, substance, and color. A pinkish misty sculpture formed. The shape reminded me of Gloria, the older woman from opening night, who'd tested Fausten's breath with the hand mirror.

"An old lady!" someone yelled.

I startled and glanced at Brenda. But it seemed yelling was normal PuB audience behavior. Brenda was nodding in agreement, captivated by the thick pink smoke. Its old-lady shape flashed once in a single pulse of bright strobe.

"Old?" the yeller clarified.

The smoky old lady flashed twice, then dissolved, and the smoke gathered again, taking on a new form: a giant pink gift box. Dashes of bright smoke radiated from the package as if it were shiny and new.

"A present?" Madison guessed.

The gift box dulled in color, vanishing slowly as the lid lifted and the bottom fell away, revealing its contents: a smoke-formed dress. A huge, twinkling sales tag hung from the sleeve.

"A dress?" Madison said. "A wedding dress?"

"It's new!" someone yelled.

The smoky dress flashed brightly two times.

"Something new?" Madison said.

Still forming its next depiction, the smoke flashed brightly three times fast.

The crowd applauded.

Madison beamed.

I leaned toward Brenda. "So it's like charades?"

"Yeah, or Pictionary," Brenda said. "The smoke draws the answer to your question, word by word, and then the light flashes when you guess right."

Fausten's smoke formed another image. This one moved, like flip-book animation. A woman rifled through clothes in a closet. She selected a dress and held it up to a friend, then nodded and handed off the dress.

"Borrowed" and "Something borrowed" echoed throughout the crowd.

The smoke flashed three times fast.

"I know it," Madison said. "Something old, something new, something borrowed, something blue."

The smoke flashed brightly, three times fast.

Madison bounced. "I've already got all that. Thank you. Thank you so much."

She stepped down the stairs, but behind her, the smoke continued swirling. A tendril slithered after her. The crowd yelled for Madison to go back, that her answer wasn't finished.

Madison looked a question at Guy.

Guy hesitated, glancing at the PuB on her throne, but he ultimately welcomed Madison back to the stage.

Fausten's smoke collected at her feet. It swirled, tighter and tighter, condensing and deepening in hue. Its flirty pink color became an angry red.

Guy's showbiz smile faltered. His hands went to his pockets, then patted his hips—and his smile disappeared altogether. He looked at Fausten, then out at the crowd, at me. I raised my brows in question, but he didn't respond in kind. He backed into the wing, disappearing from sight.

Fausten's red smoke began forming a shape. It was so small I couldn't make it out.

The house leaned forward in rapt silence.

The red shape grew bigger...bigger... I realized what it was.

"A shoe!"

The smoky red heel flashed once.

Brenda elbowed me. "Good one."

Madison sounded unsure. "I've got shoes."

The smoke did not flash its gratifying confirmation.

High above the smoky shoe, a blood-red dot blinked into existence, then slowly fell, its bright red color becoming a matte and dirty gray. It dropped into the smoky high heel and disappeared into the toe.

"And a silver sixpence in her shoe."

The bone-saw voice gave me chills, and I half rose out of my seat to look behind me.

Nechai. She might have written me a check, but she still creeped me out. She was standing at the back of the house, watching the smoke through her blue-tinted glasses.

No, not watching the smoke—watching Fausten. Always watching Fausten.

Light flashed brightly on the stage, three times fast, confirming Nechai's guess. The crowd applauded, but many people murmured in low, uncomfortable voices. Brenda chuckled.

Nechai smirked and left the house.

I faced front and leaned toward Brenda. "What's funny?"

"Just some old gossip."

"Like what?"

"Shhhhh," said the woman behind us.

Brenda leaned closer and spoke softer. "Just that old rumor that Fausten Cotter's hiatus last year was due to a botched magic trick. Supposedly, she forgot the words."

I still didn't understand, but Brenda's cocked eyebrow said it was gossip intended for the gullible, so I let it go.

Onstage, Madison had lost her giddy. "What's a sixpence?"

Fausten sat motionless. I got the feeling she wasn't listening. Maybe it was just me, but I got the feeling Fausten wasn't smiling behind her veil so much as seething at the closing house doors.

Guy stepped out of the wing, his shoulder muscles tense and his right hand clawed. He was holding something, something the size of a tennis ball, wrapped in red-and-white plastic.

"A sixpence," he said, his face unreadable, "is an old British coin."

Madison fretted her fingers. "Where do I get one?"

"Check online," someone yelled.

"Those are mostly fake," said someone else.

Madison bit her thumb like if she didn't get a sixpence for her shoe, then her wedding would be for naught.

The smoke swirled again, forming a vaguely human shape that extended an unmistakable hand. The hand splayed its fingers wide, as if showing us its palm was empty, then twisted, flashing its knuckles; nothing up its sleeve.

The smoky hand reached for Madison.

Madison stilled, her lips disappearing between her teeth.

The smoky hand reached alongside her head and pulled something out from behind her ear. The item was too small for me to see, but Madison's eyes widened. She laughed and clapped.

The crowd cheered.

What could only be a sixpence hovered in the air, even as the smoke that had produced it retreated from the spot.

Madison held out her hand. The sixpence fell into her palm, and she held it up for all to see. Light glinted off the metal.

"How'd they do it?" whispered a girl behind me. The lady who'd shushed us said, "Probably tacked it to a wire and then gave it a little shake." She demonstrated on the girl, who giggled.

Strobe lights flashed all over the stage.

Fausten's smoke retreated to her hand. When it was nothing more than a smoldering flicker of pink in her palm, she curled her fingers one by one and returned her hand to her lap.

After a few more audience questions, Fausten's show was over. The girls and I gathered our things.

"What's next?" I asked.

The bachelorette didn't answer. She had her elbow on the armrest and her head in her hand.

"Madison's not feeling well," said Hannah.

I bet. She'd prefunked pretty seriously, then drank like she was just getting started once she got here.

"So we're calling it a night, then?" That was my vote. I wanted to get home to Andy. Fausten's smoke trick remained a mystery, but I had a feeling that, once again, just being around her would help me move things forward with Andy.

"It's not even midnight," said Sasha.

"Well, Madison should probably go home," I said. "Who wants to go with her?"

"We should probably all go," Brenda said.

"Forget that," said Sasha. "Coming, girls?"

The sheep, all bundled in their wool coats, looked at each other, wondering what to do. Raquel shrugged and scurried up the aisle after Sasha.

"Let's get her home," Jade said to the rest of us. "We can go out again after, if you still want."

"I can call her a cab." At the back of the house, Petty pushed through the last of the stragglers and strode his lanky legs down the aisle. He was dressed in sweats and his hair was flat. "You guys can go."

To my surprise, half the remaining girls left. The other half looked to me. I looked a question at Petty.

"It's okay," he said. "I'm used to it."

"Don't you need to help Fausten?" I asked.

"Nah, she's—"

"Resting?"

He shrugged. "She had a feeling our girl here wasn't feeling well after the smoke. Told me to come check on her."

That seemed unlikely, but Petty was peeling Madison's hair from her face, tucking it behind her ear, helping her up, so... "Okay. Thanks, Petty."

"Thanks, Petty," said the girls.

I got a shoulder under Madison's other arm, and Petty and I helped her to the lobby, where we propped her on a bench. She was out.

"Go," Petty said. "Really, it's okay. I'll make sure she gets in the cab."

"You're sure," I said.

"Yeah. Have fun." He went into the ticket booth and picked up the phone.

Outside, the girls were huddled under the awning, deciding where to take the party.

"Quiet," Hannah said. She pointed to the phone against her ear. "Carlos is asking Andy about proposing."

Fear scoured my gut and threw up in my throat. I swallowed it back down and tried to stay cool. "And?"

Hannah held up a finger. Then, "He laughed."

"He laughed?" I said.

She shrugged. "That's what Carlos said."

My whole body warmed with tingles.

He'd laughed.

He wasn't denying it.

It didn't seem real, not even when the girls crowded around me, congratulating me again, and with even more enthusiasm now that they had Andy's confirmation. Because that's exactly what it was: confirmation. If Andy was still against getting married, he would've said so.

So he must've decided to make it official.

Soon.

I'd have a proposal by the end of the weekend!

I bounced with squee. We didn't need a bachelorette; our party was filled with the engaged! Both the recently and the oh-so-soon-to-be.

I linked arms with Brenda and hip-checked Hannah. "So," I said. "Who's up for more fun?"

CHAPTER 49

DAPHNE - 35 hours left

I woke in the theater's ballroom. Costumes and old blankets from the storeroom were strewn on the floor. We'd capped the night with a slumber party.

Or so I'd thought. I was the only one left.

I changed out of my costume and into my real clothes. It was too early to call Andy for a ride, so I headed outside. The streets were quiet save for runners training in groups for the next marathon. Impressive, really. I could barely walk straight.

Andy was awake when I got home. More than awake. He had his all-in-one printer set up on the kitchen table and was working on his laptop.

"Hey," I said, heading straight for the fridge. It took some digging, but I found a 7-Up. I popped the top and took a sip. Ahh, much better.

The all-in-one made some laser sounds. I walked around the cabinets and leaned against the counter. Andy kept his eyes on his computer screen as he typed, but then he clicked the mouse and closed the laptop.

I took another gut-soothing drink and sat across from him at the table. "What did you guys do last night?"

Andy looked at me, closed his eyes and exhaled through his nose, then he got up and moved closer to me.

My stomach churned, and not because I was hungover. It churned in sync with Andy's nervousness. With anticipation. This was it; I could feel it. It was happening. It was actually happening. I sat up straighter and bit my top lip to keep from grinning so wide.

Andy sat in the chair next to mine. He wasn't exactly kneeling at my feet, but whatever. I moved my hand to my knee, just in case he wanted to hold it as we entered the next phase of our lives.

His knee shook the table. He wasn't one for serious talk. If he had something to say, he just said it. But he had this look on his face, like he couldn't make the transition from thoughts to words. He rubbed his hands on his pants.

I touched his fingers, offering him encouragement.

"I know you're not happy I don't wanna get married," he said, pulling his hands away from me and hiding them in his armpits, "but nine calls to yell at me about it isn't cool."

"Nine calls?" I said. "I called you once."

Andy got out his phone.

I got out mine, too, then stopped, remembering I'd called him on the theater's phone.

"I called you once," I said. "I let the girls think—"

"We're engaged. Yeah. I heard. In the first message."

"That's the only message I left."

He scoffed, shaking his head as he scrolled through his voicemail. He pressed play and hit speaker. "*You won't propose, adamantly deny giving me this ring, and now this girl, this Ericka girl. I wish my shoe had hit her in the face. She'd be less glib with no teeth.*"

I chilled from marrow to skin. I'd thought that just the other day. *Thought* it, but never said it. I would never say it.

Andy selected another voicemail.

"I didn't do that," I said, loudly, trying to drown out the message. My head throbbed. The earworm was dancing in its cocoon. "Turn it off. Please? Just turn it off. I didn't do that."

Except it was my voice.

"*All that work, all that ruining of the wedding dress, just to convince my boyfriend, who supposedly loves me, to do so forever. I fulfilled my part of our deal, but you still won't commit. Not to me anyway. But to a job? What about me, Andy? What about us?"*

The message ended with an audible click, and Andy's thumb scrolled for another choice piece. I clapped my hands over his phone.

"So, this isn't your voice?" he said.

"Delete. Please. Just delete."

"So, this isn't your number?" He set his phone on the table so we could both see the red number followed by a parenthetical nine.

"That's not my number, that's—"

"The theater's number."

"But I only called you once," I said, each word slower and more confused than the last. They sounded like lies, even to me. "I didn't..." I rubbed my forehead. I didn't know anymore.

Andy blew out a breath. "I know you need a place to stay."

"What?"

"It's fine," he said. "You can stay here while I'm gone."

My body tensed its every cell—but my inner shields offered me no protection. The time to circumvent this moment had passed. They let me endure it alone. My eyes saw his every fidget. My skin felt his every breath. My ears heard his every word.

"I'll take the couch until then," he said. "It's only a couple of weeks."

My hands found my elbows and squeezed. "You're taking the internship?"

His gaze drifted to his laptop.

So that's what he'd been doing when I'd walked in—he'd been sending the form. I reached for him, but he leaned away from me. I wrapped my arms around my shoulders and hid my mouth in the triangle they made. "It's her, isn't it?"

Andy scoffed and shook his head.

"It is, isn't it?"

"It's us, Daph."

I wedged my hands between my thighs. I'd always admired the way Andy could just say what he meant.

Not so much anymore.

"It used to be so easy," he said. "Now it's just tired."

I laughed to avoid crying. The way he distilled things to the essence of how he felt. No facts, just truth. Just his straight-up opinion. Just impossible for me to rebut without sounding like a four-year-old.

"And not that this deserves an explanation, but Ericka... First, she glommed onto this guy in group, and he was into it for a while, until he wasn't anymore and she made group hell. So when she switched to me, I figured I could keep the peace, you know? Play nice to her—and mention you a few hundred times so she'd get the hint."

I pinched myself. That was why he'd picked her up before bringing me my shoes. Why he'd introduced me with hard emphasis on *girlfriend*. I'd thought he'd said it like that for my benefit. It had been for hers. "Why didn't you just tell me?"

He sighed. "I don't know. When I didn't have to think about it, I didn't."

I made a face, because that was the weakest excuse I'd ever heard.

"Oh, okay"—he sat up straighter—"why didn't you tell me about Guy?"

My gaze darted to the window and back, because that question—it had come out of nowhere. "Nothing to tell. He's a turd. Everyone knows."

"Really? That's funny, because I heard you two posed together."

I stared at him. That had been a last-minute thing at a private benefit party.

"Ares and Aphrodite." Andy mimed the adoring statue pose and made kissing sounds.

"How do you—?"

"Conlin told me," he said. "You know—when I should've been at group but came to pick up *you*."

I stared at a piece of lint on Andy's knee, wanting to get it, wondering if he'd mind the excuse to touch him. "Guy"—*bleh*—"why would you even think that? That was—"

"Nothing. I know. Same here."

Oh.

We sat there for a while, me staring at him, him staring at something I couldn't see. We sat there until his breath stopped making long, deliberate airy sounds through his nose. Until his knee stopped bumping the table.

Calm once more. Nothing going on with Ericka. I couldn't explain those phone messages, but it was okay. We were calm once more.

I moved to give him a hug, to make up, to be together, but he leaned away from me.

"I'm sorry," I said, hugging my elbows. "I don't remember making those calls. But I promise I won't ever do it again."

"It's not the calls."

"Then I promise I won't ever forget that I trust you."

He shook his head and unplugged the all-in-one.

"What, then?" I said.

Everything about him rounded down: his eyes, his mouth, his shoulders. He lifted the lid of the scanner. On the glass lay the acceptance form. He picked it up with two fingers, as if lifting the weight of a death note. His Adam's apple bobbed and his cheeks reddened.

I could keep it together no longer. "What, then?!"

The paper crackled in his fist.

My calm broke in a choked and wheezy gasp. He'd sent it, but not because he wanted to go. He'd sent it to boost his resolve, to give himself strength. He'd sent it so that he couldn't change his mind.

About me.

He sniffed and struggled to keep his voice steady. "You care more about telling people you're married than about just being with the right person."

I dropped to my knees and wrapped my arms around his waist. "You're my person."

He banged the back of his head against the wall. He didn't like what he was doing to us—

"You won't be happy until you're hitched."

—but he was doing it anyway. I clung to him tighter. He curled himself around me, pressing his chest against my back, digging his fingers into my side. He placed a long, sniffled kiss on the back of my head and laid his cheek on my hair.

"So go ahead," he whispered. "Go do that."

CHAPTER 50

FAUSTEN

Judging by all the buzzing around my bed, the flies numbered in the thousands.

Do flies eat bacteria? I should have had Petty push the netting aside so that they could eat the little buggers helping my flesh decay.

The restoration we'd tried to perform last night, with ingredient courtesy of the bachelorette, hadn't healed my skin so much as it had left my situation...urgent.

I had a new plan, of course, and even now, Petty was setting it into motion. But I was tired of just sitting here, rotting, waiting for Daphne's convenience.

I pulled myself into her head.

She sat in the dark, in an out-of-the-way corner of Andy's apartment, on the floor between the couch and the sliding glass door. Arms wrapped around her legs, chin on her knees, a crayon in her fist. She rubbed her thumb along its length, increasing the pressure, daring it to break. She'd walled herself into her tiny fortress with a backpack, army duffle, and a moving box too full to close. Her laptop shuffled through pictures of her and Andy. She sniffled, feeling gutted and eager to try anything.

And I had just the suggestion.

Come to the theater.

She winced and rubbed her head. She didn't think she could stay at the theater. Conlin might let her, if she asked, but the theater had no shower, no cell service, no windows. The theater was a giant coffin.

But where else could she go? She couldn't go to her mom's. Mom wouldn't risk anything ruining her latest engagement. She could stay at Andy's place, but she didn't want to, not when he didn't want her anymore.

You could get him back.

How?

Get off the floor.

Daphne tipped onto her side and buried her tears in her knees.

As if she were a poster, I pushed my influence through her eyes and into the open air. She rubbed her temples. Using our connection to access my speck of influence in her head gave Daphne headaches. But now that my own oil had been harvested, that speck was the only method I had left to project my will.

I created a wind. The curtains covering the sliding glass door billowed like the door was open and needed to be shut. It was close to freezing outside, and so was the breeze, but instead of checking the door, Daphne lifted her chin and let the wind whip her hair about her face, accepting its sharp lashings as if it were a punishment.

Pathetic.

I slid the balcony door open. The real freezing wind caught the loose papers in Daphne's moving box and scattered them over the floor. Daphne got up and closed the door, then gathered the pages, including my crumpled poster. She snorted at the damned thing, blaming it for her misery.

She dropped to the floor and started scribbling. Her crayon, a white crayon, one of the last of Harry's originals, had been so rarely used that it still had its tapered end. *Not anymore.* She scribbled it flat, big heavy zigzags across my veiled face. The crayon slid over the poster's glossy finish, barely leaving smudges of white where the paper was black, but her raging hand marred the paper. She scribbled until it ripped, then sat back and exhaled, feeling better.

Daphne stood, leaving the poster on the floor. She picked up a pamphlet about shelters and services for the homeless. She hadn't needed this pamphlet back when she'd persuaded Andy to let her move in, but finding it now felt right to her. She clutched it to her chest and stood taller, closing her eyes. She would do anything for Andy, and if Andy wanted her gone from his life, she wouldn't make him wait. She wouldn't treat him the way he had treated her. Teasings? Delays? No. If Andy wanted her gone now, she'd give him what he wanted now.

I, however, didn't want her at a shelter. The little buggers feasting on my flesh were so ravenous I could hear their crackling even though I was focused here.

I used my influence to flick Daphne's lights, but it didn't get her attention. She was too in her head to notice, too worried that she'd be broke forever, homeless forever, single forever...or like her mom.

Could I risk something more drastic? I didn't want to project my influence too much. Daphne might think she was having another hallucination and run screaming for the nearest MAX train to her mom's house, new fiancé or no. She'd be out of my range of influence, and I wouldn't get another chance.

Daphne took a key off her key ring and set it on the kitchen table. Should she leave Andy a note? No, notes are to ease the minds of people who care about you, and Andy didn't care about her, not anymore. She left the closet door open, her drawer pulled out, so that he would see right away, *I'm gone. You never have to see me again.*

She double-checked her phone, making sure it was charged and loaded with minutes, just in case he called.

Using the belt from her robe, she tied a garment bag, filled with my white dress, her wig, and her blue shoes, to the front of her backpack. She put the backpack on, then slung the duffle across her body and picked up the moving box. The shelter brochure lay on top. She held it in place with her chin and hefted everything to the entryway, leaving my crayon-marred poster behind.

She opened the apartment's front door.

I crumpled up the poster and rolled it across the carpet, past Daphne, and into the brightly lit corridor.

"What the—?"

Daphne had told Guy numerous times that she wasn't superstitious, that she didn't believe in anything paranormal, but our connection buzzed with the energy of her enlightenment.

Everyone believes once it's happened to them.

I encouraged her belief. I uncrumpled the poster so that she could see my ripped face staring back at her through the veil. But I didn't project my influence. Daphne associated projections with hallucinations, and I didn't want to remind her that she used to be scared.

But I needn't have worried. Daphne imagined a projection herself, and she welcomed her old enemy. Of course her postergeist would come. She thought nothing was more natural than a heartbreak-induced hallucination, and she wasn't going to fight it.

She embraced it.

She dropped her stuff where she stood and left it all behind, figuring she wouldn't need it anymore, not where she was going. She'd follow my poster anywhere, over the chain-link of Vista Bridge if that's where her postergeist took her.

She suspected it would.

It wouldn't. I had something else in mind. But I loved the commitment.

I rolled the crumpled poster past wedding dress shops and jewelry stores. Daphne moped along behind it, wondering if the diamond solitaires always sparkled this much or just when people were recently dumped.

Neither. I'd boosted their shimmer and infused the air with romance. Couples clasped hands and leaned in for a kiss. Daphne stared, wondering why them and not her? So funny, her need to get married. As if a ceremony made for lifelong security, let alone happiness.

They don't deserve it like you do, do they, Daphne?

You should be holding hands.

You should be wearing a diamond.

You should be buying that dress.

"I did everything!" she cried, oblivious to the people watching her.

One of those people approached. "You're the Pin-up Bride."

My fan shoved a notebook and pen into Daphne's hands, then pulled out his phone. It had a sticker of me on its case, but he still gushed over Daphne like she was me.

"Do you mind?" He snapped pictures, not caring if she did, and had them posted online before she found a blank page in his book. "To Brian," he instructed.

I let her write what she wanted—that it was a pleasure meeting Brian on the street—but when she signed at the bottom, I bumped her hand. I didn't care if the signature was scribbled, so long as it didn't read *Daphne James*.

With one fan making a success of it, more fans approached Daphne. I wanted them to adore her, but not yet, not like the amulet was the star and I was so easily replaced.

All the attention distracted Daphne from feeling lost without Andy. She didn't think she needed to follow the crumpled poster anymore, and she began to feel weird about having done so in the first place. She shifted to avoid seeing it. Someone asked her for another picture. Daphne grinned and huddled close, stamping my poster flat. As soon as she stepped aside, I plumped the poster back up and rolled it over her foot with the weight of a bowling ball.

"Ow," she said.

I didn't feel bad. I didn't feel bad about anything I had planned for her, not anymore.

I rolled the poster to the end of the block and around the corner. She followed it, limping slightly, but only to exact her revenge.

I rolled the poster down Park, just fast enough to stay ahead of her. But she started to slow down. I tried to urge her on, but she resisted. My fans had left her feeling confident. Her mom had survived heartbreak. Maybe she could too. And maybe she could devote her Andy-less extra time to understudying *me* in Conlin's new show.

I needed to crush her feelings again. My plan required her cooperation, and she wasn't so willing when she felt good.

But at least she was still headed where I needed her to go.

Her shoe kicked up something shiny on the sidewalk. It skipped along the concrete and landed heads up in front of the theater's ticket booth. Daphne bent for a look-see. She didn't recognize the profile, but when she realized what it was—"Madison must've dropped it"—she picked it up.

The crumpled poster had accomplished its mission. I rolled it off the curb and into a puddle, where it softened to mush.

I shifted my focus out of Daphne and into the ticket-booth poster so I could check on Petty's progress with the plan.

But the person in the ticket booth wasn't Petty.

The person in the ticket booth picked up the phone but then noticed Daphne, standing outside the window, and put the receiver back in its cradle. "Ms. James?"

Daphne jumped and stuffed the coin into her pocket. She looked around, not seeing anyone.

Conlin tapped the window. "I was about to call you," he said, and he left the ticket booth.

On the counter lay the crux of my plan, a white gift box with pink-and-mint-green ribbon. But where was Petty?

The main door creaked open. Conlin said, "About the show tonight—"

"I'm already working it," Daphne said.

"No, I mean... Why don't you come inside."

"What's going on?" Daphne said. "Is Fausten okay?"

Sweet Daphne and her genuine concern. It almost renewed my remorse for her.

She followed Conlin into the ticket booth. The light streaming through the window kept the tiny room warmer than the rest of the building. For now.

Conlin leaned against the counter, hiding Daphne's gift. I couldn't tell if that was by accident or design.

"Just between you and me," he said, "I'm tired of her and her excuses. This time it's a rash. She can't perform because"—his deep voice rose a mocking octave—"the makeup might aggravate the rash."

Daphne shifted her weight. "You want me to pose?"

"And do her act."

My influence surged, rattling the poster's glass.

I hadn't brought Daphne here to fill in for me. Canceling Aphrodite was one thing, but not even Guy would agree to replace me in my own act.

Besides, I could do the show. It might take more makeup, a roomy housedress maybe, but I had another weekend in me. Probably two.

But this wasn't the boys' fault. Petty had told Conlin we were canceling Aphrodite and nothing more, I was sure of it. As usual, Conlin had taken the information he liked, forgotten the rest, and twisted the circumstances to suit himself. I'd respect him for it if it wasn't always causing problems for me.

Daphne glanced at my poster, its glass still rattling with aftershocks. "I can't do Fausten's act."

"Sure you can," Conlin said. "You've seen her show. Park and Vargas do the heavy lifting. Ms. Cotter just sits there."

My influence lashed at his face. He blinked and rubbed his cheek, frowning at the ticket window.

"You impressed me on amateur night," he said, moving the glass globe to cover the window's money hole. Hilarious. As if his attacker were just a harsh breeze. "And you've had a certain somethin'-somethin' lately, ever since that night Ms. Cotter posed with your boyfriend."

Bravo. Even Conlin was succumbing to Daphne's possession of the amulet.

But Daphne still wasn't ready to agree. She wanted to do the show, and the earlier encounter with my fans coupled with Conlin's praise suggested she *could* do the show, and do it well. But she glanced at my poster, at my veiled eyes glaring back at her. Even if she could do the show, she wasn't sure she should.

You shouldn't.

Daphne winced and rubbed her head. She was okay with that. The main reason she wanted to do my act was to show Andy, and there was no guarantee he would come. But she was becoming more and more okay with that too. Every bit of praise she received convinced her further that, with or without Andy, she would be okay.

I had to get her back to their sad apartment.

I pushed my influence into the room and nudged the gift.

It's for you.

Daphne ignored the white gift box moving on the counter. She thought people who felt good shouldn't hallucinate.

Conlin didn't see the box move, but he did see Daphne glance at it. He slid the box toward her—"It's for you"—but when she reached for it, he pulled it back. "It's for doing the act."

No, it wasn't. It was just a gift, no conditions. Instructions, maybe, but no conditions. Conlin was twisting the gift into a bribe to get Daphne to do the show. But worse, Daphne was mishearing him. Daphne thought the gift was something to use *during* the show.

And something about that worried me. I had intended for Daphne to use the gift in the privacy of her apartment, but I had a terrible feeling that if she used it onstage, it wouldn't work out well for me.

How to fix this?

I could knock the box from Conlin's hands. But what would that do other than break its contents? It wouldn't correct their assumptions. And too many inexplicably moving things could scare

Daphne. She might not use the gift at all. She might even throw it away.

I could get Petty down here, have him explain the gift to Daphne and undo everything Conlin had said. But interfering with the gift or clarifying its purpose could raise Daphne's suspicions about its *real* purpose. And that could raise her suspicions about me.

Conlin held his bribe out to Daphne, and I could think of nothing to do about it that wouldn't make things worse. He shook the box, trying to tempt her. If he broke what was inside...

Daphne caressed the pink-and-mint-green ribbon and found the tag that read, *To Daphne, From Fausten*. She showed it to Conlin. "She knows?"

"Her idea."

No. No. No!

Daphne glanced at my poster again, only this time she smiled in gratitude. For the gift. For the opportunity. For the depression-busting encouragement. She took the box from Conlin and clutched it, lifesaver-like, to her chest.

Conlin said, "So, you'll do the show tonight? You'll do Ms. Cotter's act?"

My influence surged, slamming the glass like thunder.

Daphne flinched and inched out of the ticket booth. She'd had enough of the strange energy in the room, but she was otherwise cheerful and confident as she assured Conlin that she would see him tonight, ready to pose.

So confident that she stopped hugging the gift. My plan rattled inside the box as it bumped against her leg.

Be careful. You need that.

She didn't listen. She imagined Andy's face as she performed my show, and his face became one of hundreds admiring her from the seats. She let the gift dangle, practically forgotten, and I couldn't make her do otherwise.

Would she use it? If she used it, I'd be a new woman. My only fear was that she'd decide she didn't need it.

But I had a nagging worry that Conlin's changes had somehow wrecked the plan. But how? His changes just meant that if Daphne used the gift at all, she would use it onstage. There was nothing inside the box to suggest she shouldn't. But that was fine. If the plan could work in her apartment, then it could work anywhere.

And let's be real. This was a spectacle meant for the stage. And what a show it would be. For the finale, I'd take center stage in my new, influence-wielding, amulet-wearing body. And the crowd would cheer. For me. For my recovery. For my manifesting destiny as a living legend, as theater's finest performer ever.

"Oh, Ms. James," Conlin said.

Daphne let the outside door fall against her with a thud. "Yeah."

"You still have that new wig," he asked, "and Ms. Cotter's white getup?"

"Yeah," she said, reentering the ticket booth.

"And those blue shoes?"

"Uh-huh."

"Good. You'll wear those tonight."

Daphne said okay, but my instincts wailed that it wasn't. Something about Conlin's direction. *New wig. My dress. Blue shoes.* They were spot-on instructions.

So why did they feel like a threat?

"Anything else?" Daphne asked. Conlin said no, and she waved goodbye. With her left hand.

I suddenly knew what was wrong.

New wig, borrowed dress, blue shoes. But that wasn't everything of mine Daphne would wear. I'd been right to worry, but not because Conlin had changed the plan's venue from the apartment to the stage.

He'd changed the costume. Daphne could've worn anything at home, but performing onstage required she wear an outfit. My outfit.

If Schadenfreude was still here, she'd be cackling herself to death.

I gathered a lethal burst of influence. But as much as he deserved a lashing, I couldn't strike Conlin. I was the golden goose, but his were the hands that gathered the golden eggs. This was Conlin's theater. The doors didn't open without him.

And I couldn't disrupt the plan. My body was out of time, and that gift held my only chance.

Me or Daphne. Tonight, one of us would fall sacrifice on the altar of the other's stardom.

I had five hours to make sure it was her.

CHAPTER 51

DAPHNE - 27 hours left

I rushed into the apartment eager to share my news with Andy, but he wasn't home, and the stuff I'd left in front of the door reminded me why. The empty apartment felt hostile without him, like it knew it wasn't our place anymore, only his.

He doesn't want you.

I winced at the pain in my head, in my heart, and sucked in a breath, trying to maintain my confidence. Andy might not have wanted me anymore, but other people did. Conlin, Fausten, her fans.

I set the white gift box on the kitchen table and pulled off its pink-and-mint-green ribbon. I still couldn't believe that Fausten wanted me to perform in her place tonight, that she'd given me this gift to help me shine.

Me!

The whole walk home I'd tried to guess at its contents: a lucky charm, a push-up bra, a mini fog machine...

I lifted the lid, releasing pink-and-mint-green tissue paper and a heady whiff of peaches.

On top was a note.

Hi, Daphne,

I once had the same question about Guy that you have about Andy. The same question your

> bachelorette friend asked about her fiancé. I wasn't kidding when I told her how to guarantee a happy relationship. But I left out the secret ingredient. It can be tricky. I should know.
>
> The rumors about me are true. I did botch a trick. It backfired because I didn't know the rhyme's last line. But you <u>do</u> know it. You'll do it right.

I lifted the tissue paper. At the bottom of the box lay a pink folder like the one I'd found in Petty's desk drawer the day I'd answered Fausten's fan mail.

The folder held a single sheet of paper. I recognized the fancy stock, the eight stylized words written in four lines. They were still hard to read, but I knew now what they said. I couldn't remember Madison's question, but I'd never forget the smoke that had formed the answer: *Something old, something new, something borrowed, something blue.*

A hard-pressing hand had added a fifth line to the page: *And a sixpence in your shoe!*

Nechai had mentioned, at the benefit, that Fausten had done something wrong. *It was your incantation*, she'd said. *Your words. You borrowed them, but you didn't say them correctly. You didn't say the whole thing.*

Had she been talking about this rhyme? What had Fausten been trying to do—

Keep reading.

I winced and glanced at Fausten's note. It had more to say.

> I've seen the way Andy looks at you. Sometimes people just need a little nudge...

I read those lines again and again, knowing exactly the way Andy looked at me, knowing exactly the doubt we needed to fight. I hadn't realized the Pin-up Bride had been paying attention to Andy and me, but she was right. Andy had cried this morning. He didn't want us broken like this. He wanted us together.

The ellipsis after *nudge* trailed to the edge of the page. I flipped it over.

So nudge him.

"How?"

The box jerked. I looked around for what might've moved it—nothing, me—then glanced inside. The box's last item was familiar in ways I both knew and couldn't remember, ways that made my upper lip curl.

A vial. Fausten had wrapped it with another note. I shook the box, making the vial rattle and roll in the bottom. The scent of peaches sweetened until it smelled like they had been rotting in the trash for days—and the note slipped free. I plucked it from the box.

When the time is right, say the magic words and place things true of Andy in a circle around you. Then touch him with this magic potion. ☺

Magic potion? The vial had a pink-and-mint-green label. Wasn't it just one of her pheromones souvenirs?

Thanks to her note's smiley face, I figured that it was, that she was kidding.

But the postscript suggested she was serious.

P.S. The sixpence? It's in your pocket.

My skin tingled as I dug it out and set it on the table. How could she have known that I had found—no, that I *would find*—a sixpence? Her soothsaying warmed me to the possibility that her gift was more than just superstitious bunk, but nothing could keep her secret ingredient from giving me the heebie-jeebies. The substance was glittery but not clear. The thick yellowish goo thudded back and forth in the vial, never fully blending with an unsettling glob of reddish brown.

Like a bad batch.

Fausten had been absent from the stage—from life—for over a year. Gunk in a vial probably wasn't to blame, but it still wasn't worth the risk. I wanted Andy to choose me. I wanted him to realize on his own that he'd made a mistake. And anyway, these pheromones probably didn't even do anything, aside from smell like peaches. Petty had said Fausten never used them herself.

I repacked the gift and put the lid back on the box. Then I went and turned on the shower. I needed to wash the morning off me and prepare for the show. Tonight might be the pivotal moment that changed my life. But at the very least, wowing the crowd could earn me a permanent place on the stage. After graduating next term, I could put science and my scholarship woes behind me. Theater fans didn't care if I passed physics, and they didn't care if I got into med school. If I did well tonight, maybe I could do well on my own.

I got out of the shower and called Andy. I wanted him to know what he'd be missing. After two rings it went to voicemail. He was avoiding me. His voicemail asked me to leave a message, but I didn't. Leaving messages was how I'd gotten dumped in the first place. I left him a note on the table.

> Conlin asked if you'd do another job with the Pin-up Bride. No posing this time, just an audience plant. I'll leave your ticket at will-call. Thank you,
> D

I rubbed my temple. The shower had failed to ease the headache I'd had all morning.

I dropped my towel and picked up the shirt I'd been wearing earlier. It passed the sniff test, and anyway I'd be changing again as soon as I got to the theater. I slipped it over my head and wandered into Andy's room—

Put these on.

I pulled on a pair of sweats I found on the floor and shoved my feet into the nearest shoes. They felt a little big, but my head felt a little better—

Get your backpack.

Good idea. I didn't want to leave a mess for Andy. I unzipped my backpack and swiped everything on the table into the main compartment: key, coin, crumpled acceptance form—

Take the gift.

My bags were full. I put on my backpack, slung the duffle across my torso, and grabbed my moving box. I probably could've balanced the gift box on top of the moving box, but what did I need it for? I nudged it across the kitchen counter, walked around to the other side, and dumped it into the garbage under the sink.

Pressure pierced my forehead. I dropped the moving box and staggered under the weight of the lopsided duffle bag. The cabinet door banged opened, and the garbage toppled onto the linoleum. A piece of its contents rolled onto the carpet and collided with my foot.

I looked down, not sure which was most strange: that I was wearing Andy's blue sweats; that I was wearing Andy's favorite shoes; or that, lying between my feet, tempting me to pick it up, was Fausten's pink-and-mint-green-labeled vial.

Just in case.

I rubbed my head and tried to soothe the earworm's anxious throb.

Andy wanted us to be together. He'd remember that when he saw me perform as the Pin-up Bride. I'd be fulfilling my end of our deal. I'd be embodying the kind of girl he'd said he'd marry. He'd realize that truth with the audience looking on. He would.

And if he didn't...

Well...

CHAPTER 52

DAPHNE - 24 hours left

My stuff and I took the elevator downstairs. The doors opened onto the lobby—and Ericka. She had her pink scarf around her neck and a dreamy look in her eye. She smiled at me, sweetly at first.

"Andy's not here," I told her.

It took her a moment to realize who I was, but once she did the sweetness turned glib. "Yeah, he forgot his backpack and didn't want to come back to get it. He's having a rough day."

She held up two sets of keys. One set dangled Andy's house and Jeep keys. The other dangled his fig leaf.

I gave Ericka a sweet, if tight, smile of my own and resisted the urge to attack her with Andy's words about her. Or with a better-aimed shoe. No crazy ex-girlfriends here. Andy had said he didn't like her, and I would trust him, like I'd said I would, even if we were broken up at the moment.

Ericka said, "He didn't think you'd be here."

"Just leaving." I leaned my backpack against the elevator to hold it open and invited Ericka to squeeze inside.

"The lock sticks," I told her. "Make sure you lift up on the key." I jiggled my hand to demonstrate.

"Thanks," she said, unsure.

I stretched the corners of my mouth. "You're welcome," I said. Then I leaned toward her. "Can I borrow this?"

I grabbed her scarf and yanked it over her head, pulling it out of the elevator just as the doors closed and messing her thick dark hair to boot.

As I wrapped myself in the pink scarf of Andy's little girlfriend, the earworm hummed with approval.

Now he'd definitely come to the show.

I lugged my stuff into the theater's storeroom and dropped it near the upholstery cleaner. My hands shook, and not from fatigue. In less than an hour, I'd be nuding it up for Fausten's fans.

I stripped off my clothes, put on the hip scarf and my robe, and headed back to the lobby, growing more nervous with every step through the house. What would Andy think when he saw me posing as Aphrodite? I hoped he stood in my line of sight. I wanted to see his face when he changed his mind about us.

I just hoped that seeing me naked and clinging to Guy didn't validate his decision to leave me.

At the top of the aisle, I took a deep breath and peeked out the house doors.

"There you are," Petty said. "Finally. Lose the robe."

I didn't move. I didn't like what I saw at the foot of the grand staircase. Petty was standing next to Fausten's platform, which was completely bare save for a painter's drop cloth and a hand-painted A-frame sign.

"'*The Fairest*'?" I said, reading the sign. "What's 'The Fairest'?"

"You are," he said. "Or Aphrodite is anyway. Get up here. And leave the robe."

I did as he asked. Too slowly, apparently. He grabbed my arm with his freezing hand and forced me onto the platform.

Petty popped the lid on an aerosol can and spray-painted my feet. The droplets felt like needles. And the color was wrong.

"Tan?" I said. "What happened to beige? Tan won't match the Aphrodite wig. And where's Guy?"

Petty crossed his arms and inspected me with a scowl. "Where's your wig from the benefit?"

On Petty's orders, I went back to the storeroom to get my Fausten Cotter wig. And I did so with a skip in my step. The PuB wig was long enough to cover my boobs.

I returned to the lobby with the wig looking like a halter top thanks to my generous application of double-sided tape.

"*Ewgh,*" Petty said, "You've pulled the hair so tight it has no life."

He grabbed at the strands. I clapped my arms over my chest and blocked him with an elbow.

"I don't have time for this," he said. "Just take it off. Fausten never looks this embarrassing."

I didn't want to look embarrassing, but—

"Take it off."

I turned my back to Petty, pried the strands from my chest, and tossed him the wig. Then I tightened my hip scarf.

"Don't get attached to that."

"What?" I pressed one arm tighter to my chest and spared the other to protect my hip scarf. "What do you mean 'don't get attached'?"

Petty took the wig to the bar and dug some hairstyling tools from a bag he had sitting on a stool.

"What do you mean, Petty? And where are the gold Ares props? Where's Guy?"

"Change of plans," he said. "Fausten thought *The Judgment of Paris* might suit you better."

"Is Guy playing Paris?"

"Just you tonight."

"Alone?" My teeth chattered. A tiny part of me approved: no need to confuse my off-right-now boyfriend by pressing my nakedness against a nude Guy. But despite my mantra that he would, Andy probably wouldn't come to the show tonight. And posing with Guy felt infinitely safer than posing alone. Fausten's fans could get grabby. Especially when...

"Wait, where are the ropes?"

"Worry about finishing your paint, Daphne. Doors open soon."

I picked up the paint can and did as he said, because he was right, but—"Where are the ropes, Petty? If Guy's not posing, I at least want the velvet ropes."

Petty brushed out the wig, ignoring me.

The house doors opened. Guy came in pushing a cart of rope stands. Thank goodness. He placed a stand beyond the curtain line, creating a glorious ten-foot buffer between me and the rest of the lobby. Fausten was lucky to get an arm's length. I sent him some silent appreciation.

Petty looked over his shoulder. "No ropes tonight."

"What?!" The shock almost felled me from the platform.

Guy, who had yet to look at me, kept setting up the stands. "She's not posing without ropes."

"No ropes," Petty said. He dragged an already-placed stand to the cart and came back for another. Guy blocked his path and stared him down.

Footsteps hurried across the ballroom overhead.

Petty made a hands-off gesture and backed away from the stands, but his pursed lips said he expected to soon get his way.

Footsteps thundered down the stairs.

Conlin stopped on the middle landing and tucked his shirt into his glittery pants. "Park! House lights are flickering. Go fix 'em. You two, doors in five."

Petty smiled at Guy. Guy glared back.

"Did you hear me?" Conlin asked.

"Yeah," Guy said. "Tell Petty the ropes stay up."

"Of course they're up. Why wouldn't they be up?"

Petty crossed his arms and pouted.

"But not there." Conlin fast-footed down the stairs and moved a couple stands closer to me, about two arm-lengths away. "Put 'em here."

Guy and Petty continued their stare-down.

"Lights, Park. Go," Conlin said, and he hurried toward the ticket booth, ignoring their standoff.

Still staring at Petty and without moving his feet, Guy reached for a rope stand and dragged it to where Conlin wanted it. "You gonna help?" Guy asked Petty.

Petty huffed and returned to the bar to finish styling the wig.

After setting up the last stand, Guy finally looked at me, and the anger in his eyes shifted to something like concern. It didn't make me feel better.

"Let me get your back," he said, making a give-it-here gesture.

Covering my bits, I awkwardly handed him the paint can and turned around. The spray on my back was gentle, a light mist compared to Petty's needles. When the spray stopped, I stepped off the platform and Guy removed the drop cloth. Then, before I could step back into place, he leaned in close to me.

"If I'm not back by curtain, come find me," he whispered, his breath tickling my neck. "I have something I need to give you."

"But you have to come back."

Guy helped me onto the platform, then walked backwards toward the house doors, like he needed to keep an eye on me for as long as he could. Like he was trying to convince himself that I'd be all right for the next hour without him.

But he had to come back. He had to man the lobby while I posed. He couldn't leave me alone with the fans. I didn't trust Petty to keep me safe.

Guy opened the house doors and pushed the cart through. "Okay?" he mouthed.

I shook my head. It wasn't okay. He had to come back. He had to guard me. But he vanished into the house.

Petty finished styling the wig. "Here, put this on."

"Fausten doesn't wear her hair like that," I said.

"Just put it on."

I did. Petty had fluffed the wig so much it looked like a puffy vest, one short enough to show my unimpressive underboob.

Conlin yelled from the ticket booth. "Doors. Go, go."

I faced the wall, then peeked over my shoulder in a pose that I hoped accomplished flirty, yet maximum, modesty.

"What are you doing?" Petty said. He grabbed my shoulders and tried to turn me.

"What are *you* doing? This is her pose." *More or less.* After seeing her first show, I'd spent some time in front of the mirror imitating Fausten's Aphrodite-in-a-clamshell pose. Except my version minimized the sideboob and the ass crack.

"Not tonight." Petty turned me until my bits were facing the whole of the lobby. "Tonight, you're Aphrodite after winning the judgment of Paris."

He handed me a pink apple with a mint-green leaf and positioned me with my feet together, one knee slightly bent and covering the other. Shoulders back, chest high, underboob maximized. He told me to hold the apple at eye level, like I was appraising it before taking a bite. I didn't think I could hold my arm like this for a minute, let alone an hour, but that wasn't the worst of it. By the time Petty was done primping me, I'd traded my hip scarf for a fig leaf.

"Quit frowning," he said. "You look great."

Sure I did. I felt nothing like the goddess who was decidedly fairer than both Hera and Athena. I felt more like a sacrificial pig willingly taking the apple.

Conlin opened the front doors, engulfing me in a chilly breeze. But it was the voices that got me shivering. We'd never announced an understudy. Our guests were expecting the real deal. What would they do when they got me?

People entered the lobby. When they saw me, they hurried toward the boundary set by the velvet rope, and their wide eyes gawked at the racy full-frontal view.

And they smiled. I was a treat. And not just because Fausten hadn't done Aphrodite in a while. I was giving them a new pose, a new experience.

I spent the next several minutes trying to retreat into myself, trying to distance my self from my body and from the reactions of Fausten's fans. I didn't know how else to be a living statue worthy of them, worthy of Aphrodite and of Fausten Cotter herself.

After a while, something pulled my gaze from the apple and into the depths of the lobby. A tall figure was meandering through the crowd. I gasped, almost dropping the apple.

Head down, shoulders slumped, hands shoved in his pockets. He looked like he was having a rough day, just like Ericka had said. But I didn't see Ericka. Just Andy. I pulled up taller and willed him to look my way. To remember us.

Andy lifted his head and scanned the room. His gaze passed over me.

And didn't come back.

I swallowed and focused on the apple, hoping that the heat in my face wasn't dissolving the paint.

Maybe he was still mad at me.

But he wouldn't have come at all if he was completely against me. And it wasn't like he'd noticed me, frowned, and looked away. His gaze had passed over me same as it had passed over everyone else.

So maybe he hadn't realized the statue was me. The other patrons didn't seem to notice. They were all smiling and taking pictures like I was Fausten.

But Andy hadn't even looked at the statue. He'd shown no interest in coming to this end of the lobby to check it out. He'd walked directly into the house, to find his seat.

Because he only had eyes for me?

Tingles of truth rippled down my neck and across my shoulders. Fausten was right. Andy wanted us to be together. He just needed a little nudge.

"You're doing great," Petty said, pulling me from my thoughts. He picked up a velvet rope stand.

"Put that back," I said.

"Shh. Just keep doing what you're doing."

Petty moved the stand to the side, then picked up another and moved it too. A few people offered to help him, and soon my protective barrier was gone.

And the crowd moved closer. So close, I couldn't see the closest in my periphery. So close, the closest fans could touch me.

And they did.

They kissed little trinkets and placed them at my feet, then touched my calves.

They pressed their palms together and bowed their heads, then touched my arms.

They made the sign of the cross, then touched the hollow of my throat.

One lady placed a garland of pink flowers around my neck, exposing my breasts as she pulled my hair through and fluffed it back into place.

And Petty let her. He lit tea candles and handed them to people, telling them to place them at my feet. Someone said the flames might trigger the sprinklers, but Petty assured us it wasn't a problem, the alarm was manual.

"Go ahead," he said, handing out candles. "Make an offer, say a prayer. Wish her well, and thank her for everything she'll be doing for us tonight."

And so they did, not one of them complaining that I wasn't Fausten Cotter. They believed. They believed, and they transformed me into something more than Aphrodite, marble statue.

I became their shrine. I stood frozen amidst fire and let Fausten's fans touch me. It was the least I could do to thank her for the opportunity she was giving me tonight, and my resolve settled me into the pose, held me present to the whole of my domain. I took in everyone.

Including Nechai.

She was at the bar, sipping from a tumbler. Her posture was casual, but how she watched me was not. I tried to look without looking, without moving my eyes—Fausten wouldn't move her eyes—but I wasn't as good as Fausten.

Our eyes met. Nechai tilted her head, and her lips curved into a satisfied smirk. She knew I wasn't Fausten. Everyone else was fooled or forgiving, but not Nechai. I was grateful to her and her money, but seeing her made nightmares flash in my mind. Images of the creepy fan hurting the Pin-up Bride.

I focused on the apple, hoping that averting my eyes would discourage Nechai from coming any closer.

It was all I could do.

Petty handed out more candles; people placed them at my feet. I glanced back at the bar.

The creepy fan was gone.

But I felt her. Nechai. I felt her hiding among the crowd, inching closer. I fought an urge to look around for her, to make sure she wasn't behind me. Every molecule in my body strained against my will to stand still, but I couldn't let Fausten down.

The lights dimmed their five-minute warning.

And someone touched me.

I flinched, and my heart began beating so fast all over my body that I couldn't tell if the touch hurt or which direction to swing in order to bat the person away. And then I heard it, her bone-saw mumble.

My skin prickled; my head burned: the earworm didn't like it either.

A light in an alcove burst with a pop.

"Fausten!" Petty cried, and footsteps pounded up the stairs.

The lobby lights returned, and I quickly glanced behind me.

Whoever had touched me was gone. But they'd left me a present.

Something dripped from my finger and slid, warm and wet, down my leg.

CHAPTER 53

DAPHNE - 20 hours left

"Are you okay?"

I risked a quick look down. It was a patron. Petty had left me alone with the fans, most of whom were now bottlenecking through the house doors.

I was cold, tense, and something slimy was sliding down my left leg. But it didn't hurt. It was warm. Gross. But not painful.

I set my jaw, and my attention on the apple, and nodded once. The lobby would clear in less than five minutes. I could hold the pose until then. It's what Fausten Cotter would do.

I waited until Conlin's booming voice had started the show, then dropped the pose and inspected my hand, my leg. Both looked fine and were dry to the touch, but my skin still phantom-felt the slime. I rubbed a smudge of gunk off the cabochon, then crouched low and blew out the candles.

After a show, I'd sometimes find stuffed animals or flowers in the house seats, but Fausten's fans had never left gifts for the statue. And these gifts were weird. Crosses and Buddhas and worry dolls. Well-wishes on napkins and photos. Drinks from the bar, still brimming with liquid and offered with straws. The platform looked like the site of an impromptu tragedy memorial.

I tiptoed through the gifts, donned the robe and undies I'd left behind the bar, and took the grand staircase to the hall of dressing rooms.

The other performers were talking and laughing in the greenroom, but I couldn't share their mood. Petty had abandoned me. The fans had groped me. Andy had overlooked me.

But he was here. That had to count for something.

The crack beneath Petty's door was dark. I banged on it anyway.

"I'm right here." Petty grumped down the stairs and came loping down the hall. His skin looked pasty and his hair was flat. And he brought with him the faint scent of something sweet and rotten.

"What's that smell?" I asked.

Petty wiped his hands on his skinny jeans, leaving dark marks on the material. "Get inside," he said, unlocking the door and ignoring my question. "I'll need every second to make you a presentable fill-in for Fausten."

He sat me down on the white leather couch and perched himself on the edge of the coffee table, next to his arsenal of makeup. He closed his eyes and took a moment to breathe...but when he opened them again, his knee began to bounce.

"Everything okay?" I asked. "You look as nervous as I feel."

He pumped product into his palm and rubbed it between his hands. "Just want to get back to Fausten."

"Right. The rash." I rubbed at the phantom slime on my left hand. "She doing okay?"

"She's—"

"Resting?"

He glared at me, sustaining it while he spread the product on my face. "You're wearing the dress you borrowed, right? The blue shoes?" He scowled at my bare feet.

So that was it. Petty was worried I'd ruin the show. I rubbed at my hand. So much for getting a pep talk.

Petty wiped concealer under my eyes and dabbed it with a sponge. "I saw Andy in the lobby," he said.

"Me, too. But he didn't see me."

Petty selected an eyeliner. "He saw you. He just didn't *know* it was you because he was too busy *looking* for you. You know? Look up."

I hoped that was true. I'd come to the same conclusion, but it was nice having it seconded—even if by Petty. Andy had come. Alone. Because I'd asked him to. Because he wanted to see *me*, not anyone else.

"What if he doesn't realize it's me onstage?" I said. "It won't impress if I have to explain."

"He'll notice. He just needs a little nudge." Petty winked. "You brought everything, right? The stuff? The oil?"

"You said Fausten doesn't use that stuff."

"You're not Fausten," he said. "Look at you. You've got limp hair and a little boy's torso."

I gaped at him.

"But you've got decent legs. Put them in a short skirt and some blue heels—you're welcome—and you're closer to capturing the Pin-up Bride. But it's still not enough and you know it. Andy's not the only one you need to impress tonight. The crowd's wonderful when they're satisfied, but you don't want to see their nasty side. And if you're serious about Conlin promoting you to the stage, well, *I* wouldn't snub a good luck charm."

But I had. I'd snubbed Fausten's good luck charm. My chest tightened.

Petty finished my makeup and pointed at my fluffed wig. "Take that off."

"Why? What's wrong with it?"

Petty went to the desk and brought out a dark wig with pink and mint-green streaks, styled to long, wavy perfection. "Fausten wanted you to have something brand-new," he said. "Look." He joggled the wig and the overhead light picked up strands of black, pink, and mint-green tinsel. "This one's got shimmer."

I pulled off the old wig. "Can't argue with shimmer."

Petty styled me in the new wig and handed me a mirror. I couldn't believe what I saw. Petty had outdone himself. I handed back the mirror and rubbed my hand.

"You keep doing that," he said. "You need some lotion?"

He handed me a tube. I squeezed a drop onto the back of my left hand and massaged it in. "You know that rich benefactor, Nechai?"

"Chaiprasit?" Petty slid the mascara back into his kit. "Yes, I know her."

"Did you see her?"

He stilled. "Here?"

"She mumbled something and then—"

"You saw her here? Tonight?"

"She's always here."

Petty squinted at me and then his gaze shifted to the wall behind me, to his giant poster of the Pin-up Bride.

I shivered. *It's just a poster. (Don't hallucinate.)*

Still looking at his poster, Petty said, "She do anything?"

I swallowed and flicked the fingers of my left hand. It felt fine, but, still, it wasn't. "I think she wiped something on me."

The lights blinked.

Petty grabbed my feet and yanked them into his lap. I fell back against the couch, arms flailing. His fingers probed my arches and the cracks between my toes.

"Where?" he said.

"Here." I waved my left hand.

Petty dropped my feet. They clunked unladylike on the table. I scrambled to tuck them beneath me, sweat beads forming beneath my wig.

Petty eyed my left hand like it was contagious. "She say anything?"

I shrugged. "Prayer? I don't know. I don't even know if it was her; it was dark. But that's what everyone else was doing. Which was weird, by the way. And the candles."

Petty lifted my hand and peered down his nose as he tottered it under the light. I didn't know what to make of the expression on his face, but it had me squirming on the couch.

"Why'd you make it sound like tonight would be different from what Fausten usually does?" I asked. "Why all the gifts?"

"Last rites of sacrifice," he said, his voice lower than usual.

I shivered. "What?"

The lights blinked. He looked up at me, then chuckled. "You should see your face. I told you: fan appreciation night." His thumb rubbed the cabochon. "What she wiped on you—do you know what it was?"

"I dunno. Slimy?"

His face paled and his eyebrows invaded his blue hairline. "Like saliva slimy or oily slimy?"

"Gross slimy?"

"Maybe she cursed you."

"*Cursed me?*"

He nodded, his eyes earnest. But he couldn't be serious. This was ridiculous. I was being ridiculous.

"Nechai gave me money to keep me square with Conlin," I said. "She wouldn't hurt me."

She *hadn't* hurt me. My hand was fine. Everything was fine. It might not have even been her.

The lights blinked again. Petty glanced at the poster, then shook his head as if clearing it. "Sorry, you're right. Faus and I were watching scary movies last night; I can get carried away. Your hand's okay to perform?"

"Yeah. It doesn't hurt." I wiggled my fingers to show him. "It was just...creepy."

"She is creepy. With those blue glasses?" He shuddered, then smiled. Sort of. He stood and pulled me up too. "You look great. Just play your part tonight and everything will go as Fausten planned."

Except I'd snubbed her good luck charm.

Back in the storeroom, I dressed in Fausten's skirt and corset and buckled on the blue T-strap peep-toes. Petty had implied that these shoes were from him, but I knew they, like the dress, had come from Fausten. Even back then she had deemed me worthy—of Andy, the stage, her secrets.

I didn't feel worthy. Success is sexy. Fausten knew that, and she'd given me everything I needed to make tonight's performance a success and to secure my future with Andy. But it was only by strange happenstance that I was now holding her gift.

I put the vial in a pocket I'd found in the PuB skirt. The vial fit perfectly, and I didn't think that was a coincidence. It made me feel worse. I wished I'd followed her instructions to the letter and gathered things of Andy's, but taking her good luck charm onstage was the best I could do now.

I took the elevator to the trap room, weaved my way through the posts supporting the stage, and lay atop Fausten's platform.

Thud.

I startled.

Light split the elevator doors, and someone stepped out of the brightness. "Daphne?"

"Guy?"

He found me with the beam of his red flashlight. "Here, take this," he said, coming over. "It'll keep you *sa—*" He heaved and stumbled into the nearest support post.

I sat up. "Are you okay?"

"*Just put...this in...your pocket.*" He held up a well-used red-and-white plastic takeout bag.

I scowled. "I don't want your trash."

He looked at the rumpled plastic and puffed a pitiful laugh, then took something out of the bag. "*Here.*"

It resembled a baby food jar, except the contents looked as nasty as the takeout bag

"What's it for?" I asked.

"*Just put...it in...your pocket.*"

It looked too big to fit. "What's in it?"

"*Herbs...and...**come on.***" He reached toward me, face askew, arm straining to set the jar on the platform. "*Just herbs,*" he said, "*Just herbs and...and...*"

And blood.

I jerked on instinct, hitting the jar. It skittered across the floor, glass scraping concrete, and ricocheted off a post.

Guy made a lumbering effort to collect the nasty and bring it back to the platform.

I kicked out. "Get that away from me."

"*I know...it's foul,*" he said. "*So...is she.*"

He tried to shove the jar into my costume. I swatted his hands.

"*Daphne, stop.*"

"You stop." I peeled his fingers off me and shoved.

He backed away. "*You talk...to Madison?*"

"Madison? Why? Why are you talking like that? What's going on?"

"*She's...gone. Fau—*" He groaned and keeled over as if punched in the gut.

Above us, the audience clapped.

My head throbbed. Cold mist dispersed from beneath the platform and surrounded me like I sat in a cloud.

Guy raised both hands as if in surrender. One hand held the flashlight, the other, the jar of blood. He stepped closer, leaning forward as if fighting an invisible force.

"*I'm just...gonna—*" He grabbed my skirt, his fingers finding the pocket and ripping the seam. Fausten's vial slipped free and clinked on the platform. I clambered to find it before it rolled off the edge. *Where is it?*

Guy fumbled the flashlight, and its red beam shined on the vial.

"*Fuck me,*" he said. He reached for the vial, but I grabbed it first and stuffed it back into my pocket.

Guy stumbled backward and collapsed against a post, his face so contorted, I couldn't tell what he was thinking.

He held out his jar of nasty. "*Trade me.*"

Above us, the audience roared with applause.

The trapdoor slid open, illuminating the trap room—and the haze. I thought the haze was part of Fausten's act, but Guy's eyes widened as the haze thickened into mist, into fog, into a pall of sweet peaches.

He laughed this defeated whimper of a laugh, and his eyes pleaded with mine. His only movement was a tremor in his left hand. The jar of blood.

Please, his expression said. *Please, just take it. Just take it.*

The gears beneath me rumbled and the platform began to rise.

Guy grabbed my arm and pulled. I clung to the other side of the platform, but misty condensation made my hand slip.

"Let go," I said, rising closer and closer to the underside of the stage. If Guy didn't let go, I'd lose a limb when the platform pushed me through. I fought harder. "Guy, let go."

"*She doesn't...help.*" He reached for my skirt, my hip, my pocket. "*She takes...control.*"

Around me, the mist sizzled.

Guy screamed and let go of me. "How?!" he wailed, his voice normal but pained. "There's no posters down here!"

Heart pounding, soul crying, brain numbing to the struggle happening on the ground. I lay in position, flat on my back, and brushed the wig strands off my neck. I pointed my toes.

Guy groaned—and glass touched my hand. I flicked it away, my body twisting, and something slipped from my pocket. The vial—

Glass shattered.

"Shit," Guy said, but his voice was muffled by the mist as it surrounded me, forming a tunnel that forced me to only rise, to only react, like the girl I'd long wanted to become.

CHAPTER 54

DAPHNE - 19 hours left

I rose from the stage in a cloud of mist with a spotlight shining upon me.

The house was silent. And no strobe light flashed to cue my next move.

I sat up anyway, letting my ribs lead the way, and jazz-sat to the right, putting my back to the audience. I swung my legs over the side of the platform, and—

Crap. I'd forgotten the dark sheet.

No matter, keep going.

I stood and swayed my hips, slinking my arms up the sides of my body as I turned to face the audience, glowing like Fausten, impressing like Fausten, exuding power like Fausten. I hit a high V, and the crowd erupted with cheers.

But their reaction to my entrance was nothing compared to the response I got next.

Fausten's throne glided up behind me. I took a seat as a lanky human in full-body matte black exited among the shadows stage right, cuing Guy's entrance, stage left.

But stage left remained empty.

Standing in the wing, Conlin shrugged his sequined shoulders and pointed at himself, offering to stand in for Guy.

I shook my head no, and I rose. "Volunteer?"

The audience went wild. I'd never heard them cheer so loud, not even for Fausten—but I knew what had them so excited.

Guy always did Fausten's talking, but tonight I spoke for myself. Tonight, I wasn't *like* Fausten Cotter.

I was better.

Arms shot up. Not a single holdout in the house. I scanned the crowd, looking them over. I flirted. I teased.

I chose.

The lucky volunteer skipped down the aisle in a pink PuB shirt and a white hat with the veil pushed back. I invited her to sit on the throne.

"Really?" she asked.

No reason for it to go to waste.

Omigod, she mouthed at the audience as she rushed to the throne. She plopped herself down, gripping the armrests and bouncing a little. *I'm sitting in the Pin-up Bride's chair!*

"What's your question?" I asked.

She said something, but I was suddenly too anxious to listen. The question didn't matter if I couldn't deliver the answer like Fausten. Petty and Conlin had both told me to just sit here and hold out my hand, that everything else was under control, but I didn't see how that could work.

"Fausten?" said the volunteer. "Is that right?"

I had no idea. My hands tingled with a feeling like threads slipping through my skin.

Sweaty palms or the act's magic at work?

Guess we'll find out.

I stretched out my left arm...

And my hand produced a mist. It happened slower for me than for Fausten, but mist poured from my fingers and spread throughout the stage. It formed pictures. The audience yelled, the mist blinked, and my first volunteer left to the soundtrack of catcalls, cheers, and applause. My chin lifted and so did my confidence.

I could do this. I could so do this.

I answered another two questions and then the mist crept into the house, all the way to the back third of the right section.

It was choosing its own volunteer.

The mist illuminated someone special, someone sitting on the aisle, next to a vacant seat.

I drew in a deep breath. This was it: our breakthrough or my swan song.

"I've got a surprise for you." I scanned the crowd, giving myself a pause and each delighted face a dedicated moment of my appreciation. "It's something new. Well, maybe not entirely new. I've tried something like it once before."

Was that true? I didn't know, but the words felt inspired, and everyone jumped to their feet like they knew what I was talking about.

Everyone except the next volunteer.

Andy sat hunched in his seat. He had his elbow on the armrest and his hand pressed to his mouth. His eyes frowned at the stage.

He was frowning at me.

Did he know who I was?

He had to. He wouldn't look at Fausten Cotter that way.

"Are you ready?" I asked.

Andy's frown deepened. He sank further into his chair and shielded his face with his hand. He didn't want to come onstage.

And I didn't want to force him. I wanted to be wanted. I wanted someone who wanted me. Andy had made his decision about me this morning, and apparently it was final. Calling him onstage wouldn't impress him; it would only make him mad. He was here tonight, but only because that's the kind of person he was. The kind of person who, even after uncoupling, I could count on.

Either that or he was here for Ericka's scarf. The empty seat next to him was probably saved for her.

I swallowed the sludge in my throat and pointed a vague finger at

Andy's section, at somebody, anybody. It didn't matter who if it wasn't Andy.

I expected some posturing from the fans, but there was no confusion. They all knew who I wanted.

They clapped the back of Andy's seat and shook him by the shoulder. The stout guy sitting near him took him by the arm and encouraged him to get up. Andy remained hunched in his chair, resisting their every pull.

But he couldn't resist the mist.

It swirled around him, seeping between him and his seat. Andy clung to the armrest, but he still began to rise. The mist thickened until he popped out of his chair and stumbled into the aisle. He glared at me.

He turned, trying to leave, but the mist blocked his path. Andy leaned into it, fighting the mist, but even as he struggled, the mist held him upright. His feet barely brushed the ground as the mist carried him up the stairs.

It carried him to me.

Onstage, Andy scrambled to find his footing. The audience cheered for him, but it didn't put him at ease. He angled his body toward the stairs, trying to run, but the mist had him cloaked. He rolled his neck and shoulders like it was strangling him.

I fidgeted, not knowing what to do.

Ask.

"Do you have a question?"

Andy jammed his hands in his pockets, scowling at me like I was entirely familiar and therefore all the more disenchanting.

I steadied myself against the throne. Everything was fine. I was *fine*. And I would continue to be fine. Look at what I'd already accomplished. I was filling in for the best act in the region.

I exhaled slowly, trying to believe myself, trying to believe that I'd be fine without Andy. But I suddenly needed a hug. My hands found my elbows and squeezed.

"Daph?"

I looked up at Andy. His expression softened, and the mist surrounding him dispersed until there was nothing but Andy, a spotlight in all the darkness. No one but Andy, not for me.

He crossed the stage and wrapped me in his arms and his scent of peppermint gum. He hugged me tightly. I tried to match his strength, willing him to do the thing he always did.

And he did. He kissed the top of my head and lingered there a moment, puffing breath against my hair. "I miss you already."

I choked out a sob and squeezed him tighter, trying to hold it together, to hold us together.

He laid his cheek on my head. "I didn't mean for you to move out," he said. Fausten was right. All Andy needed was a little nudge. "Stay. Finish school. Settle your scholarship." He swayed us side to side. "It's only a few months."

I waited for him to say more. But my body bristled with every silent second.

And after those few months? Would I be kicked out after those few months or would I be invited to Chicago? The need to know worsened my headache. I rubbed my temple, trying to remain calm. "What do you mean 'it's only a few months'?"

"I mean you can stay in my apartment."

"But just for school?"

Andy stiffened like a statue in my arms. I glanced up at him, wishing I hadn't complained. *James girls don't complain.* But I couldn't be sure he was reacting to me. He looked puzzled by something happening behind me.

My dark assistant had set up a stand near the proscenium wall. On it were a few things I recognized.

Andy pulled out of our hug. "Are those my sweats?"

I plucked the navy-blue fabric off the stand and held them up by the waistband. And I laughed. Fausten was a saint. Far from holding a grudge about me ignoring her gift, she'd had our dark assistant cobble together for me the items she'd asked me to gather. She'd anticipated this moment, this rift between me and Andy. And I knew that she was here with me now, guiding me through it.

"You see these blue sweats?" I said to the crowd. "Andy used to make me pancakes in these sweats, cuddled me on the couch in these sweats, let me borrow them when he begged me to stay over."

Andy half smiled, a wistful smile, but he still looked wary.

I held his blue sweats to my nose. I'd worn them here, but they still smelled like him. I closed my eyes and inhaled his scent. *Please. Please, not for the last time.*

I tossed them aside.

Andy watched the sweats slide stage right, then looked at the crowd. He stepped closer to me and spoke quietly.

"Why am I here?"

"You tell me." I turned toward the stand. It held something else I'd worn here tonight.

"You see these shoes?" I held them up, one in each hand, so that the crowd could see where the soles of Andy's ECCOs had worn through, where he'd already had them repaired. "Andy's had these shoes since ninth grade. They're his favorite. He was wearing them the night he told me..."

For a second I forgot who I was. I smoothed the PuB's skirt and adjusted the veil.

"The night he said he'd marry a girl like me."

The crowd roared. Whistles. Applause. I tossed the shoes stage left and struck a pose, taking in everything around me: the stage, the lights, the crowd. I might have started this endeavor to meet Andy's requirements, to persuade him to make good on what he'd promised, but in the process I'd discovered myself. I wasn't a dank-lab biologist. I was *this*.

I held up my hand, and mist hovered in my palm, captivating everyone, swirling like a vortex star.

This. This was who I was.

Andy's eyes widened, his pupils swirling in sync with the mist. "How are you doing that?"

"I have more than fulfilled my end of our bargain," I told him. "Don't you think?"

"I wanted Daphne," he said, his eyes sad, his palms pleading, "the one before winter break, before we went to my parents' house and Mom sent you home and I didn't leave with you."

"Then don't leave me now."

He rubbed his neck. His gaze trailed from me to the stand. It still held more of his stuff.

I picked up a piece of paper that was twice crumpled, first by Andy's fist and then by me brushing it into my backpack.

"You see this form?" I asked the crowd. "Andy got a new job. He's leaving me for Chicago."

"I can't quit the internship," he said. "Not after waiting till last minute to take it. But I think it'll be good." He grabbed my hand. "A head start."

"You mean a *fresh* start?"

He frowned.

"And do you know why he's so eager to get to Chicago?" I asked the crowd.

With thumb and forefinger I picked up the last item on the stand. The scarf I'd borrowed from Andy's would-be girlfriend. Pink with hints of mint green.

"It's a great color," I told the crowd, "but it's not mine."

"Boo!"

"She'll probably want this back." I tossed the scarf at Andy and turned back to the crowd. "It's time for Andy to perform his part of our deal," I told them. "Can you guess what his part is?"

The audience applauded and yelled out their guesses. Andy puzzled his brow at me.

"It starts with *Will...you...*" I pressed my lips together, prompting the word that starts with *M*.

Andy's expression shifted. He glowered at the spotlight, the audience, the stand, now empty of his things. He leaned closer so only I could hear.

"You put on a costume, call me onstage, and I'm supposed to propose? Is that it?"

"You put up this same fight when I wanted to move in with you, but you loved it, you know you did. And I'm not following you to Chicago without a commitment, Andy." He grimaced, so I said it again. "I want nothing to do with you without a commitment."

He looked at his feet.

"We can justice-of-the-peace it first thing Monday, before class, before you leave. I can transfer to school in Chicago. We can move what we've got going on here to there."

His face flinched again, but this time it wasn't with pain. It was dread. "I don't want this following me."

"We've been dating for years," I said. "If it was all for nothing, then why are you here?"

"Not for this." He flicked at my costume and all its drama with a scowl. "That thing I said about the poster? It was a joke. Sarcasm. But you made it your only hope. I would've given you what you wanted after graduation, probably, but now..." He shook his head. "I don't know what happened this term, if this was a fluke or stress or what, but you remind me—"

"Don't say it."

"—of your mom."

"No, I don't."

"Worse. You're unstable—"

"Don't even—"

"You remind me of my mom."

"Then why fight it!?" My raging body stumbled backward and hit the stand.

New items rattled on top.

And you know what to do with them.

I did. I was nothing like our moms. They would never perform like this. They would never do for someone what I had been doing all term for Andy.

But they would have no problem giving someone a permanent nudge.

"Then why fight it?" I said more calmly. "Our moms are cute, they're coddled, and they're cared for. So why fight their method?" I leaned toward him and whispered, "It works."

I addressed the crowd. "Should we get him in the chair?"

Andy shook his head and turned to leave, but I didn't want him to go—and the mist made sure I got my way. It surrounded him, stopping him midstride and jerking him in a circle to face me. His eyes flashed with a fear that hurt my heart. I couldn't look at him.

But I could make this right.

I gestured for Andy to sit. He didn't want to, but the mist forced him onto the throne.

"Did I thank you yet, for coming?" I said to the crowd. They whooped and hollered. "Because tonight is special. You're all here to witness—nay—to empower a love that needs a little glue."

The crowd went wild. Andy gripped the arms of the throne, trying to wrench himself away, but he couldn't leave his seat.

"Daphne." The strangled whisper came from the wing, from Guy.

I ignored him.

"You know the poem," I told the crowd. "Say it with me. Say it with feeling."

I inhaled through my nose, taking the mist deep into my lungs and savoring the moment.

"Something old."

The words stretched across the stage, each letter forming from the mist.

A spotlight shone on Andy's old shoes.

"Something new."

The words shifted, brightening as the audience said them too, and the spotlight moved to highlight Andy's acceptance form.

"Something borrowed."

We spoke in chorus, and the mist shifted, spotlighting Ericka's pink scarf.

"Something blue."

The spotlight moved to Andy's navy-blue sweats.

Then it trailed stage left, to the stand, where it glinted off a shiny silver coin.

I picked it up. "And...," I said, prompting my fans.

"And a sixpence in your shoe!"

"*Her* shoe," someone corrected.

My grin faltered. I tried to remember the rhyme's precise words. *And a sixpence...and a* silver *sixpence in your...her...?* I couldn't remember.

The mist swirled around Andy's old ECCOs and lifted one shoe by the heel.

I hesitated. Was the sixpence supposed to go in Andy's shoe?

And if it was, wasn't it supposed to go in the shoe he was wearing?

I looked at Andy. His eyes were wide with awe and disbelief at the mist still lifting his shoe. But when his eyes met mine, he scowled. He wouldn't be doing anything for me anytime soon. But he still wanted us. I knew he did. He just needed help overcoming his resistance.

I dropped the sixpence into his old ECCO and tried not to question what I would've done had I not worn his shoes here myself.

With the sixpence deep in the toe, the mist set down the shoe and swirled itself around the stand.

One last item stood tall. Its pink-and-mint-green label faced away from me, and the gap between its ends did little to hide the vial's unsettling contents.

Still, I reached for Fausten's gift—

And my inner shields shivered, begging for my attention. But they were too weak to rise.

They were still too overpowered by the earworm.

It was ready.

So was I. I looked into the lights, out at Fausten's fans. They cheered for me because they thought I was her. They were waiting for her to triumph. I felt my shields' concern, but if I didn't finish this, I'd render Fausten a fool in front of her fans. I'd be committing another flop on behalf of the Pin-up Bride.

And yet I knew her fans would continue to love her. No matter what.

And why?

I picked up the vial of glittery fluid dotted with clumps of reddish brown. Pin-up Bride pheromones. Basically perfume, right? Harmless. But what if the rumors were true and it was something more? If one tiny vial of putrid oil could make millions of people love the Pin-up Bride, then certainly it could make one Andy McBride love me.

I raised the vial high, toasting with the crowd. They raised their drinks, urging me on with their clapping, their cheers, their love.

And then they quieted with anticipation.

"*Daphn—*" Guy cut off the end of my name like he was choking, but I couldn't do anything about that right now. Guy was fine. He'd be fine.

I pulled the stopper from the vial.

Andy jerked away from the smell, and I couldn't blame him. It was fetid and sour, with a hint of rotten peaches.

And he was right: we didn't need this stuff. What if it didn't work? What would he think of me if he ever realized what I'd tried to do to him?

I closed my eyes and bent closer to the only person I might ever mutually love, but only partway. I wanted him to prove to me that we didn't need this stuff. Prove it by meeting me the rest of the way. He needed to meet me the rest of the way.

Get up and meet me the rest of the way.

The mist lifted him, and he angled toward me. Our lips touched. Andy's moved against mine. More than a kiss.

Words.

"Let me go."

I froze. Had I heard him correctly? I wasn't sure, but it didn't matter. The thought was there and I couldn't make it go away.

If only I could have made him see things clearly, see them how I saw them. I wrapped my arms around his neck and kissed him harder. Kissed him just one last time.

He pulled back. "I'm wrong about you, aren't I?"

So, so wrong. Wrong about shaming me, wrong about dumping me, wrong about leaving me behind. I wasn't pushy or erratic. I was focused and determined. A survivor. And I was worthy. I'd been nothing but the do-what-I-must kind of girl he'd told me he wanted.

"That was you this term, wasn't it? The real you."

Yes. Exactly yes. I could make it on my own, but we were better together. Did he know that? I pulled him closer, but he wrested away from me.

He slid off the throne.

And he dropped to one knee.

I grabbed his hand. He let me hold it as he gazed up at me with glossy red-shot eyes. As he rolled his neck and shoulders.

He said, "I don't like the real you."

"You may not have a choice."

I tipped the vial.

And around me rang the whirl of an alarm.

CHAPTER 55

DAPHNE

I fumbled the vial. It fell to the stage and rolled against the base of the throne, but not before splattering its last drops of oil on my hand.

In my head, the earworm stretched new wings and made a triumphant fluttering that bloomed throughout my body to the surface of my skin.

"Daph?" I could barely hear Andy over the alarm. He clutched his stomach and looked up at me with dreamy eyes. Oil glistened like lip gloss on his cheek. His lips twitched a smile and his fingers lifted, reaching for me.

Reaching for us.

My heart swelled, rivaling the earworm. The oil had worked: Andy was mine again. I helped him onto the throne and climbed onto his lap, hugging him to me, kissing him everywhere. Mist swirled in celebration around us, sparking in bursts, popping like fireworks.

Andy was too weak to lift his arms and hold me back, but I knew he would recover, and I could help him until then. I squirreled my fingers beneath his arms and flopped them over my shoulders. He nuzzled his head against my neck and moaned—but I couldn't tell if it was more sigh or more groan. I pulled away and studied his face. His brow was creased and his lids were heavy.

He clutched his stomach and groaned. "Why is this happening to me?"

The alarm stopped. All was quiet, but the silence deafened me in the wake of Andy's question.

Someone cleared their throat. "Ms. James."

In the wing, Conlin waved for my attention, then pointed at the audience.

I could see only the first few rows in the glaring light, but the fans all looked tense, unsure if the alarm had been part of the act or a warning they should obey. They awaited my cue.

I hopped off Andy's lap. He fell forward and hung over the armrest. I bent to him and patted his face. "Andy?"

He didn't react.

"*Ms. James.*"

Stupid theater and its faulty wiring. I pulled up tall and whirled on the audience, spreading my arms wide and strutting to the edge of the stage. I forced my lips into a show-must-go-on smile. *Just part of the act, folks. Show me you love me.*

The audience's muted clapping said they still weren't sure.

But they were about to be.

The doors at the back of the house banged open and someone rushed in screaming—

"FIRE!"

The audience panicked.

Smoke burst from the Pin-up Bride posters, filling the house with mist. It descended on the seats and covered the audience like a peach blanket. But not to smother them. Oh no, the smoke wouldn't hurt Fausten's fans. It cradled them, protecting them from each other like they were eggs in the hollows of its crate.

I couldn't say the same for Conlin.

Conlin came around the proscenium wall, to the edge of the stage. He held up his hands. "Ladies and gentlemen, please stay cal—"

A white streak flashed from the light rack and struck him in the chest. He collapsed where he stood, his sequined suit glittering as he fell. His head cracked the stage.

I screamed and dropped to my knees at his side. "Conlin?" He looked unharmed, but he wasn't moving and I couldn't rouse him. I couldn't find a pulse.

"Everybody out!"

Halfway down the left aisle, Guy was pushing his way through the haze-covered crowd. He palmed the apron and vaulted onto the stage, wincing in pain. Steam burns covered his hands and face.

But at least he was alive.

My voice squeaked as I pointed at the lifeless body before me. "Conlin."

"Can't help him," Guy said. He bent over me and ran his hands over my hips, checking the pockets in my skirt. "Where is it?"

"Where's what? Stop." I pushed him away. He grabbed my hand and pulled me to my feet—then stilled and looked at his palm.

His palm glistened with oil.

"Shit." He looked around, head whipping as he searched for something on the floor.

Behind him, Andy sat crumpled like a doll on the throne, still hanging over the armrest. He was so still. Too still.

Guy crouched next to him and picked up the vial. He held it up to the light, then flipped it over. Nothing more came out.

He met my eyes. "You don't know what this is, do you?"

I glanced at the vial, at its pink-and-mint-green label, but I was more concerned about Andy. I couldn't tell if he was breathing.

Guy screamed at me. "Do you?!"

"Love charm."

It sounded foolish, and for a second I doubted myself, doubted that it had worked. But that warm, satisfied feeling still fluttered in my head and in my heart, that swelled, fulfilled feeling.

I lifted my chin. "It *was* Pin-up Bride pheromones." *Was*, but not anymore. Now it was the glue that would bind me and Andy.

Guy laughed without humor and rubbed his hand through his hair.

I pointed at the label—but then peered closer. The label was pink and mint green, but it didn't say *PBP* like I'd expected. And yet its fancy calligraphy wasn't unfamiliar. I suppressed a shudder and told myself everything was fine. The contents were close enough. "It says so right there: *NEC Romantic Oil.*"

"That's not a brand," Guy said. "It's camouflage."

I frowned at the vial—and my synapses started to fire. My stomach rolled.

"Read it together."

I shook my head. I didn't want to read it, but even though I'd stopped my mind from combining the words, my body didn't need it to. I was suddenly cold, and no amount of rubbing my arms could make me warm. My body shivered, knowing the truth of what Guy was telling me before my brain deigned to understand. I swallowed a rise of bile.

"It's necro—"

I covered my ears, trying to stall my understanding, but I knew the word. *Necro.* A Greek prefix. I didn't want to think about what it meant, about what it meant for Andy. So still. Like Fausten holding the Aphrodite pose. Like Fausten tipping like a tree without trying to stop the fall. I didn't like the feeling brewing in my stomach as I opened my eyes upon Andy. I looked away and saw Conlin, lying at the edge of the stage. Eyes no longer seeing, lungs no longer breathing, heart no longer beating.

Necro.

Andy bolted upright and his chest expanded with breath. He wasn't like Conlin. *Not yet.* His eyes closed and he winced like he was battling something inside him—and losing.

"Andy?" I shook his shoulders, and he screamed. No words, just agony. His back arched and he toppled off the throne. I caught him before he hit the floor, but his neck twisted at a gut-wrenching angle, and he didn't try to adjust it.

Necro.

Necromantic oil. I'd used necromantic oil, oil of the dead, and I'd used it for love. On *my love.*

I licked my thumb and rubbed feverishly at the crusted oil on Andy's cheek, knowing that love and death may flirt, but they can't play together long.

The mist hovered around us, thickening and crackling in wait—and giving off a new scent. Same, but different. Yet still familiar. I sniffed, trying to place it.

Guy pulled me away from Andy, but I shrugged out of his grip and returned to my task. I had to get the oil clumps out of Andy's hair. I thought I could save him. I thought I could, if I could just get all the oil off him.

"We gotta go," Guy said, still tugging me. "We gotta get you outta here."

"I'm fine! Fix Andy."

"You're fine *now*." Guy grabbed me under the arms and tried to drag me toward the wing, but I broke away from his concern and stumbled back to Andy.

"There's nothing you can do for him," Guy said. "If he's not dead already, he'll be fine in a minute. But in a minute you'll be..."

"I'll be what?" I asked.

But it was like Guy's words themselves had triggered the change. I suddenly recognized the mist's odor and felt the appropriate fear. The mist smelled like peaches, like Fausten and the theater, except now the smell was spoiled. It smelled like the putrid oil. But more troubling was the kindred sensation I felt in my gut. A numbing infection was blooming within me and already speckling with rot.

"I'll be what?" I asked again.

Guy's mouth turned down in something like pity.

The stage rumbled beneath us and the lights flashed like a strobe.

The smoke began circling around us. Corralling us.

And out beyond the fans still immobilized by the mist, the house doors closed, then locked with an echoing click.

"What's happening?" I asked.

Guy paled.

"Fausten," he said. "She's coming."

CHAPTER 56

DAPHNE

The trap in the stage floor dropped six inches and began to slide open. A stench covered in vain with perfume permeated the stage. I covered my nose, my mouth, but I could still taste it. The bittersweet tang of chemicals and rotting peaches.

Guy tilted his head. “Do you hear that?”

Something buzzed in the depths of the trap room, getting louder. Coming closer.

Guy picked up the stand that had held Andy’s stuff and swung it against the proscenium wall, breaking off the top. He flipped it over, turning its feet into a makeshift mace.

He dragged the throne away from the hole and helped me get Andy behind it. “Hurry,” he said.

Flies burst through the trap. I yelped and tried to shield Andy. Guy swung his mace, but it only focused their attack. They swarmed over us, pricking our skin.

Guy kept swinging. Kamikaze bodies littered the stage at his feet, but there were more to replace them. So many more that they shaded the stage. I grabbed the pocket of Guy’s coveralls and tugged him toward the floor. He crouched next to me, heaving for breath. His face and arms sprouted welts.

The flies circled us, reflecting light off their metallic stingers as they joined the mist, creating a boundary like a rushing river in full sun. And just as uncrossable.

The hole in the stage grew wider. The wind and lights stilled. All fell silent except for a faint noise coming from the trap. A crackle. Like puffed rice cereal spoiling to sludge in its milk.

The platform rose from the stage. Petty sat upon it in his matte black bodysuit. He had his hood down and his hands bare, and in his lap he cradled—*Oh gawd.*

Petty scooted off the platform and laid Fausten on top, brushing what remained of her hair over the edge. He tugged the hem of her white baby-doll dress over her potbellied stomach.

They'd said she had a rash, but this was no such thing. The skin of her arms and legs glistened with the ooze of cracking wounds. I'd seen the likes of them before, in one of my grosser biology classes. They'd made us watch a video about a body farm, about the four stages of decay.

Fausten looked like decay's second stage: the bloating stage. And yet, despite her distended body, her putrid stench, her rotting skin, the Pin-up Bride took on a glow.

The glow flashed as her body spasmed—as I screamed.

Fausten was death coming to life, like Frankenstein's monster, only Fausten's life-giving energy source wasn't electricity.

Fausten wiggled her toes and my feet went numb.

She bent her knees and I couldn't feel my legs.

She arched her back, and I cried in pain, at the pinching crunch in my spine.

Guy got an arm around me and pulled me to the other side of the throne, away from the platform, away from Fausten Cotter. But I had to see her. I craned my neck over the armrest.

She scooted around on the platform, trying to face us. Petty held out his hand to help her, but she shook her head. He stepped aside, yielding the spotlight to her. She perched on the edge of the platform, dangling one ballooned gray foot.

"Finally." Fausten's voice croaked like she hadn't used it in years. She coughed and covered her mouth with a gloved hand. Swollen fingers strained the seams. She looked around, taking in her surroundings. Andy's shoes and sweats lay at the edge of the stage.

So did Conlin.

"I'd had enough of him," Fausten explained. She tilted her head and steam rose from Conlin's body as his skin, his insides, disintegrated, leaving a stain on the floor. And even that evaporated.

Beside me, Guy crouched on his toes, gripping his mace.

"While we're at it..." Fausten nodded in our direction.

Guy yelped and dropped his mace. His hand sizzled—he cradled it against his chest—but his fallen mace dissolved into mist, disappearing like Conlin.

"Now, then..." Fausten pointed at Andy's old ECCOs. Petty gathered them for her and set them next to her on the platform. She picked up the left shoe and tipped the coin into her gloved hand, then took it between her thumb and forefinger. Light glimmered off the silver sixpence.

"Something like this protected *you* that night," she said to Guy, "from my ee-vil. Nechai put it in your shoe. Did you notice? It saved you. And it did this to me. Tonight it saved Andy."

Andy still lay on the floor. I couldn't tell if he was breathing. *Please, breathe.*

"Hmm," Fausten said. "Maybe it didn't save him." She pouted for a second, then perked up and grinned at Petty, foam bubbling at the corners of her mouth. "Let's save Andy for later."

"No!"

Petty stepped toward Andy, but I threw myself on top of him, and Guy helped me drag his body behind the throne. Not that our efforts mattered. Some unseen force seized Andy's ankle and yanked him from our grasp. His body slid across the stage and thudded against the platform.

Fausten poked him with her rotting toes.

"He was perfect," she said. "I can see why you liked him, why you'd force him. He should make a decent oil, don't you think? He dumped the love of his life today."

"Andy." I tried to go to him, but my limbs were weak. Guy had no trouble holding me back.

"Let her go, Guy. I want to see her. See her as me."

Guy tried to keep hold of me. But the earworm beat its wings against my frontal bone as if trying to fly to Fausten, and I staggered toward her. My throbbing head blurred my vision.

Fausten smiled at me from behind her veil. "You were good tonight," she said. "All that walking and talking. They loved you."

She gestured at the captive fans behind her—most still hovering in their seats, a few floating in the aisles, all of them wrapped in their smoky protective shells—and her capped sleeves cut into the rotten bloat of her arm. It festered and oozed.

"You had Andy's stuff," she said, hiding the arm behind her back, "but you also had mine. Did you notice?"

The heel of her dangling foot squished as it thudded against the platform, releasing flakes of something black I told myself was just dirt. I swallowed hard and shook my head.

"I didn't either," she said. "Not until Conlin said so. Look at you. Costume borrowed from me. New wig to look like me. Blue shoes." She chuckled. "Petty put those out for you. The color was luck. Good choice." She reached for Petty. He hustled to her side and let her squeeze his fingers, beaming with pride as pus seeped through her glove.

With Petty's help, Fausten slid off the platform and stood.

Guy managed to stand too and stepped in front of me. I peeked around his shoulder.

Fausten stepped closer, trailing ooze on the stage. "You're wearing my something-old, too," she said. "I thought it was a year and a half, tops, but part of that gem is older than time. I regret giving it to you, but I'm glad you're still wearing it." She leaned to the side, the better to see me around Guy. "Do you know why?"

Guy grabbed my hips with both hands, keeping me behind him and out of Fausten's view. He inched us further away from her—but the buzz of circling flies warned us we'd never get far. Guy's grip on me tightened.

"Don't bruise Daphne, Guy. I need her."

"Fuck you," he whispered, and his muscles flexed.

He'd known what the words would cost him.

Fausten tilted her head and Guy went rigid. The back of his neck turned red. Steam rose from his skin.

"Guy?" I tried to step around him, but he looked over his shoulder, and his face...

"*Don't,*" he said, begging me through unmoving lips. I couldn't fathom the pain he was enduring for me, but I couldn't let him do it for nothing. I leaned against him and buried my face in his back. *I'm sorry, I'm so sorry, I'm so sorry...*

Fausten screamed, "Get out of my way!"

Guy flinched, but he didn't back down. Fausten lowered her chin. A white streak burst from the light rack and struck Guy in the chest, throwing him into the wall of fog and flies. He screamed, arching his back against their stings, and collapsed in a heap on the ground.

Fausten's gray and rotten body stood barely two arm-lengths away from me now, and there was nothing left to come between us. She pushed back her veil and smiled at me, showing the roots of her sour teeth.

The empty vial lay on the ground. Fausten stooped to pick it up, but she wobbled on her feet and pitched forward. Petty caught her, putting a steadying arm around her bloated waist.

"Muscular atrophy," he said quietly, just for her.

"It'll come back," she said. And, weak and rotting or not, she lifted her head high, like the goddess she was, as her loyal servant did her bidding and bent down to pick up the empty vial.

"This oil was mine," she said, taking the vial. "Do you remember?"

I didn't, but I would.

"I didn't think it would hurt, but it did. Bad." She rubbed her chin. Moist black flakes flittered about the stage, stinking up the air.

"Nechai wasn't able to collect it all," she said. "But that was a good thing in the end. Do you know why, Daphne? Do you want to know why?"

The earworm knew why. And it wanted out of my skull. It bashed against the bone like an immortal version of one of those kamikaze flies. I rubbed my head, but my fingers were too weak to soothe the pain.

Fausten stepped closer and extended her free hand. Her swollen fingers stretched in my direction. "Do you?"

I shook my head, barely moving it.

"It's good," she said, "because it let me keep using my influence. It's how I performed my act. And now that you've used my oil"—she lifted her chin, and mine jerked up as well, my muscles contracting, complying—"it's how I'll control you."

"*Don't.*"

Guy was alive, but he couldn't pick himself up off the floor. He couldn't help me.

No one could help me.

Fausten flexed her fingers—and my left hand rose to meet hers. Light sparkled off the cabochon, casting rainbows throughout the house.

"It's beautiful, isn't it?" She tugged on the band, but the ring wouldn't budge. Her soiled satin gloves were too slippery. "Petty?"

Petty grabbed my wrist and stepped between me and Fausten. He pinched the ring—and gasped, snatching his hand away and stumbling backward. He nursed his smoldering fingers.

Fausten frowned. Or so I thought. It was hard to tell. Her distended tongue mangled her mouth.

"It's fine," she said. "We'll get it when we're done."

I shivered. "Done doing what?"

Unseen energy seized my hand and pulled me closer to Fausten, sliding my arm along the length of hers. Our breaths mingled. Her sternum squished beneath my palm as her nails gouged into my chest. I screamed.

Feeling left my fingers, abandoned my toes. That feeling—my life force—amassed at my heart and poured into Fausten's hand.

Her puffy arm shrank to normal and took on color, a glow of life.

She shook her head and her hat fell away. Her hair grew thick and lush around her shoulders. Her eyes brightened. Her lips pinkened.

She simpered at Petty, exalted and perfect. "Told you."

Petty was too giddy to be chastised. He kissed her gloved hand, still soiled, but now more delicate in size.

I felt constricted inside my body, unable to feel it. Unable to control it. My head fell forward—and I stared at a silvery iridescent cord protruding from my chest.

Fausten looped the cord around her wrist and yanked.

Crack!

The earworm broke through my brain barrier and forced itself into my neck. But it wasn't quite free. It wanted to flow, like my life force, into Fausten's hand, but it fluttered in my jugular, unable to make its way.

Something pulled it toward my left arm.

My left hand throbbed, wearing the source of the earworm's fear. The earworm didn't want to be anywhere near the ring, but it was slipping down my shoulder.

Fausten wound the cord around her arm, trying to reel the earworm toward her. Every rotation made my poor swollen heart strain to keep pounding—but each flooding contraction strained the shimmery cord.

It snapped.

"No!" Fausten cried.

The cord became goo in her hands. But the bit that was still inside me bucked like a hose under pressure: the earworm was screeching and beating its wings, frantic at being left behind.

Fausten's revived eyes went wild with crazy. "Fine, then, I'll take you! I'll take you like Schadenfreude tried to take me, but unlike that suicidal hag, I—Always—Win."

Fausten pressed her palm to my chest, and the energy she'd stolen from me poured back into my core.

My hand dropped to my side. My feet flattened on the floor.

Fausten's life glow faded, and her beauty rotted away.

"Ha!" she cried, victorious even as her jaw stopped working, as half her bottom lip fell to the floor.

I tried to look away, but I couldn't move.

She still had ahold of me. She still had control.

Decomposing flesh peeked out of Fausten's gloves. She flailed her arms at Petty. He grabbed a glove and peeled it from her arm, popping black blisters in its wake. She cried out, and I did too; I could feel it happening: her skin festering into wounds, her muscles peeling from bone.

She thought it was worth it. Yellow ooze dripped from her ears. Pus bubbled from her gaping maw. But she thought it was worth it. She thought this humiliating moment of pain was worth the trade.

Her body for mine.

The last of Fausten's skin dripped to the stage. She wore nothing but red sores, white pus, black rot. And even that gave way. She melted into goo, liquefied into a mess on the stage, until all that was left was a soft spot in the wood and a hovering, ghostly haze that resembled the Pin-up Bride.

The ghostly haze contracted, becoming a tiny white orb. It circled around us, brightening as it gained speed, as it gained strength.

She dived toward me, but I still couldn't move, and my hand jerked, stricken with pain.

Even as nothing, Fausten Cotter was winning.

She was on my finger. She'd reclaimed the ring, but she wasn't stopping there.

Get out.

I didn't hear the words so much as feel them—in my hand and in my head. A piece of Fausten was inside me, always had been, and she was no longer willing to share. The ring grew hot as she burrowed for a vein. She wanted my heart, but she needed the earworm.

And the earworm created space for her. It crowded my soul to the edges of my body, pushed it through the pores of my unyielding skin.

The five million holes worked like sharp metal mesh severing trillions of nerves. My body shook.

But the earworm's efforts weren't enough: My finger hurt, but it was still mine.

Fausten couldn't get past the ring.

It's not working!

"It isn't *going* to work," said a distant voice.

Not Guy. I could hear him straining behind me, trying to reach me.

Not Andy. He still lay lifeless by the platform.

Andy.

"The ring," Petty said. He was standing at a tense angle, rocking back and forth on his heels as if resisting the urge to flee. "Let her take off the ring."

My stiff body relaxed, and I stumbled forward. I could suddenly move.

"Take it off," he said.

I didn't trust him, but what else could I do? I pinched the band and pulled, but the ring wouldn't budge.

"Let Guy try," Petty said.

I thought he was talking to me, but he must've been talking to Fausten, because Guy was suddenly on his feet. He grabbed the ring but only howled in pain and yanked back his hand. He sucked on his singed fingers.

"Spit on it," Guy said.

My mouth was too dry.

Guy's spit only burned.

I yanked and yanked, my elbows jabbing, my antsy feet dancing, but I couldn't get it off.

"I'll get you something to loosen it," Guy said. I tried to tell him not to go, but my words slurred, and he couldn't have heard me anyway, not over his roaring battle cry. He charged through the wall of flies, braving their stings and leaving me alone. With Petty.

Petty pulled out his box cutter.

"No," I said.

He slid it open. "It's all we've got."

"Guy's getting something." He had to be. But even as I said it, I knew Petty was right. My finger was blue and turning black. The ring was tightening, and no amount of lube would free me. I might not even need the knife. The ring would snap my finger.

Petty grabbed my hand but couldn't bear the ring's defense. He held out the box cutter, handle first. "You have to do it yourself."

I shook my head, dread pumping my frantic feet. "I can't."

"You have to."

I looked for Guy, for a second opinion, but he still wasn't back. And my finger—

Upchuck in my throat. I swallowed it down and grabbed Petty's knife, bracing my hand on the platform. My trembling fingers tipped the blade against the band, but the ring was so tight and my finger so swollen that blood rose with no pressure. My stomach rolled.

Petty raised his fist to force the blade, but I jerked my hand away. Blood dripped on my skirt.

"*No.*" There had to be another way. Guy would return. He would. He had to. I grabbed my wrist, trying to squeeze off the pain, but the earworm was battering at my collarbone with determined ten-pound wings that were just as painful as Fausten.

"It hurts," I said. "It hurts."

Everything hurt. My finger. My chest. My head. And the pressure, the pain, kept building. I closed my eyes, searching for relief in the black of my eyelids.

A bright streak flashed behind them—and speared my hand to the platform.

My mouth, my eyes, popped open. Nothing but air and heat and a hole in my hand. And instinct. The knife stood by itself, erect at my knuckle. I raised my hand—and slammed my palm on the blade.

My finger fell. It grazed my foot and rolled in an arc toward the throne, trickling blood on the stage.

And the earworm was free. It abandoned my memory and burst from my knuckle, leading the way to open air for the swarm of fog and flies. The wind died down as they dispersed.

Petty showed me upraised palms and backed away.

And Andy…

"Andy?"

I…I couldn't…

CHAPTER 57

DAPHNE - 17 hours left

My head bounced against a bony lemon-and-formaldehyde-scented chest. Someone was carrying me. And I feared I knew who. I tried to squirm, tried to kick my legs to the ground, but it wasn't working. I wasn't sure I was moving at all.

I heard my name in the distance. Was it Andy? I tried to yell for him.

"That's not Andy," said my captor, and her bone-saw voice confirmed my fear. She adjusted me in her arms. My head bounced harder against her chest: she was suddenly in a hurry. "That's Guy."

"Guy?" I tried to look for him, but everything was blurry.

"Daphne?" Guy was getting closer.

My captor moved even faster.

"Nechai?" Guy said. "What are you—Daphne!" Guy's warm hand squeezed my shoulder. I tried to look at him, but my eyes wouldn't stay open.

"Oh shit," Guy said. "What happened to her finger?"

My finger? It didn't hurt. I tried to touch it with my thumb.

Nechai said, "Petty has her finger."

"What—why?"

"He wanted the ring."

Guy's warm thumb rubbed my knuckle. "She needs a doctor."

"They can't help her, you know that. They'll just ask questions you can't answer."

"But she's still—"

"She's not, though. Look."

"Look at what?" I asked, but there was no response. Maybe I wasn't loud enough. "Look at what?" I said again, but the words came out like *wuhwuhwuh*, if they came out at all. "I want to go to the doctor," I said. "Doctor."

"No," Guy said, but he wasn't speaking to me. It was a distressed *no*, the *no* of someone witnessing the truth of something he doesn't want to believe.

"I tried," Nechai said, "but I can only protect people from others. I can't protect them from themselves."

"But she's—"

"Even if you got her to the ER, they'll just bag her once it's done. Let me take her."

No.

"For what?" Guy said. "You didn't help Fausten."

"No one could help Fausten."

Guy scoffed. "But you can help Daphne?"

"I can take her now," she said, jostling me like I was getting heavy. "I've got the station wagon."

No. Please no.

Guy's warm fingers opened my eyes. His own eyes were downturned, his eyelids puffy, his face still covered with steam burns and stings. I tried to shake my head, tried to tell him that I didn't want to go with Nechai—that I'd taken him to the doctor once, that he needed to take me to one now—but his frown of concern only deepened.

"The mist is gone," Nechai said. "The spectators won't stay stupefied for long."

Guy let go of my eyelid. It stayed open just long enough for me to see him rub his face and run his hand through his hair.

No, Guy, please. Please, no.

"Okay," he said, "but I want to carry her."

Guy carried me outside and I couldn't do anything about it. I couldn't see. I couldn't move. I couldn't talk.

But I could hear—

A car door unlatched. Something slid closer to me, then screeched open, metal grating on metal. Hard wheels rolled toward me on the concrete.

I could feel—

Guy set me down on cold pleather, laid me back, and pulled my legs straight. Light from a streetlight warmed circles on the backs of my eyelids. A cold breeze drizzled rain on my skin as they rolled me headfirst on bumpy pavement.

And I could smell—

They raised the gurney's legs with a screech and slid me into the back of a vehicle. Nechai's station wagon. It smelled like a hearse.

Someone opened the hearse's driver's-side door and crawled over the seat, positioning themselves above my head. They smelled like lemon and formaldehyde—and jasmine deodorant. Nechai. She grabbed the gurney and pulled me in further.

"You can't come," she said.

My slow, heavy heart tried to beat faster at this, but the effort only hurt.

"Why not?" Guy said.

Nechai's calm breathing puffed on my face.

Guy's thumb tapped my ankle.

A car drove by. Water splashed my feet. The silence was worse than the gurney's screeching.

What were they doing?

What were they planning to do?

Guy's warm hands grabbed my ankles and pulled. The pleather pushed up my skirt and squeaked up my back.

Nechai's cold hands grabbed my shoulders and tugged me by the armpits, but she didn't have Guy's strength.

Guy yanked my calves, then grabbed my thighs. Another pull and he had my hips.

Nechai grabbed my ribs. She heaved and pulled, but she was hunched over me, constrained by the cab space. She didn't have Guy's leverage.

"Still not today," she said. And she let go.

Guy grabbed my waist as Nechai started the engine.

"Shit," he said.

The smell of exhaust mingled with the scent of death. The gear shift nocked into drive.

Guy rotated me, knocking my cheekbone against the side panel.

Gas fueled the hearse.

Guy yanked me out, pulling me into his arms as the hearse pulled away. My feet hit the ground, gouging my heels, but Guy protected the rest of me. He lifted my legs, cradling me in his arms. And he ran.

Guy put me in the front passenger seat of another vehicle. It smelled of motor oil and greasy fries.

He put a pillow behind my neck and reclined the seat. He opened my eyes. This time they stayed open.

I could see the van's gray pinhole-upholstered roof and the theater's loading bay door. It was rising.

Guy got in the driver's side and started the van. It cricket-chirped as he pulled us onto the street and drove slowly past the buildings of downtown Portland. I sent him some mental reminders about how to get to the hospital, but instead of stopping at one, the van picked up speed. Green signs passed overhead, listing the miles for destinations like Salem, Eugene, and Ashland.

We were on the freeway, headed south. Away from everyone who could help me.

My chest heaved. My cheeks warmed. A lump formed in my throat.

"Don't cry," Guy said. "Whatever you do, don't cry. You can't cry."

Why not? I asked, but only in my head, and the uselessness of my words just made me feel more helpless.

"Don't cry, don't cry," he said.

Pressure built behind my eyes to a searing pain, like my tear ducts were passing a stone.

"Hold on," Guy said. "I'll help you, just hold on."

But his words only hurt, and the need to sob continued until I gave in.

"No—shit." Guy put his hand against my eyes. "Shit."

He pulled out the pillow. My head fell back, and I lost my view of the freeway signs. I stared at the gray upholstery, trying to make sense of the pinholes, of what was happening to me.

The van veered right, onto bumpy road. My head flopped against the door frame. Guy slowed us to a stop and put the van in park. He straightened my head. I stared at the gray ceiling again, sniffling, my cheeks wet.

"Fausten cried too, the night she..." He blew out a breath. "She wiped her tears, and they glommed onto that ring."

Guy squeegeed my cheeks with the side of his pinky.

"I hated that ring," he said. "I hated it when she first got it, when it was all brown and weird, but I really hated it when it was beautiful."

He tilted my head toward himself and cupped his hand below my eyes.

"I'm sorry," he said, his eyes pleading with mine. "I—I tried—I..." He trailed off, covering his face with his free hand. But I knew what he wasn't saying. He'd warned me.

Or at least he'd tried.

When my tears stopped falling, he lifted his hand from my temple. In his palm was a misshapen crystal. My tears. They'd pooled together, like mercury, and solidified into a gem. It looked like the cabochon in my ring, only a different color. A golden rose.

"I don't think we're supposed to see these," Guy said. "They're supposed to stay inside." He tapped his chest—then pressed the rock to my lips. "You need to swallow it."

I shook my head and clamped my jaw shut. I couldn't feel my teeth grinding—just my consciousness rattling in my head—but I must've been doing something, because Guy couldn't open my mouth.

"You have to. I'll never get you back if you lose it. When Fausten gave you hers..."

He didn't finish, but he didn't need to. I remembered the black pus on the knuckle of Fausten's ring finger. The slime of her feet on the stage. The stench. She'd given me her ring, and she'd started to rot.

Guy stuffed the rock in my mouth. My thick tongue fought his fingers, but he won. He forced the rock into my throat. I tried to swallow, but the ability was gone. I choked.

"You have to relax," he said, pushing his fingers so far down my throat that his wrist was scraping my teeth. "Please. Just relax."

But I wanted to fight—to at least try—even if it only made things worse. And it did. Fighting made my whole body so tense I could feel the blunted end of all the life I would never live. Relax? I couldn't relax.

But I could surrender.

The crystal left a spicy tingle behind as it slid down my throat and settled heavy in my stomach like a boulder thirty times its size.

"I'm sorry," Guy said, and he sat there for a moment, looking at me like he expected me to answer him.

Even if I could've, I didn't know what to say. I'd already said, already done, too much.

CHAPTER 58

DAPHNE - mere moments left

After hours and hours of driving, the sun came up and the evergreens shifted to palm trees. Guy pulled the van into the parking lot of a building that looked familiar. I'd seen it in the blown-up pictures that had been hanging in Fausten's room: the club in the background of the photo of her and Guy.

The sun was high overhead, not west enough for the club to be open, but Guy got out anyway, leaving me in the van.

When he came back, he opened my door and stuck his head in so I could see his face. He looked tired.

"Sometimes I could hear Fausten," he said, "but I haven't heard you."

I tried to speak, but words were difficult to form, even in my head.

Guy's eyes narrowed. His lips disappeared between his teeth. His head tilted, like he was trying to receive my signal. But he eventually sighed and his head left my view.

I would've cried from frustration, but my lungs couldn't draw in air, let alone make my chest heave; my blood couldn't rush to my cheeks to redden my face; my eyes held no more tears. There was just an aching sensation all over, but strongest in my belly. And I knew why.

That's where my soul was hiding.

Guy was right, though, about keeping the gem, the ringsel. I could feel it, its energy pulsing within me. All my lost, vital parts were still here, inside my body. They just weren't positioned where they could be useful.

The van's back door creaked open. Something scraped along its metal floor, then made a screeching sound and a thud. Wheels rolled on the sidewalk. I remembered the gurney, and my insides shivered. But these wheels sounded bigger.

Guy opened my door. He tipped my head to his chest, lifted me from the front seat, and set me gently into a chair. The wheelchair.

My weight was too heavy on one hip. It didn't hurt, but I wouldn't have sat like this if I could help it. But I couldn't help it. I couldn't adjust and I couldn't ask Guy to adjust me either. I was stuck like this.

Guy wheeled me to a stage entrance and pushed me inside, down a long, dark hallway, to what looked like a lobby. He sat on a bench against the wall and wheeled me to face him.

"Can you hear me?" he said. "Blink if you can hear me."

I blinked like a butterfly.

I blinked like my eyelids were hummingbirds, like my lashes alone could cause a tornado or save the world.

He squinted and peered closer, inches from my face.

I'm doing it, I said. *Can't you see me? I'm doing it. I'm doing it.*

He looked away and puffed his cheeks, raked his fingers through his hair.

Please. I blinked at him with everything I had. *Please, Guy. Please know that I am in here.*

CHAPTER 59

DAPHNE - now

Guy massages my skin with oil. He does this every day. It was awkward at first, but I'm caring less and less that I'm mostly naked. I'm not prone to bedsores, so he says, but dry, scaly skin is apparently a problem. Either that or this is just how Guy took care of Fausten for all those months, and now he's transferred the habit to me.

As Guy massages me, he tells me about his progress on finding a cure. Today he says he's found another lead.

"But don't wait for me," he says. "I know you can save yourself."

If I could sigh, I would. I'm sure this daily encouragement is also left over from the days of Fausten. And I'm sure she found it just as tiresome as I do.

After my morning massage, Guy sits me in the wheelchair in front of the window so I can look outside. He does this every day, and every day the ringsel in my stomach shivers.

I don't know what it means.

At night, Guy puts a pillow beneath my head, making sure all my hair is off my neck. He closes my eyes when he's ready for bed and opens them when he gets up.

But I prefer them closed. It's easier to pretend I'm not like this when they're closed.

Guy scans the Portland news and reads me anything important. Since I'm missing along with Petty, Fausten, Guy, and Conlin, the media decided I ran away with the circus.

Madison and Sullivan are missing too, but no one has suggested their disappearances are related. I assume they went the way of Conlin, their bodies disintegrating into nothing. As I sit in this dark motel room, at a distance from the window, watching a traffic light cycle through its colors, listening to the constant hum of the air conditioner, waiting for nothing, hopeful for nothing...I don't know whether or not I should envy them.

As for my mom, she insists that I've been kidnapped. At least she did for a news cycle. After her fiancé—now husband—got a new job, she reportedly moved to Seattle and now can't be reached for comment.

And then there's Andy.

I try not to think about Andy.

He's not in Chicago. According to an article Guy read me, Andy "turned down a lucrative position at a Midwest marketing firm in order to continue the search for his missing girlfriend."

His girlfriend. I long to know who phrased me that way, Andy or the reporter. And I long to know if he's still looking for me. Guy hasn't read me anything new about him lately. Seems the news has moved on to other tragedies.

My eyelids are closed, but I don't really sleep anymore. The night is quiet, even with the window open to the summer breeze and the traffic. I listen for Guy, for the sound of his breathing, but I don't hear him, don't feel his warmth next to me on the bed. He's probably in the bathroom. Though I don't remember him getting up.

When it's quiet like this, it's beyond silent. I never noticed how much my body made noise until I couldn't hear it anymore. The general hum, the subtle radiation of life. Maybe it's not really audible sounds, but a feeling or a sixth sense. Whatever it is, I don't have it anymore.

I hear a creak out in the hallway. I expect the door to open and Guy to enter, but instead, there's another creak. It's cautious. Too uncertain to be Guy. It's the noise of someone who doesn't want to be heard.

My senses sharpen.

The door opens. Guy usually greets me when the door opens.

There's no greeting now.

"She's here."

I haven't seen or heard a non-Guy human in I don't know how long. The light flicks on, backlighting my eyelids. Static footsteps brush the carpet. The bed squeaks. There's a warmth at my neck. They're checking my pulse. I wait for the verdict, but my visitors must be communicating with looks and gestures, because they don't say anything.

Or maybe I'm imagining them. Dreaming. Hallucinating? Maybe they're not here with me at all.

Oh, but they're here. The mind may fool itself, but the shivers of the body never lie.

Wind blows through the open window, bringing the scent of palms and the distant noise of crickets. The constant chirping gets louder, closer, becoming distinctly mechanical. I know that sound. I've come to appreciate that sound.

But I don't like hearing it now.

Guy's van slows to a stop just beyond the window. I wait for the engine to turn off, for the door to open, for Guy to come in and—and I don't know. Save me?

He's already done the best he could.

The van idles, chirping softly.

A woman says, "I'll call it in." She brushes against the doorway as she leaves the room.

A moment later, the mechanical chirping grows louder. The van's tires roll off the uneven parking lot and onto the smoother street.

Guy drives slowly for a block or two, then guns the gas. I appreciate his hesitation, and I agree this choice is best. I am thankful for Guy. I wish him well.

But without him, what will happen to me?

As I repeat a mantra to avoid imagining what my intruders might want to do with me, I feel my inner shields quiver, trying to surface and offer me comfort. They do that now and then. But the one thing I have that still works is my mind, and I berate them until they are nothing. My shields weren't strong enough to rise and keep me out of trouble when I most needed them. What good are they to me now?

But they keep quivering, reminding me that they're still here.

Whatever. I still don't want them.

The noise in the room is busy after that. Quiet in general, but busy with movement, a movement that ends with a rustle of plastic.

The intruders aren't as gentle as Guy when they lift me and set me inside.

CHAPTER 60

DAPHNE - three unzips

Zzzzip.

A harsh, bright light shines on the back of my eyelids. The air smells earthy and pungent, of rot and decay, but also of lemon and disinfectant.

I hear the click of something electronic.

"Daphne Lynn James." The voice is male and professional. "Twenty-two-year-old female. Sixty-three inches. A hundred and fifteen pounds. Arrived in a Snuggie."

I feel the heat of the man's body as he moves around me. He says my left ring finger has been severed at the knuckle but notes no other signs of trauma. He sounds surprised by this. He says I'm very clean, very well groomed.

"Likely cause of death..."

Death. No one has suggested this about me before, and the use of the word now, so decisive, makes my insides strain against their cage.

But life doesn't flash before my eyes. If I want to review anything I've done, I have to go there on purpose.

I don't do that anymore.

Warm sensations alight on my feet, my hand, my head. My eyelids open for a millisecond. My lips part, then close.

There's an electronic click and the recorder stops.

The only sound is the man's breathing.

"Cause of death unknown," he says slowly, "and, it seems, not quite complete."

He touches my fingers, my cheeks.

"No external evidence of blocked arteries. Blood tests show no signs of heart damage. She said you had massive bruising and a hole in your hand. Not anymore, though, do you?"

Another electronic click.

"Cause of death: takotsubo cardiomyopathy." He says this with disbelieving amusement, and I find myself sharing his sentiment, because he has to be kidding.

I died of a broken heart?

He finishes his notes and closes me up in the bag with a zip.

I hear the muffled sigh of pressurized air being released. Hands rustle my plastic and slide me on my back, headfirst. There's a whoosh of wind at my feet and the suctioning click of a sealed door.

The air is cool now. Freezing, probably, but cool is all I feel.

Some while later, the door at my feet clicks open. I'm slid out again, onto a platform that rumbles beneath me to the sustained sound of rolling wheels.

I'm unzipped, and a warm, diffused glow backlights my eyelids. The air is full of lemon and disinfectant again, but no death. Not this time.

A door opens to my right.

"Mrs. Kramer," says the man from before. "I'm Dr. Talbott. Thank you for coming."

A presence begins to sob as it moves near my head. The woman hasn't spoken yet, but I already know who she is.

Something uncomfortable swells in my chest.

"*Daph,*" my mom whispers. Her cold hand caresses my cheek, but she quickly pulls it back. "She's warm." She presses the flat of her palm to my forehead, then the back of her hand, then both hands to my cheeks. "Why is she so warm? And she looks so—how can she—?"

"A medical miracle."

My mom cries harder. It's strange to miss someone who's right here with me. Strange to want to cry and not have the ability. I don't bother trying to talk to her. Doing so only builds pressure in my body, and the swell in my chest is already too much. With no way to release it, the effect of stress takes days to go away.

"Mrs. Kramer," the doctor says, "there's something delicate I'd like to ask you. Can we talk in my office?"

Mom's hand trails the length of my bagged body and moves away from me. The doctor zips me up, and the door to my right opens again. But it doesn't close in time.

"Mrs. Kramer, have you heard of the Willed Body Program?"

My mom groans a negative.

The last unzip comes quickly after that, and the final moment is eager.

I'm on another gurney. There's a bump and then a cacophony of sound from the wheels. Something warm heats my body through the plastic bag. I imagine myself rolling along jagged pavement beneath an August sun.

At least I hope that explains the heat. I'm not ready to be cremated.

A vehicle door opens, and the gurney's legs screech up. I'm slid inside, and the warmth of the sun is replaced by the warmth of a closed-up car.

The engine revs and the vehicle backs up before going forward.

The ride is smooth. Freeway driving. In my head, I sing "ninety-nine vials of oil on the wall."

I've sung to zero before we stop.

Doors open. Wheels roll. People say greetings and laugh. A big belly laugh. There's something sinister about the exchange. I shrink away, within myself, but there's no escaping this situation. My body contains me better than any prison.

The gurney's wheels roll softly muffled, then loud and echoey, softly muffled, then loud and echoey. I'm being rolled on a hard floor sparsely covered with rugs.

And then there's silence. I wait in it for hours.

And there's no warning before I'm unzipped.

The light around me is soft, barely enough to penetrate my eyelids. But the smell. It's like day-old tuna marinated in cat piss, served with a side of compost.

It's decay stalled with formaldehyde.

And it's everywhere.

I hear a squeeze dispenser and running water, then two slaps of plastic. I've heard that sequence before, the washing and gloving of hands. Pressure builds in my head, my chest, but I can't help it.

The Willed Body Program.

A fire lights in my belly. But it's not me, it's my shields: *You can overcome this, Daphne.*

They don't care if I want them, they're here. My body tingles, and the hairs on my limbs stand tall, rising, like my inner shields.

Their comfort wraps my heart. *It could still beat, Daphne.*

Their calming hushes my brain. *Try to relax, Daphne.*

I find that last one funny, but only because I'm high on terror, and the request seems impossible. Tense is my immobile body's constant state. I do my best.

But gloved fingers are lifting my eyelids.

Blue-tinted glasses look down at me.

"At last," Nechai says. She smirks at me, and the tops of her cheeks press into her frames. She removes them, and her yellow-green eyes study mine.

"Hello there," she says. And then she steps out of my view.

An angled mirror stretches across the ceiling above me, and in its reflection I can see the wall beyond my head. There's a poster hanging there. A poster done in shades of white on a black background.

My opportunity, my muse, my trigger.

I want to close my eyes, to instead see Mom happy and Guy free and Andy somewhere searching for me...

But all I can look at is her.

AUTHOR'S NOTE

Thank you for reading! I am thrilled that you picked up this book, and I hope that you enjoyed it. Whether you did or not, I would greatly appreciate it if you would please leave a review (a line or two is enough) on your favorite bookstore's website and on Goodreads. Raving or raging, your reviews contribute immensely to the success of a book, and I am grateful for your help. I can't do this without you.

Thank you again,
Megan Bledsoe

ACKNOWLEDGMENTS

Ladies and gentlemen, boys and girls, and those of you entertained by acknowledgments!

For your reading pleasure, I will now attempt to thank everyone, yes, everyone who helped me get here. I expect half of you probably won't remember me, because I've been at this for years, but that's okay. I remember you.

Thank you to the writing craft gurus who taught me in person and left me with memories, notes, and handouts I'm still referencing years later: James Scott Bell, Larry Brooks, Jeffrey Deaver, Monica Drake, Diane Holmes, Clark Kohanek, Margie Lawson, Donald Maass, Brian McDonald, Lorin Oberweger, Alice Orr, Beth Revis, Carrie Ryan, Tom Spanbauer, Christopher Vogler, Eric Witchey.

Thank you to the writing craft gurus who wrote something I read that noticeably elevated my craft: Shawn Coyne, H.R. D'Costa, Will Dunne, Joseph Paul Gulino, Jack Hart, Stuart Horwitz, Dara Marks.

Thank you to the authors of books I read that stoked the initial spark of GIRL, INC's inspiration: Joan Carroll Cruz, *The Incorruptibles: A Study of the Incorruption of the Bodies of Various Catholic Saints and Beati*; Andrew L. Erdman, *Queen of Vaudeville: The Story of Eva Tanguay*; Martin Pistorius, *Ghost Boy: The Miraculous Escape of a Misdiagnosed Boy Trapped Inside His Own Body*; Mary Roach, *Stiff: The Curious Lives of Human Cadavers*; Daniel Stashower, *Teller of Tales: The Life of Arthur Conan Doyle*; Trav S. D., *No Applause—Just Throw Money: The Book That Made Vaudeville Famous*; Thomas R. Tietze, *Margery: An Entertaining and Intriguing Story of One of the Most Controversial Psychics of the Century*.

Thank you to the Fort Vancouver Regional Libraries and in particular its ILLiad department for getting me SO. MANY. BOOKS. I heart the library.

Thank you to the variety arts performers living in or drawn to the Portland, Oregon area—and to the Alberta Rose Theatre, where I saw most of them—for the entertainment and the milieu details.

Thank you to the ER doctor at PeaceHealth SW Medical Center who answered my questions about his med school gross anatomy lab—and gave me the gem "Juicy Mama Lucy," the name of his cadaver—while gluing the tip of my pinky back on. (I had an accident with the veggie peeler.)

Thank you to the family and friends who occasionally asked me about my "stuff" and stout-heartedly proceeded to offer me encouragement despite my self-preserving stinginess with the details: Leah Bledsoe, Aaron Chamberlain, Sharon Creek, Kaye Reiter Fleming, Courtney Mertes Garcia, Dr. Chad Kleven, Vickie Nygard, Michelle Rusk, Kelly Sawyer, Buddy Van Hook, Roni Ziegler.

Thank you to the friends who read or otherwise helped me with my earlier stuff: Nikki Campbell, Angie Chastain, Annie Graye, Andrea Nimmo, Richelle Royal. And thank you to the writers who exchanged work with me over the years: Erin Anderson, Holly Hughes, Cindy Phillips, Shawn Raiford, Deborah Brink Wöhrmann. Those earlier projects of mine didn't go anywhere, but I still appreciate your help.

I've sent hundreds of queries for different projects over the years, but only two agents ever sent an explanation with their rejection. Even though your reasons were understandably limited to a mere handful of words, your comments helped me find the path forward. Thank you, Ann Collette and Molly Ker Hawn.

Thank you to three writers/editors who, despite not knowing me at all, generously offered to review a partial: G. Elizabeth Kretchmer (first fifty pages), Dayna Mahannah (first seven pages), and Michelle Rascon (query and first five pages). Many extra thank-yous to Dayna, whose comments noticeably elevated my craft.

Thank you to the writers on Scribophile who read and commented on scenes from the first chapter: Sanchi Arora, J. S. Drake, Kate Lillystone, Earl Noble, John Patrick, Kat Tsa.

Big thank-you to Eliza Dee for editing every page, for phrasing issues not only kindly but in ways that inspire solutions, for being so patient and so wise, and for helping me do this thing with confidence. All errors are because I didn't listen to her. (Except for open/closed/hyphenated spelling errors. You can blame some of those on *Merriam*. I know I do.)

Big thank-you to GIRL, INC's beta readers: Anna Bledsoe, Mary Bledsoe, Chad Nygard, Elaine Weedman. And a big thank-you to Lisa Bledsoe for helping me fine-tune its presentation.

An additional trillion thank-yous to Mary Bledsoe, Queen Beta, chanter of **You Need To Make It Interesting!** and **If that's what you mean, then SAY IT!**, creator of the *Not Good/Excellent* rating system, head cheerleader, top sponsor, and overall best mom in the universe. But for you, and in too many ways to list, this book would not exist. Big thank-you also to Kurt Bledsoe. He never read my stuff because he hated to read (though he loved audiobooks), but he still found ways to show his support: I remember him coming home with a bookcase to store my growing piles of craft books, and I remember him preparing the very first draft I wrote (yes, the vomit draft) of my very first project for my mom to read (poor Mom): He hole-punched it, stuck it in a three-ring binder, and hand-titled the cover, THE BOOK. (Mom gave it a *Not Good.*) Thank you, Mom and DAD.

Thank you to the pugs for getting me up in the morning, keeping me on a healthy schedule, and making sure I get a walk in every day.

Thank you to Chad Nygard for sharing me generously with my writing time; for being strangely helpful with fight scenes, stakes, magic systems, beta-comment interpretation, and for not complaining too much about the consequences of being exposed to story craft; for hugging out my lows and for hugging out my highs... For lots of things, really. Thank you, Chad.

And to you, kind reader, thank you for picking up this book and for giving its story a chance. I hope it exceeded your expectations.

(And if it did, I hope you'll share it with friends.)

JOIN THE READER LIST

Want more?

Join my Reader List at **meganbledsoe.substack.com**. You'll get updates, exclusive content, and other goodies from me about once a month.

Make sure to read the welcome email. At the bottom, there's a link to a page of stuff that's just for readers of this book. The password is *postergeist*, all lowercase.

Talk to you soon!
Megan

ABOUT THE AUTHOR

Megan Bledsoe takes inspiration from the world's unexplained but still undeniable phenomena. She used to be an attorney but now writes in the Pacific Northwest, where she lives with her family. This is her first novel. Find her online at meganbledsoe.com.

TYPE CREDITS

Agreloy by Gluk, SIL Open Font License via glukfonts.pl
Bangers by Vernon Adams, SIL Open Font License via googlefonts.com
Bergamot Ornaments by Emily Conners/Emily Lime, Desktop End User License via myfonts.com by Monotype
EB Garamond by Georg Duffner, SIL Open Font License via googlefonts.com
Foglihten by Gluk, SIL Open Font License via glukfonts.pl
FoglihtenBlackPcs by Gluk, SIL Open Font License via glukfonts.pl
FoglihtenNo04 by Gluk, SIL Open Font License via glukfonts.pl
FoglihtenNo07 by Gluk, SIL Open Font License via glukfonts.pl
Mansalva by Carolina Short, SIL Open Font License via googlefonts.com
Open Sans by Steve Matteson, SIL Open Font License via googlefonts.com
Outbacker by Greg Nicholls/Rook Supply, Desktop End User License via myfonts.com by Monotype
Roboto by Christian Robertson, Apache License Version 2.0 (open source license) via googlefonts.com
Rubik Puddles by Luke Prowse/NaN, SIL Open Font License via googlefonts.com
Rustic Printed (Stamp) by Edi Gunawan/Edignwn Type, Desktop End User License via myfonts.com by Monotype
Sancreek by Vernon Adams, SIL Open Font License via googlefonts.com
Tinos by Steve Matteson, Apache License Version 2.0 (open source license) via googlefonts.com
The Best We Could Do by Thi Bui, Chank Diesel/Chank, Desktop End User License via myfonts.com by Monotype

www.ingramcontent.com/pod-product-compliance
Lightning Source LLC
Chambersburg PA
CBHW020504310726
48979CB00016B/2780/J

* 9 7 9 8 2 1 8 1 8 7 3 4 7 *